SUNDANCER

SUND

ANCER

shelley Peterson

Illustrations by Marybeth Drake

KEY PORTER BOOKS

Library and Archives Canada Cataloguing in Publication

Peterson, Shelley, 1952-
        Sundancer / Shelley Peterson.

ISBN 978-1-55263-842-2

I. Title.

PS8581.E8417S96 2006   jC813'.54   C2006-903135-5

ONTARIO ARTS COUNCIL
CONSEIL DES ARTS DE L'ONTARIO

The publisher gratefully acknowledges the support of the Canada Council for the Arts and the Ontario Arts Council for its publishing program. We acknowledge the support of the Government of Ontario through the Ontario Media Development Corporation's Ontario Book Initiative.

This book is a work of fiction. Names characters, businesses, organizations, places, events, and incidents are the product of the author's imagination or are used fictitiously. Any resemblance to actual persons, living or dead, events or locales are entirely coincidental.

We acknowledge the financial support of the Government of Canada through the Book Publishing Industry Development Program (BPIDP) for our publishing activities.

Key Porter Books Limited
Six Adelaide Street East, Tenth Floor
Toronto, Ontario
Canada M5C 1H6

www.keyporter.com

Text design and electronic formatting: Martin Gould

Printed and bound in Canada

09 10 5 4

To David, as always,
and
to my own Sundancer,
who didn't have a Bird to tell his story to.

Prologue

July had been lazy and hot, and August started out the same. The country road was dusty, and quiet except for the occasional passing vehicle. Only the clear, burbling sound of a wren's birdsong sporadically broke the boredom. A faded sign flapped lethargically against a gate. On it, a big grey horse jumped over the words "Saddle Creek Farm." The sign needed fresh paint, and one of its hinges was broken.

Suddenly, the stillness of that Friday afternoon was shattered by the distant roar of a big engine. Big tires speeding over gravel pelted small stones in all directions. Then, the sharp, unmistakable sound of steel against steel. *Thump, crash, thump, crash.* Relentless, powerful, steady. The rhythmical beat continued, ever louder as the big rig neared.

A large navy-blue horse trailer turned into the Saddle Creek driveway in a cloud of dust. "Owens Enterprises" was boldly painted in gold lettering along the shiny new aluminum sides.

The furious pounding increased as the truck stopped in front of the century red-brick farmhouse with the green door and shutters. Two scowling men stepped out of the vehicle and strode around to the back of the van. One carried a long whip, the other a sturdy broom.

The man with the broom dropped the ramp while the one with the whip prepared to enter the van. Without warning, a magnificent, lathered chestnut horse shot backward off the

7

trailer and shoved both men aside. A broken leather lead shank dangled from his torn halter.

Now the muscular, haughty creature stood braced and prepared to fight, like a heavyweight champion in the middle of the ring. With nostrils flared he snorted loudly. His sleek, sweat-drenched body vibrated with energy. His delicate ears were pricked to catch all sounds. His intelligent dark eyes were intense, his classic head alert to any threat.

The men circled him menacingly. Loudly, they cursed their bad luck at being assigned to deliver this dangerous and ornery horse. Swearing at the recalcitrant animal, the men moved in closer. They cornered him, using a sturdy oak rail fence and the horse trailer as barriers. The horse tossed his fiery mane. He shook his head wildly, which sent remnants of leather flying. Vigorously he pawed the gravel driveway, then sniffed the air with suspicion. Neck arched and tail high, he spun to face every direction in turn, looking for a way out.

To humble him, the one man snapped his long whip hard across the horse's flank, leaving a bleeding welt. As the trapped creature spun to face his attacker, the other smacked him across the head with the broom, following through with such a whack that for a moment the animal was stunned. He staggered, dazed. The whip came down again, *whoosh*, landing across his back and tearing the flesh over his kidneys. The broom was raised to strike his face.

As the man with the whip prepared to throw a rope over his head, the mighty chestnut got his bearings. He bucked, twisted, and shot out a double-barrelled kick, missing his targets by inches.

I have nowhere to go, nothing to lose.

The men hollered their outrage. The horse assessed his options and made his decision. He would not be caught. From a standstill, he rocked back on his haunches and effortlessly sprang over the solid four-rail fence into the front paddock.

With cat-like agility, he spun as he landed then defiantly stared at the men. He raised his head high and whinnied with ear-piercing intensity. Then, he turned his back, kicked out dismissively, and ran off to stake out his chosen territory. Bucking and rearing and prancing and diving, the fearsome chestnut raced around his new domain. He leaped and dove and kicked the sky. The earth trembled as he pounded the inside perimeter of the paddock.

The engine of the big rig roared to life. It was gone as quickly as it had arrived. As the noise receded into the distance, the dust settled and the little wren resumed his song.

Nothing at Saddle Creek Farm would ever be the same.

1

THE NEW HORSE

It is time to tell my story.

I am big and I am beautiful. When I run, I run like the wind, and when I jump, I jump like a deer. I am a winner.

ALONE IN THE PADDOCK, the sleek chestnut gelding grazed. He methodically trimmed the blades of grass close to the ground, left to right, right to left, as far as his neck could reach. He took a step and began again. Row after row. Step after step.

A woman and a girl leaned on the fence and observed him closely, an old yellow dog at their feet. A quiet breeze ruffled their hair and gently rippled their clothing. The woman, forty-ish, lean and sinewy, smoothed her fair hair from her face and muttered, "What the deuce are we going to do with him, Bird?"

The girl said nothing. The hot August air blew her unkempt hair into her eyes, and she made no effort to remove it. Her arms were skinny and brown with the sun.

He'll be my horse, she thought. No one else's.

Tell me your story, handsome. She aimed the thought in the horse's direction. No response.

The horse had been delivered earlier, while Bird and Hannah were out checking the fences. Bird wished she'd been there to see his arrival. Their vet, Paul Daniels, had practically begged Hannah to take him in. A favour, he'd said. An underdog in need. Bird could relate.

Lazily, the horse took another step and began a new line of grass. He casually swished his tail to rid himself of flies.

Bird studied the horse closely. He was extraordinarily handsome. Sixteen hands, two inches tall, she guessed. His legs were long, fine, strong, and straight, correct in every way. His neck was elegant, with a graceful curve along the top line of his body, connecting his delicate ears to his generous withers and across the gentle slope of his back to his perfectly rounded haunches. Every movement he made was graceful, and his coat gleamed a fiery copper.

And yet, something about this horse was not quite right. Underneath his calm exterior, as he mechanically grazed and pointedly ignored them, was a nervousness, a jumpiness, that Bird found disquieting. He didn't trust them. He didn't trust anyone.

"Poetry, eh, Bird?" said Hannah. "He's like poetry in motion."

Hannah sighed and turned back to the house. "Don't be too long, hon. Supper's almost ready." She stopped for a moment, waiting for a reaction. There was none. Alberta, nicknamed Bird, continued to stare at the animal.

"Don't get any ideas, young lady. Nobody can handle this horse. That's why he ended up here. Saddle Creek: farm of last resort. I'll add that to our sign, if I ever get around to fixing it."

Hannah Bradley shot one last glance at the new horse and headed for the house. She left the girl, the dog, and the horse alone.

Now, finally, the gelding raised his eyes to meet the girl's. They assessed each other, neither one making a move.

Talk to me, beautiful horse. Tell me your story. Bird willed the big horse to respond. *I know you can hear me.*

The horse simply stared.

Why are you so suspicious? You have nothing to fear with me.

The horse didn't so much as blink. He dropped his head back to the grass and continued grazing. Bird crouched down on her heels and began to rock gently. Although she was growing fast, Bird was still small for her thirteen years. She used that to her advantage now, as she manoeuvred her body under the lowest rail of the fence. She inched her bottom over to the post and quietly leaned her back against it.

In spite of spindly legs and oversized ears, Bird was pretty in her own unique way. Deep sable eyes graced her elfin face. Often they were dull and expressionless, but at other times they were lit by flashes of intelligence and sensitivity. Right now, they were almost entirely covered by her dark brown bangs that were badly in need of a trim. Impatiently, she pushed the hair off her face and continued to stare at the horse.

Now that Hannah had gone, it seemed quiet in the paddock. The yellow dog dozed in the grass at her feet. The horse grazed in the field. Bird watched and enjoyed the silence. All at once, the horse stopped and looked directly at her, as if waiting for her to say something.

Don't look at me, Bird thought with a smile. Alberta Simms hadn't spoken a word for seven years, and she wasn't about to start now.

Bird was Hannah's niece, the daughter of Hannah's younger sister, Eva. Eva had dropped Bird off at Saddle Creek—farm of last resort—two years earlier, on her way to another new life, with another new man. As far as Bird could tell, this was Eva's way. Bird's father was a cowboy from Calgary who left when Eva told him she was pregnant. He rode off into the sunset never to return, Eva was fond of saying, and had never even phoned to find out if the baby was a boy or a girl.

From the time Bird could remember, Eva seemed to change jobs often, which meant picking up and moving to a new place.

She was always hoping for something better, more interesting, less boring. Eva had changed boyfriends often, too, always hoping for someone better, more interesting, less boring. The one constant in Bird's life, until the day she moved in with Aunt Hannah, was change.

Now, sitting at the edge of this field with this beautiful horse, Bird could feel Hannah watching her from the kitchen window.

What was she worrying about now? The traces of a fond smile formed at the corner of Bird's mouth. She's worrying that I don't talk. She's worrying that I don't fit in. She's worrying that I'll never be normal. Most of all, she's worrying about school. And with good reason.

On the last day of classes, Stuart Gilmore, the principal of the Forks of the Credit School, had told Hannah that Bird could not come back. The school was simply not equipped to handle her. He'd given Hannah a list of alternative schools, and for the last few weeks Bird had watched as Hannah tried to find her a place. She'd had no luck with any of the public schools, and she couldn't afford the fees at the private ones. Now it was August, and at the top of Hannah's to-do list—posted conveniently on the refrigerator door—was a note to call Stuart Gilmore. Bird figured that Hannah planned to ask one more time.

Bird hated school. The kids were mean. But if she had to go back, the Forks of the Credit would be better than unknown alternatives.

Hannah called from the kitchen window. "Bird! Supper's ready!"

Bird was hungry, but she disliked the confinement of sitting properly at the table, and she detested being constantly coached on her manners. Reluctantly, she scrambled back under the fence.

Come for dinner, Hector. Bird stroked the dog on her way

past. He raised his head and thumped his tail.

Yummy. I've been hungry all day.

So what else is new? Bird smiled. *What do you think of the new horse, Hector?*

I don't trust him. You shouldn't either.

Bird nodded slowly and patted Hector's head. *He won't talk to me yet, so I don't know what to make of him.* Bird hadn't faced this before. Most animals responded to her immediately, delighted that a human could not only talk to them, but also understand what they had to say.

She slowly raised her hand and stretched it out toward the horse. The haughty chestnut lifted his head. Bird tried again to reach into his mind. *Talk to me. Tell me about yourself.*

The horse gave Bird a bored look, then turned his back, providing a perfect view of his welts and cuts. They would heal nicely with proper care, but so far the horse had not allowed anyone to get close to him, let alone treat his wounds. Earlier, when she'd first spotted him, Bird had taken the water hose out to the field. She'd stood on the fence and created a fountain that he had eventually walked into to cool off, so at least the wounds were washed out. She'd tried to squirt Wonder Dust, an antiseptic powder, into the nastier gashes but had only been somewhat successful. Tomorrow she'd try again.

Not for the first time, Bird wondered what had happened to this horse. How did he get those cuts, and why had he ended up at Saddle Creek? *What did they do to you, beautiful fellow?* Bird waited a moment for an answer then ran to the farmhouse without a backward glance.

Late that night, the quiet of the farmhouse was disturbed by the telephone ringing.

In her darkened room beside Hannah's, Bird was instantly awake. The walls of the old farmhouse were thin, and Hannah's voice, drowsy with sleep, travelled easily into Bird's room.

"It's late here, Eva. I was asleep."

Eva. Her mother. Bird wiggled out of bed, placing two bare feet on the wooden floor. She crept quietly down the stairs, avoiding the creaky floorboards, and made her way into the kitchen where the extension hung on the wall beside the fridge. Softly, she raised the receiver to her ear. Her mother was laughing about the time difference. Hannah was not amused.

"It's one A.M., Eva. This better be good."

"Randy asked me to marry him."

"Congratulations."

"You don't mean that. I can hear it in your voice."

"Eva, it's the middle of the night. Tomorrow I have to get up early to take four horses to a show. I don't know Randy. I've lost count of how many times you've been engaged, and last night your daughter threw her dinner at the wall because she wanted dessert first. Excuse me for my lack of enthusiasm."

Bird cringed at Hannah's words and waited out the long silence on the line.

"Actually, Hannah, that's why I'm calling."

"Speak to me, Eva. I'm not good at riddles at one in the morning."

"Randy wants to meet my family, so we're coming to visit in a couple of weeks. I've told him all about you and Daddy and Mom, but he doesn't know about Bird."

Silence again. Then Hannah's voice, more awake now. "You said he doesn't know about Bird?"

"Yes."

"What doesn't he know? Her existence or her unusualness?"

"Both."

Bird listened closely. She could hear the intake of air as Hannah took a deep breath. "So, when are you going to tell him?"

"It's not that easy, Hannah. He adores Julia. But I know he'd have a hard time with Bird. It might change things."

"Reality sucks."

"I don't know why I called, you make me so mad!"

"So why *did* you call, Eva?"

Again, there was a pause, but this time Bird could feel a crackle of energy on the line. Something big was about to happen.

"Can you tell Randy that Bird is your daughter? There. I've said it."

In the darkened kitchen, Bird felt like she'd been punched in the gut. She fought the urge to smash the phone against the wall and knock everything off the counter.

Hannah spoke calmly, quietly. "Let me get this straight. You want me to tell Randy that Bird is my daughter. Is Julia still yours?"

"Yes, Randy loves her."

Bird thought of her little sister. A pretty, cheerful nine-year-old. Chatty, charming, and well adjusted. Blonde and beautiful like their mother.

"Look, Hannah." Eva was still talking, faster now. "Don't go all holier than thou on me. You know I couldn't take Bird with me to California. She was in school and she had her friends..."

"Friends? Since when has Bird had a friend? And Bird had to change schools anyway when she moved in with me. We both know why you left her here, so at least be honest with yourself if not with me. Or with Randy, for that matter. What kind of marriage are you—"

Eva cut her off. "This is going nowhere. I've already told Randy that you have an autistic child, so it's done."

"Eva!" The line went dead.

Bird stood listening to the dial tone until it stopped. The recorded message played, "Hang up. Please hang up now."

Finally, Hannah tumbled the receiver back into its cradle. Bird hung up, too, then sank down to the kitchen floor with her back against the wall and her knees drawn tightly to her chest.

Autistic. The magic word. It was spoken. Bird had sat through enough "sessions" to know that it was a popular amateur diagnosis for a grab bag of disorders. She had to admit that she exhibited some of the clinical symptoms. She was frenetic at times. Distracted. She'd always been extremely sensitive to noise and light and sudden movement, and was prone to outrageous tantrums when thwarted. She detested change in routine. She didn't speak, she rocked, she could rarely look a person in the eye. But there was so much more to her than that! More than anyone could see. Sometimes Bird thought that Hannah came close. It was Hannah who'd found the one doctor who'd disagreed with the others.

Hannah explained to him that Bird had begun to talk at a normal age. By kindergarten she was already reading and had a vivid imagination. She interacted with people. She was somewhat shy but made friends easily. Kids and animals were drawn to her. In fact, she had an uncanny ability to understand what people and animals were thinking. Then, everything had changed when she was six. Only Bird knew why.

The doctor had looked her in the eye and pronounced her an "elective mute."

"It's not that she can't talk, Ms. Bradley," the doctor had said in a kind, gentle voice. "She chooses not to." Bingo, thought Bird at the time.

Now, a small tear of self-pity dripped onto Bird's sleeve. Her stomach was in knots. Her own mother was ashamed of her— too ashamed to call her her daughter. Suddenly the farmhouse seemed too small. Bird needed to be outside in the fresh night air, with nothing around her but the night and its noises.

Saturday morning dawned too soon for Hannah. Sleep had eluded her after her sister's call. A little after three she'd gotten up for a glass of water and had spotted something in the field. It was the white fabric of Bird's cotton pajamas shining in the moonlight. There she was, sleeping in the field with Hector curled up beside her and the new horse standing close by. Hannah had approached quietly, not wanting to panic the horse, but he'd been watching her from the moment she'd neared the fence. Hector sat up and thumped his tail on the ground, happy to see her. Bird jerked, settled, then stared at Hannah defiantly. Hannah couldn't think of one good reason to bring her back to bed by force, so she retrieved a couple of heavy horse blankets from the barn and gently tucked her in. The horse never moved.

Now, in the light of day, Hannah looked out her bedroom window to see Bird dragging the blankets across the field. She looked happy.

To Bird, the morning smelled delightful. Dewy grass, clean air, horse smells, new wood from fence repairs, and mouldy horse blankets, damp with dew. I bet camp smells like this, she thought. Or home on the range, when the cowboys go out for weeks at a time to bring home the cattle. Cattle drives, they're called. Bird breathed deeply and smiled.

Hector walked stiffly beside her, wagging his tail. After a moment, the new horse followed. Bird awkwardly managed to push the blankets over the fence, then reached to pat the horse's face. He turned away and stuck his nose high in the air.

Bird tried once more to reach him.

Big horse, will you talk to me?

The chestnut swung his head around and looked at her passively.

Who made those cuts across your back? Who hurt you?

The horse looked startled for a brief second, then closed down again. He turned away from her and moved into the paddock to begin his day of grazing. He ignored her, but Bird could see that he was keeping her in his field of vision. She watched for a minute, pleased that she'd gotten through, however briefly. There is damage piled up in that horse, Bird thought, as she began her morning chores. And no one will get through that damage until he decides to let them.

At Saddle Creek Farm, the heavy work was done by two trusted employees, John Fraye and Cliff Jones. Daily, they mucked the stalls, scrubbed the buckets, and kept the farm looking neat and smelling fresh. They put out the horses for their turnout time wearing blankets or boots, depending on their owners' requests. Seasonally, John and Cliff kept the lawns cut and the fields free of burrs, and plowed the driveway clear of snow. At all times, they dealt with the surprises and emergencies that were part of life on a horse farm.

Bird's work was lighter, and she took pleasure in it. With Hector following, Bird began cleaning and filling the outdoor water troughs. Another of her responsibilities was to check gates, fences, and loafing sheds for any needed repairs. It was an important job, and one that Bird took more seriously after three horses had run down the road and almost caused an accident after she had failed to call attention to a faulty latch. "If a horse can get into trouble," Hannah repeated time and again, "he will." It was Bird's daily duty to minimize the possibilities.

While she worked, John and Cliff led the horses out to the fields. Hannah's horses were out all night in the warm summer months, but the boarders' horses were kept inside. If the animals were to decide, Bird knew, they'd all be out in the cooler night air and inside during the heat of midday.

Duties done, Bird stretched up her arms and admired the blueness of the sky. She filled her lungs with the fresh morning air and sighed contentedly. Hector plopped down by the barn door in the sun. She knelt, ruffled his fur, then cast another glance at the new horse. The enigma.

Her eye was caught by the unmistakable figure of her aunt as she marched toward her from the house. Even from a distance, Bird could feel her stressful mood. Hannah strode up to Bird carrying a small brown paper bag. She was dressed to ride.

"I made you a bacon sandwich. You must be starving." She held out the bag. Bird felt immobilized, uncomfortably alert to Hannah's clipped speech and quick movements. She didn't take it.

"I've got to get going. Do you want to come to the show with me? I'm taking Kimberly and Jo and Peter and Melanie."

Bird could only stare. Hannah was upset, and suddenly Bird knew why. All the joy of the day drained away as Bird recalled last night's phone call from her mother.

Hannah spoke firmly. "Bird, answer me. Look, how am I supposed to deal with you? Do you want to come with me or not?"

With a heavy heart, Bird looked down. No, I don't, she thought. I want to be alone.

She glanced up and saw her aunt's worried eyes. She felt sincerely sorry for Hannah. It's not her fault, Bird thought, that her weird sister burdened her with a weird kid whom she now wanted to disown. I shouldn't be so difficult. I should get my act together and go to the horse show. I could be a help. Bird looked back down at the ground and studied a line of ants as they paraded past in the dirt. But no. She felt too upset. Best to avoid the company of people today. Today, when no one was around, she would get up on the new horse's back.

"Look, make you a deal. You'll stay here with Cliff and John unless you're in the truck by the time the horses are loaded. And if you decide to stay here, whatever you do, you are *not* to get on the new horse's back."

Bird looked up at her aunt quickly. Was she that transparent?

Hannah thrust out her arm and dropped the paper bag with the sandwich. Bird caught it. Hannah smiled briefly. "Good reflexes."

A short while later, Bird watched as Hannah pulled away with the rig, four horses safely aboard. "Saddle Creek" was emblazoned in green, grey, and red on the sides of the white truck and trailer. Saddles, bridles, boots, wraps, and grooming kits were stowed in the tack room at the front of the horse trailer, as well as a safety box fitted for every possible emergency.

Two cars followed. One with Jo's mother driving Jo and her best friend Melanie, and one with Peter and his mother. Kimberly always met them at the shows, a subject of discussion at the barn as this left the preparations up to Hannah.

Bird climbed on the fence to eat her bacon sandwich and watch the new horse. Hector had moved from his usual position at the barn door to lay on the ground at her feet. He kept one big brown eye on Bird's sandwich, hoping for a spill.

I'm happy you stayed.

I'm happy to spend time with you, Hector. Bird leaned down to rub his soft yellow head.

Can I have a bite?

You had your breakfast. This is mine.

It's going to be an unhurried day, she thought. Good. Lots of time to sit and understand this horse. Bird felt her sadness fade away as she ate and watched. She loved how the sun danced on the horse's coat. She admired his motion. He moves gracefully, like a dancer, she thought. And he's the orangey colour of the sunset. That's it. I'll name him Sundancer—Sunny for short. Even though there's a darker side to him, too. He's a veiled horse, like the wild mustangs of the ancient Indians. A mystery horse with hooded eyes and many secrets—secrets that even Paul Daniels doesn't know.

Unfortunately, what Paul Daniels did know was shocking.

He'd told them that, one time, Sundancer had been in a trailer accident. Because of a faulty hitch and rusted undercarriage, the horse trailer came loose from the truck on the highway.

Unguided, it smashed into a hillock on the side of the road, knocking the horse from his feet and sending him sliding under the chest bar. He was lucky. Had the trailer gone into the two lanes of fast-moving traffic, things could have been much worse. As it was, Sundancer survived with nasty scrapes and a lifelong distrust for trailers.

Another time, as he was being led down the road behind another horse, he pulled free and began to gallop away, dragging a long rope. He ducked in behind a farmhouse, jumped a hedge into the back garden, and leaped out over another hedge. Unfortunately, that second hedge sat at the edge of the Niagara Escarpment, the rocky ridge that runs through the Niagara peninsula. The landing was thirty feet down into big rocks. Again, he was lucky, because if he hadn't stopped rolling there, he would have gone a hundred feet more. That time his injuries almost killed him.

Sundancer had many idiosyncrasies, too, that Dr. Daniels mentioned. Some were obvious, like his dislike of trailers and his fear of heights. Others were harder to understand.

He always assumed that a person was going to hit him with whatever they were carrying, be it broom, water bucket, pitchfork, or hairbrush. He was suspicious of everyone. The first of his nine trainers tried to desensitize his nervous nature with noises, pokes, and slaps, all of which led to a fear of surprises. Sundancer took to hiding in his stall, shaking, anticipating the next scare. He scooted alarmingly fast when touched on his sides. He had a penchant for running away, as well. No fence had been high enough or strong enough to keep him in. Bird wondered if Sundancer would run away from them. More likely it was a matter of when.

Bird gave Hector the last bite of her sandwich and wiped away the crumbs. She waited for the man who'd come up behind her to speak.

"Hello there, Bird."

Bird didn't look around. She knew it was Paul Daniels by the feel in the air. His aura, perhaps. Whatever it was, it was good—safe and intelligent.

She also sensed that his son, Alec, might be sitting in the car. She glanced over quickly to sneak a peek. Yes. There he was. So far, he hadn't moved to come out. That was good. Bird always got agitated when he was around. It wasn't Alec's fault. It was just that Bird had always had a bit of an interest in him. He was his own person and had his own thoughts, unlike the other boys in her class who ganged up to make fun of her. Bird thought he was cute, although that wasn't the common view. He wasn't the most popular guy at school, and he got into trouble for asking too many questions, but Bird liked him just the same.

"Good-looking horse, isn't he? Have you named him yet?"

Paul knew that Bird never spoke, but he always tried. Bird appreciated his efforts to treat her like a normal human being. It was more than most people could manage.

"I was glad when your aunt said she'd take him in. Didn't know where else to try. Didn't even have a second choice. I thought of Abby Malone because she's so good with problem horses, but she's going off to school in New York next month, and good for her. She's worked hard for it." Bird could hear the smile on the vet's face.

"Is he settling in?" Paul sat on the fence beside Bird. Not too close. Just the right distance. "Sure looks it. Horses like it here. They settle in faster here than anywhere else I know."

They sat in silence for a while, both engrossed in the new horse.

"I don't know why I saved him, Bird. I've never done this before."

Bird found herself looking at the man beside her. Dr. Paul Daniels had a quiet, leathered, handsome face and a relaxed, lanky body. He was old. Probably as old as Hannah. Over forty at least. Most of all, though, he was a person she could trust, if she ever needed to trust someone.

Paul turned to meet her eye, and Bird could see acceptance in the vet's face. She didn't look away. She met the man's gaze and held it until they both turned back toward the field at the same time.

Sundancer suddenly lifted his head in a fluid motion and stared at the driveway. Hector began to bark. A silver sedan stopped at the kitchen door and a nice-looking man in a golf shirt and khakis got out. He slammed the car door shut and walked to the house, combing his fingers through his short greying hair, oblivious to the man and the girl on the fence.

As he was about to knock, Paul called out, "Hi there, Stu. Come to see Hannah?"

Stuart Gilmore, the elementary school principal, spun around. "Paul! Didn't see you there." He walked toward the fence with a warm smile on his face. "Hello, Bird. I came to speak to your aunt about school this fall. She called yesterday and left a message."

His demeanour was more energetic than the vet's. He moved with a slight self-consciousness and some other tension that she couldn't quite define. Ah, yes, she thought, suppressing a grin. He was here with bad news about school. Good.

"Is Hannah here?" Stuart spoke to the vet, not to Bird.

"Don't know," answered Paul. "Her truck's gone. She's likely off to a horse show with some of her students. Right, Bird?"

Bird nodded.

Stuart looked at his watch. "I was hoping to catch her. I guess I'll have to call in later tonight."

The rush of confused emotions emanating from Paul Daniels was so strong that Bird almost fell off the fence. Jealousy. Hmm.

"I was thinking of stopping by the fairgrounds." The vet

climbed off the fence and stood to his full height. "I'll tell Hannah that you were by."

Well, well. The vet liked Hannah and saw the principal as competition. Interesting. Bird couldn't quite figure out why Dr. Paul would bother. As far as she knew, Hannah wasn't interested in romance. He was wasting his time.

She chanced another quick look at Alec. He was listening to music through his earphones, gyrating in the front seat and singing along to a wild tune that only he could hear. He caught Bird looking and stopped dead. He gave her a sweet, crooked smile and an apologetic shrug.

Bird grinned. Then, because she felt happy, she mimicked the way he'd been moving around and throwing his head. She was stopped cold by the surprised look on his face.

He thought she was making fun of him! Bird was mortified. She hadn't meant to hurt his feelings or make him feel stupid. She wanted to hide in a dark hole and never come out. Head down, she ran for the house.

2

Bird

I am not vicious, but I have a mean streak from my grandfather on my mother's side.

BIRD WAITED UNTIL CLIFF AND JOHN finished their Saturday morning chores and took off for breakfast at the Coffee Bean Cafe. Then she slipped out the kitchen door and climbed over the fence into the front field. In one back pocket of her jeans was a vial of Wonder Dust; in the other some apple slices. She deposited a plastic bag containing a brush, comb, and hoof pick on the ground beside the fence.

Her plan was simple: Gain his trust, disinfect his wounds, groom him, then get on his back. She had about an hour before the men returned. Plenty of time. Horses generally took to her right away, but this one was different. Some time alone would surely help.

She watched for a few minutes, then approached the new horse with confidence. *Sundancer. That's your name, better get used to it. And you'd better get used to me, too. I'm not going away.*

The gelding lifted his head gracefully and looked at Bird. Then he casually turned his back. Bird walked around him in a wide arc and faced him again.

Let me fix your cuts, Sundancer. They'll hurt if they get infected.

The horse turned his back again and took ten steps in the opposite direction. Bird followed, positioning herself so that he could see her peripherally. Not wanting to seem threatening, she avoided making eye contact by keeping her head tilted down.

Every time the horse moved, Bird moved, too. If he turned right, Bird would counter, turning him left. If he turned around, Bird would circle him to make him face the other direction. A slow dance, thought Bird, but at least I'm leading. She had seen Hannah perform this exercise with countless horses. It required patience, but eventually the animal would give up and allow himself to be caught. Out of boredom, if nothing else.

Time for the apple, Bird thought. She stretched her hand toward Sundancer, palm upward, with an apple slice on it. The horse looked insulted. He snorted and trotted away. Bird couldn't help but laugh. He'd just let her know that he couldn't be bought. This was going to be interesting.

Bird placed all the apple slices on the ground in a little pile and stepped back. She waited as Sundancer grazed his way over, then greedily munched up the apple bits, never taking his eye off her. He ate every one and looked for more. This was more like it.

I gave you the apple pieces, now can I put this powder on your cuts? It won't hurt.

Suddenly Sundancer reared up, forcing Bird to jump back. The horse spun and dropped back to earth, then trotted away. As he moved across the field, Bird admired his fluidity. His shoulder action was tremendous, with his front hooves flicking out firmly before hitting the ground. His hind end powered his forward movement, and with no discernible effort he was across the large paddock and circling back at a canter.

He carried his head level with his shoulders, and his elegant neck was arched and muscular. Bird watched, transfixed, until she realized that he was coming toward her with his ears flat and his eyes cruel. He was rapidly gathering speed. It looked for all the world like he was going to mow her over.

In an instant, Sundancer had turned the tables. He was

going to make *her* dance. Bird was stunned, her mind frantically searching for options. She couldn't outrun him, and besides, that would send the wrong message. Scared as she was, she wasn't about to let him win. There was only one choice: She would have to trust that he didn't want to kill her. And she wasn't at all sure.

Bird waited until he was three strides away. Then she jumped as high as she could, flapped her arms like a bird, and screamed at the top of her lungs.

Startled, the horse veered sharply to his right, avoiding her by mere inches. Then he stopped and turned. He snorted and shook his head up and down. Agitated, he lowered his head and began to paw the ground. This was not good news.

Struggling to catch her breath, Bird looked him right in the eye. She growled like a lion and loudly clapped her hands. She strutted like an angry male gorilla, swinging her arms toward him while jumping backward to the fence. She hoped it didn't look like she was making a retreat.

Confused by her antics, the horse stretched out his neck and curled his upper lip to get her scent. Bird took advantage of this moment to scramble backward up the rails of the fence and out of danger.

Sundancer was jubilant. The horse knew he had won. Relaxed now, he cantered around the field tossing his head and kicking up his heels. He never once looked at Bird.

Later, Bird sat on a pile of old saddle pads in the window of the tack room, cuddling kittens. Hector lay on the laundry in the corner, and nearby, the old mother cat groomed herself, happy to have a babysitter. Three of her litter had survived; all fluffy and soft, multicoloured and purring loudly.

More cuddles, please. The calico rolled on her back and looked at Bird expectantly. *More.*

Scratch my back, girl. The tabby nudged her hand, trying to capture her attention.

I'll catch you! You're a mouse! The white and ginger kitten pounced on Bird's wrist with her tiny sharp claws.

Calm down kitties, or your mother will fire me.

The week before, one kitten had died. He'd been tiny and his back legs had defects that didn't allow him to walk. It had been very sad.

After the incident that morning with Sundancer, Bird had busied herself with cleaning tack, picking small rocks out of the pastures, grooming horses, and pulling manes. Now, it was nearly seven o'clock and still muggy and hot. Idly, Bird stared out the window at the driveway.

Hannah would be back from the show any minute with lots of stories to tell. Bird smiled and snorted. She wondered if Dr. Paul had dropped by to see Hannah after all. If he had, he'd wish he hadn't. Horse shows were always stressful and Hannah usually had more than she could cope with as it was. She did too much of the work herself, which drove her crazy and made it easy for her students to take advantage.

Bird had been to enough shows with Hannah to imagine how the day had gone. They'd be coming home with ribbons, no doubt, as Hannah was a good coach and the horses were well trained. But by now, Kimberly was probably threatening to sell Pastor for some silly reason. It happened every time. Chances were that Jo had thrown up at least twice, and Hannah would be lucky if Peter showed any interest at all in looking after Zachary, his long-suffering mount. Sweet Melanie was the least likely to cause trouble, but she was easily distracted and needed Hannah's constant guidance.

Bird sighed. Perhaps she should've gone to the horse show with Hannah after all. She could've given Hannah a hand and avoided the whole episode with Sundancer.

Suddenly, Hector started thumping his tail and whining

happily. Singing, really.

She's home! She's home! She's home at last!

Good ears, Hector.

Bird looked through the window and watched Hannah steer the big rig through the stone gates with care. Bird noticed a red-haired passenger beside Hannah. It was Kimberly. Odd. The students usually went home with their parents after the show.

She patted each kitten one more time and jumped down to help.

By the time the rig pulled up to the barn, Bird was there to open the side doors and pat noses while Hannah dropped the loading ramp to the ground.

Kimberly got out of the truck to help. She raised her hand in a little half-wave. Bird waved back. She liked Kimberly. She could be mean and selfish, but Bird sensed a kind heart.

"Kimberly's staying for dinner," said Hannah as she backed Pastor down the ramp. "Lavinia...her mom...is tied up with something and can't get away. She'll pick her up later."

Bird looked at Hannah as she spoke and then at Kimberly. Kimberly was staring hard at the ground, kicking up dust with her riding boot. She's embarrassed, thought Bird. She feels like she's in the way. And Hannah is angry, but not with Kimberly. Lavinia strikes again.

Together, they unloaded all the equipment and the four tired, sweaty horses. They hosed them off with cool water and tucked them into freshly bedded stalls with buckets of water, hay, and their evening grain.

Bird made her way to each stall, dropping apples into the horses' feed as a special treat. At Pastor's stall she stopped for a moment to rub his ears. Kimberly had ignored him ever since they'd arrived.

What happened today, Pastor? Why's Kimberly mad this time?

I dumped her on her head at the show.

Why?

She wasn't paying attention. She was showing off, kicking me in my sides and yanking at my face. I showed her.

That was mean.

She wasn't hurt. She'll pay attention next time.

I hope you know what you're doing, Pastor.

Are you kidding? I trained four kids before Kim.

Bird chuckled and patted his honest, reliable face.

"Thanks, Bird. You're a great help," said Hannah, wiping her dusty hands on her pants. "You too, Kim. It's rather pleasant looking after them, isn't it?"

"Yes. I guess. I don't do it too often."

"It's never too late to start. Hungry?"

"I'm starving."

"Good. Let's go make some dinner." Hannah tousled the girl's red curls with affection.

"Come on, Bird, let's go clean up."

Bird nodded. She was hungry, too.

Exhausted, Bird and Hannah and Kimberly walked from the barn to the house. The shadows were getting longer and the leaves in the maples were fluttering slightly. Bird hoped that the heat wave might be lifting.

As they were passing the front field, Bird's eyes fell on Sundancer as he peacefully grazed. The elegant chestnut gelding seemed to glow in the light of the evening sun. Nobody would guess, she thought, what a maniac he'd been earlier that day.

Kimberly's back stiffened with attention. "Who's that? I've never seen him before."

"Dr. Daniels sent him over yesterday. A gift horse. He warned me four times that this horse is unrideable."

"So he's vicious?"

"Vicious sounds horrible. Let's just say he's unpredictable."

"You mean he has a mean streak?"

"Maybe. Maybe not. We'll see."

"What's with that, anyway? Why do some horses have a mean streak?"

"Usually it's the way they've been handled. Rarely it's the way they were born, but it does happen."

Kimberly nodded, unable to take her eyes off him. "He's gorgeous. What's his name?"

"I didn't ask. There's been so much trouble in his past, I've decided to rename him and start again."

"If I owned him, I'd name him Phoenix, after the fire bird that rises out of his own ashes. He's the colour of flames."

His name is Sundancer, thought Bird.

Hannah looked at Kimberly and smiled. "Well, Kimberly. What a good idea. You have poetry in your heart. You keep it hidden, don't you?"

Kimberly sniffed and yawned. "Whatever."

"Too late, Kimberly," smiled Hannah. "I've already seen it."

Bird took a last look over her shoulder before she ran off toward the house.

Hannah and Kimberly reached the house a moment later.

"Stuart!" exclaimed Hannah.

Stuart Gilmore, the school principal, was standing at the kitchen door in khaki pants and a white shirt with the sleeves rolled up.

Stuart jumped. "Hannah! You startled me." He put his hand over his heart and grinned. "And hello, Kimberly."

"Have you eaten? We were just going to fix some dinner. You're welcome to join us."

"Wonderful," he said jovially, following Hannah and Kimberly into the house. "If you're sure I'm not imposing."

"As long as you're not expecting gourmet fare. We'll barbeque some hamburgers and be lucky to find something for dessert."

"Sounds perfectly delicious," the principal said. "In fact, for dessert, I'll treat for ice cream at Best's."

"Now *that* sounds perfectly delicious." Hannah looked around for Bird as they went into the kitchen. "I'll just wash up and get out of these dusty clothes. I've been in them all day. If you see Bird, could you ask her to cut some lettuce in the garden, pick a few ripe tomatoes, and pull up some green onions?"

Before Stuart could respond, Bird crawled down from the top of the refrigerator where she'd been listening and observing. She took the scissors out of the drawer, grabbed a plastic bag, and, without looking at either adult, headed for the garden. The faster the tasks were done, she reasoned, the sooner they'd eat.

Stuart was nonplussed. "Does she do that often?"

"Do what?"

"Appear out of thin air."

Hannah laughed. "She's stopped surprising me. Bird sees, hears, and understands everything. Plus, you never know where she is."

"I'll make a note of that."

"Make yourselves at home, both of you. There's iced tea in the fridge and I'll be down in a few minutes," said Hannah over her shoulder to Kimberly and Stuart. She hurried upstairs to shower and change.

When Hannah emerged fifteen minutes later, bathed and dressed in a fresh blue cotton shirt and clean jeans, Stuart was sitting at the kitchen table talking to Kimberly. Bird was washing lettuce in the sink.

"So, I hear you're off to Cardinal Cardiff School next month," said Stuart. "We won't have you back at Forks of the Credit?"

"Well, it's time I started getting a real education. And there's a much better calibre of girl at CCS. I should be making friends with the people I'll associate with all my life."

Over at the sink, Bird tried hard not to laugh. She could almost hear Kimberly's mother speaking.

"Heavens, Kimberly," Hannah said. "It sounds like you're more than ready to leave us."

Kimberly blushed. "Well, it's not that I don't like it here. And I love my friends and everything. And I'm not saying that Mr. Gilmore and the teachers are bad or anything. My mother went to CCS, and that's what she says." Kimberly twisted a lock of curly red hair as she spoke. She stopped when she realized that Bird was watching her. "Hannah, why is Bird looking at me like that and not saying anything? She's creeping me out."

Bird stopped washing and stared at the other girl. This was the side of Kimberly that she didn't like—the side that spoke before thinking, that didn't care if someone's feelings were hurt.

"Bird will say what she wants to say, when she wants to say it." Hannah noisily collected cutlery from the drawer and placed dinner plates on the counter.

"But she never does, does she? I mean, say anything," countered Kimberly, studying the other girl closely.

This time, Hannah didn't answer. "Kimberly, wash your hands thoroughly please, then set the table for me. Bird, thanks for cleaning the lettuce. Will you please slice the tomatoes and make a salad?"

"And what can I do, Miss Bradley?" teased Stuart.

"You can start the barbeque and prepare the burgers. And get moving! We're all so hungry we could eat a horse."

"Yuck!" exclaimed Kimberly. "That's disgusting!"

Half an hour later, dinner was on the table. Hamburgers with pickles, onions, ketchup, mustard, and tomato slices shared space on their plates with leafy green salad lightly tossed with vinaigrette. Hannah was the last to sit down, and she bit into her burger hungrily.

"Your message light is blinking," noted Kimberly with her mouth full.

"Thanks," responded Hannah. "I'll check it later."

"What if it's my mother?"

"It can wait until we eat, Kimberly." Hannah took another bite before the eager look on Kimberly's face made her reconsider. Reluctantly she put down her burger and went to the answering machine. She pressed "messages."

"Hannah, it's Eva. We'll be there the weekend before Labour Day; Randy, Julia, and me. Can we stay with you? Mom's place is too small, and Dad, well, you know. He likes his privacy, and I don't want Randy to be alone with him for too long. The old twenty questions routine."

Bird slouched in her seat. The sound of her mother's voice took away her appetite.

Eva's voice rattled on. "Can you be a dear, Hannah, and have a dinner party for us? Invite Mom and George, Dad and whomever he's dating now. I know you won't have a date; ha ha ha ha; you never do. Don't get touchy, now. Call me back today, but not too late. I need my beauty sleep now more than ever! Bye-bye! Call me back."

Bird stared at her burger and willed herself to eat. So, her mother was really coming. Wonderful. At least she'd get to see her sister.

"Eva never needed beauty sleep." Stuart's voice interrupted her thoughts. "She's one good-looking gal."

Hannah nodded. "Mmm."

"And nice, too," Stuart continued. "I've only met her a couple of times, but I remember how she makes everyone around her feel special."

Specially stupid, Bird thought.

"Wow, does she ever talk a lot!" exclaimed Kimberly. "What's with the baby voice? And who's Eva, anyway?"

"Eva's my sister," answered Hannah. "Bird's mother."

"Bird's mother? I didn't know Bird had a mother. Why doesn't Bird live with her, not you? Is it because she doesn't talk? Her mother talks so much, no wonder Bird doesn't say anything!"

Kimberly didn't see the plate coming. Smack in the face with all the fixings. She sat for a second in shock, onions and mustard dripping down the front of her shirt. Then responded in kind, hurling her own plate at Bird. Bird ducked.

The plate, loaded with Kimberly's entire messy dinner, missed Bird's head by inches and shattered on the wall behind her, a mere inch to the left of the window. Immediately, the kitchen became a war zone. Bird leaped at Kimberly and tackled her to the ground, knocking over two chairs and shoving the table aside on the way.

Kimberly fought back, screaming indignantly. "Get off me, you savage! Hannah! Get her off me! Now!" The girls scrambled and wrestled each other with all their might.

After a moment of shock, Hannah and Stuart sprang into action as well. With a great deal of effort, Hannah was able to grab Bird by the arms while Stuart successfully contained Kimberly. Each pair retreated to a separate corner of the kitchen. All were panting with exertion and covered in condiments.

Bird struggled against Hannah's grip, a low growl coming from deep in her throat. She stared hard at the red-headed girl across the room. Do you see me now? Can you tell that I'm here?

Kimberly's eyes were wide with surprise as she returned Bird's look.

Hannah and Stuart assessed the damage, not letting either girl go. Aside from the broken dishes and splattered food, the only injury was a scrape under Kimberly's right eye where Bird had scratched her in the tussle.

"What a mess. I'll take Bird, Stuart. Can you manage Kimberly?"

Stuart nodded, raising an eyebrow. "No fatalities. I think we're okay."

"The medicine chest is above the microwave. You might want to disinfect that scratch. Human nails and all that."

Hannah took Bird to the washroom where she sponged off as much of the dinner as she could. "These are guests, Bird!" she exclaimed, rubbing at the stain on the front of her own shirt. "You don't throw food at guests! You don't throw food at all!"

Bird set her face in a stubborn grimace. And guests should be polite to their hosts, she thought. What did Hannah expect her to do? Let Kimberly insult her? She just didn't get it.

"What will Mr. Gilmore think? He's the principal of the school for heaven's sake! What do you think your chances are now?"

Bird wearily appraised her aunt. She didn't get this, either. Bird didn't care about her chances. Right now, she didn't care about anything.

By the time they returned to the kitchen, Stuart had righted the table and chairs, and wiped the floor. Kimberly's tiny wound had been bathed with antiseptic soap, sprayed with Solarcaine, and bandaged at Kimberly's request. Kimberly sat in a sulking heap.

Hannah took a deep breath and forced a smile. "Okay, girls, let's start again. Who'd like a new burger?"

"I want to go home."

"Kimberly, your mom'll be here by nine thirty. We've got a little time, so you might as well make the best of it. Have something to eat."

"Forget it!" She glared across the table at Bird. "She's a maniac!"

I can be a maniac, sure, thought Bird.

Once again, Bird growled from deep in her throat, and Kimberly sprang out of her chair. "She's scaring me! On purpose! What is she? An animal?"

We're all animals, reasoned Bird.

Stuart quietly intervened. "You insulted her mother, Kimberly. Maybe you should apologize."

"I don't apologize to animals!"

"Apologize, please." Stuart's tone was kind but firm.

"If she apologizes first." Kimberly stuck out her jaw.

Bird slowly touched her face with her index finger, on the place where she'd scratched Kimberly. Then she lowered her head and placed her hand over her heart, watching Kimberly closely all the while. I can be nice. Can you?

"Bird has apologized," Hannah said, amazed. "And very nicely, too. Well done, honey. Now it's your turn, Kimberly."

The girl's eyes filled with tears. "I don't know why I should apologize! She attacked me and cut my face open!"

"But you insulted her mother and called her an animal."

"But I like animals! That wasn't an insult!"

"Come now," coaxed Stuart. "You meant it as an insult. Apologize, and we can forget this ever happened."

"Okay! I apologize! But..."

"Let's leave it at that," said Hannah quickly.

Bird smiled at Kimberly. First a small smile, then bigger and broader. Kimberly was suspicious at first but then seemed to realize that it was sincere. She put out her hand. Bird looked at it, unsure how to react. Kimberly began to withdraw it, feeling silly. Suddenly Bird grabbed her hand, then dropped it, embarrassed. Kimberly smiled at her and said, "Can we try to be friends? Not like normal or anything, but friends?"

Bird smiled back. Mission accomplished.

Later, at the ice cream parlour, the girls sat side by side on a bench licking their cones. Bird wondered if they looked like friends to the people passing by. She hoped so. She looked at Kimberly. Kimby, she'd call her if she ever talked. Kimberly was too adult, too formal. Kimby was a girl who needed friends, thought Bird. Real friends who cared about her for herself and not for the clothes she wore or the cool holidays she took with her dad. Show-off stuff. Underneath all that, Bird could feel a goodness in Kimberly, and a creative swirl. Orange and purple. She offered her chocolate fudge to Kimby to sample. Kimberly took a lick, smiled, then held out hers for Bird. Bird smiled back broadly and tasted Kimby's rocky road.

Bird cast her eyes to the bench on the other side of the parlour door, where Hannah sat talking with Mr. Gilmore. She could tell they were talking about her now, and she strained to hear their conversation.

"Stuart, I need to ask you something. And of course you'll answer honestly and I'll accept what you say." Hannah breathed deeply, then blurted, "What are Bird's chances of a place at Forks of the Credit? I haven't had any luck getting her in anywhere else. That I can afford, I mean."

Bird waited for the principal's answer, fingers crossed. The tantrum at dinner should've done the trick.

Stuart sat in thought for a moment. Finally, he said, "I think we can try again."

Oh no, thought Bird.

"Thank heavens," whispered Hannah with pure relief. "I didn't know what I was going to do if you said no. Thank you, Stuart."

"Hannah, I can't promise that she can stay."

"I understand."

"I hope so. Tonight at dinner was a good example of the problem. Bird reacted to Kimberly's prods swiftly and violently. Not much has changed since last year."

"But she apologized. I've never seen her do anything like that before."

Stuart smiled. "That's what changed my mind."

I can't believe this, thought Bird.

"I came over tonight to tell you that we couldn't have her back this year. Now I think there might be hope after all."

"She'll be there, first day of school. With bells on."

"Hannah, I must caution you. I can't jeopardize the entire class for one child. If she causes too much chaos..."

"I know."

"If it doesn't work out, it won't be for lack of trying."

"Thanks, Stuart," Hannah said earnestly. "And I'm sorry about your shirt."

Stuart looked down at his white shirt, now stained forever with mustard. "Invite me to dinner when Eva's in town and we'll call it even."

"Deal." Hannah smiled. "You can't know how much this means to me. And how much this will mean to Bird."

More than you know, thought Bird sadly. I hate school. Everyone thinks I'm a freak. Even I feel like a freak when I'm there.

Bird sat dejected. School started soon. Her life as a free person was over. She let her melting scoop of chocolate fudge fall to the ground.

By ten o'clock, Kimberly's mother still hadn't shown up. There was no answer on Lavinia's cellphone, and no one was home. Bird noted that Hannah had left four messages, just in case.

"Kimberly?"

The girl looked up from *Horse Sport Magazine*, where she and Bird were checking out some shiny new horse trailers. They particularly liked the Four Star three-horse slant with a dressing room.

"You're in the guest room tonight. Bird's blue nightgown will fit nicely, and here's a spare toothbrush. Towels and soap are in the linen closet at the top of the stairs."

"But Mom'll be here any minute!"

Hannah smiled gently. "Don't worry. Climb into bed now, and when she comes, I'll wake you up. We all need our sleep. Bird, you too."

Bird was already yawning at the welcome thought of bed, but Kimberly looked uncertain.

"Aren't you tired?" asked Hannah. "You've had a long day."

"Yes, actually. Very tired."

"Then come along. Bird'll show you to your room. You can get some sleep before your mom arrives."

Kimberly's eyes filled with tears. "Do you really think she's coming?"

"I'm sure she is."

Kimberly whispered, "I think she forgot me."

"Your mother wouldn't forget you," Hannah said lightly. "She's just been held up."

"At her boyfriend's house!" Kimberly spat out. "She always forgets about me now that she has her precious boyfriend!"

Hannah reached out to her, and Bird watched as Kimberly's anger dissolved into tears. She felt sorry for her new friend. She knew exactly how she felt.

"Don't you worry." Hannah gave Kimberly's shoulder a squeeze.

"He's old, too! As old as my grandfather. It's disgusting. And she acts like a baby around him. He buys her everything she wants and likes her to wear teenager clothes. Ugh!"

Hannah patted her back and listened.

"Mom doesn't spend any time with me any more."

A little later, when Kimberly's head started to nod, Hannah helped her upstairs. Bird ran ahead and opened the guest room door and turned down the bed. The minute Kimberly's head hit the pillow, she was asleep.

Bird kissed her lightly on the cheek. She hoped that the

sleeping Kimby would think it was her mother. It's hard to live without a mother's love, thought Bird. Even for a short time. She turned out the light and quietly closed the door.

The phone rang loudly, cutting through the stillness. Hannah ran to her room to answer it, not wanting to wake Kimberly. "Hello?"

Bird peered through the crack in the door. Hannah sat on the edge of the bed, her shoulders tense. It had to be her mother.

"Of course, Eva, you're welcome to stay—Julia and Randy, too." Hannah's voice was light, but Bird knew that she was making an effort to sound happy and relaxed.

"A real family. That sounds good. I'm happy for you, Eva."

Hannah smiled sadly. "Of course I mean it, Eva."

In the dim light of the hall, Bird felt actual pain as her heart filled with grief. She choked back a sob so Hannah wouldn't know she was there. Bird had no illusions. Her mother's "real family" didn't include her.

3

ABBY MALONE

On the ground I'm a pet, but on my back all friendship ceases. This is a problem.

BIRD WOKE EARLY THE NEXT MORNING and dressed quickly. She'd spent much of the night thinking about her mother and hadn't got much sleep. But the new day was bright and sunny, and she wasn't going to waste another second on Eva. Today, she would deal with Sundancer.

She thought about the strange horse as she pulled on her socks. His refusal to communicate with her bothered her. It made her feel handicapped, like a normal person. He was an enigma all right, but Bird had made a vow. She would not be defeated.

As she passed the guest room door she was careful not to disturb Kimberly, who was still fast asleep. She didn't want to awaken Hannah either. This was something she must do, and Hannah could not know.

Bird crept down the stairs and tiptoed into the kitchen, where she filled her pockets with carrots and sugar cubes and grabbed an apple from the fruit bowl. Thus fully armed, she walked out to the field. Sunny looked up, stared at her, then aloofly resumed grazing.

Hector waddled down from the barn wagging his tail. *Nice day. Sure is, Hector. Did you sleep well?*

Never better.

How's the arthritis?

Same as usual. You're not going in there again, are you?

I think I am, Hector.

He's going to kill you. Stay away.

I know you love me, but I have to do this.

I'll be watching.

Bird smiled and rubbed his soft, yellow head. *You're a good dog.*

She climbed up on the fence and considered her plan. Bird had noted the way Sundancer had relished the apple slices the day before. Now it was time for something new. If this horse wouldn't let her come to him, she'd make him come to her.

Slowly, she climbed down into Sundancer's field. She placed carrots and sugar cubes about a foot apart in a row beside the fence. Task completed, she sat down in the grass at the end of the row and began to eat the apple as loudly as she could. *Crunch. Crunch.*

Sundancer did his best to remain uninterested, but as Bird continued to enjoy the delicious treat, Sundancer got more aggravated. He was missing out, and he didn't like it one bit.

Sundancer grabbed the furthest carrot from the ground, eyeing Bird. He ate it, then took a sugar cube. As Bird had hoped, he moved closer and closer as he ate his way along the row. Bird sat still, moving only her jaws as she slowly devoured the apple. Visions of yesterday's mad charge danced in her head. She was ready to leap out of the way should Sundancer decide to knock her over. But so far, so good.

Fifteen minutes passed before Sundancer's nose was at the apple. Bird shifted her weight and turned her back to him. She took another nibble.

Sundancer's neck stretched out to follow the apple. He nudged Bird's arm. She pushed back. Bird shifted again, forcing Sundancer to follow her.

She let him have a taste. He tried to take the whole thing, but Bird stopped him at a bite. Then another. She put her hand on his jaw and stroked him while he enjoyed his hard-won prize. He didn't move away.

Very slowly, Bird stood and offered him the rest. As he gobbled the apple, she seized her moment. In one fluid motion, she grabbed his mane in both hands and jumped lightly onto his back, using the fence rail as a springboard.

Now, that wasn't so bad, was it?

Hannah awoke feeling refreshed and calm. It was Sunday, the least hectic day of the week. She stretched and opened the curtains to look out at the day.

She froze. In the paddock directly opposite Hannah's window, Bird was sitting astride the new horse. Bareback.

As she watched, the big chestnut exploded. He reared up and twisted. Hannah gasped as Bird crumpled into a heap in the dirt. The horse casually kicked up his heels, put his nose to the ground, arched his back, and bucked. His rear legs shot straight up in the air and kicked at the sky. Then he turned and looked at Bird. Bird stood up, brushed off her clothes, and walked toward him.

In her blue cotton nightgown and fuzzy leopard-spotted slippers, Hannah tore downstairs and out the door. "Bird!" she yelled. "Bird!"

Both Bird and the horse turned to look. Hector wagged his tail and barked a hearty welcome. Hannah kept running until she got to the fence.

"Bird," she panted, awkwardly climbing over the rails, "what did I tell you about this horse? He cannot be ridden. We have to do this one step at a time. We must retrain him, like he's a two-year-old. He is unsafe! Do you understand?" Hannah spoke far louder than she probably intended in her effort to get through to Bird. "Do you? Nod if you understand."

Bird nodded. Actually, she had just begun to understand.

"Then why the heck did you get on him?"

For the same reason people climb mountains, I guess, Bird reasoned.

The horse was gloating. Bird saw it. There was an arrogant, superior look of satisfaction in his eyes, as if he'd won a contest. Which, in fact, Bird acknowledged he had. Sundancer two, Bird zip.

Hannah saw it, too, and stared at him. She had her work cut out for her, and it was work that needed to be done now. If Sundancer believed he could push people around, he would try to get his way in everything, until finally he would no longer be useful. She just hoped it wasn't already too late.

She reached out quickly and grabbed his halter before he could move away. "Bird. Get me the lunge whip, my gloves, and a lead line. Fast. I need my riding boots and the socks that are in them, too. Please. They're right by the kitchen door. And my jeans. They're in the basket on the washing machine."

Bird ran off to do as she was bid. This was going to be good.

Ten minutes later, Hannah stood rooted to the ground in front of the proud chestnut gelding. They were in the round pen—a circular enclosure measuring sixty feet in diameter, surrounded by six-foot-high, solid oak walls. It was a valuable training area, and Hannah used it often to teach young horses.

They had interrupted Cliff's morning chores, and he joined them now, a curious look on his face. "Hannah, it's six thirty in the morning."

Hannah turned away from the horse's haughty gaze for a brief second to look at Cliff. Three years earlier, he'd come to the farm from the racetrack. He was tall and gaunt and full of horse knowledge.

"Don't worry, Cliff. I haven't gone insane, or at least not more than usual. Bird was just dumped by pretty boy here, who thinks it's funny. I don't think he should get away with it, and now is always the best time to sort out a problem."

Cliff nodded. "Give you credit, Hannah. If anyone can fix this rascal, it's you. Need a hand?"

"Can you get the gate?"

Cliff nodded.

Bird watched from the stands as Hannah untied the rope from the horse's halter. She flicked the lunge whip and yelled, "Get up!" The horse turned to look at her, eyes hard and challenging. "Get up!" Hannah called again, flicking at his hind end. The horse sat back on his haunches, sprang up in the air then dove down with a mighty buck. He turned his back to Hannah and kicked out at her, missing her by inches.

"Get out of there, Hannah!" cried Cliff. He, too, was watching from the stands, and Bird could see the fear in his eyes and hear it in his voice. "He's going to kill you!"

Hannah flicked the whip harder. "Don't worry, Cliff, this has got to be done. Get up!" The horse bucked again, sending a rear hoof at Hannah's head.

"Let me do it, Hannah. Or send him back. He's not worth dying for."

"Get up!" Hannah called, chasing the horse around the pen. "Cliff, I'm not going to die. Please. You're distracting me."

Now the horse was galloping in a circle around Hannah. "Good boy!" she cooed, keeping her whip pointed at his rear. When he slowed, she flicked the whip and called, "Get up!" Around and around he went. No more bucks, but his eyes still challenged.

Bird watched, chastened. She'd failed. Again. No other horse had ever blocked her out this way. She hoped Hannah would be more successful. If she wasn't, Sundancer would be useless.

Out in the pen, Hannah changed the rules. She put the whip in her right hand and stopped Sundancer's action. The big horse skidded to a halt and spun his rear toward her, preparing to kick. She snapped the whip loudly, sending him around the other way.

With ears pinned back and tail swishing, he was the picture of a malevolent spirit. Even so, there was no disguising his majestic carriage and his natural grace. His action was smooth and liquid, and he moved around the pen with effortless athleticism.

Hannah was relentless. Around and around he ran, Hannah on his tail, snapping the whip and yelling, "Get up!" She never once touched him, but it was plain that she meant business.

Bird admired the way her aunt worked. Tough lady, Bird thought. Her instincts are right, and she knows what she's doing. Sundancer needs this lesson. He is the most pigheaded horse I've ever met, and he feels superior. Maybe this will make him worse, but it's worth a try. He's not good for much as he is.

Twenty minutes later, the horse was flagging but still obstinate. Hannah kept after him.

Bird understood exactly what her aunt was doing. The whole idea was to have him submit. That was the only way he would respect Hannah enough to allow himself to be trained. Many horses hardly resist at all.

In wild mustang herds, the matriarch, or dominant mare, chases a wayward youngster away from the herd and keeps him away until he begs to be included in the group. If she doesn't let him back in, he will be alone and therefore vulnerable to predators. Young fillies and colts soon learn to behave themselves according to the rules of the herd, or die. Monty Roberts, John Lyons, and other respected trainers base their taming technique on this facet of equine behaviour. Bird had read their books, and she knew from her own experience that they were correct. This was what Hannah was doing now.

Sundancer was breathing hard. His nostrils were flared and bright red. Sweat poured off him.

Cliff interrupted again. "Hannah, he's going to burst a lung."

"Better dead than dangerous. He's no good to anyone this way. He has to submit. He can't be the boss." Hannah let him slow to a trot but kept him moving forward. The horse stopped, sides heaving. He faced Hannah and stared at her with hard eyes and a stiff jaw.

"Move on, you stubborn fool!" she cried.

He reared up and lashed at her with his front hooves. Hannah snapped the whip at his feet. He jumped and spun.

Bird had never seen a horse react like this. Usually it took no more than fifteen minutes before the head dropped and the jaws chewed. Then it was a nice, quiet time for saddling up and beginning the training process. But Sundancer did not want to be bettered by anyone. Already thirty minutes had passed and the horse looked like he'd never submit. Hannah was tiring but determined. Who, Bird wondered, would outlast whom?

Sundancer kept moving, trotting now instead of cantering. His bucks and kicks were becoming minimal, and his energy was rapidly being depleted. Still he eyed Hannah with suspicion. How long could he go on like this? Or Hannah, for that matter?

As Bird pondered, the unimaginable happened. The big chestnut gelding sat down on the ground. He simply dropped his rump onto the dirt and skidded to a stop. Then he fell down on his side, breathing hard.

Bird involuntarily rose to her feet.

Hannah ran and crouched beside him. A moment later, she stood, hand on her hip. "You should see his eyes, Cliff!" she shouted. "He knows exactly what he's doing. He's trying to rest without submitting."

She flicked the whip. "Get off the ground! Up! Up!"

Hannah one, Sundancer zip, thought Bird with a smile.

The horse was startled. He had not expected Hannah to persist. He staggered to his feet, then put his head down and rushed at her. She jumped out of his way. Crack went the whip. "Raaaaaa!" she hollered, sounding more like a lion than a human. "Raaaaaaa! Get up!"

Bird could see that Hannah was mad. "Move on!" she cried again as she forced him into another round of circles.

Finally, two long minutes later, the big chestnut dropped his head. Hannah watched closely as he trotted around with his nose almost touching the ground. When his ears began to flick toward her, indicating that he was paying attention to her, she softened her voice. "Good fella. Good boy."

His jaws started to chew. He was declaring defeat. His tongue licked his upper lip.

"Whoa. Whoa, boy. Good fella."

Now the gelding stood quietly. His eyes were lowered, his posture gentle. Sweat dripped off his body, creating a damp spot underneath him in the sand. Hannah walked up and placed her hand on his neck. He quivered at her touch, then relaxed.

Bird jumped down from the seats. She was impressed. Hannah hadn't given up. Now, Bird could finally have her chance.

"Cliff, the saddle and bridle, please," Hannah said.

Cliff entered with the tack and helped Hannah put on the saddle pad, saddle, then tightened the girth. They slipped the bridle over his head and fastened the buckles. The horse made no move.

"Hannah, you're so exhausted you're shaking. No way you're getting up. I'll do it," Cliff said.

"I'm a big girl, Cliff."

Bird tapped Hannah on the back. Hannah turned to see who was there, and before she could react, Bird had pulled herself up onto the horse's back.

SUNDANCER

"Sun...dan...cer," she croaked.

"Bird!" Hannah hesitated for a moment, deciding how to react. Her eyes blurred. "You named him Sundancer? Well, then, Sundancer it is."

Hannah led Sundancer around the pen with Bird sitting proudly atop. Bird could feel that his attitude had changed. He was mellow and sweet. He was going to be okay. She signalled to Hannah to let go of the reins.

This is just what I imagined, thought Bird. He's big and strong and even after his workout there's more energy in him than I've ever felt in a horse before. Power. Wildness. Danger. His ears are flicking around, picking up every sound and reading every nuance. He's sensitive beyond what's good for him. Each sense seems magnified a hundred times. It must hurt him to live each day.

Hannah did the right thing, Bird thought. Now it's up to me to earn his trust. He doesn't trust because he's worried about being tricked. *I won't trick you, but you don't know it yet.*

Every human tries to trick me.

Sundancer?

Who else is here?

Well, I won't trick you.

Why should I believe you?

Because you can hear what I think.

Hmm. But you can hear what I think, too, girl. I didn't know humans could do that.

Some can, I guess. I can't be the only one.

You're the only one I know. Still, don't count on getting the better of me, girl. I'm very smart.

I'm smart, too.

I'm smarter. I scared you silly.

True, but I came back for another try.

And I dumped you. I can do that again. Any time I want.

Do you know what "putting down" means?

No.

It means putting to sleep. Permanently. Understand something, Sundancer. You were going to be put down because you're dangerous. You're here for your last chance at life.

You're making that up.

No, I'm not.

I don't want to die, girl.

I'm glad.

The woman thinks she got the better of me. She didn't.

She shook you out of your snobbiness.

What do you mean?

You wouldn't talk to me before.

Oh.

You'd better treat her well. She owns the place.

So?

So it'll be game over if you cross her.

She wouldn't do that. I'm the best-looking horse here. By far.

Hannah always says beauty is as beauty does.

Crap.

"Ohmygawd! Look at Bird! She's riding Phoenix! He's bee-you-tyful!" Kimberly's shrill voice surprised Sundancer, and the chestnut gelding's head shot up. He was immediately tense. He skittered sideways and threw his head around to find the source of the noise.

There's nothing wrong, Sundancer.

The horse let out a big breath.

He's always waiting for punishment, Bird thought.

Because I always get punished.

You won't get punished here unless you deserve it.

That's what they all say.

That's because they don't know better. Here, we understand horses.

I'll be the judge of that.

"Kimberly, you know how to behave around horses," Hannah scolded in hushed tones. "Look what happened. You scared him."

"I know, and I'm sorry, but I didn't expect this! I woke up and didn't know where anybody was, and I looked all over the place and I finally came here. I thought you said he was unrideable."

"Today's the first day. We'll know more about him as we work him."

"Can I get on?" Kimberly asked.

"No, Kimberly. We're going to take it slow."

"But Bird's riding him."

"Bird was bucked off this morning. She's now back up."

"Phoenix looks awesome."

"He's got a new name. Bird named him Sundancer."

"Right. She can't talk."

"She said, 'Sundancer' when she got on. Sundancer is his name."

"When I buy him, I'll name him Phoenix."

Moments later, Jo, Melanie, and Peter arrived. Soon, everyone was talking at once.

"Who's that horse?" asked Peter. "What's his name?"

"Is that Bird riding him?" wondered Melanie.

"Can't be!" exclaimed Jo. "That's the new horse. My mother told me to stay away from him. She says he's mean."

Hannah turned to face them. "Yes, yes, and yes. Yes, it's the new horse, and his name is Sundancer. Yes, Bird is riding him. And yes, I've heard stories about him, too. That's why we worked him into the ground before Bird hopped on. Literally."

"He's good looking," said Peter. "I like his colour, except for the sweat. Which is all over him."

"And check out his shape," added Melanie. "He's got excellent conformation."

Hannah nodded her agreement. "But beauty is as beauty does. Never forget that."

"And I am definitely going to ask my father to buy him for me," said Kimberly. "Or my mother's new boyfriend. He's old and rich. We'd kick some butt. The judges for sure would notice him."

"What'll you do with Pastor?" asked Jo. "He's a cool horse."

"Do you want to buy him? As of yesterday when he bucked me off and made a fool of me, he's for sale."

"I'll never sell Gem," answered Jo loyally.

"Whatever, but Pastor runs rings around her."

Hannah sensed a quarrel about to start. "Kids, all of you. Get your tack cleaned and your horses groomed. Kimberly and I brought them home and bedded them down after the show. We didn't fuss with them. They still have their manes and tails braided."

Kimberly whined, "Can I please ride Phoenix?"

"No, and his name is Sundancer."

"I'll always call him Phoenix. You said it was a good name."

"It is a good name, for all the reasons that you said. But you have to admit it's rather special that Bird named him."

"Just because she never talks?"

Hannah smiled at the girl's persistence. "Exactly."

Kimberly grimaced and went off to catch up with the others.

By now Hannah's stomach was rumbling with hunger. "Bird, let's call it a day and get some breakfast."

Bird nodded. She pulled the reins to stop Sundancer so she could dismount. He reared up so suddenly and so unexpectedly that Bird slipped in the saddle.

I'm not a plow horse, you know!

She threw both arms around his neck and managed to stay on. *What's your problem?*

Don't pull at my mouth. I've got blisters from the last bozo who rode me. Just relax your legs and sit back.

You didn't need to rear up.

I made my point, didn't I?

Hannah rushed to take the reins. "Well done, Bird. Now sit tight while we get him quiet again."

Sundancer threw his head and sidled. *This is boring, woman. I've had enough.* He pushed against Hannah, testing her authority again.

"We've got to end on a good note. We can't let him win, Bird, or all our work today is worthless," warned Hannah.

Bird sat quietly while Hannah led him. *I meant what I said about Hannah, Sundancer. Give her a break.*

I'll think about it. Begrudgingly, Sundancer walked nicely again.

Hannah brought the gelding to a halt. "That's enough. We'll quit while we're ahead. Take your feet out of the stirrups and slide down."

Bird did as she was told and safely alighted on the arena floor.

Peter came running at full tilt, waving his arms. He yelled loudly, "Hannah! There's a coyote outside the barn!"

Sundancer panicked. His eyes glazed and showed white all around. Hannah braced herself and held on to the reins as he pulled and reared.

Easy, Sundancer. Easy, boy.

No answer. He'd shut down again.

"Sorry, Hannah," panted Peter. "I didn't mean to scare the horse. But there really is a coyote. Right outside!"

"Calm down, Peter. Speak softly." Sundancer reared and walked on his hind legs. He'd begun to sweat heavily again.

Behave yourself!

Bird got no response. Interesting, she thought. He's truly so frightened that he can't think.

"But what about the coyote?" asked Peter shrilly. He jumped up and down with anxiety.

"Peter, please. Calm yourself. Don't worry about the coyote."

"Can I help?" asked a young woman in jeans and half-chaps. She had come in through the side entrance.

"You sure can. I'll hold this rascal. Can you get his saddle off?"

The girl efficiently unfastened the girth and removed the saddle while Sundancer twisted and jumped around. "Done. What about his bridle?"

"I'll take it off once I get him to the field."

"I'll help."

Bird followed silently as they led Sundancer through the barn and back to his pasture. The young woman opened the gate, and Hannah led the prancing horse into the field. After turning him to face the gate for safety's sake, she quickly and carefully slipped the bridle over his ears and dropped the bit from his mouth. Sundancer reared up, twisted, and threw himself into a gigantic buck. Hannah closed the gate behind her and let out her breath.

"What a devil," she muttered.

"No kidding," agreed the younger woman. "I heard he was here. I came over to see him. He's everything I was told, and more."

Hannah turned to look at her visitor. "You're Abby Malone. I would've recognized you right away, but I was a little preoccupied." Hannah smiled. "You were a teenager when we last met. I'm Hannah Bradley. So Peter really did see a coyote."

Abby nodded. "Yes, he sure did. Cody. I'm sorry he caused all that trouble."

Hannah shook her head and laughed. "This horse was causing trouble before you came."

From the bushes, Bird took a good look at the person

standing beside Hannah. Abby Malone was close to Hannah's height, and slight. She possessed self-assurance and directness. She was fair and attractive, with a natural good humour that was appealing. Bird guessed her age at about twenty. She listened to their conversation.

Hannah inhaled deeply. "I'd better get this over with. I don't know if you remember, but my father is Colonel Kenneth Bradley."

Abby nodded. "I know. That's not something I'd forget."

Bird studied her more closely. From family lore, Bird knew that Abby's father was Liam Malone, who had been her grandfather's lawyer for many years. Kenneth Bradley had accused him of stealing money from the family trust fund, and Liam had been sent to prison, based on false testimony. It was Abby's detective work that had uncovered the truth and resulted in Liam's release from prison. Kenneth was later convicted of stealing the money himself, from his own family's fund, and served time in jail.

Hannah was talking now. "I'm very sorry about what you and your family went through because of my father. I can't explain why he did those things. I'm still embarrassed."

"No need. We got the letter you wrote after the trial. It meant a lot to all of us. In fact, my father kept it. But that's long over now."

"I hear that your father's doing great. I'm glad." Hannah smiled.

Bird emerged from her cover and stood beside Hannah, head down. She wanted to get closer to this young woman who had a coyote.

"Hi," said Abby. "My name's Abby. What's yours?"

Bird said nothing, just stared.

"This is my niece, Alberta," Hannah interceded. "Eva's daughter. She was born in Calgary, and my sister named her in memory of the clear air and the smell of pines. We call her Bird."

"I like both names. Alberta and Bird." Abby paused thoughtfully. "Birds can fly. They simply open their wings and they're in a place all their own. Do you do that?"

Bird said nothing, but studied Abby with interest. *I like you,* she thought. *I think you might understand me. A little.*

4

SUNDANCER

I am apprehensive. I wait to see what the new humans want.

HANNAH INVITED ABBY TO STAY for breakfast and the younger woman accepted. With Bird tagging along, the three went inside the house and sat at the kitchen table. The buttercup-yellow walls were bathed in morning sunshine and a slight breeze fluttered the gauzy white curtains. They helped themselves to toast and jam, scrambled eggs, a bowl of fruit salad, and steaming coffee.

It wasn't long before the talk turned to the new horse.

"Bird's named him, haven't you, hon?" Hannah looked proudly at her niece.

"What did you decide to call him?" Abby leaned forward as she spoke, genuinely interested in what Bird might say. For a moment, Bird considered answering. She quickly changed her mind and focused on her hands, now folded neatly in her lap. Abby didn't give up. "Oh, you don't need to be shy with me, Bird. I won't bite, promise."

Bird looked up and saw an open, encouraging smile. She knew she wasn't being fair, but she just couldn't help it. She looked to Hannah for assistance.

"It's not you, Abby." Bird heard the note of resignation in Hannah's voice. "She doesn't speak."

"At all?"

Hannah shook her head. "Not at all. To anyone."

"Why not?"

"That's the million-dollar question, isn't it, Bird?" answered Hannah. "The doctors call it 'elective mutism,' which basically means that she can speak, she just chooses not to. I've heard it called 'selective mutism,' too."

"Really." Abby's brow furrowed. Bird saw the look that passed between the two women. Abby felt sorry for Bird and sorry for Hannah. She didn't understand. No one did. Bird thought about leaving, walking out of the kitchen so Abby and Hannah could talk about her to their hearts' content. But before she could push her chair back from the table, Abby spoke again.

"I'm sorry you don't feel like talking, Bird, because I bet you have some interesting things to say. But sometimes, I think I know how you feel. Sometimes quiet is better, right? It gives you a chance to listen."

Once again, Abby smiled at her. This time, Bird decided to smile back.

"Actually," said Hannah, "today was a big leap forward. Today, Bird spoke for the first time since she was six. Only one word, but she spoke."

"And what word was that?"

"She said 'Sundancer' when she got on the gelding in the round pen."

Abby's eyes widened. "Good name. Why did you name him that?"

Hannah looked at Bird, waiting to see if she might offer an explanation. When none came, Hannah just shrugged. "I haven't given it much thought. I guess because his coat is brightly coloured, like sunshine, and he skitters and dances in his movement. Good reasons."

Abby nodded. "True. But when you told me she'd named him Sundancer, I thought of something different."

"What?"

Abby paused, then said, "He totally reminds me of Dancer."

Hannah nodded. "Absolutely, he does. Same manner, same colour. Nobody knows Dancer better than you, Abby. Well, besides Hilary."

Abby Malone smiled. Abby and the great equine athlete Dancer had won the Grand Invitational a few years back. They'd made local history. Owned and ridden in his prime by Hilary James, the stallion was regarded by many as one of the finest horses in Canada. He still lived at Hogscroft, the nearby farm owned by Hilary James' family.

"Earlier, you said that you heard Sundancer was here," said Hannah. "What do you know about him?"

"Well, he was bred at Owens Enterprises. His sire is California Dreamin'," said Abby. "And the mare is Princess Narnia, one of Owens' finest. From a thoroughbred jumping line of the U.S. Equestrian Team."

Bird wasn't surprised. She'd ridden Sundancer. She knew how special he was.

Hannah, however, seemed more than a little surprised. "How do you know this?"

"A good friend of mine used to be a groom at the Owens stables."

Hannah whistled. "That breeding makes this gelding extremely valuable. Why'd they let him out of their sight?"

Bird stared at Hannah. After this morning's episode, the answer to that question should have been obvious.

"He was a problem right from the start. He reacted extremely badly to training; even putting a halter on him was a big deal. I was told that they worked for two months to get a saddle on his back."

Bird nodded. She believed it. Sundancer had a naturally suspicious nature. Even under perfect conditions, he would've been a difficult horse to train.

Abby continued. "He went through trainer after trainer.

They all gave up. Finally, after trainer number nine was smashed into the kickboards and almost killed, your vet was called in to destroy him."

"Paul Daniels."

"Yes. He filled me in yesterday when he was treating Moonie's ulcerated eye. My regular vet is on a training course, and Dr. Daniels was on call," Abby explained. "He convinced the manager to give the horse one last chance. That last chance was you. When you took him in, Hannah, you saved him."

Hannah considered this new information. "Most times the decision to euthanize a horse is a good one. It's not taken lightly, especially with an animal as well bred as Sundancer. There must have been solid reasons for each of these trainers to give up on him. No one likes to admit defeat."

No kidding, thought Bird, remembering her humiliating first encounter with the horse.

"You're right. Especially pros. His reputation is pretty bad."

"He's stubborn and proud. I know that from our session this morning. He doesn't like to be dominated."

"And he's ultra-sensitive. Apparently he's been like that right from the start. He would've done well in the wild."

"That's an idea. I'll let him go free." Hannah chuckled, then said, "Paul doesn't usually rescue horses. I wonder what possessed him this time."

Abby shrugged. "The horse is gorgeous, young, and healthy."

Hannah wondered, "Who owns him now? Paul? Me? I don't have any kind of deal. I need to speak with Paul and get this straight. Now that I know his origins, I want things to be crystal clear."

"I don't blame you."

Hannah pushed back her chair. She grabbed a paper bag and began loading it with leftovers from the table. "How are Pete and Laura Pierson these days?" she asked, changing the subject. The Piersons were almost surrogate parents to Abby. They lived close by and were a fixture in the community.

"Fabulous," answered Abby with a wide smile. "As interesting and welcoming and wonderful as ever. I see them all the time."

"They must be getting on in years."

"I suppose, but I want to be just like them when I'm old."

Hannah glanced at Bird, making sure she was finished with her breakfast. "Kimberly hasn't had anything to eat. Bird, do you mind running out with this egg sandwich and banana? She'll be at the barn."

Bird rose to leave, sorry that the visit with Abby was drawing to a close.

"Well, time for me to get going," said Abby, rising from her chair. "Chores, job, you know. Thanks so much for breakfast."

"Thanks for all the information. Come by any time."

"I'd love to see how Sundancer's doing."

Hannah smiled at the young woman. "Wonderful. Maybe you could help? I mean, if we decide we can do anything with him."

Abby wrote her phone number on a piece of paper. "I'd love to. Call me whenever you want. I don't leave for school for a few weeks."

"By the way, where's Cody?" asked Hannah.

"Somewhere close and hidden. You never know where he is, but you'll see him follow me when I leave." Abby smiled at Bird. "Goodbye, Bird. See you soon, I hope."

Bird looked out the window as a shadowy four-legged figure slid from tree to tree, following Abby Malone on her bike. She watched until they were out of sight and then ran for the barn, Kimberly's breakfast clutched in her hands.

"Bird pushed me first!" exclaimed Melanie.

"And she ran into me like a bulldozer!" stated Peter.

"She just went crazy," explained Jo. "It's amazing that she didn't hurt anyone."

"I told them not to bug her about Phoenix," said Kimberly smugly. "I told them about her tantrum last night at dinner."

Hannah sighed and rubbed her temples. Ten minutes ago she'd been in the kitchen, cleaning up after breakfast. Now this. "Let's start at the beginning. Bird brought Kimberly's breakfast to her."

"That's right. She did, and I thanked her. It was delicious, Hannah, thanks. I sure was hungry. Then..."

"I'll tell it!" snapped Melanie. "She came over as we were talking about Sundancer, or Phoenix, or whatever his name is..."

"Only I can call him Phoenix," corrected Kimberly.

And only I can ride him, thought Bird.

"And I said that my mother said he was crazy," said Jo. "Well, my mother did *and* she said that he should be put down before he kills somebody."

"And Kimberly said that we should be careful what we said in front of Bird," added Peter. "That she might go crazy, too, like Sundancer..."

"And Melanie said that she's already crazy," said Jo. "That's when Bird attacked Melanie."

Peter jumped in. "When I got her off Melanie, she ran away, then turned and tried to bowl me over. I tripped her and she fell on her nose." He started to laugh then stopped himself, eyeing Bird warily.

Bird lunged at Peter, ready for another go, but Hannah's firm grasp stopped her in her tracks. "Did you listen to what each of you said?" she asked.

They all nodded. "It's the truth," said Jo. "That's what happened."

"Then can any one of you figure out what might have upset Bird?"

It was Kimberly who finally spoke. "We called her crazy. We hurt her feelings."

Bird looked at Kimberly. You're catching on.

Hannah nodded. "Good girl, Kimberly. You remembered from last night. Bird has feelings, just like each of you. She doesn't talk, so she registers her hurt and displeasure in other ways." Hannah turned to face Bird. "Not that I condone violence in any form, Bird. You know better."

"Everyone owes everyone else an apology. Now, let's shake hands all around so we can head out for a ride. It's a beautiful day."

Here we go again, thought Bird, as she reluctantly shook hands with Hannah's students. Most muttered an apology, but only Kimberly looked at her when she spoke. Bird acknowledged her effort with a small smile. To her delight, Kimby smiled back.

Half an hour later, they emerged from the stable one at a time, leading their clean and unbraided horses. Bird listened as they chatted about the latest coloured leg wraps and special flexible stirrups. Everyone wanted the newest thing in saddle pads, and no one could stand the old hard riding caps. Just as they were mounting their horses, Kimberly's mother arrived in her black Suburban.

"Oh, no!" exclaimed Kimberly. "Hide me!"

This is going to get interesting, thought Bird.

"Too late. She saw you," whispered Melanie.

"Kimberly!" called Lavinia Davies. "Get in the car."

"We're just leaving for a hack, Mom. Please can I go? Please?"

"I don't think so, Kimberly." She glanced impatiently at her diamond watch. "I'm running late."

Bird looked at Hannah and saw her own feelings mirrored in her aunt's face. Who did this woman think she was? First, she abandons her daughter for an entire night. Then, she shows up and demands that Kimberly leave. Bird glanced at her sort-of friend. Kimby looked as if she was about to cry. In a rush, Bird remembered Eva's late-night call. She knew just how Kimberly felt.

"Good morning, Lavinia," Hannah said from the shiny black back of Charlie, her Percheron thoroughbred hunt horse. Bird smiled. Hannah wasn't even trying to hide the anger in her voice.

"Oh, Hannah, so sorry about last night. I couldn't quite manage to drop around. But I know you understand."

Hannah responded, "Actually, you're quite right. I understand perfectly."

"You're a sport, Hannah. Kimberly, let's go."

Before Kimberly could open her mouth, Hannah spoke again. "Lavinia, you said you'd pick Kimberly up yesterday at the horse show. You're a day late. We'll be no more than an hour."

Without acknowledging the astonished look on Lavinia's face, Hannah turned her horse toward the open field. Bird grinned broadly. Good for you, Hannah, she thought. It's about time you grew a backbone.

Peter on Zachary followed close behind Hannah, then Melanie on Radar, Jo on Gem, Bird on Jeremy, with Kimberly at the rear on Pastor.

They trotted across the field and slowed to a walk down the rocky path at the edge of the woods. Ducking branches, the horses waded across shallow, muddy Saddle Creek. They picked up a controlled canter once they were on firmer ground. One by one, following Hannah, they jumped the old fallen log, then a wooden coop, and found themselves skirting a growth of fir trees beside a meadow. Down a grassy slope at a brisk trot they went, then cantered along the path into another woods. Bird loved this area. It was full of jumps where trees and limbs had fallen across the path. Singles, in-and-outs, triples, all under two feet high, but difficult because there were so many.

You're a good horse, Jeremy. Bird gave her mount a firm pat on the neck. *I like riding you.*

Thanks. I try my best.

66

What do you think of the new horse?

He's nothing but trouble. He thinks he's too good for us. Put me in a field with him and I'll kick the tar out of him.

He's had some bad experiences.

So have we all. Be careful, Bird.

Interesting, thought Bird. Straight from the horse's mouth. There was truth in what Jeremy said. Lots of horses were ill treated, but not all posed a danger to humans. Lots of horses had bad experiences, but most learned to trust when treated well. So what was different about this horse? Bird vowed to find out. After their ride, as soon as she put Jeremy away, she'd get on Sundancer's back again.

Just then, Pastor reached forward and took a bite out of Jeremy's rump. Jeremy kicked out in retaliation, and Kimberly let out a scream.

"Your horse kicked at me!" Kimberly yelled. "Keep him under control."

Bird looked back at Pastor. *Why did you bite Jeremy?*

Because I felt like it.

Is it out of your system, Pastor? Feel better now?

Actually, I do.

Good. Don't do it again.

Jeremy piped in; *No big deal. He bit, I kicked; we're even.*

"You should hit him!" continued Kimberly. "He's got to learn not to kick!"

Too late, now, thought Bird. No wonder horses get messed up. By the time people get around to hitting them, the horses have forgotten the whole thing.

Once out of the woods the six horses walked single file down the gravel road until they reached another path. This one led into the riding club where a good cross-country course was kept in safe condition.

"Can we do some jumps?" called Melanie.

"I want to practise the drop," chimed Jo.

"And I want to get Zachary over the barrels," added Peter.

"Not today," answered Hannah. The kids all groaned. "The horses were at a show yesterday, and we've done enough jumping today already. Let's head back now."

"Hannah?" Kimberly had to yell to be heard. "My mom would wait, right? She said she would."

Bird could hear the anxiety in Kimberly's tone, and wondered if Lavinia had left. Moms did that sometimes; that much Bird knew for sure. Fortunately, she needn't have been concerned. Lavinia's Suburban was parked at the barn in full sight when they came around the corner.

The kids dismounted and amused each other with horse horror stories. The time a loose horse had jumped into a field of cows and led the herd back to his barn, surprising the horse owner no end. Another time a horse spooked on the road and landed on the front bumper of a car. The stories kept coming as they untacked their horses and sponged them off amid gales of laughter.

Bird thought of the stories she could tell about Sundancer. How he thought he was better than all the other horses, and smarter than all the humans. How sometimes he got so scared he couldn't think. How...She stopped herself. They'd think she was crazy if she said those things out loud. Maybe she was.

Dr. Paul Daniels arrived and walked up to Hannah as she untacked Charlie. Finished with her own grooming, Bird quietly walked over and sat on a bale of hay near where her aunt and Dr. Daniels stood. She chewed silently on a piece of hay and listened.

"Have a good ride?" asked the vet.

"Wonderful. It's a beautiful day."

"Less humid, for sure. I came to check up on the new gelding."

Hannah turned to face her vet, saddle over one arm, bridle in the other. She looked him in the eye. "He's an outlaw. I tried to gentle him this morning. He didn't respond normally. At all."

Paul took the saddle from her and they walked to the tack room. Bird thought about following but decided against it. She was in the perfect position. She could hear them talking but they couldn't see her. She'd wait until she had all the information she needed, and then she'd slip away. She had some business with Sundancer.

"I need to know who owns Sundancer, Paul. Liability and all that."

"I hear you. It's not clear. Owens' stable manager called to have me put him down, but when I saw how good he looked, I asked if I could take him. They were happy to get rid of him, no questions asked."

"And you never asked for proof of ownership? You didn't buy him for a dollar?"

"That would've been too clever. No. I didn't think of it. We can't all be perfect, Hannah."

"If you're trying to make me mad, it's working," said Hannah. "I need to know who's paying his bills, who he belongs to, what I can and cannot do with him. If he's yours, you have the right to instruct me on how you want him fed and maintained, and you'll pay me the first of each month. Same as any owner." Hannah took a breath and continued. "If he's mine, then I'll buy him for a dollar, and I'll need a receipt, signed by his former owner."

"He's dead. Samuel Owens passed away."

"Who inherited his horses?"

"That's not clear. It's probably a company."

"So who had the right to give him to you?"

Paul paused. "I assumed the manager, but I didn't ask any questions. It seemed like a good idea at the time."

Hannah sighed. "You know how the saying goes? When you assume you make an ass of u and me."

Paul was thinking about how to respond when both of them saw the same thing. In the paddock, visible through the tack room window, Bird was sitting on Sundancer's back; no halter, no bridle, no saddle, no nothing. Just a girl and a horse.

They stopped talking and watched.

Bird stroked his neck gently, from his ears to his withers. Again and yet again. It seemed as if the horse was hypnotized. He stood quietly with his ears drooped and his lower lip hanging. His eyes were half-closed.

That feels good. Keep doing that.

Talk to me, Sundancer. Tell me why you went crazy in the barn this morning. What scared you so much that I couldn't get through to you?

Don't stop patting me. I feel better now.

Bird felt light and relaxed on his back. Her legs hung loosely, her back slightly hunched. Her eyes were closed.

I will never hurt you, you know. And I will never let anyone else hurt you. Tell me what happened at the barn.

I don't want to think about it.

Okay. Maybe one day you'll let me understand why you're the way you are.

Suddenly the gelding shuddered violently. Bird, eyes still closed, saw what was in his mind. Was it his imagination or a memory of a real event? She saw a man coming at him with a pitchfork, yelling harshly and waving his arms. A dark stall. No way out. Sundancer reared, striking the man with a front hoof. The man fell and Sundancer ran out of the stall. Out of the barn. Down the road. He ran and ran. He couldn't stop.

From the tack room window, this is what Hannah and Paul saw: Sundancer, for no discernible reason, suddenly reared up, struck out, then raced off.

In an instant, everyone was in motion. Hector started

barking in panic, and Hannah ran through the barn. "Paul, get help!" she yelled over her shoulder. "I'll try to stop him!" Once outside, she climbed the fence and ran for the middle of the field where she'd be closest to Bird if she fell.

On the horse ran, head down, legs stretched to the limit. Bird's fingers clutched handfuls of mane and her legs clenched tight.

It was the yelling that set him off in the barn, she thought. It was a memory; a flashback. When Peter ran in waving his arms and yelling about the coyote, Sundancer just stopped thinking. He's living in a dream and no one can reach him. She clung to him like a burr.

Sundancer raced faster. We're flying, Bird thought. We're not even touching the earth. I've never felt power like this before.

Hannah caught sight of Bird's face. She looked calm and determined. But the horse was another story. A chill went down Hannah's spine as she looked at his face. The gelding's eyes were closed.

"Please, Lord above, save this child," prayed Hannah. She could not begin to imagine how many things could go wrong.

Drawn by the confusion, Hannah's students plus Lavinia, John, and Cliff all came running. Hannah put up the palm of her hand, signalling them to stop and stay where they were. They stood at the fence, shocked by what they were watching. Paul had his cellphone to his ear.

Still running flat out, Sundancer rounded the far end of the paddock and made straight for Hannah. As he approached the fence, Hannah saw his eyes open. Seeing both Hannah and the group that had gathered behind her, the horse skidded to a halt. Bird kept going, over his head and through the air. She landed flat on her back.

Sundancer was scared. He reared up and twisted, then raced off for the other side of the paddock, as far away as he could get.

"Bird!" Hannah called. "Bird!" The girl lay still. Hannah ran fast, Hector following hard on her heels. Hannah knelt beside her in the warm grass. Bird's colour was greying; not a good sign. Hannah tilted her niece's chin up and probed her mouth to find her tongue. Bird had swallowed it. Hannah scooped it out of the back of the girl's throat with her forefinger, and listened with extreme relief to the gurgle and gasp of Bird's lungs filling with air. Hector whined in sympathy at Bird's side.

Paul caught up. "Don't try to move her, Hannah. She may have damaged her neck or spine. The ambulance is on its way."

"Bird, honey. Are you awake? Can you say something?" Hannah crooned. "Open your eyes, Bird darling. Show me you're conscious."

The girl lay silent, eyes closed, breathing shallowly.

Hannah didn't notice the horse until Hector growled. Sundancer had made his way back across the field. Now, he stood beside Bird and slowly lowered his head. He breathed into her nose. Hector growled again, but then backed off. Sundancer moved his lips over Bird's face, trying to stimulate her into consciousness.

I didn't mean to hurt you, Bird girl. I don't know what happened.

Bird didn't know where she was. Sweet horse breath warmed her face as her world turned around and around. She struggled to open her eyes and found that her stomach was queasy.

"Sun...danc...er," she said aloud. Her voice was raspy, unused. "Sun...dancer." Then everything faded to black.

5

Eva

I have everything I need here. A salt lick. Water. Hay. Grazing land.

BIRD FLOATED ABOVE HER WHITE BED in the white room with white lights and people in white gowns. Nothing hurt as they twisted her limbs this way and that. Nothing bothered her as they moved her through big, hollow machines, and rolled her through bright rooms and down long halls. She felt nothing except a pleasant dislocation. She was out of time and place.

She'd had a special glimpse into Sundancer's mind. Fear. Flight. There was much more to see when he was ready to let her in.

She floated above Sundancer as he stood in the dark field. He was alone. He was eating something he liked very much from a bucket.

Sundancer, can you hear me?
Bird. Are you dead?
No. I'll be fine.
Good. I'm sorry. Come home.

Bird smiled sleepily. They'd made a connection. It was a good start.

Hannah, Paul, and Alec sat quietly in Bird's room. She had heard them come in, had heard their whispered words as they wondered when she would open her eyes. She was feeling better now, but she wasn't ready yet. It was nice to sit quietly in the dark, letting her thoughts wander their way through her head. But how exactly did she get here? Bird struggled to remember. Hannah had come with her in the ambulance, she remembered that. And there had been many strangers looking at her; feeling and moving parts of her around. She'd slept. At some point, she'd heard Stuart Gilmore's voice, but maybe she had been dreaming. She'd slept again for a while. For how long, she didn't know.

Bird was flattered that Alec had come. Bird tried to focus. Alec. Where did he come from? He hadn't been at the farm when Sundancer dropped her in the field. Dr. Daniels must have brought him from home. He must have wanted to come, or he wouldn't be here. Bird felt a small thrill. But...maybe he didn't want to be at home. The thrill in her chest subsided. She knew the situation. Alec's mother had left a few years ago. At first, everyone had assumed that it was a typical divorce, but it was more than that. Mrs. Daniels had left more than her husband, she'd left her son as well. No one had seen or heard from her since. Bird knew exactly how Alec must feel. Why stay at home if there was no one there?

The door to the room opened again, and this time Bird decided to look.

"Bird!" Hannah jumped up from her seat to hug her niece before turning her attention to the doctor.

"Mrs. Simms?"

"No. I'm Hannah Bradley, Bird's aunt. Alberta, that is. Simms."

The doctor looked puzzled. "Say that again?"

"I'm sorry. I'm not very coherent." Hannah held Bird's hand tightly as she spoke. "Alberta Simms is my niece, and I'm her guardian. My name is Hannah Bradley."

He nodded, then smiled. "Pleased to meet you. I'm Dr. Jonathon Molesworth. May I speak in front of this gentleman?"

"Yes. Sorry again. This is my friend, Paul Daniels."

"Good evening, Mr. Daniels, Ms. Bradley, the good news is that Alberta has no fractures. We did all the tests, particularly for spine, neck, and skull. She has suffered a concussion, as you're aware. But there might be a serious problem. Although she has shown signs of awareness, she's not speaking."

"She doesn't speak."

"Excuse me?"

"Bird, or Alberta, hasn't spoken since she was six years old. She spoke normally before that."

The doctor nodded, thinking it over. "Has she been diagnosed?"

"Her family doctor believes she's an elective mute."

"Well." Dr. Molesworth looked intrigued. "You don't run across that very often. If that's the case, then she might be recovered enough to go home tonight. We can use the bed. You must keep a close eye on her, though, waking her every two to three hours."

"Of course." Hannah sounded relieved. Bird looked around the room, catching Alec's eye. He smiled and held up an envelope. He'd bought her a card. Bird tried to smile back.

The doctor was still talking. "If she cannot fully waken at any time, or appears disoriented, bring her back here immediately and ask for me. I'm on call all night."

"Thank you, Dr. Molesworth. Very much."

Hannah reached down and ruffled Bird's hair as the doctor left the room. "You gave us quite a fright, young lady. I don't think I've ever been that scared before."

I'm sorry, Bird thought. But I'm not the one you should be worried about. Sundancer's more scared than you or me.

Soon, a nurse arrived to wheel Bird down to Paul's car. Paul and Alec drove them home and helped Hannah get Bird to the door.

"Thanks. I'm very grateful," said Hannah, holding Bird by

the waist to steady her.

"My pleasure entirely," said Paul. "We're happy to be of assistance. I hope you feel better soon, Bird."

"Me, too," mumbled Alec. He looked awkward.

Bird smiled feebly and nodded. She needed her bed.

"Call me if you need me, Hannah. Promise?"

Hannah smiled wearily. "I promise. It's good to have friends at times like this. Good night, folks." They waved goodbye and drove away.

Hector had slipped into the house when he thought no one was looking. Now he was curled up as small as possible on the dog bed in the kitchen. Bird pretended not to see and hoped that Hannah wouldn't notice. Hector used to be an outside dog, but he was getting old, and Bird was happy to have him in the house.

Hannah gently tucked Bird into bed. "I'll be waking you every couple of hours, Bird. You're going to hate me, but we have to do it. What signal do you want to make so I know you're totally awake?"

Bird sleepily placed her two thumbs on either side of her head and wiggled her fingers. She laughed silently, along with Hannah.

"Well, you haven't lost your sense of humour. Now get some sleep, and I'll call your mother," said Hannah as she turned off the bedside lamp and made her way to the door. "I spoke to her earlier and she's worried sick."

Yeah, right, thought Bird.

Bird waited until she heard Hannah pick up the phone in the next room. She turned her light back on and reached out to grab the card that Hannah had placed on the nightstand; Alec's card. Bird opened it with shaky fingers. On the front there was a picture of a fully bandaged person in a hospital bed with both legs in traction and a thermometer sticking out of a gauze-wrapped head. The caption read, "The other guy." Alec had drawn horse ears, a tail, and hooves into the picture, making the figure in the bed look like a bandaged horse. Bird smiled. Inside, Alec had written, "Next time, stay on. Get well quick, Alec."

Bird smiled broadly. She loved his sense of humour, and she was more than a little relieved that he wasn't angry about the other day. He'd just made everything okay. Bird flicked off the lamp and put the card under her pillow. She would sleep on it. Maybe forever.

Suddenly, light from the hall spilled into her room.

Hector, what are you doing here? Didn't the stairs hurt your legs? Hector looked up into Bird's face and cocked his head. His ears stuck out straight on either side. *I'm here to protect you, Bird girl.*

Thank you.

I won't give you a lecture, but I warned you.

I know you did.

That horse cares about you, girl. I learned that today.

Thanks for telling me that, Hector.

But be careful he doesn't hurt you again. He won't mean to, but he might. Sleep tight, girl.

Now that you're here, I will.

Satisfied, the old yellow dog flopped down on the floor mat and slept.

It was one week after the concussion, and Bird felt her old self again. She was dying to get on Sundancer, but Hannah had forbidden her from riding Sundancer, at least for the time being. Bird knew that Hannah was nervous, and that the numerous reports of Sundancer's crazy behaviour were very much on her mind. Hannah had worked him every day for the past week on the lunge line, but she felt he wasn't ready yet for a rider. Also, she'd told Bird that she wanted to get on him first, to try to figure him out. It was certainly true, Hannah always said, that you can't read a horse until you're on his back.

Bird agreed, but she had a secret. And she'd keep it from Hannah until the time was right.

Sitting at the kitchen table, Bird watched as Hannah put down the phone. Eva had called to say that she and Randy and Julia had taken an earlier flight. Instead of waiting for Hannah to pick them up, they'd rented a car and were on their way.

So, it was really happening. Eva was coming to visit. Now. With another boyfriend.

Bird shuddered. Over the years, Bird had seen many different sides of her mother, but the one that was the hardest to accept was the person Eva became when she was with a man. Better to just let things unfold, thought Bird, than to think about the visit too much. At least she'd be happy to see Julia.

Hannah was just as upset as she was. She stood, arms folded across her chest, staring out the kitchen window. The tension was visible in the hunch of her shoulders. Bird hated to see her like this, especially about Eva. She wanted with all her heart to help. Bird went to Hannah and put her arms around her waist. Breathe deeply, Bird willed Hannah. Deeply and slowly. In...out...in...out.

Hannah, pleasantly surprised, hugged the girl back. "Thank you, Bird. I feel better now." Bird kept hugging her while Hannah continued, "Okay, Bird. How are we going to handle this? We haven't met this Randy yet, so let's give him a fair chance, okay?"

Bird let go. That was a lot to ask. She'd never liked Eva's boyfriends. Not one. Randy wasn't likely to be any different. Tears sprang up in her eyes.

Hannah bent down to wipe them away. "We're in this together, Bird. We'll do our best, and make them all feel welcome. Okay?"

Bird made a fist and clenched her jaw. This wasn't fair! None of it! Her mother shouldn't be allowed to come and go as she pleased; to just show up and demand that everybody love her and whatever new man she'd dragged along. It wasn't right and yet it was happening and there was nothing she could do about it. She punched at Hannah in utter frustration. There was no energy in it, and the punch fell short. Her fist relaxed.

"It's only three days, Bird. We can do it."

Easy for you to say, thought Bird. Eva's your sister, not your mother.

Hannah looked at her watch. "It's two o'clock. They'll be here by three, I'd guess. And probably tired and jet lagged. We'll let them unpack and have a cold drink, then do something for a few hours before dinner. Go for a drive around the area, show them the sights. Take a walk. A ride. Whatever they wish." She looked at her watch again. A nervous habit, thought Bird. "Time to bathe and change into clean clothes."

Bird grimaced, then stuck out her tongue.

"Bird." The tone of Hannah's voice told her not to argue. "I want your mother to see I'm taking good care of you." Bird was not convinced. "Not dress-up clothes, just clean jeans will do. Now scoot, they'll be here in less than an hour. Leave me some hot water."

Less than an hour, Bird thought. Time enough.

Bird made for the stairs, then waited. She heard Hannah rummaging in the fridge, then in the cupboard. Soon, the sound of chopping echoed through the hall. Bird quickly snuck outside, across the yard, and into the field with Sundancer. She pulled the old bridle out of the upside-down pail where she kept it hidden. Bird had fashioned it from discarded bridle pieces with a forgotten snaffle bit. She gave a low whistle.

Sundancer, get over here. We don't have much time.

Rule number one. Never hurry a horse. It upsets us.

Are you upset?

Not at all. Just thought I'd give you some free advice.

Bird rolled her eyes. *Stand still for the saddle, will you? Open your mouth for the bit. One minute while I fasten the buckles and slide up the keepers. Okay, I'm ready.*

What do you want to learn today?

Dressage. I saw it on television. Do you know any moves?

Do I know any moves? Does a horse like oats?

So stop joking and get moving.

Okay. Let's skip. Here's how we do it. Hold on.

On cue, fifty minutes later, Hector barked. Bird was clean and dressed.

"Bird, it's them! Are you ready? Come on downstairs!" Hannah ran to the door. She opened it wide with a smile plastered on her face, ready for company. Ready for Eva.

"What the heck are you playing at?" asked a startled Paul Daniels.

Hannah's smile vanished. "You say the nicest things," she snapped.

"No, really," he persisted. "You scared me with that plastic smile. Who are you expecting?"

"Eva and her daughter Julia, and Eva's new boyfriend Randy."

Paul nodded and exhaled. "That explains it. Relax, Hannah. You don't need to be anything but yourself."

"I'm not trying to be!"

Sensing an argument brewing, Paul got down to business. "I've just been over at Owens. Sundancer's ownership might not be easy to secure."

"No surprise there."

Bird sat on the stairs, out of sight, listening attentively to the conversation. She knew that Sundancer didn't understand the human concept of ownership. He belonged to nobody. He would decide who had the right to ride him, and as long as he was fed and had shelter, he didn't bother about what amount of money he was worth. But Bird cared a lot—she didn't want anyone to have the right to come and take him away.

"Owens' manager called me to euthanize him," Paul continued. "According to their books, he's dead. So, if he's dead he can't be sold with or without papers, even for a dollar. Nobody sells a dead horse."

"I get that. And therefore they can't legally transfer ownership." Hannah considered this. "He's a valuable horse...on paper."

Paul snorted in agreement. "Are you thinking insurance fraud? It wouldn't surprise me."

"But you're the vet they called. If he's written off as dead in their books, wouldn't you have had to sign a death certificate?"

"Any vet will do. They know enough not to ask me to fiddle anything."

"I'd hope not. But you think someone else might?"

"Let's just say I've learned not to trust anybody in this business. The manager did say...Hannah, are you going to invite me in, or are we going to have this entire conversation in your doorway?"

"Paul, my sister will be here any minute..."

"And it would look bad if you were having a chat with your vet?"

Hannah laughed at herself. "You're right. Please come in."

Bird made herself as small as possible, hardly daring to breathe as the two adults passed the stairs to the living room. They sank into comfortable chairs and continued to talk.

"You were saying something about the manager?"

"Yes." Paul nodded. "He thanked me for saving him the trouble of organizing the dead animal removal people. Plus the expense of the euthanal cocktail. But even so, he won't draw up an ownership transfer or purchase agreement. The horse's name was Prince

Redwood, by the way."

Prince Redwood? Bird almost laughed. No way. She'd have to tease Sundancer about that.

"So he can't sell or give him to us, but is it fair to assume that he won't claim him back, either? I mean, if a horse is dead...?"

"He can't be claimed back. That's about it," said Paul, stretching his legs out in front of him. "Does that satisfy you?"

"Partially. I wouldn't mind having it on paper."

"Right. And the wording would be, 'We hereby agree not to reclaim a horse we previously stated is dead.' Not likely."

"I see what you mean. I guess I have to go along with it."

Bird sat quietly. This sounded like something that could easily backfire. But she couldn't think of an alternative.

Hannah asked Paul, "So, who owns him. You or me?"

"I have a proposal." Paul sat forward. "How about we own him jointly. I'll pay the board and you do the training for free until we decide if he's redeemable."

"And if he is redeemable?"

"We'll set a price and sell him, fifty-fifty."

"And if he's not?"

"I'll euthanize him, like I probably should've done in the first place."

"What if I want to own him, once he's trained and ready to sell?"

"Let's say that if you want him at any time, then you pay me back what I've paid in board until that time, not a penny more."

"Sounds like a fair deal. I'll think it over."

On the stairs, Bird slumped forward and put her head in her hands. Sundancer must behave himself or he'd be euthanized. Put down, destroyed, killed; there were many ways to say it, but it came to the same thing. His life hung in the balance. Her work was cut out for her.

"I've been wondering, why did you save him, Paul?" asked Hannah.

"It was stupid of me, I know. I'm a vet; it's part of my job to put animals down." Bird heard a squeak as Paul rocked back in his chair. "But there was something about that horse. A dignity. A regal quality. He was overlooked at the Owens stables, one of many. Bypassed. Labelled as a problem. I felt that he possibly hadn't had a fair shake. I looked into his eye and he stared right back. Insolent fellow, I thought. And some whim overtook me. I admit I was thinking of you, how you'd be the one to realize his potential. Call me anything you want, and I've already called myself that and more since Bird's concussion, but when you said you'd take him, I thought it was meant to be."

Bird was touched, and a little surprised. It was the longest speech she'd ever heard Paul Daniels make. She liked him more every time she saw him.

Hannah gave a short chuckle. "I appreciate your high opinion of my skills, but I'm not sure I'll be able to live up to it. Look, let me have a day or two to decide?"

"Sure."

"It's tempting to have you pay the bills. That's a very generous offer."

"I got us into this."

"But I supplied the refuge."

Bird nodded to herself. The deal was as good as done. Hannah could never turn her back on an animal—or person, for that matter—in need. It was fair, as Hannah had said. But Sundancer was on borrowed time. Bird would have to make him understand.

Outside, Hector began to bark. They all heard the sound of tires on gravel, then a car door closing.

"Get your strange and scary smile ready, Hannah, your sister's here."

"Get lost," blurted Hannah, then started to laugh. "Was it really scary?"

"Really scary," answered Paul with a grin in his voice.

Bird quietly moved to a higher position on the stairs. She wanted to see, but not be seen, when Eva arrived.

But it wasn't Eva this time, either. It was Stuart Gilmore. Hannah greeted him as Paul made his way out the front door. "Good afternoon, Stuart. It's nice to see you."

"Hello, Hannah, Paul," Stuart said heartily. "I was just passing by and thought I'd drop in."

Paul gave Stuart a level look. "It's no business of mine."

Stuart stopped in confusion. "Did I interrupt something?"

Bird stifled a laugh as Hannah gave Paul a stern look. It was funny! As usual, Hannah had no idea what was going on. It was clear to anyone looking—anyone but Hannah—that Paul was jealous.

"Not at all, Stuart," answered Hannah, smiling in an attempt to make up for Paul's rudeness. "Paul and I were just talking about a horse problem. My sister Eva's on her way, and I've got a few more things to..."

"Great," said Stuart. "Good timing. It'll be nice to see Eva again." He smiled broadly and made no move to leave.

Bird watched as Paul looked from Hannah to Stuart and back again. It was an awkward moment. Bird was dying to find out what would happen next. It was like one of those soap operas that some of the kids at school watched. Who would get the girl? Except that the competition was all in Paul's mind. Stuart saw Hannah as a friend. This was too good! Bird wished that Kimby was here with her.

Hannah was spared the necessity of reacting, as a car was coming far too fast up the drive.

Let the games begin, thought Bird. She scooted down the stairs and out the back door, around the house and up the big oak overlooking the front door. She settled in just as the red sedan came to a jerky stop in front of the house.

Eva was the first to emerge. She was dressed from head to toe in her favourite colour: pink. Her bleached-blonde hair was swept up in curls, caught in a pink polka-dot bandana. Her pale-pink skirt was short and pleated like a schoolgirl's, showing off her lean, well-tanned legs. Her bright-pink T-shirt was stretched tightly across a chest that looked larger than Bird remembered. Pink ankle socks under pink high-heeled pumps and matching lipstick completed the outfit.

On the front porch, Stuart's jaw literally dropped while Hannah simply stared.

Bird felt ill.

"I'm sooo mad!" pouted Eva as she tottered up the walk. "Randy insisted he knew the way. He wouldn't listen to me and we kept getting lost!"

A grim-faced man opened the driver's door and stepped out of the car. Bird examined him carefully from her perch. He smoothed his skin-tight designer jeans with his hands and brushed imaginary lint from his body-hugging powder-blue sport shirt. His round face featured a thick, dark moustache, and he had a great head of curly brown hair. Bird wondered if it was dyed. His highly polished shoes gleamed in the sunlight. Arrogant but insecure, thought Bird. Time will tell.

Next out was Julia. Nine years old now, she'd grown since Bird had last seen her. Bird's heart lurched as she took in her sister's outfit. Julia was dressed exactly like her mother, but in miniature. It was all wrong. She was pretty, but she looked wan and tired, and more than a little nervous. Don't worry, sister. I'll find you later, when no one else is around, thought Bird.

Bird watched as Eva gave Hannah a huge hug. "It's sooo good to see you!" She looked over Hannah's shoulder at Paul and Stuart. "You must introduce me to your handsome friends."

Where did the Southern accent come from? Bird wondered.

"Of course," said Hannah politely. "Eva, I'd like you to meet my vet, Paul Daniels. And this is Stuart Gilmore, the principal of Forks of the Credit School. Gentlemen, I'd like to introduce you to Eva Simms, my sister."

"Your much *younger* sister," Eva drawled, then giggled.

Paul shot Hannah an amused look.

Stuart, for his part, was smitten. "It's nice to see you again," he said.

Eva batted her eyelashes at him, forming an appealing, questioning look on her face. "When did we have the pleasure of meeting? I *never* forget a handsome man, and I *absolutely* never forget a gorgeous one!"

Stuart flushed as pink as Eva's shirt. "It was five years ago at the Theatre Orangeville fundraiser. You modelled a red flamenco skirt."

"Oh, yes! At the Tijuana Tribute! What fun!" Eva danced in a circle flashing her white teeth, pretending to throw her skirts around. "Ai ai ai ai!"

Was this really her mother? Bird felt sick with embarrassment. Why did Eva always have to flirt, always have to be the centre of attention. Nothing had changed.

Randy joined the group with his beige topcoat over his arm, carrying luggage. He was shadowed closely by Julia.

"I'd like you all to meet Randy Band," said Eva. "And my precious little daughter, Julia." She pointed out each person. "Correct me if I get mixed up. Hannah, of course, Paul, and...Stuart? Am I right?"

"Perfect!" gushed Stuart. Eva smiled at him coyly.

Bird was momentarily distracted by a red squirrel. He was angry about his space being invaded.

"Chee chee chee chee!"

Quiet, Red. I'm only here for a minute, until they go into the house.

This is my tree!

It's my tree, too. Hush! I can't hear!

The squirrel lifted up his tail and scrambled irately away.

While Eva and Randy exchanged pleasantries with Paul and Stuart, Bird saw Hannah observing Julia. Bird knew what Hannah was thinking. She was thinking the same thing. Something had changed. Julia was just as pretty in her blonde, blue-eyed, fragile way, but she seemed more tentative and subdued. But they hadn't seen her for two years, and so much can change in that time. Perhaps it was only fatigue from the long flight. Plus, Bird noted, Julia was wearing mascara and the same shade of lipstick as her mother's. How stupid.

Julia felt her aunt looking at her and turned. "Hello, Aunt Hannah."

Hannah gave her a big hug. "Julia, I'm so glad you're here. I haven't seen you for ages. Welcome back to Saddle Creek."

"Thank you. Where's Bird?" Julia asked. "I'd really like to see her."

Hannah took her hand. "She wants to see you, too, but there are too many people here for Bird. She'll show up."

I certainly will, thought Bird. Don't you worry, Julia.

Eva interrupted them. "Hannah. I brought Randy all the way from California to meet my family, and you haven't even said hello!"

"Hello, Randy, and welcome." Hannah shook Randy's hand. He was shorter than Hannah by an inch or two, and sturdy. Bird guessed that he might be a good deal younger than Eva. "I'm Hannah, and I'm very pleased to meet you."

"Pleased to meet you, too. You don't look anything like I expected. You're attractive." He sounded surprised.

"Why, thanks," said Hannah.

Paul smothered a laugh with a short cough. "I'm on my way, folks," he said as he strode to his truck. "Nice to meet you all. See you later, Hannah. Call me when you decide."

"Right. See you, Paul," called Hannah.

"Decide?" squealed Eva. "Has he asked you to marry him?"

"No, Eva. It's about a horse."

"Hannah! I was kidding. You're always so serious."

Reluctantly, Stuart started walking toward his car. "I guess I have to go, too. It was wonderful seeing you again, Eva. You're just like I remembered. Goodbye Randy, Julia."

"You don't have to go yet, do you?" Eva pouted.

"I'm sure he's a busy man," said Randy forcefully. He took Eva's arm and began to steer her toward the house.

"Yes, I must, but I'll see you again." Stuart got in his car and rolled down his window. "Your sister promised to invite me for dinner."

"Oh, goody. Bye, Stuart!" Eva blew him a kiss.

"See what I have to put up with?" Randy said to Hannah. "She's a terrible flirt. All the time. I can't turn my back for a minute."

"Oh, you big, strong man. You're jealous." Eva kissed him on the lips, and Randy appeared momentarily mollified.

Bird rested her head on the strong trunk of the tree. She felt exhausted. They would be here for three whole days.

Down on the front steps, she heard Hannah think the same thing.

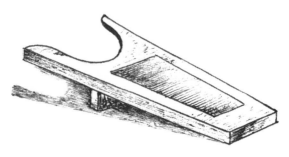

6

COMPANY

I am smarter than most people, and most people do not understand this about me. It causes problems.

EVERYONE DISAPPEARED INTO THE HOUSE. It was safe for Bird to come down.

All yours, Red. See you later.

Not too soon, I hope.

Bird climbed the fence and went over to Sundancer. She needed to tell him what she'd overheard between Dr. Paul and Hannah in the house.

I've got something to tell you, Sundancer.

As she neared, the horse visibly stiffened up. *Don't come any closer, Bird girl.*

Why not?

Just don't. The big gelding flattened his ears and threatened to kick.

Bird was alarmed. *What's wrong, Sunny?*

Nothing. I'm having a bad day. It happens. Now scram before you're sorry you stayed.

You were fine earlier. You taught me to skip! Has something happened?

Don't push it. Get lost.

Okay, but I'll be back. We have to talk. It's important.

Bird made her way back to the house feeling hollow inside.

She didn't know what was worse: Sundancer ignoring her, or having him send her away. She thought she'd gotten through. Now, she wasn't so sure. Not for the first time, Bird was struck by the unique nature of the new horse. He had moods to reckon with. She needed to learn this and be patient.

Bird quietly crept in the back door. She hopped up on the kitchen counter and wiggled into the space on top of the fridge. It was one of her favourite listening spots. People rarely looked up when they were talking, and she'd heard many interesting things at this post. Kitchen, hallway, living room—Bird could hear it all. She momentarily put her worries about the horse aside. It was time to find out what was going on with the people.

Hannah led the way into the living room followed by the faithful Hector, who was limping painfully. "Let's get everybody settled," she said brightly. "I'll show you to your rooms, and then we can talk about what you'd like to do this afternoon." To Bird, her voice sounded forced and overly cheerful.

"Can you hang this up for me?" asked Randy. He handed Hannah his coat. "It's a Burberry. I got it in England." He sniffed proudly. "Belted."

"Of course," Hannah answered. Bird couldn't see what was transpiring in the hall, but she heard every word clearly. "It'll be right here in the hall closet."

Bird heard the clinks of hangers as Hannah found one for Randy's coat.

"Let me," said Randy. There was a scraping sound as he squeezed all of the other coats over to one side of the closet and hung his separately. "There," he said. "This is how I like it hung, not touching other coats, and with the belt flattened properly in the loops."

Bird chuckled. Ooh, I could have some fun with this.

"I'd like to see Bird now, please, Aunt Hannah," said Julia softly. "If I could."

"I didn't forget, Julia," replied Hannah. "I'm not sure where Bird is, but she knows where you are. You know what she's like; she's probably waiting until she can see you alone."

Bird smiled. True.

"Talking about Bird?" asked Randy as he shut the closet door. He whispered audibly, "To tell the truth, living in a house with an autistic child is not my idea of a good time. Eva had to talk me into this visit. I'm not proud of it, but there, I admit it. I'm honestly not looking forward to meeting her."

Hannah's voice was cool. "Bird's not autistic. She has elective mutism. She chooses not to talk, but aside from that, she's perfectly normal. In fact, she's exceptionally bright."

"Eva says she's autistic," stated Randy. "In my book, if the kid doesn't talk, she's autistic."

Don't even bother, Hannah, thought Bird. It's not worth it.

Hannah took a deep breath. "Randy, it's not always as simple as we'd like. Bird has decided not to talk. We don't know why, but we do know she's able to. Two weeks ago she said a word."

"She said a word?" asked Eva from the living room. Bird heard her high heels clack-clacking into the hall. "What word?"

"She named a horse. Sundancer. The one she fell off."

"Sundancer? Bird named him? You didn't tell me, Hannah!" Eva was angry. "You kept it from me? Bird's first word since she was six!"

"Calm down, Eva." Randy sounded annoyed. "What's it to you, Eva?"

"I care about Bird." Eva replied quickly, reining in her emotions. "She's my niece, after all."

"No, Mom," corrected Julia, "She's your d—"

"Come, sweetie!" sang out Eva loudly. "Let's bring our bags upstairs. Auntie Hannah said you can sleep in Bird's room. We're going to have such a fun time!" Eva kept a running monologue all the way up the stairs. "We'll go riding, we'll see animals.

There are kittens, I'm sure!"

Julia's smaller heels clacked up the stairs as she followed along.

"You love pussycats, don't you, darling? Randy does, too!"

Hannah walked into the kitchen, unaware of Bird. She talked to herself under her breath. "It'll be fine. It *will* be fine. Only three days."

Bird watched as Hannah plugged in the kettle then artfully arranged freshly made banana bread and chocolate brownies on a plate. She placed the cups, the creamer and sugar bowl set, and the teaspoons with the fancy inlaid handles on her best tray. She also took a pitcher of lemonade out of the fridge, which she carried out to the screened-in porch off the kitchen and put down beside the coffee. With bright-blue napkins, a bowl of overflowing fruit, and a fresh flower arrangement, the table looked beautiful to Bird and ready for the finest company. Too good for Eva.

"Where's Bird?" asked a small voice. Julia stood behind Hannah with her toes together, wearing pale-pink jeans and a tiny, tight white halter top that showed off her navel and flat little-girl tummy. Bird expected that Eva would show up in the same outfit.

"Julia! You surprised me," exclaimed Hannah. "Bird will find you in her own time, honey. I was just getting ready to serve tea. Are Randy and your mom ready?"

"Not yet. They're in their room."

"Do you want to go and tell them tea is ready when they are?"

It was time. Bird descended from the fridge, surprising them both.

"Bird! There you are!" Julia grabbed her sister tightly. "I miss you, Bird. Come back with us, please?"

Bird drew back from the hug first and took a long look at her sister's outfit. Something needed to be done. Bird disappeared into the laundry room and quickly emerged with one of her own clean white T-shirts. She put it over Julia's head and Julia worked her arms through. Bird smiled. Much better, she thought. Julia smiled back.

"What are you wearing?" cried Eva as she stormed into the kitchen. Bird stepped back and slid behind the door. She wasn't ready to face her mother. Not yet.

"Take that off! It's miles too big!"

Bird peeked around the door frame at her mother. I knew it, she thought. Eva wore a much-too-tight halter top and overly snug pink jeans, just like Julia's. She pulled the white T-shirt off Julia before her daughter could protest. It caught one of Julia's earrings and she winced in pain.

"What right do you have to dress my daughter?" Eva demanded of Hannah.

"I didn't dress your daughter. Your other daughter did." Hannah glanced in Bird's direction and Eva swung around to look.

Here we go, thought Bird.

"Bird?"

Bird stood back and looked her mother over. Her dark eyes scanned Eva from her pink barrettes to her navel ring, to her high-heeled sandals. Then she looked coolly into her mother's face.

"Don't look at me like that," whined Eva. She was disconcerted and turned on Hannah. "Fine welcome. I haven't seen her in two years and that's all I get? A gross stare? What have you been doing to her, Hannah? She wasn't this bad when I left her here."

Bird's stomach began to ache. Her mother hadn't seen her at all. The only thing she cared about was how people saw her.

"Let's have tea, shall we?" Hannah said lightly, ushering them out to the porch. "Then we'll get outside and enjoy this nice day. We'll go for a ride through the woods."

Bird could not imagine sitting down for tea with her mother. She waited until the group made their way onto the porch, then slithered back up to her fridge-top lookout as Randy joined the others at the table. He looked like he was dressed for a part in a western movie. New black cowboy boots, new jeans, white cotton shirt with buttons undone to show off his chest, all topped with a black cowboy hat.

"Howdy, Randy," Hannah said. Bird giggled quietly.

"Hannah," said Randy gruffly, "you're making fun of me."

"Not at all," answered Hannah. "You look ready for our ride. I'm glad, because there are horses out in the barn getting tacked up. As soon as we like, we'll head out to the range. I mean, out for a ride."

In the stables, Cliff had prepared horses for the guests. Sir Galahad had been brought out of retirement for Randy. Stately and slow, the old fox hunter with his regal bearing and glossy mahogany coat pleased the eye and boosted the confidence of any rider.

Lady Sadie was the perfect choice for Eva. The beautiful and dainty quarter horse with her bay coat and black points was elderly now, but in her prime she had been a ribbon winner for the barn. Hannah had even asked Cliff to put pink leg wraps on the mare to please Eva. She squealed happily when she saw them.

Bird lingered at the stall door, watching Sundancer graze in the field. He was tense, still. She could tell by the way he moved. *I wish I could ride you again today.* Bird imagined how they would sail over the fields farther and farther from Eva and Randy. She waited for a response, but none came. Reluctantly, she turned her attention to Eva and the others.

Cliff was having a hard time taking his eyes off Eva, who was posing for him shamelessly as Randy glowered.

Even Julia looked angry. She caught Bird's eye and frowned,

S U N D A N C E R

then focused on her pony instead of her mother. Sturdy and dependable, Timmy did his job with no complaints and pulled no fast ones. Cliff had braided pink ribbons into his black mane and wrapped his legs in pink. Timmy was somewhat grumpy to be dressed in such a silly manner.

You still look masculine, Timmy.

Easy for you to say, girl. You don't have pink ribbons in your mane. And if you did you could take them out.

"Why can't Julia ride this one?" asked Eva, puckering her lips. She was standing at the stall of Sabrina, a delicate chestnut Welsh pony with flaxen mane and tail, and a white blaze down her feminine face. "It looks just like the pony I rode when I was Julia's age. Gingerbread Man."

Here comes trouble, thought Bird.

"Uh...because...uh," stammered Cliff.

Hannah answered for him. "Because Sabrina is not for beginners, Eva. She's really feisty."

"And really pretty," cooed Eva. "Her mane is the exact shade of our hair! Wouldn't Julia look bee-oot-iful on her?" Eva stroked the little Welsh mare's upturned nose and ran a finger along her shiny chestnut coat. "Wouldn't she, Cliff?"

Yes, Bird thought. Julia would look bee-oot-iful on Sabrina. For one minute, max.

"Timmy's a handsome guy, too," said Hannah, throwing a cold look at Cliff. "And he'll get her home safely. Sabrina, on the other hand, might decide to turn around and run back to the barn."

And leave Julia on the ground, Bird finished.

"Let's let Julia decide," Eva persisted. "Julia, which pony would you like to ride. That fat one, or this *gorgeous* one?"

Julia said, "I'd rather ride the fat one today, thank you. When I've practised a bit, maybe I'll ride Sabrina."

Smart choice, thought Bird, impressed with her sister's good sense.

But Eva was upset. "No! I want you to ride Sabrina. You'll look so pretty on her."

"Just do as Eva says, Hannah," grumbled Randy. "She'll be mad all day if you don't."

Hannah spoke clearly, and Bird could hear anger creeping into her voice. "Eva, Julia will be safer on Timmy for a hack outside, and her safety is my responsibility. I'll make you a deal. When we get back, I'll tack up Sabrina and Julia can ride her in the arena."

"Why not now?" Eva said to Cliff, totally ignoring Hannah.

"Because Timmy's tacked up." Hannah stepped between them. "Let's get outside and up on our horses."

Eva sulked. "I don't want to go now."

"I told you," Randy snorted. "If you don't give her what she wants, she'll be mad all day."

"I can have Sabrina ready in two seconds," Cliff piped in.

Hannah glared at Cliff. He shrugged his shoulders helplessly.

Randy took charge. "Put Julia on Sabrina in the arena. If they get along, we go outside for a ride. Easy." He folded his arms. "If you know what's good for you, Hannah."

Hannah was ready to burst, but it was the look on Julia's face that upset Bird the most. She stood meekly, expressionless. All life and energy was gone.

Hannah saw it, too. She knelt beside her niece. "Julia? Are you feeling okay?"

Julia trembled slightly. "Yes, Aunt Hannah. I'll be fine, but I'm scared. I don't know how to ride. Should I get on Sabrina?" She glanced over at Bird, who nodded.

"I'll stay right with you, sweetie. You'll be fine."

"Sabrina's ready!" shrieked Eva. "Darling Julia, you'll look so pretty on her. Randy, did you bring the camera?"

"It's in the house," he answered. "I'll go get it."

"Hurry! This'll be too cute! I'll frame this picture and set it next to the one of me on Gingerbread Man when I was nine. Julia, come!"

Bird gave Julia a small wave, then climbed up to the hayloft, which looked over the arena. The perfect place to watch.

Hannah and Julia walked into the arena where Cliff was holding Sabrina. "Honey, stand over there. I'm going to lunge Sabrina until Randy comes back with the camera. It'll get some of the pep out of her."

Hannah attached the lunge line and clicked. Sabrina raced into a bucking canter. Around and around she tore like an animal possessed, while Julia stood outside the kickboards and watched in horror.

By the time Randy returned, Sabrina was already tiring. Hannah merely said, "Whoa," and the pony slowed to a halt.

Hannah rolled up the lunge line and called to Julia. "Come in, sweetheart. She's good and tired. Let me pop you up into the saddle." Bird felt sorry for Julia. Her sister was stiff with fright as Hannah lifted her up. "There you are. Don't worry. Grab the front of the saddle. Good. Now just relax. Take a deep breath. Very good. I'll lead her. You just sit there, okay?" Julia nodded stiffly.

Hannah led Sabrina around the arena at a walk. Slowly Julia began to relax. "That's better, Julia. This weekend, when your mother and Randy are busy doing something else, why don't you and Bird and I go for a ride together?"

Julia smiled brightly. "Yes, let's! And I can ride Timmy." She looked up at the hayloft. Bird gave her the thumbs-up.

"Randy's got the camera!" Eva yelled. "Hannah, get out of the picture!"

"I'm not letting go until Julia's ready," Hannah called back to Eva.

"Doesn't she look just like me, Hannah?" Eva enthused. "The spitting image? Daddy used to call me his sugar pie, remember?"

Hannah nodded.

"What did he call you, Hannah?" Eva asked. "Julia, you know. What did Gramps call Auntie Hannah when she was a little girl?"

Julia didn't answer.

"Something sweet?" Eva prompted.

Julia remained silent.

"Julia, you can say it," Hannah said softly. "I don't care."

"But it's not nice."

"It's not bad. I don't mind one bit." When Julia clamped her mouth shut, Hannah called out, "I remember, Eva. He called me lemon pie because I was so sour."

"And I was sooo sweet! And Julia is just like me."

"And Bird is like Hannah," added Randy. "That's what Eva always says. Where is Bird anyway, Hannah? We haven't been officially introduced."

I've been here all along, Bird thought. Randy was just like her mother—he didn't see what was right in front of him.

"I want to be like Hannah and Bird, too," said Julia so gently that it was hard to hear what she'd said. She looked up at Bird for support.

"What did she say?" Eva asked Hannah.

"I said, I want to be like Hannah and Bird," called Julia strongly. "I don't want to be a sugar pie!"

"Julia, that's enough!" exclaimed Eva.

"I want to be a lemon pie if Bird and Hannah are!"

Eva seethed, "I said that's enough!"

Sabrina didn't like the anger or the noise. She lifted her head and stiffened her neck.

"Easy, pony," soothed Hannah. "Julia, stay calm." Sabrina tossed her head. "Easy, girl," said Hannah, as she patted the small mare's neck and walked her away from the tension. "Grab her mane with both hands, Julia, just in case. It won't hurt her."

"We have to take the picture!" Eva insisted. "Hannah, come back here. Julia is my daughter, not yours. You can't just walk away like that."

This is getting ugly, Bird thought. I've got to do something.

Hannah spoke in as conciliatory a way as she could muster. "Can this keep until Julia is on the ground? Sabrina is reacting to your tone of voice."

"I can speak how I want, when I want!" Eva opened the heavy wooden gate into the arena and marched in with her pink high-heeled sandals flapping dirt up onto her tight pink jeans.

The feisty mare put her weight onto her back legs and began to lift her fronts. "Sabrina, no!" Hannah gave the pony a stern reprimand.

Eva continued her march toward them. Hannah spoke firmly, "Eva, please. Stay back until I get Julia down."

"Not until the picture is taken. And never, ever, turn away from me when I'm talking." Eva was red in the face. She didn't seem to notice how close she was to Sabrina. The skittish pony took a small sideways hop and landed squarely on Eva's left foot.

Eva howled. "Randy! Randy! I'm crippled!" She doubled over. Tears flowed as she sobbed and hobbled toward the arena gate.

Randy opened the gate and grabbed her arm. "See what you've done?" He shot a nasty glare at Hannah. "This is not rocket science. You should just let her have her way." He held Eva as she limped away dramatically.

Hannah stood holding Sabrina. Little Julia sat in the saddle, completely deflated. "Mommy's going to be mad for a very long time," she whispered. Then suddenly, her face brightened.

Bird led Timmy into the arena. She handed his reins to Hannah and helped Julia down from Sabrina. In less than a minute, Julia was on Timmy's back and Bird was on Sabrina and the two of them were walking quietly around the arena.

Bird had Sabrina walking over poles on the ground, spaced for ponies' strides. Julia followed, mimicking Bird perfectly. Everything Bird did, Julia tried to copy. Julia would make great progress in just a few days.

Bird dismounted and opened the doors to the outside. She shot a questioning look at Hannah, and Hannah smiled. "Just an easy ride today, Bird, okay?"

Bird nodded. She led Sabrina out and Timmy and Julia followed. Bird was up in the saddle in a second, and the two girls grinned and waved at Hannah as they rode away for a pleasant hack in the woods.

This is the way it should be, Bird thought. Julia and me together, growing up as sisters. Not sisters like Hannah and Eva. She wondered for the first time about her mother as a child. Had she always been this selfish and spoiled? And why was Hannah so different? Sugar pie and lemon pie.

As they rode past Sundancer's field, Bird saw Cliff walking out with a halter and lead rope. Sundancer saw him, too.

Lookee here, Bird girl. I'm getting another baby session.

Has he been on your back yet?

No. He's still making me obey ground commands. Whoop-de-doo.

Today might be the day. Behave yourself, Sunny.

I can't promise.

Yes, you can. You have control of your actions, Sunny.

Not always. Sometimes I lose my temper.

I know, but try. I overheard Dr. Paul and Hannah talking and you're on probation. If you're bad, they'll put you to sleep. Permanently.

Is that what you wanted to tell me earlier?

Yes, Sunny. But you were too grumpy to talk.

I feel better, now. I'll behave myself for Hannah.

Good. It's important.

Bird and Julia walked on, waving to Cliff as he slipped the halter over Sundancer's head. She grinned broadly. Hannah had no idea what she and Sundancer were up to. Hannah believed that she was training him from the beginning, one step at a time. Bird didn't want to upset her plans, and anyway, Hannah's work was complementary to Bird's. The more this horse was worked, the better he would become.

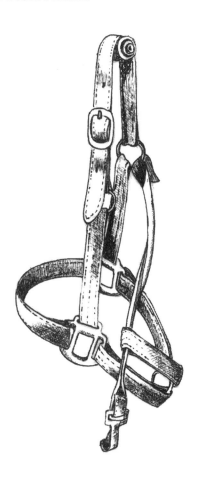

7

THE NEW LOOK

I like two people; the one and the little one.

BIRD AND JULIA CAME IN from the barn flushed and happy, covered in mud, and all wet from hosing down the squirmy ponies, and each other. As they were taking their shoes off at the door, Bird noticed her mother and Randy across the room.

Eva was sitting on Randy's lap in the armchair near the kitchen fireplace. Bird realized that this was the first time he'd really seen her. She gave Randy a level look and allowed him to study her. He seemed nervous—the way some people get around animals. I knew it, Bird thought. He's no different from all the others.

Hannah carried in giant old towels to wrap around the girls. "Randy, this is Bird," she said as she passed a towel to Bird. "Bird, I'd like you to meet Randy."

Randy nodded at Bird. "Hello." He was definitely uncomfortable. He looked at Eva, then Hannah, unsure of what to do or say.

Bird smiled sweetly. She waited until Randy started to smile back, then made a sudden lurch toward him. Randy jumped out of his skin, causing Eva to leap off his lap. Bird laughed loudly. Julia snorted then covered her mouth.

"Bird! Behave yourself," warned Hannah. Randy looked like he was going to speak then decided against it. He gathered his pride and resumed his seat with a loud sniff. Eva glared sulkily at Bird as she nestled herself again on Randy's lap.

Hector had waddled into the kitchen on the girls' heels, tracking in a line of muddy paw prints as he headed to his blanket.

"That smelly old dog has no place in a house," sniffed Randy, grumpily. "Doesn't anybody groom him?"

Bird tensed. *Nice. Taking out your frustrations on a poor dog,* she thought.

Hector knew he was in trouble. His ears drooped and his eyes looked bewildered as he slunk to his bed.

Julia ran to the sink, grabbed the dishrag, and began to follow Hector on her hands and knees, erasing his prints as fast as he made them. Bird stared at her sister, amazed. A minute ago, she had been carefree and happy. Now she was anxious and upset.

"Yes, we groom him, Randy," said Hannah as she dried Bird's dripping hair with a towel. "He gets dewormed, defleaed, and all his yearly shots, but he's not fancy. He's a farm dog. We love him just the way he is."

Eva smirked and rubbed Randy's neck. "How you show love to a dog is in how you care for him. That's what Randy says. Randy treats Bartholomew like a prince. He would never allow him to get like that." She pointed at Hector. "All tufty."

Bird sat down on the floor beside Hector. *You didn't do anything wrong, Hector.* She rubbed his ears as she glared at Eva and Randy.

Tell that to those two.

They don't know anything.

I'm so embarrassed, girl.

They should be embarrassed, not you. I bet we can think of a way to make that happen.

"You can rest easy. We take care of all our animals, including our dog," said Hannah staring warily at Bird. She had long since learned to be extra sensitive with the animals that Bird loved.

Eva and Randy weren't so aware. "But it's a little different on a farm with all the mud and burrs." Hannah tried to get Bird's attention. "We take good care of Hector, don't we, Bird?"

"You should see Bart's wardrobe." Eva ran her fingers through Randy's hair as she spoke. "He has a coat for all occasions. A winter coat, a rain coat, a light sweater..."

"Even a Burberry coat that matches mine," Randy added. "For spring and fall. With a belt."

You've just given me an idea, Burberry man, Bird thought.

"And his bed is tartan. Black Watch from Scotland. He's a Scottie dog, you know," boasted Eva.

"Wonderful. Together you must be quite the sight." Hannah changed the topic. "Did you girls have a good ride?"

Julia jumped up from the floor, dirty rag in hand. "It was terrific! I love Timmy! We went on the path along the cliff and through the woods. We even trotted and I can almost post now! We came back the other way and went in a pond to clean the ponies' feet and we rode past a whole lot of other people on horses. Big horses, too. Can we ride again tomorrow, Aunt Hannah?"

"Sure can," she answered. "I'm so glad you had fun. You'll be a super rider by the time you leave. Now, both of you, get upstairs and shower and change, then come down to set the table."

Bird was out of the room before Hannah had finished her sentence, glad to be away from her mother for even a while.

In very little time, the girls came thundering down the stairs, ready for work in the kitchen. Julia's hair was clean and shiny, and she wore one of Bird's shirts. She looked much happier than when she'd arrived. In honour of Julia's visit, Bird had decided to comb her freshly washed hair and wear a top that matched her pants.

"You both look beautiful," Hannah remarked. "What gorgeous sisters! Now it's my turn to shower and change. Please set the table—and surprise me!"

An hour later, Eva and Randy descended the stairs as Hannah was lighting the fire in the old kitchen fireplace. The table was set in the best silver, on the old lace tablecloth that their great-grandmother had crocheted. The brightly coloured napkins were all different, folded artistically into the empty water glasses. In the centre of the table was an enormous bouquet of summer flowers formerly planted in Hannah's garden. The effect was riotous and pleasing, warm and welcoming.

Bird and Julia watched expectantly for their mother's reaction.

"Fabulous table, Hannah! You've outdone yourself!" she squealed.

"Bird and Julia did it all. Every bit," Hannah said proudly.

"Not really? Julia, you're a little genius! Come give Mommy a hug." Eva opened her arms to Julia, but the girl hung back.

"It was Bird, too, Mommy. Bird did most of it. All the ideas were hers, I only helped."

Randy snorted. "How could Bird have ideas? She can't even talk."

Hannah spoke up. "Bird has lots of ideas. And sometimes it's better not to talk than to say something stupid."

Good one Hannah, thought Bird. But why did her mother say nothing in her defense?

While Randy tried to figure out if he'd been insulted, Bird noted his pale-blue jacket and open white shirt that showed off his deep tan. His black pants were made of shiny fabric, and his black boots added several inches to his height. Eva wore a long pink paisley dress with a low-cut, frilly bodice. Frills edged the slit that climbed up past her knee, and her heeled sandals were covered in the same pink paisley fabric as the dress. Bird guessed that there were smaller clothes for Julia.

"Julia, honey, come put on your dinner clothes." Eva held out a miniature of the dress she was wearing, and smaller replica shoes.

Bird rolled her eyes. Right again.

"I like what I'm wearing, Mommy," Julia replied. She didn't look at her mother. "I'm comfortable."

"Now Julia, sugar pie, I had our dresses and shoes specially made. You know that. They can't go to waste."

"Do us all a favour, Julia, and do what your mother says," said Randy dryly.

Julia sagged. She took the dress and shoes from her mother and dragged her feet out of the room. Bird went with her.

By the time the steaming food was on the table, Bird and Julia had returned. They made their entrance giggling and waited for a reaction.

Bird was wearing Julia's dress with her dirty sneakers. It was much too small for her and looked ridiculous, especially with Julia's shirt on one arm and her pants on her head. Julia wore the pink paisley heels with Bird's oversized clothes falling around her knees.

Bird looked at her mother and was pleased to see that she was angry. She might have been turned to stone, except for her high colour.

"Well, Eva," said Hannah, suppressing a smile. "At least the dress isn't going to waste." Then she, too, broke out laughing, unable to stop herself.

Randy joined in, and when Eva realized that she was outnumbered, she smiled. Bird could tell it wasn't real.

"All right. Very funny. But Julia, before you get dinner you have to wear your clothes properly." Eva's smile was tight.

The laughter ceased. Bird had underestimated her mother. Eva wasn't about to let this go. She led her sister out of the room, glaring at Eva as she passed.

In a surprisingly short time they were back, each wearing their own clothes.

"Very pretty, Julia!" gushed Eva. She was the only happy person in the room. "Don't you think so, Randy?" She waited for his nod, then stood beside Julia, posing. "Don't we look like twins?" She looked at Randy, then at Hannah, waiting for a response.

What is her problem? wondered Bird. Could she not see that Julia was about to cry? Bird touched her sister's arm, trying to make her feel better.

"Yeah, doll," muttered Randy. "Now can we eat?"

Dinner passed without incident, but everyone was on his or her best behaviour. Hannah chatted gaily about the horses, the local gossip, school starting soon—anything to get through the evening. Finally, the dinner dishes were cleared and dessert was on the table. Bird noticed that Hannah had begun to breathe easier.

"Bird needs a haircut before she goes to school," said Eva.

Here we go, thought Bird.

"If she wants," answered Hannah lightly, suddenly tense again.

"Not *if* she wants. She needs a haircut."

"What's it to you?" asked Randy, his mouth full of fresh berries.

"She looks scruffy. Hannah should keep her looking pretty, that's all." Eva looked longingly at the ice cream, then patted her flat tummy and set her jaw. "Also, her clothes are too loose and drab. They don't show her off to her full potential. She needs a new look." Eva poured another cup of decaffeinated coffee and stirred in artificial sweetener. "More colour."

A new look? More colour? A tiny smile crept over Bird's face.

"Bird, would you like more dessert?" Hannah asked.

You can't distract me, Hannah. Not this time, Bird thought.

"Bird?" Hannah tried to catch her niece's eye. "Would you like some more?"

Bird stood up and left the room, just as Julia spoke up in Bird's defense. "Mommy, I think Bird looks pretty. She has her own style, that's all."

Eva harrumphed. "She sure does. Like that dog, what's his name?"

"Hector," Julia answered. "And Bird's nothing at all like Hector."

Randy laughed. "Actually you're right, Eva. They're both rather, shall we say, neglected?"

"I think you're both being mean," the little girl said. She stood up and turned to leave.

Julia stopped in her tracks. Bird was back. It had only taken a few minutes but the effect was dramatic. Everyone in the room froze. Bird smiled broadly. Her thick mop of dark hair had been reduced to chunks of different lengths, leaving her scalp showing here and there. As if that wasn't enough, she'd splashed bright red, orange, yellow, green, and blue poster paint over her clothes. For good measure, she'd streaked her hair with it, too, then wiped her colourful hands on her face.

No one knew how to react.

"Bird got herself a haircut," said Hannah to Eva.

"And her clothes definitely have more colour," added Julia.

Bird stared at her mother defiantly, and Eva glared back, ready for a fight. She was turning purple.

Hannah stood up and put her arm around Bird. "Bird, you look very artistic. _Très chic._ You've got a new look, that's for sure."

For the first time since his arrival, Randy did something that made sense. He put his hand on Eva's arm. "I think we'll go for a little walk. Thanks for a lovely meal, Hannah." He stood, then began to pull Eva's chair out for her.

"I'll go when I'm good and ready, Randy. Alberta, I will not have you putting on a show like this! Go to your room immediately!"

"Eva," Randy said, puzzled. "Let Bird's mother handle this."

She is. You just don't know it, Bird thought.

"She's doing this to upset me! To ridicule me!"

"Eva, let's go. You're embarrassing yourself."

"You don't understand, Randy. You don't understand one bit of it. Bird cut her hair and ruined her clothes to make a mockery of me."

"You're right, Eva. I don't understand. Hannah thinks Bird looks fine."

"What has Hannah got to do with anything?" Eva turned on Bird. "You...get...up...to...your...room! Now!"

Bird didn't move. This was exactly what she'd wanted. She would flush her mother out. Let everyone see what Eva was all about. No more walking on eggs.

Randy backed toward the door. "Eva! You don't yell at another person's child, even if she is your niece. Come with me now, or I'll keep on going, alone."

Bird looked at Randy with new interest. He did have a backbone, and he was getting very angry. Maybe he wasn't as easy to push around as Eva thought.

"Don't go, Randy! I'm coming with you. You're right. I don't know what got into me. Sorry everyone!"

With the slam of the door, Eva and Randy were gone. Silence.

Julia turned to Bird. "Randy thinks you're Mom's niece?" She began to giggle, then she fell on the floor in a spasm of laughter. Bird began to chuckle, then laughed so hard that she had to clutch her belly. Hannah hugged them both, caught up in the mischief. All three were a mess of laughter and poster paint.

This is what a family should be like, thought Bird. Fun and loving, not cruel and insensitive. If Eva couldn't understand this, it was her loss.

Bird and Julia helped Hannah clear the table and scrape and load dishes into the dishwasher. They scrubbed the pots and pans and swept the floor. In minutes, the kitchen was clean.

"Thanks, girls," said Hannah. "You're the best. Both of you. And Bird, I love your new look. It's completely original—it suits you."

"I agree, Aunt Hannah," said Julia, giggling again. "That's what I'd call an extreme make-over! And the best part is how Mom couldn't do anything! I wish I was as brave as you, Bird. Nothing scares you, not even Mom."

Bird reached out and hugged her sister. Plenty of things scare me. I'm just good at hiding them.

"Is there anything you want to do until bedtime?" asked Hannah.

Bird took Julia's hand and led her to the kitchen door. She looked questioningly at Hannah.

"Sure. Go outside. I'll ring the cowbell at quarter to nine. That gives you an hour to play."

Hannah had barely sat down in a chair with her book when Eva hollered through the window. "Hannah, why did you let Bird ride Sundancer? After her concussion? Are you insane?"

Hannah leaped to her feet. She ran to the door and opened it. Sure enough, Bird was trotting along the fenceline on Sundancer. Julia sat on the top rail, clapping her hands in appreciation.

The horse looked wonderful. His coat glistened in the softening rays of the evening sun. His legs strode out in perfect rhythm, strong and sound. His head was nicely tucked, his neck arched.

Sunny, Hannah and Mom are watching. And Randy, too. Mom's never seen me ride before and Hannah doesn't know we've been practising. I don't want to mess up.

I won't let you down, Bird girl. Just come along for the ride. I'll talk you through it.

Bird asked him to move into a canter, and together they sailed. He changed leads. She rode him in a small circle, then a large circle. They changed direction. Now they slowed to a trot. Shoulder-in, half-pass. They reduced speed until he was trotting on the spot. Bird sat straight and tight, giving him lots of leg.

No, Bird girl. Not like that. Put your toes slightly out, but don't dig my sides with your heels. Now, we'll canter shoulder-in. Squeeze just behind the girth with your outside leg. Yes! And play with your inside rein. Good! See how my head wants to bend just so?

Hannah was mesmerized. Bird was doing advanced dressage! She must have been riding Sundancer all along, while she—Hannah the horse trainer—had been pussyfooting around in the arena! No wonder his muscles had developed so quickly. No wonder his tone was so good.

"See, Hannah! Bird's riding the wild horse." Eva had caught up to Hannah, out of breath. Randy leaned against his car, bored by the prospect of yet another tantrum concerning Bird.

"She's doing remarkably well, too," Hannah said.

"Stop her! She'll get killed."

Hannah turned to face her sister. "Does she look like she's in any danger?"

Do you want to try something wonderful, Bird girl?

Sure, Sunny. What?

I've never tried it before. Just sit up and hang on.

Eva opened her mouth with a response, but she changed her mind. Mouth still open, she watched Bird as she quietly sat. The big horse sprang up in the air and kicked out with his back legs. He landed, prepared himself, and did it again.

"Airs above the ground!" gasped Hannah. "I can't believe it!"

Sunny, where did you learn that?

I watched the dressage horses at my old stable.

Very cool!

Thanks for staying off my mouth. It helps.

Now they were skipping together. Two canter strides on the left lead, two canter strides on the right.

It was lovely. The horse was simply stunning, and Bird had never looked more beautiful. Her crazy hair peeked out from under her black hard hat and the paint streaks lit up her face. These two unique creatures were totally compatible.

"Your daughter's full of surprises," Hannah said softly.

"She's a good rider, isn't she?"

Hannah nodded. "Wonderful. I have no idea how she learned those steps. I certainly didn't teach her. I don't know them myself. She's very special, Eva."

Eva's head tilted to one side as she watched her daughter dismount. To Hannah, she looked lonely and lost. She seemed more like the little sister she remembered.

From across the field, Bird caught her mother's eye. This is me. Do you see me now? For the first time, Bird thought that the answer might be yes.

8

THE DINNER PARTY

I'm no different than I've always been. Nothing has changed.

BIRD WOKE UP EARLY the next morning to a bright sunny sky. All was right with the world. She'd impressed her family with the dressage show last night, and she knew that Sundancer's life had been extended, at least for a while. Hannah had seen his considerable talent and his workmanlike attitude. She would have to understand that he was worth the extra effort.

She chuckled to herself. This was going to be another good day; a day full of surprises. Tonight was the dinner party that Hannah had been preparing for, and Bird had been making preparations of her own.

She got out of bed and stretched all over. She looked at her little sister sleeping peacefully on the futon, cuddled up with pillows and blankets, hugging a stuffed pink monkey. There wasn't much time left in this visit. They'd have to make the most of every minute.

Bird quietly woke Julia. They got into their riding clothes, and after a quick breakfast the two sisters ran out to the barn, followed by the enthusiastic Hector. Bird had a soft package tucked under her arm.

To the girls' surprise, Kimberly was in the aisle, brushing Pastor. She hardly looked at them as they came bursting in.

"My mother had other plans," she said without emotion, as

she combed Pastor's mane. "So she dropped me off here. And I'm coming to the party. She arranged it with Hannah."

Bird stood silently as Kimby spoke. The expression on her face was tight and sad. Bird wondered if Lavinia had arranged anything at all. More than likely, she'd simply dropped Kimby off and informed Hannah that she was staying.

Bird and Julia looked at each other. Julia wasn't fooled, either. Both girls surrounded Kimby and gave her a hug.

Kimberly began to cry. "She woke me up so early and she dumped me here and I don't have anything to wear tonight and I can't stand her boyfriend, he's so old and horrible."

Julia wiped away a tear from Kimberly's cheek. "Trust me, we know how you feel. If you want weird boyfriends, check out some of our mother's." Julia suddenly chuckled. "Bird, do you remember the guy with the false teeth?"

Bird rolled her eyes and grinned.

"Mom didn't know until I lost my front tooth and put it under my pillow. He came running in without any teeth and his hands full of money, yelling that the tooth fairy was real, that she'd visited him and now he was rich!" Julia squealed with laughter. "You should've seen Mom's face!"

Bird hooted, pleased that Kimby was laughing, too. Good old Julia, she thought.

Now the three cheerfully saddled their horses and headed out for a nice long ride on the trails along the escarpment. They were determined to make the most of their day.

As soon as they were back, Hannah put them to work. "We've got lots to do, girls," she said. "Paul and Alec are joining us, too, so it will be a full house."

Bird smiled to herself. Alec's coming. Kimberly noticed and winked at her. Bird blushed and looked away.

Hannah put the girls in charge of washing the windows, and

soon the sun sparkled through unstreaked glass. Hector's bed was shaken out and washed. The wood floors, trim and furniture were polished within an inch of their lives. Before long, the house was clean and tidy, ready for company.

There were twelve people coming for dinner, so Randy moved the kitchen table into the dining room and abutted it to their grandmother's big oak table. Eva and Hannah set it with the best of everything Hannah owned, and the girls arranged a centrepiece. Candles and ribbons and small dolls adorned colourful, fresh garden flowers.

When the preparations were complete, Eva and Randy set off to walk along the Bruce Trail, then for a drive around the countryside. Bird was happy to have them gone. Hannah was tense whenever Eva was around. She needed a break before the guests arrived, and Bird knew just the right thing.

Bird went out to the field and caught Sundancer when she knew Hannah was watching. She led him into the barn, brushed him, and tacked him up. When she placed her saddle on his back, Hannah appeared to remind her not to ride alone. Bird laughed.

"You got me, didn't you, Bird?" Hannah said smiling. "Well, I've got news for you. I wanted to start you on jumping lessons, anyway. If you're riding so well in secret, you'll be brilliant with help."

Bird took the horse by the bridle and walked him into the arena. She casually led him to the mounting block and swung her leg over the saddle.

Today, I feel good, Bird girl. I'm happy you're riding me.

That makes me happy, Sundancer.

We'll be together as one.

My brain and your legs.

I have a brain, too, Bird girl.

You think I can forget that?

"Warm him up, Bird. Today we're going to teach Sundancer about doing courses. Going over poles and through jump standards is the first step in teaching him to jump."

While Bird trotted Sundancer in large and small circles, Hannah set down four trotting poles in the middle of the arena. She put jump standards beside the poles to get the horse used to going through them when it came time to actually jump.

"Okay, Bird, keep that nice steady pace and trot him over these poles. Look straight ahead, not at the poles. He's the one who has to figure out where to put his feet, not you. You set the pace and direct him right through the middle. He'll do the rest."

Bird trotted Sundancer in an even trot and came around the corner.

"Look in the direction you're turning, Bird."

Bird looked over the poles. Sundancer turned perfectly and trotted over the poles.

"Perfect, Bird. Perfect. Okay, come through again."

Bird trotted around the ring, again turning toward the poles. Again, she did it perfectly.

"Great! Now, Bird, trot him around and come over the poles from the opposite direction."

This is getting boring, Bird girl.

Relax. Hannah thinks she's teaching us. Make her happy.

Harrumph.

Bird executed the poles perfectly.

"Honey, you're fabulous. You keep trotting. I'm going to put some poles down over here." Hannah laid four poles on the ground with standards on either side, heading sideways to the other poles. "Come on through, Bird."

Bird trotted over the poles, eyes up, steady pace.

"Good! Now continue around and go over the other poles coming toward me, then turn left and do these again."

Bird did exactly as she was told.

Time to jump, Bird, before I explode.

We will, we will. Just be patient a little longer.

"Bird, you're listening carefully and riding beautifully. Your hands are light and your legs are tight. Walk him for a minute or so, and I'm going to set up another set of poles."

Not more poles!

Patience, Sunny.

Hannah created a course of four sets of trotting poles and explained how she wanted Bird to do them.

After Bird trotted through the course, Hannah asked her to go in the opposite direction, and then mixed it up again. Bird and Sundancer completed every possible combination of trotting poles.

"Bird, I'm impressed. Walk him around until he's completely cool, and we'll call it a day."

Hold on. Surely we're not finished, Bird girl? I want to do some jumping!

Right you are.

Bird made an arc with one arm and jumped over it with her opposite hand. Then she smiled hopefully at Hannah.

"You want to jump?"

Bird nodded eagerly.

"Today?"

Bird nodded harder.

Hannah looked at her watch. She considered the request. "Why not? We may be rushing things a little, but let's go."

Bird grinned. Little did she know.

With two poles, Hannah made a low X jump between one set of standards and rolled the other two poles to either side, for ground lines. "Trot at the same speed you were going before, Bird, and canter away when you land. Everything's the same. Look over the jump at the arena wall, not at the jump."

Baby stuff.

Just do it and stop complaining.

Bird did exactly as she was told. She trotted straight at the X, looking ahead, not down. Sundancer lifted his legs over the jump. Bird went with him, cantering away upon landing.

"Way to go, Bird!" came a voice.

"Hooray, hooray!" came a higher one. Bird's eyes searched the arena. Sundancer was unperturbed. He knew people were there all along.

"Three cheers for Bird!" This was a man's voice. "Hip, hip, hooray! Hip, hip, hooray! Hip, hip, hooray!" There were several voices, chiming together, and Hannah and Bird finally located the spectators, huddled in the hayloft: Eva, Randy, Julia, and Kimberly.

"Put up another one!" called Kimberly.

"Yeah! Put up another one!" agreed Julia.

Yeah! I'll show them what I can do!

Bird smiled broadly. She looked at Hannah expectantly.

"Only if you all come down and sit in the seats where we can see you," said Hannah.

"Okay, we'll come down," called Eva. "But admit it, Hannah. You wouldn't have let us watch if we'd asked."

"You're right."

They settled on the benches behind the kickboards. Hannah had one more request. "Even though you're not hidden any more, please keep just as quiet. Bird doesn't need distractions. Although he looks like a pussycat, Sundancer has injured and frightened nine professional horse trainers. Ten if you count me. Bird is making it look easy."

Everyone quietly nodded their assent.

Hannah set up an X at the far end, and asked Bird to trot to the first X, canter away to the far X, land in a canter for three strides, then slow to a trot, then stop.

Piece of cake, Bird girl.

SUNDANCER

Bird did precisely as she was told. The audience clapped. Sundancer turned to look at them, then bowed his head to the ground, bending his knees into a curtsey.

"Holy!" cried Kimberly. "He bows! Like Dancer used to, remember?"

Bird was amazed. Everyone knew how the famous Dancer bowed after great performances, but until this minute, she had no idea that Sundancer did.

Show-off!

Why not, Bird girl? They're here for a show.

"I guess we don't applaud unless we want him to bow," said Hannah. Julia started clapping as loud as she could, and Kimberly joined in. Sundancer dropped his head, bent his knees, and bowed again.

"Cool!" exclaimed Kimberly. "I don't believe it!"

"Believe it," answered Hannah with raised eyebrows. "We don't want him to dump Bird by mistake."

Hannah set up the remaining two sets of trotting poles into Xs and explained to Bird how she wanted them ridden. Once again, Bird executed Hannah's instructions perfectly. It seemed that Sundancer could do no wrong.

"We're finished, Bird. Well done! Now, cool him out." Hannah looked at the group of expectant onlookers and said, "Applaud!"

Eva, Randy, Julia, and Kimberly clapped their hands and cheered. Again, Sundancer bowed. Bird patted his neck, then reached down and hugged him.

Thanks, Sunny. You made me look good.

Are you kidding? This was way too easy. Give me something worth jumping.

We will soon, Sunny, don't worry. I want to jump big, too.

"Bird, you were fabulous," called Eva.

"You're just like your mother," added Randy. "A real horse nut."

For a moment Bird was confused. She looked at Eva, who registered nothing. Then she remembered. She wasn't supposed to be Eva's daughter. She was supposed to be Hannah's. She looked at Randy and managed a weak smile. It wasn't his fault. He was trying to pay her a compliment.

I'm not like my mother at all. And I don't want to be. Bird turned away from the little group of spectators and patted Sundancer's neck. *One day we'll show her. We'll show them all. Just you and me, Sunny. Watch out, world.*

You betcha, Bird girl.

She knew this animal had big talent. How high he could jump was anyone's guess, but Bird expected that he could do the four-foot amateurs easily, and probably higher. Bird imagined being on his back as he cleared the big jumps with ease, imagined Eva watching from the stands, proud to call Bird her daughter.

Bird walked Sunny around the arena, cooling him out. The audience had disappeared. Why should I care what she thinks? wondered Bird. Why do I care about her at all? I'm glad that I live here, with the horses, with Sunny, with Hannah. I wouldn't want to be anywhere else. It'd be nice to have Julia live here with me, though. She's my sister and I love her. Bird shook her head. Enough. She wasn't going to let Eva ruin one more minute of her day.

Bird slid off and began to run up her stirrups.

Bird, let me show you something.

What?

How high I can jump.

Now?

Why not? It'll cheer you up.

Bird listened closely as Sundancer told her what to do. She put the first X up a foot higher and changed the second X into a three-foot vertical. The third X became a three-and-a-half-foot oxer, and she hiked the final X up to four feet.

If you have trouble on the first, I won't send you to the second.

Don't insult me, Bird girl. Bring it on!

Bird climbed back up into the saddle and trotted Sunny toward the first X. It was effortless. They cantered on to the three-foot vertical. With no hesitation at all, Sunny lifted himself over it. Bird looked at the three-foot-six oxer and steered him at it. Sunny sat back and leaped it with inches to spare. Now Bird turned the corner and cantered toward the four-foot X. She kept the pace exactly the same, relaxing Sunny and staying focused. Over they went, as smooth as silk. Just for fun, Sunny let out a kick, and Bird laughed out loud with joy. She leaned over and gave his neck a pat.

What did I tell you, girl? This is small stuff.

Four feet is nothing for you. The sky's the limit!

It cheered you up. Admit it.

You betcha, Sunny. Nothing like jumping to chase away the blues!

Hannah stood at the arena gate in shock.

Bird saw her and stopped the horse.

"That was fantastic, Bird. I mean, I'm speechless."

Bird smiled.

"Fantastic," Hannah repeated. "Tomorrow we'll jump some more, but honestly, Bird, it's not safe for you to jump alone. Especially jumps this size." Hannah smiled and shook her head in disbelief. "I'm amazed. I don't know what to say. We'll come back tomorrow, but now I need you to clean up for dinner. Gran and George are here and Gramps is on his way with his new girlfriend."

Bird nodded and slid to the ground.

"And Bird?" Bird turned. "Look at me. You must not jump Sundancer unless I'm here with you. Agreed?"

Bird nodded again. She had her fingers crossed, just in case.

Everyone was in the living room with drinks and hors d'oeuvres. Bird had disappeared from sight when the guests arrived and hidden herself in the old sideboard. It was a perfect hiding place because it had peepholes created by missing knobs. Earlier, while arranging the centrepiece, she'd moved the spare table linens and napkins to make a perfect nest for herself.

Through one of the holes, she watched Hannah carry in a tray of hot appetizers from the kitchen and offer them to her guests. Hannah was flushed from the heat of the oven, but more from anxiety, Bird knew. She looks like she's waiting for punishment. She's like that around Gramps, not anyone else. Her laugh sounds different. Forced.

Bird's grandmother, Jean, was dressed in a very expensive navy linen pantsuit with a white camisole underneath. Her pale blonde hair was puffed into a grand helmet, and at her perfumed throat hung an appropriate strand of pearls. Very proper and controlled, Bird thought. Perfect in every way, and expects others to be perfect as well. George looked almost nautical, Bird mused, in his grey trousers, navy blazer, and paisley cravat. Stuffed and stuffy. What was left of his hair was snow white, and since they'd arrived, he'd referred to his gold watch several times. It was clear that he didn't want to be there. Bird smiled in sympathy.

Kenneth Bradley—father to Hannah and Eva, grandfather to Bird and Julia, ex-husband of Jean—had decided at the last minute not to bring his new young girlfriend. Smart move, acknowledged Bird. The last thing this party needed was more tension. Her grandfather had chosen the biggest armchair in the most prominent place as his own. A permanent scowl sat on his face, making it impossible to tell if he was pleased or not. Bird studied him closely. He was aging badly. His face was red and puffy, and his belly hung over his pants. He'd retired as master of foxhounds several years earlier but still considered himself an expert horseman. The way his eyes brightened and his face beamed whenever he looked at Eva was not lost on Bird, especially compared to the bored stares he gave Hannah.

Randy crossed his legs, careful not to crease his pants. He obviously felt well dressed in his choice of clothes—orange cotton shirt and designer tan pants. He glanced at his glossy brown leather Bass Weejun loafers with pleasure and sipped on his Scotch. He appeared content. Not for long, Bird beamed from her hiding place. She had big plans for him.

Eva and Julia wore matching outfits in shades of pink: short pink pleated skirts with matching low-cut pink sailor blouses with hot-pink ties, tall pink knee socks and white Mary Jane shoes. They looked to Bird like Barbie and Barbie Mini-Me. Eva's curled hair was held off her face with a white hair band, and Julia wore a ponytail with a white bow. Julia's hair fell straight, a sore spot for Eva, because she'd come in from the barn with too little time to have it curled. That gave Bird some satisfaction, but she still felt awful for her sister.

Eva passed mini-sausage rolls with mustard dip, making sure that she bent low when serving the men. Bird gritted her teeth. Why does she need to do that? She's just like a spoiled cocker spaniel when she's around Gramps. If she had a tail, she'd wag it.

Stuart stood at the window with Paul and Alec. All three had cleaned up nicely, Bird noticed, with their jackets and pressed pants and shined shoes. Alec looked awkward in his best clothes, but he was still handsome. Kimberly stood beside him, talking animatedly about something that was making Alec laugh. Kimby had borrowed a mint-green cotton summer dress from Bird because she'd arrived only with her barn clothes. It looked nice on her, and Bird was happy to lend it, but she secretly wished that Alec wasn't enjoying her company so much.

For the moment, everyone seemed to be having a good time. And it's only going to get better, thought Bird with a tingle of excitement.

"Julia, my girl! Come sit on your gramp's knee," barked Kenneth Bradley, patting his leg. "You're getting to be such a big girl, and as pretty as your mother." He tried to force his face into a smile, but to Bird the result was a bit frightening. Julia must have thought the same, because she hadn't moved from her position across the room.

"Julia, do as Grandpa says," Eva scolded, plopping the sausage rolls on Hannah's tray. She threw back her head so her hair bounced. "I always sat on my father's knee, didn't I, Daddy?"

"You surely did, my sweet sugar pie." He patted both knees. "You come sit, too. For old times."

Eva took Julia by the hand and dragged her over to Kenneth. She lifted Julia onto one knee and then perched saucily on the other. "Isn't this fun, Julia?"

Julia looked miserable. Bird couldn't watch any longer. It was time to do something, time to put her plan into action.

"I always liked you in pink, Eva." Kenneth proudly assessed his daughter.

"I know you did, that's why I wore it. You still do, don't you?"

"You know what I like, sugar pie, and I sure like pink."

Bird slipped out of the sideboard and down the hall toward the mud room. She worked quietly, listening to the ridiculous conversation as it went on and on. She wondered briefly what the other guests thought. Especially Alec. She hoped he didn't think it too weird.

Eva continued giggling. "And doesn't Julia look nice in pink, too?"

"She surely does." Kenneth nodded and grinned. "Makes me think of you as a child."

"Are you saying that we look pretty in pink?" Eva prompted.

"You look more than pretty. You look delicious! Good enough to eat!" Bird heard a great roar, followed by pretend gobbling noises. Eva shrieked with laughter.

It was time to make her entrance. She walked down the hall with Hector waddling happily by her side, then stood quietly at the doorway, waiting. It didn't take long for the guests to notice her. She had painted her entire body bright pink and had streaked pink poster paint through her chopped hair. She wore an outfit made from pinned-together scraps of tan and plaid fabric. Beside her stood Hector, eyes bright and tail wagging, proudly wearing a Burberry dog coat.

Hannah was the first to react. She dropped the tray of cheese balls and sausage rolls. Hector lunged for them hungrily.

Kimberly shrieked, "Bird looks pretty in pink, too!" Alec and Julia giggled hysterically at the outrageous sight.

"My coat!" sputtered Randy. "My belted Burberry!" He ran to the closet, whipped it open, confirmed that it was gone, then turned back to Bird in horror.

Randy glared at Hannah. "Hannah! Your daughter has destroyed my coat. What are you going to do about it?"

At the sound of the raised voice, Hector lifted his head and looked around. Quickly, he slipped out the back door, coat and all, sated with sausage rolls and cheese balls.

Bird looked at Hannah, willing her not to play along. This is Eva's problem. Let her deal with it. She turned her attention to Eva and waited for her to make a move.

Eva slowly stood up and rearranged her clothes. She said nothing as she busied herself with putting each pleat of her skirt in order. Bird stared at her mother, completely shocked. She wasn't going to say anything! She was going to stand in a roomful of people and let Hannah take the blame for her bad behaviour. She felt a noise gathering at her throat—a cross between a growl and a scream—and looked around for something to throw. There must be something.

Suddenly, Kenneth Bradley spoke. "You're mistaken, Randy old man. Bird is Eva's daughter. From that broncobuster in Calgary." He eyed the younger man with distaste. "Whatever gave you the idea that Bird was Hannah's child?"

Finally, Bird looked at her grandfather. Who would've thought that he'd come to her rescue? But it didn't matter how or why, the secret was out—Eva's secret—and that was that.

Randy was shocked. He slowly turned his gaze from Hannah to Eva, anger turning to astonishment turning to resignation.

"So that's what's going on. That explains it." He looked directly at Eva. "That's why you get so upset about everything to do with Bird. You're her mother. Not her aunt."

Eva's pleats were now properly in order. She peeked up at Randy and batted her eyelashes.

Bird stared at her mother and waited. Nothing.

"Eva, tell me the truth. Are you Bird's mother?" Randy spoke harshly.

"Now, calm down, Randy old man," said Kenneth. "Let's not get our knickers in a knot. I'm sure there's a reasonable explanation."

Eva ran behind her father's chair and wrapped her arms around his neck.

Randy regarded her for a moment, then turned his attention to Bird. For the first time since his arrival, he addressed her like a human being. "Bird. Who is your mother?"

Without hesitation Bird walked to Hannah. She glared at Eva defiantly through her bubble gum–coloured face.

Kenneth smiled. "Good for you, Bird. Back up your mother."

Bird stared at him, stunned. Is that what he thought she was doing?

"Is everybody in on this?" asked Randy, exasperated.

Paul stood. "Not at all, Randy. You're being hung out to dry, here."

"This is none of your business, whatever your name is!" sputtered Kenneth. "This is a family matter, and we keep family matters within the family."

"My name is Paul Daniels, and I beg to differ, sir," said Paul. "With great respect, a question has been asked, and we are all implicated by our silence."

"What are you, a lawyer?" exclaimed Kenneth.

"No, a vet." Paul smiled in resignation. "But I've had a lot to do with lawyers since my divorce." He turned to Bird. "In one way you're right, Bird. In the last couple of years Hannah has become your mother, hasn't she?"

Bird nodded her bright-pink head and hung on to Hannah with her pink arms. She looked across the room at Eva, who appeared frightened.

Julia ran to Bird and Hannah, and stood rooted. "Then I want Hannah to be my mother, too. I want to stay here with Bird."

Eva shrieked. "Julia, baby! You'll make Mommy cry!"

Randy shook his head. "Can you blame her, Eva?" Clearly, he had had enough. "You pay no attention to Julia except to dress her up like a miniature version of yourself. You don't listen to what she says. You don't ask her how she feels. It's always about you. And if Bird is your daughter...well, I can't even imagine how she must be feeling."

Bravo, Randy, thought Bird. I didn't know you had it in you.

Eva whimpered.

"Careful how you speak to my daughter, boy," snarled Kenneth.

"I don't understand, Eva." Randy never moved his eyes from Eva's face. "Why did you lie about something like this? Did you think I'd never find out? Or that you'd tell me after we were married?"

Stuart Gilmore spoke up. "I'm sorry. I have to interrupt. This is terribly embarrassing." He stood and walked calmly across the hushed room and stopped beside Eva. "Perhaps Eva and Randy could speak in private. No matter what has happened, I think we all should be considerate."

"Considerate?" spluttered Randy. "Of whom? Of Eva who sends away her kid and doesn't admit to her parenthood? Of Hannah, who plays along with Eva's game? Of Bird who's all messed up because of Eva? Of Julia who wants to be a normal kid? Or of me because I don't deserve to be lied to!"

Stuart stood his ground. "I'm sure there's a good explanation."

Kenneth nodded. "That's what I said. Eva, darling, time for you to speak up. What's the explanation?"

Eva, still silent, looked at her shoes.

"Yes, Eva," demanded Randy. "What's the explanation?"

Everyone was quiet, waiting for Eva to speak.

Bird stepped away from Hannah. She opened her mouth. Nothing came out. She tried again. A squeak, then a sigh.

Julia spoke for her. "It's because Bird can't talk." She looked directly at her mother. "Isn't it?"

Thank you, Julia. Bird smiled at her sister. Eva looked at her younger daughter, opened her mouth as if to speak, then closed it again. She began to cry quietly.

Stuart said, "I'm going to take Eva out for some fresh air until she can compose herself. Come with me, Eva."

Hannah spoke up. "Not so fast, Stuart. Eva deserves a chance to explain herself." She prompted her sister. "A chance to tell her kids she loves them."

Eva turned on Hannah, tears streaming down her face. "Of course I love them! I love them with all my heart. It's so easy for you to judge, Hannah. You don't have kids, so you don't know anything about this." She faced Randy. "I did it for you, Randy!

I knew you wouldn't understand about Bird, so I said she was Hannah's daughter. There. That's the truth." With a sob, Eva rushed from the room, followed by Stuart.

The room remained quiet. No one knew what to say.

Finally, Randy spoke. "I'm going upstairs to pack my things, and I'll be on my way."

"Randy," Hannah said. "I'm so sorry about this. I'm sorry I was part of the lie. And I'm sorry about your coat. I'd like to make it up to you. Please stay for dinner? It'll be on the table in one minute."

Randy spoke sincerely. "I don't have an appetite, Hannah, but thank you. Good night to you all." He turned and walked out of the room with as much dignity as he could feign.

"Well," said Paul. "I'm starving. Hannah? Can you use some help?"

"Thanks, Paul!" Hannah smiled too brightly. "Please, everyone! Find your name on the place cards and have a seat. Bird, Kimberly, Alec, Julia! Come with me." She spun on her heel and sailed into the kitchen, followed by everyone except Bird.

Good time to get out of here, Bird thought with growing apprehension. I've caused more trouble than I meant to. She headed for the safety of her tree.

9

Hector

I don't like too many people.

FROM THE BRANCHES OF THE OLD OAK, Bird watched as Randy carried out his bags and loaded them into the trunk of his car. Every once in a while, he stole a sad glance at Eva, who stood in the shade of the tree with Stuart. Randy didn't deserve this, thought Bird. He had his faults, but he seemed a decent fellow, underneath the bravado. Bird hoped that he'd find someone who'd be nicer to him.

Through the front window of the house, Bird could see her grandfather. He was watching Eva, she thought, but there was something else—something very focused about his gaze. Bird looked into the pasture below. Sunny grazed peacefully, completely unaware of all the turmoil. Lucky guy. Bird looked down to where Eva and Stuart had been standing. They were gone, making their way up the path toward the house.

When Bird turned back to face the window, Kenneth Bradley had a cellphone pressed to his ear. Bird didn't like his intensity one bit. Something was wrong here, she just couldn't figure out what it was.

Her thoughts were interrupted by the slamming of the car door. Bird watched as Randy walked around to the driver's door. With one last look at Eva, he got into his car and started the engine. Too late, Bird noticed the patch of yellow—still dressed in Burberry—asleep on the driveway.

No no no no no! *Hector! Wake up! Move!* Bird slithered down the tree in record time and rushed toward the car. *Hector!*

Hector didn't move; he was too soundly asleep to hear her thoughts.

"Arrrrgh!" Bird screamed through dormant vocal chords. "Raaaaa!" She tried her hardest, but the noise that came out of her mouth was not loud enough for either Hector or Randy to hear above the engine noise. Waving her arms, she tried again. "Raaaagh!" It was no use.

Inside the house, Paul was carving the turkey. The remaining guests had just taken their places at the table when a horrible mix of howls and screams and screeching of brakes erupted on the driveway. After a stunned moment of shock, everyone stumbled out of their chairs and went running to see what had happened. Hannah shot out the front door first, followed by Paul.

Bird was under Randy's car, and Randy was yelling for help. Eva was screaming and trying to reach Bird, but Stuart was holding her back.

Hector lay under the back wheels. Blood dripped out of his nose and mouth as Bird gently stroked his head. His tail thumped slowly. He whined softly, eyes full of pain and love.

Stay with me, girl. Please.

I won't leave. I'm sorry, Hector. I was too late.

The car moved.

Are you hurting?

All over. The car moved backward.

I love you, Hector. I always will.

I love you, girl. Goodbye. Say goodbye to Hannah.

Goodbye, Hector, my old friend.

The old yellow dog jerked his head up, stiffened his legs, then dropped down limp. Bird swallowed. He was gone. She silently backed away and sadly climbed back up the oak tree to her perch.

As she passed her mother, Eva reached out as if to stop her. Hannah's voice cut through the silence. "Let her go, Eva. She needs her space."

"Please give me room to work," ordered Paul. "Hannah, bring my truck over here and back it in as close as you can." He threw her the keys.

"I didn't see him!" exclaimed Randy sorrowfully. "He must've been sleeping under the car. I'm so sorry."

Everyone made way for Hannah as she navigated Paul's truck. Paul opened the tailgate where he kept his medical supplies and began to prepare.

"Randy," said Paul. "Please drive your car forward. I need some room."

Randy obliged. His eyes looked hollow.

Kenneth strode over to Hannah as she stood silently beside Paul's truck. "Hannah, I'll take my leave. There's no sense crowding the place up at a time like this."

Hannah nodded blankly.

"Lemon pie, face the facts, the dinner's over. But I'd like to take a doggy bag if I may."

Bird stared down at her grandfather in shock. Could he really be that insensitive?

Hannah was too tired to argue. "Sure. No problem. The food'll go to waste if someone doesn't eat it."

Kenneth was pleased. "Eva! Come here sugar pie."

Eva came running like a child. "Yes, Daddy?"

"Get your Daddy some takeout dinner, will you? And don't be stingy. I have a healthy appetite."

"I know that Daddy!" Eva ran into the house, eager to do his bidding.

Bird watched. Her fists were clenched with tension as she

looked at the chaotic scene below. I did this, she told herself. I'm to blame for Hector's death. He wouldn't be dead if Randy had stayed for dinner. If I hadn't ruined his coat. If I talked. She watched as Paul worked on Hector. She knew it was hopeless.

And for what? I wanted to make pink look ridiculous. I wanted to pay Randy back for what he said about Hector. I wanted my mother to notice me. But I wrecked everything. Now Eva will hate me for driving Randy away. And Alec for sure thinks I'm crazy, which I most likely am. The worst thing is that Hector— my sweet, kind, wise Hector—is dead.

Bird balled up her fists and ground her teeth. Tears fell unhindered. Why, why, why do I do these things?

When she opened her eyes she saw Alec kneeling beside Hector. He looked so sad. Bird watched as he slowly and carefully removed the dog coat. She was touched by the tenderness he showed.

Sunny nickered from below her tree. Bird looked down at him. He was looking up at her. That's odd, Bird thought. Most horses don't look up. She nickered back, then climbed silently down the tree and over the fence.

I have something to say. Just now, the Tall Man came here.

What Tall Man?

The Tall Man from the other barn.

Where you came from?

Yes. From there.

What did he do?

He watched me from his car. For a small time. Then he left.

He watched you? Bird remembered her grandfather, standing at the window with the cellphone to his ear.

Only that. But I don't like him, Bird girl. He doesn't like me.

Don't worry, Sunny. I'll watch out for him.

Bird looked over to the driveway. Her grandfather was gone now, and most of the other guests were taking their leave. Dr.

Daniels and Alec were covering Hector's body with a sheet.

Kimberly held Julia's hand protectively. Stuart stood with Eva while Randy sat dejected on the steps. Silently, Bird crept closer. She wanted to be near Hector's body, but she didn't want anyone to talk to her.

"Thanks for trying, Paul," said Hannah, looking down at Hector lovingly. Tears glistened on her cheeks.

"He died quickly," said Paul.

"He was a great dog," Hannah murmured.

"The best," nodded Kimberly.

"The very best," agreed Julia. "Even though I just met him."

Randy stood and brushed the dust off his pants. "I'm sorry, Hannah," he said, without meeting her gaze. "I never meant for this to happen."

Hannah nodded and walked him toward his car.

It wasn't your fault, thought Bird. She watched him drive away. This was my doing. She looked again at the sheet that covered Hector. Me.

"I think this would be a fitting time for the funeral," said Paul to those who remained. "Don't you?"

Hannah nodded sadly as she rejoined the group. "We have the mourners assembled."

"And even the funeral feast," added Paul. "We just have to choose the place to bury him."

Bird knew just the place, and she knew that Hannah would, too. Close to the barn, under the sugar maple and on a slightly higher elevation than the house. Here was the place Hector chose to nap when Hannah wasn't home. From here he kept an eye on the farm and was the first to know when her truck pulled into the lane.

Shortly, the hole for Hector's body was dug. Hannah, Alec, Julia, Eva, and Kimberly stood quietly by the grave, and watched while Paul and Stuart gently carried Hector from the driveway and respectfully placed him at the bottom.

Paul and Stuart took turns throwing in shovels of dirt.

Cody arrived for the funeral. He'd come to honour the life of a good dog. Alone, the small coyote sat in the bushes behind the people.

Suddenly, they all heard the steady thud of hoofbeats coming fast.

Everyone turned to look.

From the front field, Bird came galloping bareback on Sundancer. He came to a full stop at the grave. Sunny dropped his front hooves lightly on the ground, bowing deeply to Hector. Bird slid off Sunny's back and knelt at the lip of Hector's grave. Tears of grief streaked the pink paint on her face. She thumped her head on the ground. She howled like a wolf. Then, exhausted, Bird fell in a heap and curled herself into the fetal position.

Sunny stretched his neck down and gently nudged her. He sniffed her face and walked his lips over her scalp to comfort her.

Hannah knelt beside Bird and stroked her sticky pink hair. She spoke soothingly. "Bird, my darling Bird. It was awful, what happened. But Hector died quickly. He had a wonderful life here with us." Bird sobbed. She was inconsolable. Hannah tried again. "He loved you, Bird. You know that. And you were the last person he saw. I know he was happy that you were there."

Bird rolled over and stared up into the sky. "Sor...ry...Hec...tor," she croaked, her chest heaving.

Hannah put her arms around her to try to control the shaking. She cried along with Bird. "It's not your fault, Bird! Oh, no, Bird. It was an accident."

Cody disappeared as silently as he had arrived.

Slowly the group made their way to the house for the remains of the neglected dinner. Hannah held Bird close. Once inside, Julia and Kimberly sat with Bird at the table with their arms entwined.

Hannah bowed her head. "Please bless this food and welcome Hector into heaven, as all creatures have a place in Your House."

"Amen."

Julia spoke. "And it wasn't Bird's fault, and Randy didn't mean to drive over him, and please know that Hector was a good dog, and faithful."

"Amen."

Bird looked at her little sister with eyes full of tears and gratitude.

Alec watched the emotional scene. "You're right, Julia. It wasn't Bird's fault. Or Randy's. It just happened. And it sucks." He looked tentatively at Bird. She glanced up from her plate for a split second, then put her head down again. She didn't know how to react.

By the time dinner was over, the sun had almost set, casting a rosy glow over the farm. Out on the driveway, Bird, Julia, Alec, and Kimberly solemnly built a little tent of wood over Hector's coat. Bird didn't want to see the coat ever again. It made her unbearably sad about Hector and reminded her of all the trouble she'd caused. She snuck in the back door and got some matches out of the mud room without disturbing the adults. Now, the pyre prepared, she struck a match and bent down to light it.

"Wait!" commanded Julia. Bird blew out the match. "I have something else to burn." She ran into the house and up the stairs. Two minutes later Julia reappeared with her arms overflowing with pink fabric.

"What are you doing?" gasped Kimberly. "Those are all your clothes!"

"I know. I'm going to burn them."

"Are you crazy? Your mom'll kill you!"

"I don't care. I hate them. I'll never wear them again. Ever!"

"She's doing the right thing," said Alec. "Those are horrible."

Bird grabbed bundles of frilly pink clothes and helped Julia stuff them under the wood while Alec ran to get more kindling. Bird winked at her sister and gave her the thumbs-up.

When everyone was ready, Bird struck another match and handed it carefully to Julia. She let her little sister light the pink pile.

In seconds the fire was roaring. They all took turns throwing more pink clothes onto the fire. Pink socks, pink skirts, pink tops, pink sweaters, pink dresses, pink tights. With each additional piece of clothing, they whooped louder. By the time all the clothes were burning, the three girls were dancing and jumping with joy around the leaping flames while Alec stamped and clapped.

From the kitchen window where she was washing dishes, Hannah noticed the flames. "Paul! There's a fire! Outside on the driveway."

Without a word, Paul grabbed the fire extinguisher from the mud room wall and headed outside. Hannah was close behind.

They stopped in mid-step at the sight of the three girls leaping around the fire holding hands.

"What's going on!" yelled a woman's voice from the dark. Kimberly and Alec jumped back and froze in terror, but Eva's daughters kept on dancing.

"We're burning my clothes, Mommy!" answered Julia. "I hate pink! I hate pink! I hate pink!"

"Julia! Bird! Go to your room. Now!" Eva appeared in the light, her face furious, made more horrible by the glow of the flames.

Stuart appeared beside her in the fiery light. "Eva, relax. They're only clothes."

"Only clothes! Expensive clothes!"

"Eva, clothes can be replaced. You should look at the motive here."

Right you are! thought Bird, as she continued her crazy dance.

"What do you mean, motive?"

"The reason she's burning them."

"Those were beautiful clothes! They were exactly like mine!"

"Those clothes were inappropriate. A child needs to look like a child."

Bird regarded Stuart with new respect. Finally, someone was making some sense.

Not surprisingly, Eva didn't agree. Her eyes slitted. "How dare you, Stuart! Who are you to tell me how to dress my child?"

Stuart didn't back down. "I'm a school principal."

No longer dancing, Julia and Bird watched while Eva made her decision. It could go either way.

"All right. But we'll need to go shopping tomorrow for 'appropriate' ones."

Stuart smiled at Eva. "Good idea."

Eva put her arm through Stuart's and smiled back at him. "And Bird can come, too, if she wants." Eva looked searchingly at Bird. "Bird, will you come with us to buy school clothes tomorrow?"

Bird was startled. Her mother had just spoken to her. She looked at Hannah with questioning eyes.

"I think it's a good idea," Hannah agreed. "I'll come, too."

Bird grinned and nodded. Tears sprang up unbidden, and she wiped them away. She felt extremely grateful, but uncertain, too. This was new.

"Good, then," asserted Stuart. "I'll pick you ladies up tomorrow morning at ten." He shook Paul's hand and turned to Hannah. "I'll be on my way now. Thank you for a delicious dinner."

Stuart leaned down and regarded Bird. "Bird, I'm very sorry about your dog." He gently ruffled her pink hair. "Good night Kimberly, good night Julia, Alec, Eva." Stuart fished his keys from his pocket and got into his car.

"We'd best be going, too," said Paul with a quick glance at his son. "It's been a long evening and I'm sure we could all use a little quiet."

Bird and Alec smiled their goodbyes. As the vet's truck rumbled down the driveway, Bird's eyes rested on the remains of the fire. A little quiet would be good.

Kimberly had brought a movie with her, and the girls settled in front of the television to watch. Hannah and Eva stayed a few minutes, then headed for the kitchen. Bird watched them go. This was going to be interesting, Bird thought. The two sisters had a lot to talk about, and Bird wasn't about to miss it. She silently relocated herself to the coat closet by the kitchen door. Perfect.

She heard a pleasant gurgle as liquid hit glass.

"Pour one for me, Eva?" asked Hannah.

"Going to join me? I'm so glad." More gurgles. "You look awful, Hannah. I'm the one who lost a fiancé tonight."

It was the wrong thing to say, and Bird could tell by the sound of chair legs scraping on the floor that Hannah was preparing to leave.

"Where are you going? I thought you were going to join me?"

"Eva. I had a tough night, too. Aside from the disastrous dinner and the drama with Randy, I lost the most terrific, wonderful dog I can imagine. If I look awful, there are reasons."

"Hannah, you're right. Please, can we talk?" Eva sounded sincere.

"Okay," said Hannah with a sigh. "You first."

"I want to get to know Bird. How do I do that?"

In the closet, Bird leaned forward, pressing her ear to the crack in the door.

"She's worth getting to know, that's for sure," answered Hannah. "But it's not going to be easy. She has a lot of defenses. That you're taking an interest is the first thing."

"And what's the second?"

"She needs to know you love her."

"Of course I love her!"

"You left her with me two years ago, remember? Then you told Randy that I'm her mother. Do you think she's getting some kind of message?"

Loud and clear, thought Bird.

"I see how it looks. But I call. And I send her birthday cards and clothes."

"You don't honestly think that's enough? Spend time with her. Take her places. Get to know her. Think about her. Be her mother."

"But how, Hannah? She doesn't talk."

"She communicates in other ways, Eva. And there must be a reason why she doesn't talk."

"Are you blaming me? Because if you are, then..." Eva stopped herself, and for a moment the kitchen was quiet. When she spoke again, her voice was different. Calm, thought Bird. Focused.

"Number one: I want to be Bird's mother and I need your help. She relates to you. Number two: I want to be a good mother to Julia, as well. I can tell she's losing respect for me, like Bird did. Number three: I want this thing with Stuart to work out. He's the one, I just know it." A little self-conscious laugh erupted from Eva's throat. "I realize how it looks—Randy is gone for one minute, and I latch onto Stuart—but Hannah, he's the best man I've ever met. Ever." She paused again, catching her breath. "I know how to catch a man, but I don't know how to keep one. And I know if this works out, my whole life will be better, and my girls' lives will be better, and I can make Stuart's life better.

But I don't know how! I need your help."

Bird was intrigued. Did this mean that Eva was thinking of staying? Was she serious enough about her wishes to change her life? A flicker of hope burned in Bird's chest as she allowed herself to imagine a life that included her mother and her sister. I'll believe it when I see it.

Hannah was saying, "I can try to help you with your kids, Eva, but if you think I know anything about men and relationships, then you're sadly mistaken."

"Men respect you, Hannah. They want to be around you. You're a friend and a real person to them. I don't know how you do that."

"Eva, you're the one with all the boyfriends."

"I can flirt. That's all I know how to do. I need your help, Hannah. Can you give it to me?"

Bird crawled out of the closet and peered around the kitchen door.

Hannah was leaning across the table to hug her sister. "Of course. If I can. But you have to help me, too."

"What help can I give you? I only know how to screw up my life."

Hannah smiled conspiratorially. "You can teach me how to flirt."

Bird sat back on her heels. Hannah wanted to flirt?

"Why, Hannah! It's Paul, isn't it?"

"Yes. And I have no idea what to do."

Bird remembered the uncomfortable scene at the door a few days earlier. So Hannah did like Dr. Daniels after all!

"I can teach you," Eva was saying. "But Julia and I have to be here to do it."

Hannah smiled and took her hand. "Deal."

10

THE SHOPPING TRIP

I never get tired. After a little rest, I am fully recuperated.

THE NEXT MORNING WAS SUNNY AND WARM. The birds chirped and sang and flitted from tree to tree. It was perfect weather for the last part of summer, thought Bird as she walked outside and breathed in the morning air.

Kimberly and Julia were still asleep on futons in Bird's room where they'd crashed the night before. It'd been fun having a sleepover. Kimby was becoming a real friend, and having a little sister around was great. Bird chuckled as she remembered the way they'd all danced around the fire on the driveway. Later, in her room, they'd recreated the scene and invented a new dance about burning clothes and feeling free. Only the three of them knew the dance and its meaning. Bird felt like she belonged. It was a new feeling. And very nice.

There was only one thing missing on this perfect day. Hector. She could imagine him clearly, with his wagging tail, floppy ears, and sweet eyes. Bird stood still and put her hand over her heart. He should be here with her now, she thought. He would've enjoyed this morning.

Sundancer pranced impatiently along the fenceline and gave a happy buck, his sleek coppery coat glistening in the morning sun. Bird got the message and walked toward the field. *I'm coming, I'm coming.* The horse watched as Bird started dragging poles and standards from the pile in the middle of the front paddock.

Bird girl, let me give you some advice here.

Sure, Sunny.

I can do fancier stuff than this. Put up a triple combination. I'll tell you how. And a water jump. I need practice. Use that blue tarp as the water. And use up all the poles today. I want to have something to look at.

You're feeling good today, Sunny.

Today, I can do anything.

Bird completed setting up the course of jumps. Carefully, she paced out the in-and-out, the triple, the oxer, and the water jump. There were ten jumps in all—red, white, blue, and green—and they ranged between three feet six inches and three feet nine inches. The widest was four feet. The water jump looked real enough, she figured. It was ten feet wide and held down with poles all around.

Does this look ready to you, Sunny?

I can't wait to get at it.

I'll get Hannah.

Hurry, Bird girl. I'll do my stretches.

Hannah was reading the paper with a mug of hot coffee in her hand. She looked up to see the lively face of her niece.

"Good morning, Bird. You're up nice and early."

Bird made her jumping signal, curving her right hand over her left in imitation of a horse going over a jump.

"Now?"

Bird nodded.

Hannah looked at the clock. "It's seven thirty. Mr. Gilmore is picking us up at ten to go shopping. I hope you didn't forget?"

Bird shook her head. She made the jumping sign again.

"Sure."

Bird dashed out the door.

"I'll be there as soon as I'm dressed, Bird!" she hollered after the girl. "Don't start without me!"

Five minutes later, with a fresh mug of coffee, Hannah leaned on the fence and watched Bird warm up. Hannah smiled with pleasure at the harmony between horse and rider. Sundancer seemed to float along the ground. His legs punched out a dynamic trot, but his hooves barely touched the ground. Bird sat lightly on his back, legs firm and heels down. Her hands were sensitive and responsive, asking only what little was required and trusting Sundancer to understand. They moved into a canter and did figure eights. Sundancer swapped his leads with ease and confidence.

This is a team, thought Hannah. There is exquisite symmetry between them.

Suddenly, the chestnut leaped, startled, and Bird scrambled to stay on.

A dark shape slunk behind a tree.

Sundancer's head rose high, his ears forward, nostrils wide open. He snorted loudly, then again.

Bird cooed at him and patted his neck.

"I'm sorry!" called a voice.

Sundancer swung around to face the voice. There was Abby Malone, running toward the ring. "Cody spooked him. I'm sorry, Bird. Are you okay?"

Bird smiled and nodded.

"Is it all right if I watch for a while?" asked Abby. "I saw you out here setting up jumps when I drove past earlier, and I got curious."

Bird nodded again, this time with an eagerness that made Hannah laugh. She continued her warm-up.

"Abby," said Hannah. "You're welcome any time."

"Thanks." Then she remembered. "I heard about what happened to Hector last night. I'm so sorry. Are you okay?"

Hannah sighed. "Thank you, Abby. It's tough. He was a great dog."

They stood at the fence watching Bird.

Abby was appraising Sundancer. "He's sure looking good."

Hannah answered, nodding, "It's all due to Bird, the rascal. She was training him secretly so I couldn't tell her not to."

Abby chuckled. "She sounds like my kind of kid."

Hannah nodded. "You can say that again. But from my point of view, it's not so funny."

"You're right, of course. Everything's great until someone gets hurt. And horses are not toys."

"They most certainly are not. Especially this one. There's an old adage I believe in: With horses, what can go wrong, will go wrong."

Bird and Sundancer were ready to begin. Abby and Hannah directed their full attention to the ring.

Remember to look over the jumps, Bird girl. Not at them.

Thanks, Sunny. I always forget.

It changes your balance when you look down, and it's harder for me to jump.

You got it.

Bird asked Sunny for a canter, and he picked up his correct lead. They circled the ring before approaching the first vertical. Over they went without effort, landing lightly and cantering five strides to the next.

You're putting more weight on your right foot, Bird girl. It steers me wrong.

Sorry, Sunny. I didn't know. Is this better?

Perfect. And keep your hands more together and down. I know where we're going better.

Right.

Keeping time like a metronome, Sunny jumped and flew, landed and turned, now heading straight for the in-and-out. Over, land, one, jump. Perfect and simple. Toward the water jump now; stride, stride, stride, stride, jump; landing a foot to spare and without anxiety. On to the triple.

Abby had been holding her breath. "They're good, Hannah."

"I know. Bird's in her own world. With Sundancer."

"Nothing else exists right now, I can see that."

Now keep your toes up, Bird girl. When we land, let your weight go into the stirrups, not on my back or neck.

I'm listening.

The triple was big and bright, three sets of verticals with three strides between each jump. Bird and Sundancer executed it with such ease that it looked simple, and they floated toward the hedge jump.

"The art of concealing art," said Abby.

Hannah nodded. "Well said."

Over the hedge they sailed, then turned toward the big oxer.

Lavinia's car had stopped in the driveway beside the ring, but Hannah and Abby were so engrossed that they didn't notice.

"Is this the horse that you won't let Kimberly ride, Hannah?"

Hannah and Abby turned at the same instant.

"Yes, Lavinia." Hannah's eyes went back to watch Bird and Sundancer land then head for the next jump, a picket fence.

"I can see why. You're saving the best for yourself."

Hannah saw Sundancer's eyes assess the picket. There was a flicker of hesitation. Bird encouraged him steadily with her legs and he listened. He cleared it with no problem, then headed to the two winged arches.

"Hannah, did you hear me? Are you listening?"

"Lavinia, I'm watching Bird. Give me a minute."

Lavinia huffed but waited.

See how I'm doing this, Bird girl? Pretty good, right?

You're having fun, Sunny. And so am I.

Give me a little more rein when we land. Let me stretch my neck.

Okay.

Yeah. That's it. It helps me with my balance.

The gelding leaped over the first arch carefully; it was new to him. He cantered five strides, turned to the right, and cleared the last arch easily.

Bird patted his neck, grinning joyfully.

Fab-u-lous, Sunny!

You didn't do too badly yourself. Except you get eager before the jumps and creep forward. I can feel it.

Really?

It makes me want to speed up when you do that.

Hannah and Abby clapped and hooted. "Super, Bird!" praised Abby.

"Bird, that was great!" called Hannah as she climbed over the fence and headed toward her niece.

"Hannah!" yelled Lavinia. "You said you'd talk to me."

"I will, Lavinia. I'll be just a second." Hannah approached Bird and Sunny. The horse was barely sweating. He was calm and cool, as he waited for Hannah to get to him. Bird slid down from the saddle and met Hannah halfway with a big hug.

"Beautiful, Bird. Beautiful."

Hannah's eyes misted. She hugged her more tightly. "I love you, Bird. I don't tell you enough."

Bird said nothing but hugged her aunt back.

Sunny nudged Bird in the back as if to ask what was going on and why was he being ignored. Bird and Hannah laughed and praised Sunny, and walked together toward the barn.

Abby and Lavinia joined them.

Lavinia was impatient. "You didn't answer me, Hannah. Are you saving this horse for yourself?"

"If you're asking if he's for sale, the answer is no. At least not until we know he's safe."

"You put my daughter on an inferior horse and ask her to compete against that Pegasus of yours?"

"Lavinia, Pastor is a very good horse. You bought him for Kimberly for very good reasons. They're having a lot of fun together."

"Well, now I want her to win some better ribbons in some bigger shows. I think she can do that on this horse."

Hannah stopped and faced Lavinia. "Sundancer is a very difficult horse. I haven't decided what will happen with him. He has good days and bad days. Today was a good day, but sometimes he's very dangerous."

"I know that's his reputation, but Bird seems to have no problem."

"Don't forget, she was in the hospital with a concussion not too long ago," answered Hannah seriously. "I repeat. He has good days and bad days."

"So do we all, Hannah. I want Kimberly to try him out. She loves him and doesn't like Pastor any more. What would be the harm?"

Hannah looked directly at Lavinia. "I have to say no. I don't want to take that responsibility. When we've worked with him more, and he's more consistently good, maybe I'll change my mind. Does that satisfy you?"

Lavinia's eyes slitted. "I know horse people. By then the price will have gone up."

"I'm talking safety here, Lavinia, not commerce." Hannah was angry. "I do not want Kimberly hurt. Do you understand?"

Lavinia didn't look happy. "I understand. But promise me this? I'll be the first to know if he's for sale?"

Hannah capitulated. "All right. You'll be the first to know."

In the barn, Abby helped Bird untack and rub down Sunny.

"Bird, I'm impressed. You ride him unbelievably well."

Bird blushed. This was high praise, coming from her jumping hero.

"I love the way he listens to you. And trusts you. It's so rare to see. I'm glad I dropped by."

Bird nodded happily and continued to groom the handsome horse. Sunny enjoyed all the attention. Abby pulled a mint from her pocket and offered it to him. The deep-brown eyes narrowed suspiciously.

"It's a treat, Sunny. I'm not trying to poison you."

Bird took the mint from Abby, then placed it on the palm of her hand. Sunny scooped it up with his lips, then licked her hand.

"Hmm," said Abby. "He gives his trust carefully."

Bird nodded as she stroked his neck.

"Do you want to compete with him, Bird? You'd be quite a team."

Do you want to go to a horse show, Sunny?

Maybe I can. But some days are not good for me.

I know, Sunny.

Bird's eyes registered caution. She shrugged.

"It'd be fun. There's a show this week less than an hour from here."

Hannah overheard the last comment from the tack room, where she was cleaning the bridle. "You're talking about going to a show?"

"Yes. There's one at Rockhill this Friday."

Hannah looked at Bird. "After what we saw this morning, Bird, I think we should give it a try. What do you think?"

Bird stood awkwardly. How can I tell them?

She reached into her pocket and retrieved a coin. She threw it up in the air. It landed heads.

"Bird, are you saying it's a flip of the coin? That you don't care?" asked Abby.

Bird shook her head.

"Do you mean maybe yes, maybe no? That you're not sure?" asked Hannah.

Bird sighed. Maybe this is as close as they'll get, she thought. She nodded.

Abby had an idea. "What if I take him in the ring first, to let him see the jumps and get used to the atmosphere of the show-grounds? Then, if you want to, you ride him next?"

Bird looked uncertain.

Good idea. Then if I'm having a bad day, she'll be the one I toss. Say yes, Bird girl.

If you're sure, Sunny. Maybe this is too soon.

If I'm okay that day, it's not too soon. I can do anything. I'm a winner.

"Abby, that's very good of you," said Hannah. "It might be just the thing to give Bird confidence."

Abby smiled at Bird. "Bird, are you on?"

Bird looked at her new friend. Abby Malone, who'd won trophies and awards and countless ribbons, wanted to help her. She'd just have to hope that Sunny would be having a good day.

She grinned at Abby and stuck out her hand. They shook.

"Great! I'll stop in tomorrow with information, and I'll take Sundancer around the course, just so he knows the feel of me." She smiled at Bird. "Okay?"

"O...kay." Bird surprised herself by speaking aloud. She hadn't meant to. She covered her mouth with her hands and began to giggle. Together, they burst out laughing.

"See you tomorrow, then, bright and early." Abby waved goodbye and left. Hannah waved back and headed to the house.

Bird walked Sunny out to his field after she'd brushed and fussed over him a little more. She opened the gate and walked him in, then unclasped his halter and let him go.

We're going to a show, Sunny. If it was today, you'd win all the ribbons, wouldn't you?

Yep.

Do you think you'll feel the same on Friday?

Depends.

Tell me how to help you, Sunny. Tell me how to get rid of your fears and demons, once and for all.

If I knew, I wouldn't have them.

The big handsome horse trotted off. Bird watched him from the fenceline and enjoyed the way the sun burnished his sleek coat, and how his muscles rippled as he moved. She would be so proud to canter into the ring on this horse.

Sundancer lay down in the grass and rolled. He gave himself a good scratching, rubbing his coat into the ground. He hopped up and shook his whole body vigorously. Bird watched the grass and dirt fall off him.

Abby and Cody were gone, and Lavinia's car was pulling out of their lane with Kimberly. Another car drove in. Silver sedan. Mr. Gilmore, thought Bird. Shopping trip.

She ran to the house, noticing that Lavinia had stopped her car to chat with Stuart. Lavinia was pointing at Sunny in the field. Bird knew that she was telling Stuart that Sundancer would soon be her daughter's horse. She slammed the kitchen door by mistake.

"Bird! Jump in the shower," called Hannah from the top of the stairs. "Stuart's driving in. He's early!"

"I'm not nearly ready!" wailed Eva.

"I am," said Julia. "I'll offer him a coffee or something, okay?"

"Good girl!" yelled Eva. "Keep him busy."

Bird passed Julia on the stairs. Julia was running down to answer the door, Bird was running up to get ready.

"Don't worry, Julia," said Hannah. "I'm coming down. You get back up and finish getting dressed. You'd think the Prince of Wales was here!"

"I heard that," smiled Stuart. "I'm honoured, I'm sure." He bowed.

"Come on in, Stuart," said Hannah, laughing. "I'm making coffee. Have one?"

"Sure. I know I'm early, but I finished my work a little sooner than I anticipated and I was in the neighbourhood and I—"

"Have always had a crush on Eva," said Hannah wickedly.

Stuart twisted his mouth. "Yes. How did you know?"

"You're not exactly subtle, Stuart."

He looked at Hannah, startled. "What do you mean?"

"Every time I mention her name, you light up like a light bulb. There's nothing wrong with it, Stuart. Don't look at me like that. I think it's cute."

"Cute? That's manly."

Hannah laughed.

Eva walked into the kitchen looking like she was ready for the tea party in *Alice in Wonderland*. Her pink and white polka-dot dress was tied in the back with a big bow that matched the one in her teased-up hair. Her high pink strapless heels clicked on the kitchen linoleum in time to the swishing of her crino-lined skirt.

"I'm ready," she sang. "How do I look?" Eva twirled around.

Stuart shared a look with Hannah. "Lovely, but perhaps you should bring along some more sensible shoes."

Eva was taken aback. "Sensible?"

"We'll be walking around stores, Eva. The kids will be trying things on. In those five-inch heels you'll be tripping all over the place, your feet will hurt, and you'll start whining to go home."

"I will not," she pouted. "I always shop in high heels."

"Just bring some flat shoes in case, Eva," said Stuart. "I'll wait."

"Well you'll be waiting a long time. I'm not going."

"Suit yourself, Eva. Hannah and I will be fine with the girls."

"You wouldn't leave me here!" retorted Eva.

"Where else?"

Eva glared at Stuart with her hands on her hips. "You're just trying to be bossy. Well, you can't boss me."

"No problem."

With a huge exasperated sigh, Eva flounced out of the kitchen. Her heels clattered loudly up the stairs, and her bedroom door slammed hard.

Bird came running down the stairs, scrubbed and ready and eager.

"Okay, everyone," said Hannah. "Jump in the car."

Hannah started the car and began to back out of her spot. Suddenly Eva came storming out the door.

"Wait, wait! I've got flat shoes on!" She did, indeed, have on flat shoes, but the outfit was twice as revealing. Pink capri pants, skin tight, with a little white halter top that didn't begin to cover her. "I couldn't wear flats with that dress, so I had to change."

Bird and Julia exchanged glances. Could their mother be more embarrassing?

Stuart got out of the car and spoke quietly to Eva. "I'm not taking you around town dressed like that," he said in a kind tone. "I want to feel proud of you. Put a shirt over that top, and we'll go."

Eva wavered. "All right, Stuart." She turned on her heel and stalked into the house, calling over her shoulder, "You win. This time."

Hannah was grinning when Stuart got back in the car. "The taming of the shrew, Stuart?"

"Someone's got to do it."

Julia was puzzled. "What does that mean, the taming of the shoe?"

Stuart laughed. "*The Taming of the Shrew*. It's a famous play by William Shakespeare. A beautiful, willful woman becomes a terror because nobody wants to stand up to her bad temper. She scares everyone, so she eventually isolates herself until she meets a man who cares enough about her to expect her to behave civilly."

"I get it," said Julia. "You're doing Mom a favour by bossing her around?"

Hannah, Stuart, and Bird laughed.

"What's so funny?" asked Julia, chagrined.

Stuart answered, "Just the way you put it, Julia. Actually, you're dead on. We're not laughing at you at all."

Eva returned with a crisp white cotton blouse tied at her waist. Finally, thought Bird. She looks like a grown-up.

Eva stared at Stuart, hands on hips. "Well?"

Stuart smiled. "Will you do me the honour of sitting next to me?"

With a grin and a flounce, Eva sat in the car next to Stuart.

Bird wondered what the next few hours would bring. She looked into the back seat and felt a small tug of happiness in her heart. Stuart sat with Eva on one side and Julia on the other, a relaxed arm around both. They all wore contented smiles. Better still, Julia had lost the wan look that she arrived with. Instead, she had rosy cheeks and her old outgoing demeanour. Eva seemed more contented, less frenetic. This was all good, Bird thought. She sincerely hoped it would last.

Julia stretched her arm forward to include Bird in the group. Bird put her hand over Julia's and squeezed. Hannah, in the driver's seat, winked at Bird. Bird knew what Hannah was thinking. She was hoping the same thing.

Late in the afternoon when the group arrived back at Saddle Creek, the trunk was full. There were school clothes and fun clothes for both Bird and Julia, and boxes of new clothing for Eva. With much chatter and laughter, they unloaded the car. Bird and Julia rushed upstairs to try on their new things. Julia didn't buy anything that was even remotely pink.

The day had been a great success. After window shopping

and checking out the stores, they'd sat down to lunch at the Tea Room in Erin and talked over what everyone wanted to buy. They'd had fun compiling lists and adding and subtracting shoes, accessories, and clothing pieces. After lunch, with their whittled-down lists in hand, they purchased their items. Everyone remained in good spirits, in part due to their frequent coffee and soda stops all day.

Now it was after six, and Hannah began to throw together a dinner of leftovers with a big salad from the garden.

Someone knocked at the kitchen door.

Hannah was surprised. She wasn't expecting anyone. Wiping her hands on the dish towel, she opened the door.

"Paul!"

"I'm sorry I'm late. I had an emergency to look after. A horse up the road needed stitches."

"Late?"

"For dinner. Eva called this afternoon and invited me." Paul saw the surprise on Hannah's face. "Just a minute here. Didn't you know she called?"

"No, but I'm very glad she did. It's only leftovers, Paul, but you're always welcome."

"Are you sure?"

Hannah smiled. "I'm very sure."

Paul couldn't miss her sincerity. He smiled back.

Good old Eva, Hannah thought. I asked for her help and I'm getting it.

Bird woke up the next morning still glowing with the new, nice feeling of belonging. She was wearing the nightgown she'd picked out on the shopping trip. It was pale green, with soft white lace ruffles. Bird loved it. She stretched lazily. She looked over at the futon and saw that Julia was sound asleep.

Quietly, Bird got out of bed and peeked outside to see what

kind of day it was. From her bedroom window, Bird saw Abby's bike parked at the fenceline. Then her eyes picked up a blurry movement behind a tree. Cody. Without another thought, she gathered up her riding clothes, pulled them on, and raced outside.

Abby was grooming Sunny in the field. She turned and waved when she spotted the younger girl. "Hey Bird, great day!"

Sunny left Abby and trotted over to Bird. He greeted her with a nicker.

I'm feeling good, girl! Let's go!

Can Abby ride you today?

Why not? If she bugs me, I'll toss her.

Please behave. She wants to see how talented you are.

I'll amaze her.

The horse nodded his head up and down. Bird patted his neck and together they returned to Abby.

"I thought I'd hop on his back today, Bird. To get a feel for him before the show."

Bird nodded with assurance. Perfect. She wanted to see Sunny jump. She'd only ridden him, never watched him.

Bird got Sunny's old bridle from the pail and slipped it over his ears. Abby had brought her own saddle, and she placed it over the saddle pad and tightened the girth.

Bird had an uncanny feeling that something was watching her. She turned to look. She saw nothing. She turned again. There. Cody.

Girl. I'll do you no harm.

I know. I'm not afraid.

Will you be my friend?

Yes, Cody. I want to be your friend. I'm honoured.

Bird felt a warmth in her heart. Cody had not spoken to her before.

Now she addressed her horse. *Behave yourself for Abby, Sunny.*

I intend to be perfectly brilliant. She will know what an outstanding performer I am. She will never have ridden a more handsome and athletic horse.

You're so vain.

Just truthful.

Sunny made his prediction come true. No horse could have responded more quickly or with more sensitivity. No horse could have jumped cleaner or turned faster. Sunny pivoted on a dime when asked. He sprang like a deer from every angle.

Bird sat on the fence beside the paddock and watched with pride. He looked fabulous.

Abby trotted Sundancer over to the fence where Bird was perched. "Do you have any idea what you've got here, Bird? This horse is a genius! He could go all the way. He's amazing!"

I told you so, Bird girl. Sunny tossed his head and pranced.

Indeed you did! Well done, Sunny.

"He's ready for the Rockhill show, Bird. Heck, he's ready for a Grand Prix! Today, I'll take his picture and go to the Canadian Equestrian Federation offices to get his passport so he can compete. I'll be back early Friday morning. I can hardly wait!"

11

THE ROCKHILL SHOW

Sometimes I feel restricted when a person is on my back. I don't want to be dominated.

BIRD KNEW IT WASN'T going to be a good day.

Don't touch me. The chestnut horse cast a sidelong look at Bird.

Give me a break, Sunny.

Why should I?

He trotted as far as he needed to go to get away from the girl's thoughts.

Bird knew from past experience that Sunny's mood would eventually pass, but not right away. And certainly not in time for his classes at the Rockhill Show. Today was a write-off.

She felt totally let down. All the preparations. Here she was in her new show breeches and white shirt. Last night she'd pulled his mane into a feathered fringe and bathed him. She'd cleaned and oiled his tack. She'd washed his saddle pad. She'd hosed down the truck and trailer.

Yesterday, Sundancer had been looking forward to going to the show and winning the championship. Today, it would not be wise to get on his back.

Bird heard Abby's bike on the gravel driveway.

Hello, friend.

Hello, friend. She didn't see him, but Bird knew Cody was near. One day she hoped to pat him, but Cody would decide when that would happen.

Abby walked up to Bird with a smile. "Are you ready for the show?" She wore cream riding pants, a white show shirt with a monogrammed rat-catcher and shiny black show boots. She radiated good energy.

Bird's face clouded. She shook her head no.

"Nerves?" asked Abby.

Again Bird shook her head. She pointed to Sunny, then made the thumbs-down sign.

"Something's wrong with Sundancer?"

Bird nodded. Maybe Abby would understand.

"Let me get Hannah," said Abby. "She'll know what to do."

Bird sighed as Abby strode off to the house. Abby didn't get it.

A few minutes passed, then the two women joined Bird at the fence, where she stood watching Sundancer. He stayed out of her range, munching grass and giving her quick, angry glances.

"Bird," said Hannah. "Abby tells me that there's something wrong."

Bird gave her the thumbs-down.

"What is it? Is he sound?"

Bird nodded. No lameness.

"Did he eat his breakfast? Drink some water?"

Again Bird nodded. She pointed to her head and made an angry face.

"You're mad about something?"

Bird shook her head no, and then pointed to Sundancer.

"You're mad at Sundancer?"

Bird gave up. Hannah could be so understanding sometimes, but she would not listen to her now. Bird sensed her determination. She was set on taking Sunny to the show. Hannah had no idea what they were getting into.

"Do you feel all right, Bird?" asked Hannah.

Bird nodded wearily.

Abby and Hannah looked at each other. Abby spoke. "Bird, I'm riding him first, remember, like we talked about. You don't even have to get on him today unless you feel like it."

Bird looked at the older girl. *You may not be on him, either, at least not for long.*

Cody whined. *Do something else today, girl, not with the horse.*

I know, Cody. But they don't understand.

You must explain.

I'm trying.

"There's something in the air, for sure," said Abby. "Cody feels it, and so does Bird."

Hannah shook her head. "If we don't go today, what will be the excuse next time? And the time after that? Look, Abby, let's load him up and head off to the show. You ride him today. Bird can come if she likes. If he's horrible, we can always turn back."

Abby smiled. "I'm in. What about you, Bird?"

Bird didn't want to go, but she dared not send Sundancer without her. She shrugged.

One exasperating hour later, in the cab of the truck, Hannah, Bird, and Abby caught their breath. Their faces were red with exertion. Finally, Sundancer was in the trailer and they were on the road. Sunny kicked and pulled, causing the trailer to lurch, which stressed the shocks and brakes of the truck.

The chestnut had avoided being caught until the pail of sweet oats with molasses mixed with apples and carrots came out. He reluctantly gave in to temptation and they slipped on the halter.

Loading him onto the trailer was a whole other ordeal. Sunny was not going to make this easy. What worked in the end, after trying bribery and persuasion and lunge lines, was a red lead line twirling behind him like a propeller. He jumped in to avoid this strange thing, and they closed him up.

Bird wondered if it was beginning to sink in yet that Sundancer would be uncooperative today.

"Is he always so stubborn?" Abby asked Hannah as they drove along.

"We've never loaded him before, so I don't know. I can't believe we didn't practise before. I didn't know it was a problem for him. I know now."

"There's always something," responded Abby. "But in the field he was stubborn, too. He wouldn't get caught. Yesterday he stood while I groomed him, without even a halter. What's going on with him?"

Bird rolled her eyes. Were they finally getting it?

"Next time, we'll put him in a stall for the night before a show."

Bird sighed quietly. *They understand how to make their lives easier,* she thought. *They just don't understand about Sunny.*

They arrived at the show and found a place to park at the end of the row of trailers. Most of the competitors had been there for some time, and were already set up with buckets and hay nets.

Bird jumped out and opened the main door to the trailer.

Sunny glared. *What are you looking at?*

Are you going to be like this for the whole day?

If I feel like it.

Terrific. I hope you're having fun, because nobody else is.

Bird clipped the lead shank on Sunny's halter. Abby put down the ramp and unattached the rear guard.

Everybody will be watching you, Sunny. You can be a big star.

I know. If I feel like it. But I don't.

Bird backed him down the ramp. He spun and sniffed the air, ears alert and tail high. His clean coat glistened and sparkled in the sunshine. Hannah brought out the tack and the three of them quickly saddled him while he was distracted with the new sights.

People stopped and stared at Sundancer. Even though he was irritatingly grumpy, Bird had to admit that he was the most handsome horse there. With his height, conformation, fitness, and attitude, he was a real head turner. His perfect head and long, strong neck added elegance to the package. Horse people knew at a glance that he was well bred. A contender.

All this was not lost on Sundancer. He preened in front of his admirers.

I am the king.

The king of horses, or the king of asses?

Smarty.

Bird sighed. Maybe he would show off and be fabulous today, maybe he would show off and be horrible.

Abby fastened her hard hat and pulled on her gloves. "Give me a leg up, Hannah? No time like the present to show him around the grounds."

Hannah cupped her hands and helped Abby up into the saddle.

"Can you get the schedule, Hannah?" asked Abby. "We'll go in every class we can."

"Good plan, Abby. He'll start to get the idea."

Or you'll get the idea, thought Bird. Whatever comes first.

Behave yourself, Sunny.

Get lost.

Bird watched Abby and Sunny prance down between the rows of trailers. Forty or fifty trucks and trailers had already arrived and horses were everywhere, being lunged, hand-walked, or ridden. Some people were stressed and nervous, some were relaxed and confident. Some horses were spooking at shadows, some were grazing at the end of their lead. The air was abuzz with equine and human energy.

"This'll be fun, Bird, you wait and see," said Hannah cheerfully. "Come with me and we'll get Sundancer registered."

Bird was reluctant to lose sight of Sunny. She feared the worst but could do nothing about it. Hannah and Abby were in control now. Or at least they thought they were.

Hannah and Bird walked to the registration tent, looking at everything along the way. They passed the concession stand where breakfast sandwiches, doughnuts, orange juice, and coffee were being served. They passed the tack tent, where people were looking at reins, bits, stirrups, and martingales. Clothes were sold there, too, in case you forgot your gloves or hat, or needed a new jacket or stock tie. Or even a saddle.

There were six rings, Bird noticed. Two warm-up rings, two hunter rings, and two jumper rings. The hunter rings had sedate jumps set up in orderly fashion to induce the horse to keep a steady pace. Traditionally, the horse would jump a line of jumps along one side, turn back into the diagonal line, come through the line along the other side, then angle across the ring to jump another diagonal line. Or any variation of that, set out by the course designer.

The arrangement of jumps in the jumper rings were multi-coloured and higgledy-piggledy by contrast, with numbers on each jump to reassure the rider that they were going the right way. The horse would be asked to jump any course the designer dictated, depending on the desired difficulty.

Ponies, coaches, mothers, horses, kids, bicycles, and golf carts were everywhere. Bird fought a feeling of sensory overload. She wondered how Sunny was doing.

Hannah and Bird entered the registration tent. It was a small place, crowded with people registering their horses and chatting. An overweight woman sat behind a long desk. She was in her early thirties with a pierced tongue and purple hair, and was trying to organize and talk on her cellphone at the same time.

"I heard it, too. Believe it! Abby Malone is here!" the woman said as she shuffled papers. She didn't look up at Hannah and Bird, she merely shoved a registration form in front of them. "No, I'm trying to find out. Marge has no idea...She's not registered yet...I know! I didn't know she was showing again, either! Nobody's seen her since the Grand Invitational when she kicked butt!...When I find out, I'll call you back...I don't know the horse, but I hear he's a stunner. Patty said he looks like a young Dancer and Karen says the same...Yeah, as soon as I know...Bye."

When the woman noticed that Hannah and Bird were still there, she said, somewhat impatiently, "Just fill out the forms and bring them back. There's a line behind you."

"I have a question concerning—" began Hannah.

"You can see I'm busy. Fill out the forms. Everything you need to know is in them. Come back and pick up your show number and pay." She motioned to the lady standing next in line. "Next!"

Hannah laughed and said to Bird, "If she only knew whose forms we're filling! We could have given her some good gossip, couldn't we?"

Bird smiled. True, she thought, but why ruin all her fun?

Hannah studied the forms. "Here we are. The fees are listed separately for hunter classes and for jumper classes. That's what I was going to ask, so I suppose she was right, I would've wasted her time. Shall we sign up for both?"

Bird shrugged. If Sunny behaved himself, he could go all day. If he didn't, they'd be leaving very soon.

"You're a big help," Hannah said to Bird as she completed the forms. "Why not go for broke. We'll enter every class we can."

They went back to the table and put the forms in front of the purple-haired lady. She glanced at them, then did a double take.

"You're k-kidding," the woman stuttered. Her demeanour immediately became charming and attentive.

"About what?" asked Hannah.

"Your rider is Abby Malone? Why didn't you say so?"

"You were too busy to talk, as I recall. Here's the payment. May I have her numbers please?"

"Is she coming in? I mean, could you bring her in here to say hello? I've always been such a big fan and she hasn't shown for ages..."

"She's a little busy right now, but I'll ask."

"Oh, would you? I'm sorry if I was a little short with you, we've been run off our feet this morning..."

"No problem. I don't want to keep you," Hannah said as she turned to leave the tent.

"I'm not so busy now. Bring her in anytime! Bye, now."

Hannah and Bird walked out. Hannah said, "Isn't it funny? We sure became more important in a hurry."

Bird froze.

Hannah walked on, still talking, unaware that Bird had stopped in her tracks.

Help me, Bird girl. Help me.

It was Sunny. Where was he? *I hear you, Sunny. I'm coming. Help!*

He was somewhere behind the tent. Bird ran, following his urgent messages.

She looked everywhere. Colour, movement, noise, confusion. Her eyes scanned the crowd as she ran. *I'm on my way, Sunny.*

There, in the walkway beside the jumper ring, people were scrambling to get away. Up reared Sundancer, pawing the air. Abby held on to his neck tightly. Bird ran as fast as she could, dodging fleeing people and golf carts. The horse walked on his hind legs, then dropped and reared again. Whinnying loudly, he spun and stumbled. His knees hit the ground. Abby was thrown hard and lay quiet.

Bird jostled through the crowd. She arrived at the sweating, wild-eyed horse just as he was about to rear again.

Sundancer! I'm here.

The horse's eyes rolled around and looked at her. *Girl. Where have you been?*

I'm here now.

I was afraid.

I know. What happened?

The jumps. Pain! Nails in poles. Electric wire.

What are you talking about? They're just jumps.

No! I remember!

That was before, Sunny. These jumps won't hurt you. I'm here, now. Everything is all right.

The big horse exhaled with a huge snort. He shook his entire body, then dropped his head onto Bird's shoulder and gave a shudder.

Good boy. You'll be all right now.

She patted his neck and rubbed his ears. Sunny let out his breath.

Bird looked down. Abby hadn't moved. A large crowd of people had gathered. Cody stood over her. He guarded her fiercely, teeth bared, growling deeply. Nobody could get near her.

Hannah stood helplessly. "Well done, Bird! Now can you see to Cody? We've got to help Abby."

Bird knelt and looked at Cody. *Friend?*

The coyote looked away. He had to decide if he could trust her. He was frightened and wanted to be anywhere but there, but he could not leave his Abby.

I will help her, Cody. Is she alive?

She has breath but no movement.
Are any bones broken?
I know not.
She needs human help, Cody.
Promise to help her. Nobody can hurt her. Promise me this.
I promise, Cody. Kill me in my den if I break my word.

The coyote understood this solemn pledge and trusted that the girl would honour it. He looked at her meaningfully, then slunk away and disappeared from sight.

"Thank you, Bird," called Hannah, kneeling beside Abby and holding her hand.

"Abby?" Hannah murmured. "Abby, can you hear me?"

The young woman moaned. "Oh, my head."

"Abby, the ambulance is here. Can you tell me what day it is?"

"Friday, Hannah. And my name is Abby Malone, and Bird is standing beside us with Sundancer, who seems remarkably calm."

"Good, good," said Hannah.

"Don't worry, I'm fine. I had a little tumble, that's all."

"You were knocked out, Abby."

"No I wasn't. I was resting. I'm fine. Don't let them take me to the hospital."

"Let the medics look at you, Abby, and let them decide."

"Hannah, I'll be there all day, then they'll send me home and tell me to wake up every three to four hours."

Hannah chuckled. "You've been through this before."

"More than once. It's a hazard with these horses."

Two young ambulance attendants arrived with a stretcher. After reassuring themselves that Abby's neck and back were in good order, they checked her from head to foot for broken bones and found none.

"Please let me go home," pleaded Abby. "My parents are there, and Hannah will check in on me."

Hannah agreed that she would.

Abby stood up slowly, showing the medics that she was in good shape. The crowd cheered.

The men decided that she would be fine, and after warning her of dizzy spells and such, they took their stretcher back to the ambulance.

Kids lined up asking Abby for her autograph, and adults wanted her advice on problem horses.

Hannah took her by the elbow and steered her away. "I think Abby needs to sit down for a while, folks. I hope you understand."

Bird walked back to the trailer with Sundancer, following behind Hannah and Abby. She was deep in thought. Bird felt very badly that Abby had been hurt. She should have said something about Sunny's bad mood out loud. But would they have listened? Could they have understood that Sunny's moods ran deeper than just whims?

Bird girl, I didn't mean to hurt the coyote lady.

I know that, Sunny. Don't worry.

I feel bad. Memories came back. I was very afraid. I couldn't think. I wanted to run away, get out of there.

I know, Sunny. I know. One day, you'll understand what is past and what is worth fearing now.

I hope so. I don't like feeling fear.

You're safe now. We're going home.

Bird was angry. She knew that some trainers used illegal methods to train horses to clear the rails over jumps. The theory was that if the horse got his leg ripped by a nail or felt the zing of an electric shock, the next time he'd jump high enough to clear the fence. Sensitive horses like Sunny, however, could be ruined by it. Those idiots should know better, Bird thought. She'd love to see them caught and disqualified.

They arrived at the trailer to find the purple-haired lady waiting.

SUNDANCER

"Thank goodness you're okay!" she said to Abby. "Your licence plate was on the forms, so I found your truck. I wanted to give you your money back. It's not fair to pay the full amount and not even get in the ring!"

"Thank you," said Abby. "That's very kind."

"I'm a big fan. Could I get an autograph? I watched you at the Grand Invitational on Dancer. You were amazing! A kid against the world, and you won! Is this horse related to Dancer? He looks so much like him."

"Do you have a pen?"

"Yes! Write: To my good friend Jewel, from the one and only Abby Malone."

Abby took the offered pen and paper, and wrote, "To my new friend Jewel from Abby Malone. All the best." She handed it back with a smile. "Thanks for the refund, Jewel. I guess I won't be riding today after all."

Jewel handed back Hannah's cheque. "The management has asked that your horse, Sundancer, stay away from our events until he is deemed no longer a danger. I know you understand. It's for the safety of all."

Hannah spoke up. "You're blacklisting Sundancer?"

"Temporarily. He really scared people today. We had a lot of complaints."

"But you know how it works, Jewel," reasoned Hannah. "If he's blacklisted here, he'll be blacklisted everywhere, and then it's impossible to erase his bad reputation."

Abby was upset. "It's his first show, Jewel. He just got spooked back there. He got over it. Look at him now."

They turned to observe Sunny. He looked meek and gentle, but that was not what surprised them most.

Bird had donned her helmet and gloves, and climbed up on the big, humbled chestnut gelding.

I must redeem my reputation, Bird girl.

I want to help, Sunny, but I'm new at this.

If you can stay on, I'll do the rest.

Abby looked at Bird and pointedly asked, "Will you ride in the classes, Bird?"

Bird nodded with a confidence that she didn't feel.

Abby turned to the purple-haired lady and asked, "Jewel, can we give it a try? If he takes one wrong step, we'll take him home. He should have a second chance before he's blacklisted."

Jewel looked at her. "If it was anybody but Abby Malone asking, I'd say no. But let me try." She took her cellphone from her pocket and dialed.

"Joe? It's Jewel. I'm over at Abby Malone's trailer with her and the horse. He's completely cool. Abby wants another chance before we put him on the list...No, of course she won't be riding, she can barely walk...There's some girl named Bird up on him now...My recommendation? Give it a shot...Great. Thanks, Joe."

Jewel gave Abby the thumbs-up. "There's a hunter class on now. Three-foot jumps. Come with me."

Hannah returned the cheque to Jewel. Abby handed her riding jacket up to Bird, who quickly put it on and buttoned it. Hannah reached up and tied the cardboard number over the jacket. Then she squeezed Bird's hand and wished her good luck.

Bird felt her stomach suddenly go queasy. She took a deep breath. She stroked Sunny's neck.

Okay, Sunny?

I'm okay, Bird girl. Are you?

Yeah, so far. Just so you know, the jumps are clean.

It doesn't matter. I won't touch them anyway.

But if you do, nothing will happen. No pain. Nothing will hurt you. If you touch them, they'll just roll off onto the ground.

If you say so.

I say so, Sunny. Cross my heart and hope to die.

SUNDANCER

Okay.

Finally, Sundancer's mind was clear of stress. Her job was to get him around the course at a steady pace. The class would be judged on form and rhythm. They had to look good.

Jewel led the way to the hunter ring, then spoke to a man with a clipboard. She held up four fingers.

"We're four away," said Hannah. "Are you ready, Bird?"

Bird nodded. She noticed two girls in riding attire peeking at her and giggling. Suddenly, she felt self-conscious. Abby's jacket was too big for her, and she wasn't wearing this year's cool clothes. It didn't help that she wasn't part of the show crowd. When they peeked again, she smiled at them. One was ashamed to be caught, and the other gave her a superior look. Bird decided to let it go. She had more important things on which to concentrate.

Abby said, "Bird, you're a brave girl. No one else in this park would've got up on Sunny after what they saw him do."

Bird smiled at Abby. *And that would be the correct instinct.*

They watched as a boy on a dark bay horse was completing the course. Bird thought it had looked perfect.

He didn't get his lead fast enough to the fourth jump.

Sunny, you saw that?

Of course.

Bird smiled. She had no idea.

They watched the next competitor go in. It was a woman on a dapple grey. Again, Bird thought they were perfect.

She lands hard. Falls forward. Looks bad.

You're very critical.

So?

Bird laughed. This was fun. Abby and Hannah looked up at her.

"What's so funny, Bird?" asked Hannah. "Are we missing something?"

Bird nodded yes and patted Sunny's neck.

Two more riders completed their rounds. It was time for Bird and Sundancer. They trotted in.

Bird felt a calmness and confidence in Sunny. She halted and nodded to the judge. Sunny started a lovely, easy canter on his left lead, before Bird had time to ask. Bird was merely a passenger.

They went over the first jump, a white oxer with shrubs inside. They landed lightly and rode five easy strides to the next, which looked the same. They jumped it, then cantered twelve collected strides to the next hurdle, a green picket fence with red impatiens. Four strides, then another green picket fence. Now they turned left and came down the diagonal line of three blue verticals. Sunny kept his pace light and even, like clockwork. After the line, they turned right and took the opposite diagonal line, which was two yellow and white oxers, then turned left and finished over the two that they'd jumped first. Eleven jumps in all, and Sunny was perfect. He landed on the correct lead every time. He kept a perfectly steady pace.

Bird patted his neck. *Holy, Sunny. That was brilliant.*

Correct.

You vain thing!

Put up with it.

Hannah and Abby were dumbfounded. They clapped and cheered and rushed to Bird and Sunny.

"Amazing!" exclaimed Abby.

"Well done, Bird," said Hannah proudly. "Good boy, Sundancer!"

Sunny felt proud and looked it. His tail was high, his head was up, his ears were pricked. People came around to praise him, and Sunny accepted it all with equanimity.

Jewel appeared, smiling broadly. "Abby," she called out. "He passed the test with flying colours. He's off the list, but he must continue to behave. Consider it a warning."

Abby nodded. "Thanks, Jewel. We really appreciate it." She

turned to Bird. "There's a jumper class in fifteen minutes. You in?"

Bird asked Sunny. *Are you in?*

Bring it on.

Bird nodded.

"Good girl!" Abby grinned. "I sure learned today who can ride this horse." She ran off to put Bird in the order for the jumper class.

Bird felt elated.

Julia rushed up. "Bird! Bird! We got here just in time to watch! Mr. Gilmore and Mom and me! You were awesome!"

Sunny stretched his neck to the little girl and gave her a sniff. She hugged his head and rubbed his ears. "Good boy, Sunny! You were totally awesome!"

There was an announcement in the hunter ring. The judge called out the winning numbers. Bird heard her number called. She took off Sundancer's saddle and gave it to Abby, then led the gelding at a trot around the hunter ring with the other seven winners. The boy on the bay won fourth. The woman on the grey got third. Bird waited while a man on a roan accepted the second-place ribbon. Sunny won first.

Bird grinned happily while Sundancer had the red first-place ribbon hooked onto his bridle. He acted like it happened every day. They trotted proudly out of the ring to wild applause by family members. Sunny stopped dead. His head dropped to his knee, and he bowed to the ground. People started to cheer.

"Let's get over to the jumper ring, Bird," said Abby. She had come running and was out of breath. "We've got to learn the course."

I hope you're good at memorizing, Bird girl.

I hope so, too.

12

THE TALL MAN

I look good when I'm fixed up.

Sundancer and Bird waited for their turn outside the jumper ring. This class was judged solely on jumping clear within a predetermined time. Form and prettiness counted not one bit. So far the competitors had been riding at a good pace, but there had been many poles down and quite a few time faults. Bird studied which angles to take and which corners to cut to make up time without pushing Sunny too fast.

Bird felt tension mounting in Sunny. She stroked his neck and cooed to him, but the horse only became more nervous. Bird feared that he might have another meltdown.

Speak to me, Sunny. Why are you so tense?

I'm not sure I can do this, Bird girl.

Why not? You've jumped higher than this.

That's not it. I cannot tell which jump is next.

You mean you haven't memorized the course?

Whatever.

Sunny. Please relax. I know which jumps to do, and in which order.

What if you forget?

I won't forget.

What if you do?

We lose.

She felt his body bristle. *Bird girl, I want to win.*

So do I, but this is our first time. Let's just go in and have fun.

I need to win.

Sunny, can you let me ride you like a normal horse? Most horses don't memorize the course.

Most horses lose.

Bird patted his neck again and laughed quietly to herself. Sometimes she found him very funny. She'd have to work at relaxing him, and help him learn to accept winning and losing equally. Bird also realized that no other rider would have been able to explain things to him or understand what upset him. He would have panicked—and probably bolted. All because he hadn't memorized the course.

Bird studied the course again. It was complicated, she had to admit, but she was on top of it.

Her number was called.

Trust me, Sunny. I know the course.

I hope so.

You jump, I'll steer.

Deal.

They rode in and Bird nodded to the judge. She wasn't sure whether or not it was required, like in the hunter ring, but she didn't want to be penalized for anything as trivial as that.

Hannah, Eva, Stuart, Julia, and Abby were lined up at the fence. Even Paul had stopped by during a break from his veterinary duties. Bird glanced at them. She didn't want to be distracted so she ignored their waves of encouragement. Sunny enjoyed the attention and showed off a little with a cow hop and a buck.

Cool it, Sunny.

What's the harm?

Pay attention.

Didn't you say we should have fun?

Bird smiled in spite of herself. She asked him for a canter

and they rode through the timer. The first jump was blue and white and oddly angled, but Sunny soared over it. They turned hard left to the brown oxer at a brisk pace, took it, then steered right. They got braced for the red striped in-and-out. The water jump was next, then the triple. After racing the water jump, Sunny slowed just in time to collect his stride.

You pushed me at that water! Don't do that!

Sorry.

Now we have a problem. Just let me go, and grab my mane.

Okay.

She let his reins loose. He popped the first of the three jumps, added a chipped stride to the second, but had his act together by the third. Bird breathed out with relief.

There, I fixed it. No thanks to you.

Good boy, Sunny.

Number six was coming up fast. It was a rainbow-coloured optical illusion. Sunny sprang over it hugely, unsure of which pole was on top. They landed almost past the point where a turn could be made, so Sunny sat back on his haunches, pivoted, and headed to the line of four jumps.

Now, that was my fault, Bird girl. I overjumped.

But you fixed it.

The difficulty of this line was that each jump was a different height but appeared the same. Horse and rider might assume they were equal, and many of their competitors had made a mess of them.

Let me do this, Bird. Look up over the entire line, chin up, and stay still. Don't look at the jumps. Close your eyes if you have to. Give me the reins. Heels down.

Sunny leaped and cleared the first. He landed, then took a stride, and another. He leaped higher for the second, higher yet for the third, then easily sailed over the last with no rails down.

There were two more jumps. Bird headed left for the white

oxer. Sunny pulled right, toward the green skinny. Bird tugged back.

That's not it, Bird girl.

Yes it is, Sunny. It's marked eleven. I see number twelve behind it.

The horse before us went to the green jump next.

He was wrong.

You better be right.

As they flew over the white oxer and cleared the last jump—a tricky narrow thing—by a foot, Bird wondered how many people had to argue with their horses. Now they moved as fast as they could through the timer. It was done.

Abby rushed to the gate and congratulated Bird.

"Fabulous ride! Great time, too. You'll be in the ribbons again."

Bird flushed and hugged Sunny's neck.

Were you right, Bird?

I was right.

Good. Then we won.

Their cheering section of Julia, Eva, Stuart, Hannah, and Paul joined them. Together they watched the last entrants make their trips.

Nobody's even close.

Don't get too smug, Sunny. Pride cometh before a fall.

I thought summer cometh before the fall.

Puns, now? Give me a break. She gave him a pat on the neck, happy to see him so relaxed and cheerful.

Again, Bird and Sunny were called in for the ribbon presentation, this time mounted.

Word had gotten out that there was a new horse to watch, and the stands were full. When the red first-place ribbon was hooked onto Sunny's bridle, he reared straight up, then dropped and bowed. People stood and cheered.

The eight horses did a victory lap around the ring with

Sundancer leading. He showed his stuff proudly. He tucked in his chin to flex his neck and shot his tail straight up. Sunlight danced on his sleek, coppery coat. His feet barely touched the earth.

Bird looked at the stands for the first time, and saw the smiling faces and supportive waves of her family. Happy tears filled her eyes.

It was time to go home. Sunny had performed well and it had turned out to be a good experience. Bird was excited with the day's results. She walked Sunny back to the trailer and took off his tack. She rubbed him with a big blue towel.

Did you have a good time, Sunny?

Yes. After the first bit.

Do you want to do this again?

Yes. I like to win.

Abby brought one bucket of water for him to drink and another to sponge him down. Hannah had a bag of fresh carrots and fed them to Sundancer one by one.

Suddenly the big chestnut tensed. Bird felt a prickle of apprehension. Cody, under the truck, growled.

"Good afternoon, ladies."

The Tall Man I told you about. Sundancer began to shake. *Get me out of here. Now.*

Come with me, Sunny.

Bird began to walk away with the big gelding on the shank.

"Where are you going?" the Tall Man asked. Bird kept walking. "Hey!" She didn't look back.

"She doesn't speak," said Hannah defensively. "She's just cooling out the horse." She looked at the man, noting the dark sunglasses and brimmed hat that hid his face. He was very tall and lean, in his mid-forties, and had an athletic build. A small brown and white Jack Russell terrier shadowed his every move.

"Is that Sundancer?" the man asked.

"Yes," answered Hannah.

"I came over to take a look at him. I watched him today. He did well."

Abby and Hannah relaxed, and smiled at him.

"Thanks," said Abby. "Let me introduce myself. I'm Abby Malone."

"Yes, I know."

"And I'm Hannah Bradley," said Hannah. "Have we met before?"

"Perhaps. The horse world is small."

Hannah was surprised that he didn't offer to introduce himself. She was compelled to ask, "What is your name?"

"Elvin Wainright."

Abby and Hannah exchanged glances. "The trainer for the Owens stables?" asked Abby.

"That's right." His wolfish smile made the women uneasy. "Sundancer looks a whole lot like a horse we raised."

Hannah swallowed. "Is that so?"

"Yes. A horse named Prince Redwood. Sire was California Dreamin' and dam' Princess Narnia. A valuable horse."

Hannah repeated, "Sounds very valuable to me."

"I think you know where this is going, ladies. Don't play dumb."

"Mr. Wainright," said Hannah, irritated, "if you have something to say, please speak your mind."

"The horse you people call Sundancer is actually Prince Redwood, and he belongs to Owens Enterprises."

"That's not my understanding."

"You must return him."

"I'm not prepared to do that."

"You are in big trouble, Hannah Bradley. Big trouble. You will hear from our lawyers tomorrow morning."

The Tall Man turned to go.

At that moment, Paul, Stuart, Eva, and Julia appeared at the horse trailer. They wore happy smiles on their faces.

"Where's Bird?" asked Paul. "We came to congratulate her on her beautiful ride."

"For that matter, where's Sundancer?" Stuart asked Hannah.

"Mr. Wainright," called Hannah. "Before you phone your lawyer, I'd like you to meet some people. This is my sister Eva, my niece Julia, my friend Stuart, and my vet Paul Daniels." She waited while the penny dropped. "Paul, Mr. Wainright tells me that I'm in big trouble because of Sundancer."

Paul spoke first. "Elvin Wainright?"

"Yes. Dr. Paul Daniels?"

"Yes. I'm the veterinarian that your stable manager called to put down a horse recently."

"I don't recall."

"I'm not your usual vet. I wondered at the time why I was asked to do it, so I spoke to you on the phone. You told me that the horse was insane, a menace to all, and needed to be euthanized for safety reasons. That was the conversation, word for word. Ring a bell?"

Elvin Wainright looked uncomfortable. "Not at all."

"In that same conversation you told me that you'd never before had the misfortune to train a horse as 'evil' and you wanted him dead ASAP."

"I have no idea what you're talking about."

"Then you have a bad memory, Mr. Wainright."

"Regardless. The fact remains that this gelding is Prince Redwood and the property of Owens Enterprises."

"Were you not aware that I was given, for no money, this horse that you wanted destroyed?"

"No." Elvin's eyes narrowed. He shifted his weight.

"Your manager was under the impression that you were more than happy to get him off the property. He spoke to you about the matter that same day, before I accepted the horse. I was in the room at the time."

"That's news to me." Elvin adjusted his hat and pulled back his shoulders. "At any rate, you have no proof. I have all his papers. I have his blood samples on file. You have nothing but your story."

Bird and Sunny returned from their walk. They casually sauntered up to Elvin. Bird slowly and deliberately handed him the lead shank.

I'm doing what you asked, Sunny. I don't want to know what you have in mind.

I think you have a pretty good idea, Bird girl. Get the trailer ready.

"What are you doing, Bird?" demanded Hannah. "He has no right to take Sundancer."

Bird winked at her aunt and put her finger to her lips. Hannah held her tongue.

Elvin put the chain of the shank over Sunny's nose and yanked it tight. "Well, thank you. At least one person here knows right from wrong. Now we can just forget all about this. Have a good day." Elvin Wainright turned on his heel and led a quiet, obedient Sundancer away. The terrier followed them, a safe distance behind.

"What are you doing, Alberta!" shrieked Eva. "You just gave away the most fabulous horse in the entire world! You just *gave* him away!"

Stuart took Eva's arm. "Relax, Eva. Let's let Hannah and Paul handle this. And Bird." He smiled at the nervous girl.

"Well, they're not, are they. Handling it, that is. They're standing there with egg on their faces. Somebody has to do something!"

Bird touched her mother's hand and gestured for her to follow. They walked around the trailer and watched as Sunny was quietly led to the huge navy-blue Owens Enterprises van. Elvin

Wainright shouted to his grooms to bring down the ramp.

"You see?" squealed Eva. "In one minute he'll be gone, and we'll never see him again. He won *first*, today! In *two* classes!"

Sunny stood quietly as the ramp was readied for loading. Two grooms came up behind him to urge him on, while Elvin led. Sunny took a few steps and started up the ramp. It appeared that he would simply walk in.

"*Do* something!" wailed Eva.

Bird held her breath.

Sunny kicked out with a speed and ferocity that astounded everyone. He narrowly missed striking both grooms in the chest, one with each hind foot, and they rolled away in surprise and fear. Elvin turned and raised his whip to strike the horse.

Quickly, Bird ran behind Hannah's trailer, opened it, and dropped the ramp. She motioned to Hannah to start the truck.

Sunny reared up as Elvin continued to hit him. They could hear each blow land, whump, whump, whump. Elvin's hollering echoed across the parking lot.

Sunny walked backward down the ramp of the Owens van, dragging Elvin as he yelled and flailed. Suddenly, the horse spun like a top and threw Elvin six feet in the air. He came down hard. The terrified grooms staggered over to help their boss as he lay on the ground. Elvin Wainright lifted his head and shook his fist at Sunny.

Sunny neighed loudly. He rose up on his hind legs and pawed the air. He neighed again. Then he dropped down and shook his head angrily. His ears lay flat. It looked as if he was going to charge. The little brown and white dog jumped through an open door into the cab of the truck. Wainright and the grooms cowered. They cried out for mercy and covered their heads.

Then, as if it was all a joke, Sunny turned and trotted back to Bird.

Get on the trailer, Sunny. Let's go!

Was I good, or was I good?

Gloat later. We've got to get out of here.

Sunny trotted into the trailer. Abby and Bird lifted the ramp behind him, secured the latches, then quickly climbed into the cab of the truck as Hannah jumped in. She put it in gear and accelerated.

"See you back at Saddle Creek," Abby called out the truck window as they drove away. "I wouldn't dally, if I were you."

Paul, Stuart, Eva, and Julia stood dazed. "We haven't heard the last of this," predicted Paul.

"Let's go," said Stuart. Elvin Wainright was now on his feet, standing with the help of his two grooms and looking extremely agitated. "This is not the time to have a reasonable discussion with the man."

They got in Stuart's car and headed home to the farm.

Dark clouds gathered in the sky, and the day went from sunny to overcast in a matter of minutes. Rain threatened but stayed at bay as Hannah drove the Saddle Creek rig into their lane. The sedan had already arrived, and Eva, Stuart, and Julia were in the house. Paul was waiting at the barn to help unload. He stood on the driveway when the truck and trailer pulled in.

Paul spoke before Hannah had a chance to get out of the truck. "I'm sorry. You were right. I should've insisted on a contract. How can I help?"

"With the horse or the lawsuit?"

"Both."

Abby and Bird unloaded Sunny from the rig, and took him into the barn to wash, feed, and bed him down. Hannah and Paul organized the truck, trailer, and tack. Paul directed Hannah as she backed the trailer into its spot. He unhitched it, and Hannah drove the truck to its parking place. They carried the saddle, bridle, blankets, and brushes into the barn and put them away.

As they worked, they talked. "Look, Paul, I know it's not your fault. But what do we do now? I can't afford a lawyer."

"I hope it doesn't come to that. If it does, we'll fight back, and I'll foot the bill. I got us into this." Paul looked earnestly at Hannah. "We've done nothing wrong, Hannah. I'll stake my reputation on that."

"Still, it'll be hard to prove. It's your word against theirs and it's all hearsay. Nothing on paper. Will the stable manager back you up?"

"No. I called him on my cell just now. He says he doesn't remember a thing."

Hannah got mad. "These people are just not honest!"

"I'll say it again, Hannah. I'm sorry I didn't get something signed. I took the horse in good faith."

"I know. I'm not blaming you, believe me."

"Look on the bright side. They might change their minds about wanting him, since Sundancer behaved so badly back there. He scared three men witless in less than a minute."

"True. He is dangerous. So maybe it's best if they take him back after all. It's plain lucky that nobody was hurt."

"That we know of. We'll hear if a bone's broken or someone's bruised."

"That could cause us some trouble, as Elvin Wainright said."

Paul and Hannah spoke in unison. "Big trouble."

They chuckled half-heartedly.

Hannah paused thoughtfully, then said, "That whole thing was rather interesting, wasn't it?"

"What whole thing?"

"How Bird handed Sunny over to Elvin but seemed to know what he was going to do. That he was going to come running back."

"You're right. She even dropped the ramp."

"And gestured to me to start the truck."

"She and Sunny understand each other, Hannah. The horse wouldn't let Abby ride him, and she's the best rider around."

"It's a little mysterious. I wonder if Bird is the only one who will ever understand him."

"I certainly wouldn't get on his back."

Hannah agreed. "We'd all be wise to leave him to Bird. There's something magic between them."

"That's for sure," said Paul. "But he's a wild card. What if he turns on Bird one day?"

Hannah looked at Paul. "Do you think I don't worry about that every time she gets on his back?"

Abby cleaned and oiled the leather in the tack room while Bird hosed Sunny down in the wash stall.

I showed those men a thing or two, Bird girl.

You certainly did.

I won ribbons today. I feel good.

I'm proud of you, Sunny. For winning. Not for scaring those men.

But I feel best about scaring those men. They hurt me. Before.

How?

I don't want to talk about it, Bird girl. I thought the jumps were going to hurt me, too.

Why?

Because. It happened before. The jumps hurt me. Those men hurt me. I don't want to think about it any more.

Okay, Sunny. Tell me about it if you want to. I'd like to know.

After they were finished in the barn, Bird and Abby caught up with Hannah and Paul on the driveway. Together they joined the others in the house. The wind had kicked up and the rain would not be long in coming. A sudden gust of wind slammed the door forcefully behind them.

Eva and Stuart had made mushroom and cheese omelettes, toast, and salad. Julia had set the table. They'd made every effort to create a cheerful atmosphere in the kitchen, with the threatening storm outside. Everyone was hungry and tired and deep in their own thoughts, so there was silence as the food was consumed. The weather change and the events at the show had affected their mood.

Finally, Julia put down her fork and spoke. "Bird, I've never seen anything more beautiful than you riding Sunny today. Ever. In my whole life. One day, if I work at it hard enough, I want to ride like you."

Bird stopped chewing. She looked at Julia and smiled. Bird felt full of gratitude for her little sister's words, and even more for the swelling of love emanating from her. No matter what happened now—and she sensed that something was about to— Bird felt she could deal with it.

13

THE GREAT ESCAPE

I need to use up my energy. I have an excess of adrenaline.

AS THEY SAT EATING their steaming omelettes, there was a knock at the kitchen door. Bird's stomach tightened. She knew who it was, and trouble always came with him.

Eva was the closest, so she got up and answered the knock.

A smiling Kenneth Bradley stood at the door. Framing him, Bird saw black rain clouds in the sky, then a flash of lightning accompanied by a rumble of thunder. Pathetic fallacy, she thought. She'd learned about it in school. When inanimate objects reflect human emotions. In this case, she thought, the weather perfectly reflected her grandfather's soul.

"Daddy, what a nice surprise," Eva enthused. "Come in!"

"I will, sugar pie. Are you having a late lunch after the horse show? I'm not disturbing you, am I?"

Hannah joined them at the door. "Not at all, Dad. Please join us. I'll whip up another omelette in a jiffy."

"I've eaten, Hannah." He patted his stomach. "Got to watch my weight. I've got a new girlfriend, you know. Much younger." He winked at his daughters. "No. I'm here on business. Good news for you, Hannah. It'll make your day."

They made room at the table, and Kenneth pulled up a chair.

Abby Malone blushed uncomfortably. Bird knew why. Abby

had not seen Colonel Kenneth Bradley since that day in court, years earlier, when she'd testified against him. Bird understood why she could barely sit in the same room with him now.

Bird observed her grandfather from across the table. He was smiling broadly, looking friendly. Bird thought a giant great white shark might smile that way. Just before it ate you.

"I heard what happened at the horse show today." Kenneth looked around importantly. The indecision and uneasiness that met his words satisfied him. Briefly, he rested his eyes on his granddaughter. "Congratulations, Bird. You did a fine job of riding Prince Redwood. Well done." He reached out to shake her hand.

Bird stared at her plate and refused to react. He called him Prince Redwood, thought Bird. Guess where this is going.

Without missing a beat, Kenneth Bradley continued. "Prince Redwood surprised us all today. He's been a bit of a rascal, to be sure. His trainer always believed that some time off work would do him a world of good. He thinks he's ready now to return for some serious training."

"You're talking about Elvin Wainright?" asked Hannah.

"Yes. His trainer."

Paul asked, "Mr. Bradley, may I ask exactly how you are involved?"

Kenneth laughed heartily. "How sweet. You're speaking on my daughter's behalf. You want my credentials? I'm a director of Owens Enterprises."

Everyone was stunned. This was news to them all.

"You're a director?" asked Hannah. "Of Owens Enterprises?"

"I'm on the board of the company. I'm also a horseman, as you well know, and thereby very involved in the operations of the stables. Elvin is a valued employee, and I trust his opinion. By the way, he told me the entire history of this horse." He glanced dismissively at Paul.

"What story did he tell you?" Paul was not intimidated.

"The correct one, no doubt, but I'll humour you. You took the horse because you were under the false impression that nobody wanted him. No legal deal was drawn up at that time, and none has been drawn up since. No papers were signed over. In other words, in a court of law, you could not claim ownership."

Paul shrugged. "Bluntly stated, Mr. Bradley. And true. But the fact is, I was given the horse outright. The staff loaded him on the Owens trailer and brought him here themselves." Paul paused, watching Kenneth for his reaction, then continued. "I had verbal assurances from Elvin Wainright and the manager. Indeed, the entire stable was relieved when I took him off their hands. They wanted nothing to do with him."

Kenneth was impassive. "Well, they do now, and they have the right."

Paul held the older man's gaze.

"Let's be adults and agree to disagree, shall we? Because I come with very good news." Bradley again smiled the shark smile. "Owens Enterprises wants to take the horse back to his rightful stable. We'll pay you for all your trouble, Hannah. Handsomely."

Bird was worried. Hannah always needed money.

"We will *not* press charges for theft. We will *not* sue for injuries sustained today. We *will* pay you for boarding, training, and rehabilitation, with a little extra to sweeten the pot. What do you think?"

Paul was dubious. "What are you offering?"

"Ten thousand dollars."

There was silence around the table. Hannah immediately thought of all the uses to which she could put the money. Bird read her thoughts and shook her head. This was going to be bad, she could feel it.

"Dad," said Hannah, trying to be fair. "Sundancer, or Prince Redwood, is a difficult horse. More accurately, he's completely messed up. He's unpredictable and strong-willed. Nobody could make him do anything before he got here. Do you think that he'll stay well behaved when you take him back? He's the same horse as the one that Elvin and your manager wanted euthanized hardly a month ago."

"Elvin changed his mind."

"What if somebody gets hurt?"

"We'll take that chance."

Hannah looked at Bird. She had tears on her cheeks and her fists were clenched. For a moment, everyone was silent. Then Abby spoke. "Mr. Bradley, you talk of forgetting the past. I hope you understand that doing so would be impossible for me." Bird gasped as she picked up on Abby's memories—thrown into a dark, smelly shed at gunpoint, door locked. She shuddered.

"I'm not referring to our past, Miss Malone. I will never forget what happened between us." He pursed his lips and squinted at her, the anger clear on his face. "You testified against me in court."

Abby swallowed her own anger. "And I'm glad I did, but this has nothing to do with us. I just want to say that there is only one rider who can communicate with Sundancer. That rider is Alberta, your granddaughter. Without her unique ability to connect with horses, Sundancer's talent would not be realized."

Kenneth smiled condescendingly. "I appreciate your sentiment, Abby, but don't try to tell me my business. I heard about what happened today. Just because you can't ride him doesn't mean that Bird is the only rider who can. Although it might make you feel better about your own limitations if that were true."

Abby clammed up. With a brief nod in Hannah's direction, she rose from the table and left the house.

"I agree with Abby, Dad," said Hannah, hoping that Abby was somehow still close enough to hear. "One hundred percent. Bird and Sundancer have a relationship. The horse trusts her, and nobody else. If you take him back, he will be just as dangerous as he was before."

Kenneth rolled his eyes. "What's it to you? He'll become our problem. I've hired Leon Parish. Tell me that he can't ride."

Bird was surprised; in fact, everyone at the table looked a little shocked. Leon Parish was widely considered to be the best rider in Canada. He had recently come out of a drug rehabilitation program and was looking for work. There was no doubt about his talent.

"If you've got Leon, you're serious," said Stuart.

"Dead serious. We'll keep his new name, Sundancer, since he's already shown with that on his passport. We feel confident that he'll be a contender at the Haverford Fair."

Paul asked, "You won't show him under Prince Redwood, his registered name?"

"No. It's easier this way."

Paul nodded. "Easier."

"I've had enough of your insinuations, Dr. Daniels. If you have proof of any wrongdoing, show it. Otherwise, I don't want to hear it again."

"Point taken. Hannah will have to think about this offer before she can give you an answer."

"Can't you speak for yourself, Hannah?" asked Kenneth, ignoring Paul.

"Paul is my full partner in this venture, so he has a right to speak. And he's right. We need to think this over. There's a lot to consider, Dad, including Bird's feelings. She loves Sunny."

Kenneth furrowed his brow. He glanced in Bird's direction and shook his head. "Sentimentality is a beautiful thing, Hannah, but don't let it get in the way of business. We're offering compensation for his training. Simple. We need not offer one cent, since no deal was made. If you don't accept, we'll take you to court and sue you."

"You have such a way with words, Dad."

"Don't be sarcastic, Hannah. Granted, life would be easier for all of us if we can cut a deal and avoid court. But don't stretch my patience. I will take this to court. Twenty thousand is my last offer, which is roughly the cost of lawyer fees."

"Twenty?" Hannah repeated. She thought she'd misheard him.

"Twenty. Take it or leave it."

Paul caught Hannah's eye. He raised his eyebrows and nodded slightly.

"Dad, Paul and I need a moment." Hannah rose and signalled to Paul.

"One minute is all you get." Kenneth's shark smile was gone, Bird noted. She felt powerless. Sundancer's future was being decided and she could only sit and wait.

Out in the hall, Hannah whispered, "But what about Bird?"

"You and I both know that Sundancer is a dangerous horse. He demonstrated that twice today. I'd never forgive myself if something happened to Bird. Time to cut our losses, Hannah, and make a deal." Paul paused. "Also, your father's right. We could spend a lot of money on legal fees, but we have no proof of anything. If they take us to court, we don't have a prayer. We really have no choice."

Hannah saw resolve in Paul's face. He made sense. She nodded and led the way back into the kitchen.

"Twenty-five," said Hannah as she sat down. She could hardly believe she'd said it.

"Deal. You cut a tough bargain, Hannah. Chip off the old block." Kenneth put out his hand. Hannah, ignoring a queasy sad feeling, shook it. Kenneth took his cellphone out of his jacket and punched in a number.

"Elvin? Kenneth. The deal's done for twenty-five."

Bird listened in horror. She stared at Hannah and then at Paul. Neither would meet her gaze. She pushed out her chair and stiffly backed out of the kitchen, ignoring her little sister's voice calling her name. She could not stay inside, not now. She had to get to Sunny. Bird ran outside and jumped the fence. Under the darkening skies, she raced as fast as she could through the field, accompanied by a rumble of thunder.

Whoa there, Bird girl. Where's the fire?

Sunny! Hannah sold you! She sold you to the Tall Man and my grandfather.

You must be joking. No, I can see it is the truth.

It's the truth. What can I do?

You must tell them it is a terrible idea.

I can't talk, Sunny. You know that.

You won't talk, Bird girl. I know you are able.

I can't make the words come out!

You must. I will not go back. They hurt me there.

I know! Bird sobbed, burying her face in Sunny's warm neck.

I won ribbons today. Why does Hannah want to get rid of me?

You also hurt people today, Sunny. You looked vicious.

I only hurt the people who hurt me. It's fair.

What about the coyote lady? You hurt her, too.

I didn't mean to. I got scared.

I know how you see it, Sunny. I'm telling you how humans see it.

Then tell the humans how I see it! You must!

I can't!

Sunny kicked up his heels and ran off into the field. Bird knew he was angry with her for letting this happen. Bird was angry at herself, too. Why couldn't she speak when she wanted? The words always got stuck in her throat and wouldn't come out. She clenched her fists and punched the air. She tried to scream. Only a low, throaty groan came out.

"I'm guessing that Hannah took the offer." Abby's voice startled Bird, and she turned quickly, angrily wiping a tear from her cheek.

"I know how hard it must be for you, Bird. You don't want to hear this, but it's probably for the best." Abby reached out to touch her, but Bird backed away. "Sunny is a loaded gun. An accident waiting to happen. I know that. Deep inside you know it, too."

Bird shook her head fiercely. Of all people, she'd thought that Abby would understand. She wanted to tell Abby that she was wrong. Sunny was not a loaded gun for her. They talked to each other. She wanted to tell her that selling him was a huge mistake. That those people had hurt him. That Sunny would hurt them, too. But nothing came out except a strangled little squeak. How could she make Abby understand? Bird groaned as the realization hit her: She couldn't. No one would ever understand. Once again, Abby reached out to comfort her. Bird shook her head. Don't touch me! Just go away. She closed her eyes and flailed her arms. Go away, go away, go away. Before she knew what was happening, her fist made contact with Abby's chest. Bird stopped moving and opened her eyes. What had she done?

Abby jumped back in surprise as Cody charged from the bushes. He knocked Bird over and held her down, growling in her face.

"Cody!" commanded Abby. "Get off!"

Cody, I didn't mean to hit her.

You swore you would never hurt my Abby. You swore the oath.

It was a mistake. I lost control.

"Cody, get off her, now!" Abby's voice seemed very far away.

Are you mad at her?

No. I'm mad at myself. I'm mad that I can't talk and tell Abby why Hannah should not let Sunny go to the Owens stables.

Then hit yourself, girl.

I will, if you let me up.

I will let you up if you will not hurt my Abby. Ever again.

I promise, Cody. I mean it.

Cody backed away and let Bird get up. He waited for her to punch herself, as she had promised. He was satisfied when she did, but still he watched her carefully and stayed by Abby's side. Abby gave him a pat.

"What was that all about, Bird?" asked Abby. "Why did you hit me?"

Bird felt miserable. She opened her mouth and nothing came out. She punched her chest again, then squeezed her eyes shut and scrunched up her face, but nothing worked. Tears poured out of her eyes and down her face. Finally, she began to sob. The sobs made sounds from her throat, and Bird tried again.

"So...rrr...y," she grunted.

Then she ran. She ran to Sundancer and grabbed his mane.

We're getting out of here, Sunny.

Good plan. Where are we going?

Sunny dropped his head and bent his knees, making it easier for Bird to get on his back.

Anywhere but here. Let's go.

Hang on, Bird girl. We're going to fly!

Sundancer galloped lightly to the fence. Bird wove her fingers through his mane and held on to his sides tightly with her legs. He gathered his impressive strength in his haunches, sprang off the ground with no effort and sailed over the four rails with air to spare.

Bird looked back to see Abby and Cody standing in the field, staring at them through the gathering mist. She also saw the big blue Owens Enterprises horse van turning into their lane.

Just in time, Sunny!

They'll never catch us!

Sundancer and Bird raced through the fields behind the farm. The rain had started to fall, and it was getting steadily heavier. They splashed through Saddle Creek and along the ridge, heading for the woods. Sunny slowed down to a trot as they followed the dense forest trails, then moved faster into a gallop as he found better footing in the meadows. Big black and white Holstein cows looked up from their wet grass in wonder.

My legs are getting tired, Sunny. Slow down.

I'm having fun, Bird! See how fast I'm running?

Yes, I do. But you're all wet and slippery and I'm having trouble staying on.

I'm the fastest horse in the world! The best racehorses can't beat me!

Sunny, I'm serious. You might slip in the mud. Slow down!

You're no fun.

The big chestnut gelding slowed to a trot, then a walk. Then he stopped.

What's wrong, Sunny? Why'd you stop?

Where are we going?

I don't know.

I can feel that. Horses always know if their riders don't know where they're going. It's a terrible feeling. So I'll just stop here until you decide.

Let's see. We're close to Hogscroft, the James' place. That's where Dancer lives. We're not far from Abby's barn. The Piersons are very close. The Owens stables aren't far, and the Casey's farm is over there.

We need cover. I'm getting nervous out here with the lightning. Who would hide us?

The Piersons don't use their barn in the summer. Their Herefords are out and they don't have horses any more. They probably won't even know we're there.

Laura Pierson was peeling potatoes for dinner at the kitchen sink. She hummed along with the opera that was playing on the stereo and mentally planned the menu for her next book-club meeting. Laura and Pete belonged to four book-clubs, and Laura was often the main promoter. She loved the mental stimulation of reading and discussing good books with intelligent people, and tried hard to include interesting new people as they moved into the area. Which was why there were now four book clubs.

The storm had come in fast and the light had faded. The birds normally began chirping their cheerful nesting noises at this time of the evening, which always made Laura feel happy and content. She knew that tonight they were already snugly nestled in, covering each other with their feathered wings. The thought pleased her.

Laura stopped peeling and looked outside to watch a bolt of lightning. She rubbed her eyes and looked again. If she wasn't mistaken, a powerful, handsome chestnut horse with a small rider jumped over their front fence and cantered toward their barn.

"Pete! Pete!"

Pete looked up from the book he was reading, ensconced in his comfortable chair with a heating pad warming his aching back.

"A horse and rider just jumped over our fence. It looked for all the world like Dancer and little Abby Malone!"

"Abby's all grown up now, Laura."

"I'm not making this up!"

"I didn't say you were."

"Before you get your nose back in that book, I want you to go see what's going on."

"I need to finish this book before tomorrow. Book club, you know."

"You've had that book for a month."

"I'm reading it now."

"I'm glad you are, Pete, but could you look out the back? Please?"

Pete put down his book. For the peace of the family, he'd take a look, but he thought that his lovely wife might be seeing things. Old age, he mused. It does crazy things to us.

He got up out of his chair. His arthritis hurt. His back ached. His feet were numb. He looked out the back window just in time to see a girl hop off a horse's back and quickly disappear into the barn.

Pete stood there, looking at the dark barn door through the window. He sniffed and stood taller. "Laura, my love, we have company."

Laura spun around, peeler in hand. "I'll go invite her in. She must be hungry."

Bird was happy to be out of the driving rain and on solid ground again. She was shivering, and her clothes were drenched. Her leg muscles felt like wet noodles, they were so weak. Sunny was delighted with the large, clean dry stall he'd chosen, and more than pleased with the quality of hay and water.

Do you think anybody saw us, Sunny?

No chance, Bird girl. I was as quick as a bunny.

A bunny, eh? A fat, slow bunny?

What are you saying?

That the back door just opened and someone is coming.

What!

Mrs. Pierson is on her way.

Great. I guess I'll have to do the talking.

A talking horse. That'll be the day.

There's more chance of me talking than you, Bird girl.

"Hello?" Laura Pierson was dressed in a vibrant orange raincoat and matching rubber boots. She entered the barn, put down her turquoise umbrella, and fumbled for the light switch. "Hello? Please speak up, I know you're in here."

You're scaring the old lady, Bird girl. Say something.

I can't.

Do I have to do everything myself?

Staring at Bird resentfully, Sunny neighed loudly.

"Thank you, horse. That was very polite. Now, I know there is a girl in here, too. I saw you both through my window." Her hand searched the wall for the switch, to no avail. "And my, my! You both jumped that fence well."

Bird's eyes were adjusted to the dark, and she walked over and turned on the lights.

"Oh! It's you! The little girl who lives at Saddle Creek. Hannah's niece. That explains the silence. You don't speak, do you?" Bird nodded. She liked this woman right away. She was kind and gentle. Someone she could trust. "Who's your equine friend?" Laura continued. "I thought for a minute it was Dancer! That gave me quite a start. He was a brilliant champion, and a dear, dear horse."

No better than me.

Bird rolled her eyes at him.

"I feel quite embarrassed, but I forget your name. It's a province, I think, and your nickname is an animal. It'll come to me."

Her name is Saskatchewan, Sasquatch for short.

Sunny, you're so funny I forgot to laugh.

"It's Alberta, isn't it! You're Bird! Well, I'm very happy you dropped in. Is your horse looked after?"

Bird looked at Sunny. He loftily ignored her and munched his fresh hay. She nodded.

"Good. Then why don't you come in and dry off and have a bite to eat with Pete and me. We're all alone tonight and would love some company."

Go ahead, Bird girl. It's been a long day, and I need some rest. The horse show, the kicking at grooms, the great escape. Quite a day.

Okay. I hope they'll let us stay for the night.

That part's up to you. I'm just a horse.

Right.

Bird and Mrs. Pierson entered the kitchen together, leaving the rain outside. Pete looked up from his book and smiled warmly.

"Well, well! It's Bird from down the road. Soaked to the skin. I haven't seen you for over a year. To what do we owe this welcome visit?"

"Pete, dear, she doesn't talk."

"Oh, yes. That's right. Then, sit down here with me while Mother gets you some dry clothes and the dinner ready. I'll just keep reading. I have a lot to cover by tomorrow. Book club. I don't want to let Laura down. She chose this book, and I can't quite get into it. It's not my type of thing."

"Pete, the book can wait. Bird came here for a reason, and we should find out why." Laura hustled away and called back, "I'm getting some nice warm towels, Bird, and I'll find something cozy for you to wear."

Pete studied Bird's face. She cast down her eyes.

He was unsure where to begin, so he waited for Laura to return. Soon, Bird was all changed and dry. She sat warming herself by the fire, looking somewhat comical with her wet, spiky hair and oversized blue and green flannels. The sound of Bird's clothes in the dryer provided a soothing background noise.

"Does Hannah know where you are, dear?" asked Laura.

Bird's eyes flicked up at Laura then dropped down.

"I thought not. Now, Bird dear. I must telephone her and tell her that you're safe."

Bird jumped up and started for the door.

Pete was alarmed. "There's something amiss here, Laura."

"Have you run away, dear?" asked Laura. Her voice was low and sympathetic.

Bird turned from the door and stared into her eyes. If she could tell her the situation, she knew that Laura would understand. Bird opened her mouth, but predictably, nothing came out.

Pete rose from his chair with great difficulty and went to her. "Families are complicated things, Bird. We find ourselves at odds with the people we love sometimes. It's natural." He reached out and tousled her short, choppy dark hair. "Right at this minute, your aunt is at her wits end with worry. She probably wonders if you've been in an accident or kidnapped, or have fallen off your horse and are lying somewhere with a broken neck or leg, or both. We can't let her worry."

"You can stay here as long as you want, dear," said Laura. "We have a spare bed. Your horse is welcome, too. There's lots of food and water for him, and fresh bedding."

"The deal is this." Pete had to sit down again to rest his limbs. "You can stay here with us until you want to go home, but Hannah must know where you are."

Bird didn't know what to do. She wanted to run away with Sundancer, even on this stormy night. She didn't want Hannah to come and get them, only to sell Sunny to the people that hurt him. But if she got on Sunny and ran away again, these nice people would still feel it their duty to call Hannah. Bird felt trapped. No win. She walked over to the black phone beside Pete's chair and picked it up. She dialed her home number and held it out for Pete.

Laura swirled over and scooped up the receiver. She listened attentively to the rings with her head tilted expectantly.

Eva answered. "Hello?"

"Is that Hannah Bradley? This is Laura Pierson."

"No, I'm sorry she's out."

"Who is this, please?"

"Eva Simms, Hannah's sister."

"Oh, my. The beautiful little Eva. Bird's mother."

"Yes. Did you say you were Mrs. Pierson? I wasn't paying attention. We're so worried. It's horrible out there and Bird hasn't come home. Hannah's out looking for her, and I'm waiting here for Bird, just in case."

"That's why I'm calling, dear."

"That's very kind of you, Mrs. Pierson. A lot of people have called, and a lot of people are out looking for her. I'll call you when we find her."

"No, dear, you don't understand. She's here. With us."

"Bird's there? Is she all right?"

"She's perfectly fine. She's here with her lovely horse. They just popped over the fence for a visit."

"Thank heavens she's safe." Eva was overwhelmed with relief. "I'll call Hannah on her cell and tell her."

"Not so fast, dear. I want to know why your daughter ran away. Kids don't just jump on horses bareback and hide in strange barns for no reason."

Eva paused for a moment, then began the story. "Hannah sold the horse. Actually, he wasn't her horse because he was supposed to be put down and he was given away to the vet instead, but Bird did so well at the show today that the Owens barn wants him back and they're prepared to pay twenty-five thousand even though they have the papers and Bird was so upset that she ran outside and Abby saw her get on Sundancer and jump the fence and gallop away and we've been looking for them ever since and the Owens guys are really mad. They're threatening to sue and I think they mean it, and my sister doesn't have any money for lawyers, but the important thing is that Bird is safe."

"My, my. Catch your breath, dear Eva, and relax. I'm going to talk this over with Pete. He'll know what to do. In the meantime, call Hannah and tell her that Bird and the horse are safe. Sundancer, did you say?"

"Yes."

"Is he related to Dancer?"

"No, his sire is California Dreamin'."

"Really?" Laura paused for a moment. "I was under the impression that that stallion mostly shoots blanks."

"Pardon me?"

"Sorry, dear. California Dreamin' is a gorgeous stallion, but he unfortunately can't always reproduce."

"I didn't know that happened to horses."

"It doesn't matter. It's just that this horse looks so much like Dancer that I wondered. Anyway, Hannah should know they're safe, but perhaps nobody else should just yet, until we figure this out."

"I agree. I don't want those men going to your house. May I talk to Bird, please?"

"Absolutely." Laura handed the receiver to Bird.

She put it up to her ear. "Bird, it's Mommy. I'm so glad you're all right. I was so worried. I don't know what I'd do without you."

Bird squeaked into the phone.

Eva whispered, "I'm so sorry about everything, Bird. I love you."

Bird's lips quivered. Her eyes filled with tears. It was the first time her mother had ever said that.

14

THE PIERSONS

I don't care for anybody when I'm mad.

HANNAH WAS WORRIED. She had no idea where Bird would go in this storm. Bareback on an unstable horse was a bad idea on a good day.

After searching the roads to no avail, she retraced the route back to Saddle Creek. The wipers were clearing her windshield as fast as they could, but still the visibility was poor. Several times Hannah imagined that she saw a horse in the distance, but it turned out to be just her hopes painting pictures.

One of these visions turned out to be real. Not Bird on Sundancer, as she'd fervently hoped, but Abby on Charlie. Abby had thrown on one of Hannah's slickers and saddled up Charlie to follow Sunny's tracks. Hannah stopped her truck to talk.

"Any sign of them?" she asked.

Abby shook her head. "The rain's so intense I lost the trail. I thought I'd head off to look in another direction." She pointed east.

"Good luck. Don't stay out too long in this stuff."

"Don't worry, Hannah." Abby forced a smile. "She'll turn up."

Hannah smiled back, grateful for Abby's support. She waved as Abby and Charlie trotted away. The ringing of her cellphone startled her. She picked it up quickly to find Eva on the other end of the line.

"I just heard from Bird."

"You spoke to her? Where is she?" Hannah asked.

"Safe, and that's all I'll say until I know that those men won't get rough with her."

"Eva, nobody's going to get rough with Bird! I just want her home safely."

"She's safe now. With good people."

Hannah sighed. "Why am I the bad guy here? I sold a neurotic horse for good money. Bird is understandably upset, but it's actually for her own good. She could get hurt on that horse. Badly hurt. She already had a concussion, and you know what he did to Abby today. Not to mention the show he put on at the trailers!"

"I know, Hannah. I just don't trust that Elvin Wainright. He was so mad."

"He was furious," Hannah agreed. "If he'd come a minute earlier, he would've had Sunny in the van and been on his way."

"I never want to see anger like that again."

"Our father was hopping mad, too, Eva, don't forget."

Eva was silent on the other end. Hannah had no doubt that Eva was remembering their childhood and their father's frequent rages.

"I wonder why he was so mad," she continued. "It's not his horse, nor his deal. He was just negotiating for Owens Enterprises."

"Dad doesn't like anything to get in the way of a deal, Hannah. He's always been like that."

"Maybe. But I can't help thinking there's something personal here." Hannah heard a signal on her phone. "There's another call coming in, Eva. I'll see you at the house."

"Bye, Hannah."

Hannah pressed enter and picked up the incoming call. "Hello?"

"Hannah, it's Lavinia. Where's my horse?"

"Hello, Lavinia. Pastor's in the barn where he should be. Isn't he?" Hannah sighed. She did not have time for this right now.

"Not Pastor, Hannah. Phoenix. The horse you call Sundancer."

"He's not your horse."

"Yes, he is. I got him from your father. I've been waiting here at Owens' stables and now I hear that Bird stole him before they could pick him up. I want you to bring him back immediately."

Hannah was shocked. "You bought him from my father?"

"Actually, he was a gift. Your father bought him for us."

Hannah pulled over to the side of the road and stopped her truck. She put her hand to her forehead and rubbed her temples.

"Hannah? Are you there? Hannah?"

"I'm here, Lavinia. I need to collect my thoughts."

"Well, I need you to collect my horse. Pronto. And get him over to Owens' stables where I can see him."

"Just a minute, Lavinia. You're saying that my father bought Sunny for you as a gift? Why?"

Hannah listened as Lavinia sighed in exasperation. "You're always the last to hear everything. Your father and I are dating." She hung up.

Hannah's head was reeling. This was getting crazier and crazier.

Her cell rang again. She thought about not answering but decided against it. What if it was about Bird?

"Hello?" She spoke hesitantly, then relaxed when she heard Paul's voice over the line.

"I just heard from Abby. Your cell was busy, so she called me. I'm on my way over to the Piersons."

"The Piersons? Why?"

"Bird and Sunny are there. Abby dropped in to ask them to keep an eye out, and there she was, feasting on roast chicken and gravy with Pete and Laura."

Hannah turned the truck around as she spoke. "I'm on my

way, Paul. My cell was busy all right. I was just on the phone with Lavinia."

"What's up? Does she need you to babysit?"

"Not even close. Did you know that my father and Lavinia are dating?"

"I've heard rumours."

"So she's right. I'm always the last to hear. Anyway, Lavinia's under the impression that she owns Sunny, that my father bought him for her."

"I don't understand, Hannah. Your father was—"

"Was making a deal for Owens Enterprises. Or did he say that? Did we just assume? Look, Paul, I can't figure it out. I'll meet you at Merry Fields."

Hannah had nothing but questions in her head as she pulled into the Piersons' lane. Paul's muddy truck was already there.

She looked in the window of the kitchen door. The Piersons, Abby, Paul, and Bird were sitting at the table behind steaming plates of food. Bird looked unharmed. Hannah relaxed. She's safe.

Laura spotted Hannah before she knocked and rushed over to open the door. "Come in, come in, dear! I'll set a place for you. Now sit down. Don't worry about your boots, a little mud never hurts." Laura took Hannah's raincoat and pulled out a chair for her. She produced a chicken dinner before Hannah had a chance to say hello.

Bird didn't look up from her plate. She wasn't yet sure how she felt about Hannah. Her aunt had sold Sundancer, and that was unforgivable. But Bird knew Hannah's reasons and they would seem like good reasons to Hannah. Bird needed a minute to unmix her feelings. Also, she was embarrassed. Once again, she'd caused everyone anxiety, this time by impulsively running away.

"Welcome, Hannah," said Pete. "Laura, Bird needs more chicken while you're up. And gravy."

"Yes, dear. In a jiffy."

"You eat, Hannah," said Pete. "We'll slow things down and sort out this whole thing. Can't do anything on an empty stomach."

Bird glanced up and caught her aunt's eye. Now that they were here at the Piersons, things seemed better. Bird hoped that Pete was right—that they could work something out. Maybe she could forgive Hannah after all. She smiled at her aunt.

Hannah sighed in relief and smiled back.

"Charlie's tucked away in the barn, Hannah," said Abby. "In the stall beside Sundancer. Hay, water, the works."

Hannah nodded her thanks and took a mouthful of mashed potatoes and gravy. "Delicious," she said to Laura.

"After dinner," Pete said, wiping his chin, "we'll sit by the fire and start at the beginning. Laura has made phone calls to the people concerned." He smiled comfortably. "Usually things are much simpler than they seem. If everyone is reasonable and honest, we will reach an acceptable solution."

People began to arrive as the dishes were being cleared.

Eva, Julia, and Stuart appeared first. After kicking off her boots, Eva ran to her daughter and hugged her tightly. Bird was surprised at how good it felt. It had been a long time. Eva took her hand and sat down on the couch, placing Bird between herself and Stuart.

Julia wriggled her way between Bird and Stuart, and kissed Bird on the cheek. "I'm glad you ran away with Sunny," she whispered. "That awful man came with a huge van to take him, but you were gone and he was sure mad! Gramps, too! It was crazy!"

An unamused Kenneth Bradley arrived next with a subdued Kimberly and Lavinia, who held Kenneth's arm possessively. Kenneth wiped his shoes on the mat, reminding Bird of a bull pawing the earth before charging.

"Well, well," said Pete heartily. "Come in, everyone, and take a chair."

Kenneth half-heartedly shook his offered hand and sat, leaving Lavinia to fend for herself. Underneath her expensive black patent-leather rain cape, Lavinia was dressed for a party. She found seats beside Kenneth for herself and Kimberly. Kimberly didn't look at anyone.

Bird felt badly for her. She wanted to comfort her but didn't know how. Kimby, she messaged. It's not your fault. I understand. Bird was not surprised that Kimberly didn't react. She hadn't really expected her to.

The last to arrive was Elvin Wainright. He walked in with his dripping coat and muddy boots and didn't bother to remove them. He took the last available chair, to the right of Pete Pierson, looking like this was the last place on earth he wanted to be.

Laura appeared with old newspapers, which she placed under his feet to make a point. He ignored her as he checked his watch and glanced at Kenneth. Bird giggled when Laura gave her a quick wink.

"Thank you for coming." Pete spoke in a friendly but firm voice. He was clearly in charge. "We'll keep this short, as you all have things to do and so do I." He looked pointedly at the book club selection beside his chair. "Every person in the circle will tell their story in order. I ask that you keep it short. Then we will try to come to a fair conclusion." He picked up a notepad and pencil, and donned his reading glasses.

Kenneth Bradley yawned and looked bored. Bird watched him and saw his resentment toward Pete. He liked to be in charge, she thought, and when he was forced to take a lesser role, like now, he needed people to know that it was beneath him. What a sad and lonely man, thought Bird. He likes people to fear him. He plays mind games that leave everyone guessing and worrying that they might upset him. What made him like this, she wondered?

Bird brought her attention back to the issue at hand. She listened carefully as each person around the circle spoke in turn and argued their point of view regarding Sundancer.

At the end of an hour of self-justifying explanations, Pete sat back in his chair and regarded his notes. Two suspenseful minutes later, he spoke.

"Now it's my turn. Let me summarize." Pete looked at them over his glasses. "There are three things on which you all agree. One, Sundancer is extremely talented. Two, he is also extremely difficult. Three, you all want to be involved with him, particularly after he did so well at the Rockhill Show. But, there are three things that present problems. One is ownership. Two is value. Three is ridership. All agreed?"

Everyone nodded with various levels of enthusiasm.

"This horse was no good to anyone before he moved to Saddle Creek. Therefore, I propose that for the sake of the horse he remains there with Hannah and Bird."

"Outrageous!" said Kenneth Bradley.

Pete turned an icy stare at him. "Please let me continue. These are only my proposals." Pete waited for Kenneth to settle back in his chair.

"Now the question of ownership. Elvin and Kenneth both believe the horse still belongs to Owens Enterprises, even though they also recognize that Paul Daniels took him in good faith."

Elvin shrugged his acceptance. Kenneth sat back in his chair, eyes closed.

"So this is my suggestion. The deal to buy the horse for twenty-five thousand dollars is off. Hannah and Bird will train and ride him at Saddle Creek in exchange for regular training and boarding fees. Owens Enterprises remains the owner, collects prize money, and has the prestige of ownership. Therefore the actual book value of the horse need never be discussed."

Lavinia burst out. "Where does that leave Kimberly? High and dry!"

Pete looked at her kindly but with a sternness that was palpable. "You are right, there's more. To complicate things, Mr. Bradley made the deal to buy Sundancer from Hannah and Paul on behalf of Owens Enterprises but then gave the horse to Lavinia and Kimberly Davies as a personal gift."

Lavinia nodded forcefully. "Absolutely. On condition that Sundancer returns to the Owens stables and is ridden by Leon Parish until Kimberly is ready to ride him."

Embarrassed, Kimberly hung her head.

"Kenneth had no right to do that," Pete cleaned his glasses and glanced at Kenneth, "with a horse he did not own. And I suspect that Elvin had no idea that Kenneth had gifted the horse to Kimberly." Pete looked through his glasses, inspecting for smudges.

Elvin spoke up. "Offering twenty-five thousand was authorized. Making a gift of the horse was not."

Kenneth glared at Elvin and snapped, "What difference does it make if the child thought she owned the horse? There was nothing on paper. He was going back to Owens. It made everybody happy and no harm was done. Kimberly never was going to be capable of riding him, anyway."

Bird made note of his logic. It was all about deception.

"That's not true!" Lavinia blurted. "Kimberly is an exceptional rider. She just needed the right horse, and now she's got him!"

"Mom," whispered Kimberly. "Please drop it. This is getting way too complicated."

Lavinia opened her mouth to speak, then shut it when Kenneth gave her a censoring look.

Elvin asked, "Now what do we do about Leon Parish? He's been contracted to ride Sundancer at the Haverford Fair."

Pete sighed. "Let me understand this. You signed a man to ride the horse before you knew you had the horse for him to ride?"

"Yes," answered Kenneth with a smirk. "Knowing my daughter's financial situation, I felt reasonably confident that we'd had a deal."

"Really?" reacted Hannah. "Well, I feel reasonably confident that the great Leon Parish will fall on his you-know-what."

"Is that a dare, Hannah? Can you put your money where your mouth is?" Kenneth Bradley's eyes flashed.

"If Leon can ride him," challenged Hannah angrily, "you can have him."

Kenneth sneered. "Done. Tomorrow at 10 A.M." He rose from his chair and rubbed his hands.

Hannah glowered at her father. "Ten. At Saddle Creek."

Bird listened in shock. Hannah had fallen for her father's goading. She'd walked right into his trap.

Pete sighed again. People and their knee-jerk reactions. He had no choice but to conclude the meeting. He stood with great difficulty and tried to put a positive spin on the exercise. "This meeting has been helpful. The facts and understandings have been vocalized. If we all meet tomorrow morning at ten o'clock at Saddle Creek, we'll hopefully find a way to stop fighting over the poor horse." He signalled to Laura.

Laura Pierson had been quietly listening the entire time, filling coffee cups and passing cookies. "It's past our bedtime, folks. The horses are fine here tonight. No need to ride them home in the storm. See you all tomorrow morning at ten." Laura opened the kitchen door and smiled graciously.

Hannah, Bird, and Paul were the last to go. Laura gave Bird a plastic bag containing her dry clothes and handed Hannah a box of leftover chicken. "It was so good to see you people again," she said. "Nothing like a little excitement."

"It was good to see you again, too, Mrs. Pierson," said Hannah warmly. "We'll see you tomorrow. And thank you for doing this for us tonight. Nobody else could have acted as mediator."

"I doubt it was helpful," said Pete. "We didn't have agreement on one thing, really."

Paul replied, "You put everything clearly on the table. That's a good start."

Hannah looked sheepish, "I didn't help, throwing out that dare."

"Don't you worry about that," stated Pete with assurance. "You only put wheels in motion. We have to hope for a good result."

"Pete will work it out. He always does." Laura beamed proudly and put her arm through her husband's. Pete was not so sure.

That night, Bird slept poorly. Before they'd left the Piersons' place, she'd gone out to say good night to Sunny and Charlie, and check on their hay and water. Sunny had been uneasy. He worried that something bad was going to happen to him.

Everything was turning out wrong. Tomorrow Leon would ride him and things could get crazy.

Laura cursed her bladder. Getting old meant inconveniences, including nightly visits to the washroom. It was 2 A.M. Laura washed her hands and made her way back to bed.

A horse neighed loudly. She smiled. How nice to have horses in their barn again. Even for a short stay.

The horse neighed again. This time it sounded panicky. The other horse joined in. Then silence. Ten seconds later, a louder and longer neigh.

Laura looked at the sleeping form of her husband. She made a quick decision not to disturb him, and slipped on her white satin house coat and slippers. She stealthily crept down the back stairs and out the kitchen door.

Bird girl! Bird girl!

Bird awoke suddenly. She sat upright in her bed.

Bird girl!

Sunny! What's wrong?

A man is here. In the dark. He's in the barn.

What's he doing?

I kicked him, but not hard enough. He gave me a needle.

Don't let him, Sunny! I'm coming!

It's tooo laaate.

Bird grabbed the clothes she'd dropped on the floor the night before and ran downstairs. She hopped on her wet bike and pedalled down the muddy gravel road as fast as she could in the direction of the Piersons' barn.

Laura Pierson padded quietly out to the dark barn, looking in all directions as she tried to make sense of the shadows. The rain had stopped, and big mud puddles reflected the emerging moon. Slowly Laura's eyes identified the shapes. A dark jeep and horse trailer were hidden behind the barn. The hairs on her arms raised as she sensed danger. She slowed her steps and thought quickly. She was old and she was small. No way could she out-muscle. But she could out-think.

Bird had never sped on her bike this fast before. Her legs pumped the pedals relentlessly. The tires threw up a thick coat of stones and mud, covering her legs and back. Two kilometres. Two to go.

Sunny? Can you hear me?

No answer.

Laura figured that the only way the jeep and trailer could leave was down the lane and through the gate, which would've been the way they'd come in. The gate was always left open, now that the cows were in the summer pasture. She turned and almost ran to the gate. Behind her, she heard horse hooves stumbling. Then the clank of the trailer ramp being put into place. Then the sound of an engine. Charlie kept up a steady racket in the barn, kicking and neighing to sound an alarm.

She was at the end of the lane and out of breath. She grabbed the heavy metal gate and tried to pull it closed. It stuck.

Bird's thighs were burning with fatigue. She pushed the pedals harder.

Sunny, I'm coming! Hang on!

The old metal gate wouldn't move. Laura heaved on it with all her meagre weight, but it wasn't enough. The gate wouldn't budge. She heard the engine purring behind her and turned to look. The jeep was almost to the gate. Laura jumped out in the middle of the lane and waved her arms. It kept coming.

Bird was at the corner beside the school. She was almost there. She peered through the darkness. Something that looked like a scarecrow in white was standing in the Piersons' driveway. It was Laura Pierson. And a jeep without headlights, pulling a trailer, was heading right for her!

Bird's bike hit a rock. It bounced high and twisted. She flew through the air and landed on the soft muddy shoulder of the road.

The filthy jeep was not stopping. At the last second, Laura jumped out of the way. She looked hard at the driver. She recognized the face from pictures in *Horse Sport Magazine*: It was Leon Parish—she'd bet her life on it. And the smooth round chestnut bottom showing over the ramp could only belong to one horse. Sundancer.

Bird picked herself up from the wet gravel and stumbled down the road. The jeep and trailer were coming toward her.

Sunny? Are you there?

B...ir...d.

Bird heard feeble kicking in the horse trailer.

I'm right here, Sunny. I'll stop the car. I'll save you.

She stood in the road and put out her hand, signalling the driver to stop. Now the headlights came on and the engine accelerated. Bird hit the shoulder at the last possible second, then listened as the jeep crunched over her bike and dragged it to the stop sign, where it fell loose as the rig wheeled around the corner.

Bird stood and watched the horse trailer disappear in the direction of the Owens stables. Her mud-caked body ached with exertion. Sunny had been so close, but she hadn't been able to get to him.

Sunny, I'm sorry. I couldn't stop him.

I'll b...e o...kay.

Don't worry, I'll find you.

Laura came up and stood beside her. Laura was gasping for air and spoke in bursts. "We have...work to do...Bird, dear. Come with me...now."

They walked up the lane to the farmhouse. Charlie continued to neigh. The lights came on in the kitchen, and Bird and Laura saw Pete limp through the room and open the door.

"Laura? Are you out there? What's going on? Is that Bird with you? Why's that horse making such a racket?"

"Bird, go to the barn and make sure Charlie's all right," Laura whispered, breathing more evenly. Bird ran to do what she was asked.

"Pete, we were robbed. It looked like Leon Parish. He came and took Sundancer. Bird came as fast as she could on her bike, which is now lying in a heap at the stop sign. What do we do now?"

Bird was in the barn. She tried to calm Charlie down.

Charlie, we'll get him back. Don't worry.

That man came in here. We were sleeping. He stuck a needle in Sunny's neck.

Just relax. Bird stroked his side.

I want to go home now.

I promise I'll ride you back first thing tomorrow.

I know the way. Just let me out.

I can't do that. Something might go wrong.

Nothing will go wrong! Let me out!

Bird thought about the cars, the holes, the wire fences, and who knew what else Charlie might run into in the dark.

No, Charlie. I'm sorry, but you'll have to wait. First thing. I promise.

Charlie turned his back on her and settled. He pretended to be miffed, but Bird suspected he might be a little relieved.

Pete and Laura called Hannah. She answered on the first ring.

"Hannah, this is Laura. Bird's here, don't worry, but Sun—"

"I heard her leave! I've been out of my mind. What's going on?"

"I don't know how she knew to come, but Sunny was kidnapped from our barn, and she rode her bike over to help. She was a little too late. He's gone."

"Sunny's gone? Where?"

"Pete will talk now." Laura handed over the phone and sat down heavily in a kitchen chair. All at once, she was exhausted.

"Hannah, there's nothing we can do tonight."

"But what about Sundancer? Where is he?"

"Laura thinks it was Leon Parish driving the jeep, which leads me to believe that Sunny's on his way back to the Owens stables. Which is where he rightfully, if not actually, belongs. Leave it for tonight, Hannah. Please."

Hannah felt deeply tired. "I agree. I'm coming to get Bird right now. I'll be over early tomorrow morning to pick up Charlie. Thanks for everything, Pete."

Bird woke late the next morning. The storm was over and the country air smelled fresh through her open window. The sun was shining at an angle that suggested that it was around eight thirty or nine. With a pang, she thought about Sundancer. Everyone assumed he was at the Owens barn, but nothing was certain. She must find him and bring him home.

Sunny? Are you all right?

Yes, Bird girl. Don't worry.

Bird sighed with relief. *Are you at your old barn?*

No. I'm fine and happy where I am. Don't take me away.

Sunny? What do you mean?

There was no response.

Bird was confused. And hurt. Sunny didn't want to come back. She couldn't imagine what might have happened to change his mind. It was so strange. Then she remembered poor Charlie. Oh, no, she thought. I promised him that I'd ride him home.

She dressed quickly and ran downstairs. On the kitchen table was a note from Hannah. It read:

Bird, Eva, and Julia,

I've gone to Merry Fields to pick up Charlie. Have some breakfast, and I'll see you later.

Love, Hannah

That solved one problem. At least Bird didn't have to worry about Charlie. She saw from the garbage and dishes that Eva and Julia had made oatmeal with banana slices, and drank orange juice. There was also one dirty coffee mug. She put a slice of bread in the toaster and got out the peanut butter and honey. Her favourite breakfast.

Bird waited for the toast to pop, and leaned on the counter wondering what Sunny meant about being "fine and happy" where he was. She gazed absently outside, then rubbed the sleep from her eyes.

An elegant chestnut horse was grazing in the rain-drenched field across the driveway.

Sunny! You're here! Completely forgetting about her toast, Bird ran outside and scrambled over the fence.

Of course. Did you think I'd stay there?

Why didn't you tell me?

I wanted to fool you.

Well, you did! It was a good joke, but you hurt my feelings.

Boo hoo.

Sunny, your leg is cut.

It doesn't hurt. It just looks bad.

I'll put something on it later.

If you want.

How did you escape from Owens'?

I wasn't there. It was a different barn. No other horse or human in sight. Abandoned.

Where?

Same distance away, but from the other direction.

Have you been there before?

No.

So how did you find your way home?

Horses always know the way home. If it's not too far as the crow flies.

Were you locked up?

No. I jumped the stall door and a few fences and came home. Simple.

Bird and Sunny both turned to look as Hannah pulled into

the driveway with the trailer. She did a double take. Bird grinned and waved. Hannah jerked to a stop and jumped out of the truck.

"Where did he come from? When did he get here? I swear he wasn't here when I left."

I wasn't.

Bird shrugged and patted Sunny's silky neck.

Charlie neighed impatiently in the trailer.

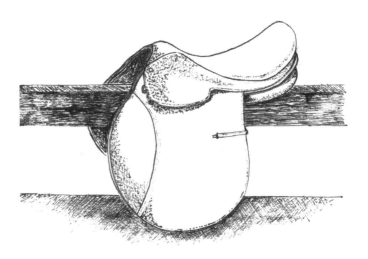

15

SHOWTIME

I want to prove I'm superior to people.

AT TEN O'CLOCK ON THE DOT, Kenneth Bradley showed up at Saddle Creek. Beside him in the big black Cadillac sat an overdressed Lavinia, looking more than a little put out. Kimberly scooted out of the back seat as soon as the car stopped. She ran to Eva and Julia, where they stood at the paddock gate.

Elvin Wainright drove in thirty seconds later.

Hannah watched from the kitchen window with nervous curiosity. She called Paul's cell. He answered on the first ring.

"Paul Daniels."

"Hi, Paul, it's Hannah. You were right. It's ten o'clock and Elvin and Dad are here with bells on. Looking like nothing happened last night and probably thinking that we'll have to break the news that Sunny's gone."

Paul laughed. "Well, well, well. According to plan. Is Abby there yet?"

"She and Bird are in the barn getting Sunny tacked up."

"Good. Has Leon Parish shown up yet?"

Hannah caught a glimpse of a dirty blue jeep driving past the window, followed by a green Ford truck. "I believe so. And the Piersons are right behind him."

"It's showtime. I'll finish up here and be right over. Five, no fifteen minutes. Can you wait?"

"No problem. See you soon."

Hannah took a deep breath. She'd need some top-notch acting skills to pull this off. Never bluff a bluffer, unless you must. She smoothed her hair and tucked in her shirt, then walked cheerfully out of the house and over to the fence.

Eva came running. "Stuart just called to say he's running a little late."

"So's Paul. Send Julia to the barn to tell Bird to slow things down by fifteen minutes."

"Okay. And I'll get some chairs for the Piersons."

"And Dad. Let's make a fuss over him."

Eva winked at her sister. "This is so much fun."

Hannah took a good look at Leon Parish. He was a young man of slight build. Good looking, but pasty skinned with heavy, sleep-deprived eyes. He wore his chaps and held his helmet by the chinstrap. He slapped his thigh nervously with his whip. So this is the man who stole Sunny, thought Hannah. He has nerve to show up here.

"Hello, Leon," she said as she walked to him with outstretched hand and bright smile. "We haven't met, although I've heard lots about you. I'm Hannah Bradley, Kenneth's daughter."

Leon gave her a cool, lopsided grin. "Hey there." If he was feeling guilty about the kidnapping, he gave no indication.

"Hannah, darling," said Kenneth, wide eyed and innocent. "Where's the horse? It's after ten." He pointed to his watch.

"He's coming, Dad. Bird's shining him up for us."

Kenneth shot a glance at Elvin.

"Can't wait to see him." Elvin looked so smug that Hannah nearly lost her nerve. She took a deep breath and smothered the impulse to get angry.

Laura momentarily distracted her by opening the big hamper that she and Pete had dragged over from their truck. "I hope you don't mind, Hannah, dear, but I brought a picnic breakfast for all of us. Coffee in this thermos, tea in this one. Raisin bran muffins, fresh blueberry muffins, cornmeal scones. With butter." Her smile was full of sunshine. Suddenly, Hannah felt much more optimistic.

Sunny was ready. His tack was clean. His coat gleamed with good health and thorough brushing. His mane was combed and pulled to a short, feathery length and his hooves were coated with shiny black oil.

Earlier, Bird and Julia and Abby had set up a course of eight jumps in the paddock, including a water jump made from an old wading pool. The jumps were on average three foot six, with lots of room to go higher.

Bird's hands were clumsy with nerves as she looked down at the paddock. She dropped the mane comb.

Abby noticed and smiled reassuringly. "It's going to be fine, Bird."

Bird wasn't so sure. So much could go wrong.

Remember, Sunny, you don't have to kill him.

Leave it with me, Bird, and stop worrying.

Julia popped her head around the corner. "Hey, Bird! Sunny looks spectacular! Mom told me to tell you to slow things down for a while. Mr. Gilmore and Dr. Paul are late."

Abby frowned. "How much longer do we have to wait? Sunny's geared up and ready to go."

"Not too long," answered Julia. "Maybe fifteen minutes."

"We'll wait five, then we'll walk him out to the paddock and let him take a look around."

Bird got more anxious.

Calm yourself, Bird girl. You're making me antsy.

I'm nervous! As far as the bad guys know, you're not here. They probably think that we think you jumped out last night and ran away from Merry Fields, but we can't admit it. They think we're bluffing.

You're confusing me, Bird girl. Relax and leave me in charge.
Don't hurt anybody, Sunny.
We'll see.

Bird patted his face. Again she looked out of the barn toward the assembled group. Stuart had just arrived and was hugging Eva hello. There were the Piersons, Lavinia and Kimberly, her grandfather, Elvin Wainright, Leon Parish, and Hannah, down by the paddock. And now Paul Daniels. The vet's truck was turning off the road. Everyone was here.

Bird fretfully motioned to Abby and Julia. It was time.

Showtime, Sunny. Be good.

Just watch me.

Bird raced down to the paddock and positioned herself beside Hannah. She wanted a close vantage point to observe reactions when Sunny came out.

All eyes focused on the equine vision stepping out of the barn, led by Abby. He shone in the sun, as if a spotlight was trained on him. His long legs were strong and fit, his haunches and chest filled out and round. He pranced on the spot and danced as he moved ever closer. Shaking his gorgeous head and arching his muscular neck, he looked like a king's stallion valiantly setting off to the wars.

Bird looked at her grandfather first. Although a smile remained plastered on his face, she could see his jaw clenched beneath his skin. Elvin whispered something in his ear, and they both turned to stare at Leon. If the look was meant to intimidate the rider, it failed. Leon was oblivious to Kenneth or anyone else. His eyes assessed the animal from top to bottom, then back again. He let out a low whistle.

Nobody spoke.

Nice work, Sunny. You really laid it on.

When you've got a crowd, play to it.

Bird chuckled as she ran to open the paddock gate. Abby

walked him through and Bird closed it after them. She turned to Leon and pointed at him. He looked at Bird with surprise, then sneered.

"What's she pointing at?" he asked nobody in particular.

"She's telling you that Sundancer is ready," answered Hannah politely.

Leon looked to Kenneth for instruction. Kenneth frowned, then nodded. He flicked his fingers forward, urging Leon to go and ride.

Leon strode out to Sunny and took his reins from Abby.

"Do you want a leg up, or do you prefer the mounting block?" she asked.

"Neither." He flipped the reins over Sunny's neck and sprang lightly onto his back from the ground.

Sunny jumped back, surprised. He rolled his eyes and hopped up on his hind legs. Bird gasped, expecting the worst.

Not yet, Sunny. First show him how good you are.

Sunny dropped down and relaxed. Leon walked him a few strides, then trotted him around the paddock. Sundancer stepped out firmly and framed up exactly as asked. When they came around to the gate again, Leon waved with one hand and yelled, "Piece of cake. He's a pussycat!"

Bird sat on the fence, slightly away from the crowd. *More like a lion.*

He's a good rider, Bird girl. I'll give him that.

How are his hands?

Soft. Quiet. And he's sitting very still.

Good.

They cantered away. Leon asked Sunny for some side passes and lead changes, then yelled out, "I'm going to jump him, starting with this single vertical."

Sunny cantered in easily, then sprang carefully over the jump. Leon grinned. "I'll take him around the course. He's a dream. What's all the fuss about? Who said he was dangerous?"

They jumped around the course of eight jumps like a fox hunter out for a Sunday ride.

"Abby, put them up!" yelled Leon. "Let's see what he can do."

Am I wonderful or am I wonderful, Bird girl?

Perfect, Sunny.

This rider is a show-off. He doesn't need to swing around so much in the saddle, but he thinks it looks cool. He's a fancy pants.

Bird laughed.

He might need a riding lesson from me.

In time, Sunny.

"What's going on?" whispered Paul to Hannah. "Sundancer's behaving like a lamb. Did you drug him?"

"No," answered Hannah equally quietly. "I can't figure it out. I thought it would be all over by now."

Abby ran out to the paddock to raise the jumps.

"Stop!" hollered Lavinia. "Let Kimberly ride him over these jumps the height they are, then we'll raise them. He's her horse."

Leon looked at Kenneth in dismay. "Not a chance."

Kenneth shrugged. "Do it, Leon. What can it hurt?"

Leon said, "Let me finish here, Mr. Bradley, then we'll get the kid up. We're on a roll."

"Who's paying you, Leon?" asked Lavinia demurely.

Kimberly sat on the ground beside Julia and hung her head.

"Kimberly, get over there," commanded Lavinia. "Leon will give you a leg up."

This wasn't part of the plan, Bird girl.

Can you be nice to Kimby, Sunny?

I'll try. Just don't let her pull on my face or kick me or it won't be pretty.

I'll try.

Bird hopped off the fence and sat beside Kimberly. She took the girl's face in her hands and looked into her eyes. Once she had her attention, Bird put her index fingers in her own mouth, pretending they were a bit. She pulled hard and then shook her head, no.

"Don't pull on his mouth?" asked Kimberly.

Bird nodded. Then she showed Kimberly her feet and mimed digging her heels in as she rode. Again she shook her head, no.

"And don't kick him?"

Bird nodded and gave her friend a hug. Together they walked over to Sunny.

I don't like this, Bird girl. I wasn't expecting this.

Just be nice. I'll be right here.

You better be.

What are you worried about, Sunny?

I've seen how she rides Pastor.

Abby gave Kimberly a leg up while Bird held the nervous horse. Bird looked up and saw a big smile spread across Kimberly's face. Bird smiled back.

"This is great!" Kimberly enthused. "I've dreamed of riding him since the first day I saw him in the field." She stroked his neck. "He's so beautiful."

Maybe she's not so bad after all, Bird girl.

That's the attitude.

Bird led Sunny along.

"Let him go!" screamed Lavinia. "Kimberly can ride! Don't treat her like a novice. What have we been spending all that money on lessons for?"

"It's okay, Bird," said Kimberly quietly. "I'm fine to ride him alone. Mom won't shut up 'til I do."

Bird wasn't sure. *Are you okay with that, Sunny?*

Depends on the kid. Sure, let me go.

They walked around the paddock once. Lavinia called out, "Terrific! Let's see him trot, Kimberly!"

In her excitement at finally being on the horse's back, Kimberly forgot Bird's advice. She kicked Sunny to make him trot, like she always did with Pastor. Sunny jumped up three feet, then shot forward. Kimberly tumbled to the ground.

Leon laughed aloud.

Lavinia came running. "You get back up there, Kimberly!" she demanded. "That was just a small mistake. Could've happened to anyone."

Kimberly moaned and held her right arm.

Sunny couldn't relax. He trotted away, full of anxiety, shaking his head wildly.

Leon was furious. "See what I was talking about, Mr. Bradley? You don't fool around with a horse like this. Now he's going to be difficult."

Kenneth glared at the young man. "You said, and I quote, 'Piece of cake. He's a pussycat.' You gave them the impression that anyone could ride him."

"You're blaming me for this?"

"I'm blaming you. Now get out there and make this all better."

"You want me to ride him in the mood he's in?"

"No. I want you to help Kimberly ride him."

Leon walked out toward Sundancer as he pranced and threw his head around. The reins dangled close to his feet. If he stepped through them, they'd trip him before they broke.

Bird watched mutely, then raced out ahead of Leon.

Sunny, come to me.

I'm finished. My nerves are shot.

How can I help you?

Open the gate and let me run back to the barn. I want out of here. I'd jump, but the reins will trip me. That fellow is coming. Quick, Bird girl, let me out before I hurt him.

Can you calm yourself?

Not possible. Let me out! Sunny reared and pawed the air.

Bird quickly unlatched the gate and let Sunny out. He ran to the barn, right into his stall, and stood shaking. Bird ran in after him.

Close the barn door, Bird. Don't let him come in.

You know people, Sunny. He'll want to fix this.

Maybe later. Take off this tack.

Leon arrived before Bird could do as Sunny asked. "Get out of his stall, girl! You'll get yourself killed. Why'd you let him go? What were you thinking?"

Bird girl, talk to him! Tell him to wait until I calm down!

Bird opened her mouth. She made a big effort to speak. Only a high-pitched noise came out.

Try again! Someone's going to get hurt!

Bird tried again, with all her concentration. "La...t...er, ple...ase."

"Have you been drinking?" Leon snorted. "Get out of my way. I've got other horses to ride today."

It was no use. Even when she did speak, people didn't listen. She sat down in a corner of Sunny's stall and buried her face in her hands. There was no telling what would happen now.

Back at the paddock, Lavinia was berating Kimberly who was sitting on the ground in tears. "When you fall off a horse, you get right back up! Everyone knows that."

"But Mom, I don't want to ride him any more. I don't want him. He's way, way too powerful for me."

"If Bird can ride him, you can! You looked fabulous up there. Think of all the ribbons you'll win, Kimberly!"

"I don't want ribbons. I want to go home. My arm hurts. I can't move my fingers."

Laura Pierson had been listening, biting her tongue. Now she moved in. "You can't move your fingers, Kimberly dear?"

"No."

Laura took a look at Kimberly's arm. "Lavinia, there's no doubt about it. She's broken her arm. Take her right to the hospital."

"That's absurd. She had a little roll off the horse."

"Tell that to her arm, dear. It's turning blue."

Lavinia could see for herself. The arm was swelling. She realized that Laura was right. She asked, "Kenneth, are you coming?"

"You take my car, honey child. I'm going to stay here to see Leon ride that animal."

Leon was leading Sunny down from the barn. He'd put a chain over the horse's nose and carried a thick crop. Sunny twisted and lunged.

"But I need help with Kimberly, Kenneth. And you've already seen him ride," said Lavinia.

Kenneth took a good look at Lavinia. He spoke slowly, quietly, and clearly. "You take my car. I have to stay. Now, your child has had an accident. Go care for her." He took his car keys out of his pocket and dangled them.

Lavinia opened her mouth, then shut it. She snatched the keys, tossed her hair, and stomped off. Kimberly followed unhappily, holding her arm to her waist. Her face had gone white.

Julia ran to her and gave her a quick hug, careful not to touch the arm. "It'll feel better soon, Kimberly. As soon as they set it."

"I hope so, Julia. Oh, no. I'm going to be sick."

Julia guided her to the bushes and held Kimberly while she emptied her stomach. "Here, take this," she said, handing Kimberly a tissue from her pocket. "And here's a mint. You'll need it to calm your tummy."

"And to get rid of this awful taste in my mouth. Thanks, Julia. You're a friend." Kimberly walked shakily to the car and climbed in.

Julia gave her a kiss on the cheek. "Good luck," she said.

"Call me later."

As soon as Julia had closed the car door, Lavinia sped off.

In the paddock, Sunny reared and hopped and pulled on the shank. Leon was tough. He yanked and grunted and fought back.

Hannah and Paul watched. "This is more like the Sundancer we know," said Hannah. "When should we stop it?"

Paul considered the problem. "It could go on a long time, and it won't get better, but they need to figure out that Sunny's not your average horse."

Bird didn't want to wait. She hopped the fence and walked steadily toward Sunny and Leon as they struggled.

"Get the kid outta here!" Leon bellowed.

Sunny, if you stop fighting, so will he.

I'm so mad I want to kill him.

No, Sunny, don't. Will you let me come to you?

I won't hurt you, but I'll still be mad.

Okay, Sunny, here I come.

"Someone, get her outta here! She's gonna get kicked!" Leon yelled.

Kenneth Bradley yelled back, "She knows him, Leon. Let her come over. Give her the horse."

"She let him out last time!"

"She won't this time, will you, Bird?" asked Kenneth, calling across the paddock.

Bird turned to look at him. She shook her head, no.

"Leon, give her the horse. That's an order."

"Fine. If that's the way you want it," shouted Leon angrily. "She's not my problem."

Bird quietly walked up to Sunny and took the shank from Leon. Leon sneered at her and huffed, "Good riddance." Then he stalked off.

Sunny snorted and danced. *I can't make this look too easy, Bird girl.*

You can make it a little easier. My arm's going to fall off.
Let the shank go slack. I'll just jump around for show.
Okay.

Hannah felt the time had come. Kenneth might not care if his granddaughter got injured, but Hannah did. "The party's over, folks. Sunny's finished for the day."

Behind her, Elvin spoke up. "Hannah, Leon did a super job of riding Sundancer before Kimberly got on. We're here today to decide this animal's fate. It's important that we get it right."

Hannah waited.

Kenneth continued Elvin's train of thought. "The horse was rattled after dumping Kimberly, but he'll get over it. What if Bird hops up and relaxes him a little, then Leon can ride him over some bigger jumps? Let's see what he can do."

"Now?" asked Hannah. She looked at Paul for his reaction. He simply shrugged.

"Yes. Right now."

"Bird?" called out Hannah. "Do you feel like riding Sunny?"
Sunny, will you let me ride you?
I won't buck you off, if that's what you mean.
Bird nodded to her aunt.

"Okay," said Hannah warily. "Bird'll get up. We'll see how it goes. If there's trouble, we stop. I don't want her hurt."

The men nodded.

Bird walked Sunny to the mounting block and scrambled up onto his back. He heaved a big sigh.

This was a good idea, Bird girl. I feel better already.
I'm glad.
Let's do some jumping.
In front of all these people?
What do you care? Are you turning into Fancy Pants Leon?
He intimidates me. He's famous.
Forget him. I'll do it for you. Just point and leave me alone.

Bird laughed and stroked his neck. *I love you, Sundancer.*
Don't go all mushy on me. We have a job to do.

Bird trotted Sundancer into the corner then slowed him to a walk. She asked Sunny for his left lead at a canter, and they steadily travelled into the first jump, a white oxer. Sunny cleared it, rounding his body beautifully. He landed and gave a happy little buck. The oxer was followed by a multicoloured in-and-out, which he made look easy. Bird and Sunny flew gently and surely over the course, ending with the purple and white triple combination.

Bird's friends and family gave her a standing ovation. Even Kenneth managed a smile. "Well done, Bird! Let's raise the bars."

Hannah started to protest, but Bird nodded happily. Together, Abby and Hannah raised the jumps three inches.

"Make the last jump in the triple higher yet," instructed Kenneth. Abby obliged.

Let me at them, Bird girl.
Take it easy, Sunny.
Don't tell me to take it easy. I'm having fun.

They cantered in again, the same as before. Sunny felt a little wild underneath her, but Bird let him have his way. The jumps didn't seem any higher, and even though they were going faster than before, Sunny made no mistakes. They came into the triple, and he figured it out with ease. When he landed the last jump of the purple and white triple, the little gathering rose to its feet again. Sunny kicked out in triumph.

Take that, Fancy Pants.

"That's enough, Bird," called Hannah. "Let's leave him on a positive note. He's been a very good boy."

Leon strode out to the middle of the paddock. "My turn now, kid. Let me show you how it's done. Put 'em up six inches."

Bird slid down. She shook her head, no.

"I said, put 'em up. Six inches."

Do what the man asks, Bird girl. I'm ready.

Bird didn't like the wild, unpredictable look in Sunny's eye. *This isn't a good idea.*

He's asking for it. It's payback time.

With trepidation, Bird raised the jumps. They were now all four foot three; the triple even higher. The course looked huge.

Leon sprang up on Sunny's back, oblivious to his mood. Sunny reared and bucked, but Leon stayed on. Sunny calmed right down, very suddenly.

Oh, no, thought Bird. The calm before the storm.

"He just needs to know who's boss," sneered Leon.

Oh, I do, Fancy Pants. I do.

Leon headed for the first jump. He steered him in straight and at a good pace, but then asked him to take off with more leg than Sunny liked.

You want me to jump, Fancy Pants? I'll jump.

Sunny soared six feet into the air, cracked his back, lowered his head, and landed hard. Leon stayed with him. "This sucker can jump!" he hollered to Elvin and Kenneth.

This sucker can stay on. I'll have to try harder.

Leon turned for the colourful in-and-out. Again he asked too harshly. Sunny flew high, landed, then took one stride instead of two, and jumped from too far back. He made an enormous effort and cleared the second jump.

Leon was left behind in the saddle and pulled hard on the reins. He was furious. "Whoa! I didn't tell you to jump!" he yelled.

They headed for the water jump. Leon pushed Sunny, pumping at him to keep him going.

Don't insult me, Fancy Pants. I never stop at water jumps.

Sunny slammed on the brakes and dropped Leon neatly in the water.

Until now. The chestnut gelding reared up and neighed loudly. He dropped his front hooves to the ground and spun around. He bucked and played and whinnied again. He was unmistakably proud of himself.

Bird worried that Leon would punish Sunny. She wouldn't give him the chance. While everyone was distracted by Leon's fall, she raced out, hopped on Sunny's back, and cantered around the ring.

Did you see that, Bird girl? Served him right.

It was funny, I'll admit.

Let's do the course. Show up Fancy Pants.

Bad idea. They're upset enough.

Then the water jump, Bird girl. I need Leon to see how easy it is when you don't hump and pump at a horse.

Okay. Leon's out of the water now.

Sunny and Bird steadily cantered to the water jump. Over they went as easily as could be. They landed carefully and cantered away quietly.

Leon came running, shaking his arms. His face was contorted with rage. He dripped with water. "Stop that horse! He can't do that to me!"

Bird could see no advantage to sticking around. She aimed Sunny at the four-rail paddock fence. They hopped over and galloped off, leaving the grown-ups to sort out the mess. The show was over.

Leon Parish had never been more humiliated by a horse in his life. "I'm out of this deal," he yelled. "I'm finished." He dumped the water out of his riding helmet and sloshed out of the ring toward his car. "There's only one thing." Leon turned to Kenneth and spoke loudly. "You still owe me for the little job I did for you last night."

Kenneth's face turned ashen. "I don't know what you're talking about. I'll pay you for your time today. That's all you deserve."

"What do you mean, that's all I deserve?"

Kenneth looked uncomfortable. "The...er...job. It wasn't done. Obviously."

Leon was affronted. "I did what I was told, and I want to be paid."

"Let's talk privately," said Kenneth in a more appeasing tone.

Elvin joined the conversation. "I handle the bills, Leon. Come to me this afternoon and we'll straighten things out."

Laura Pierson had been busy folding her lawn chair and hadn't appeared to be paying attention. "I'm sorry to interfere, gentlemen, but Leon is quite right. He did what he was told to do last night. I'm a witness."

Kenneth, Elvin, and Leon all swung around and looked at Laura in astonishment.

"Bird, too. We both saw Leon stealing Sundancer from our barn, if that was what you meant, dear, about doing what you were told to do last night."

"Then how did he get here?" blurted Elvin, tired of covering things up.

"On his own four legs," answered Abby. "He's got a cut on his leg, but aside from that, no harm done."

"He ran home?" asked Leon. "I wondered why he was here. It wasn't the plan."

Pete Pierson took control. "And just what was the plan, Leon?"

Leon looked at Kenneth, then Elvin, then shrugged. "Why not? I quit, anyway." He answered Pete, "I was told to take the horse to the old Harris barn last night, then show up here at ten." He spat on the ground.

Pete nodded. "Is that so. Well. Everything's changed now."

Elvin and Kenneth looked dismayed.

Pete continued. "Given that Leon has resigned and Kimberly has given up her dream of owning Sundancer, do we all agree that the horse will stay here with Hannah and Bird?"

Kenneth and Elvin looked at each other. They were out of options.

Kenneth nodded. "As long as it's clear that Owens Enterprises still owns him."

"Therefore you will pay all the bills, past, present, and future," said Pete. He looked sternly at Kenneth and waited for his response.

"Yes, of course," decided Kenneth, suddenly smiling. "Bird will ride him, God help her, and we will see you at the Haverford Fair next week. Enter him in the Grand Classic Event, Hannah."

Without further ado, Kenneth and Elvin stalked off to Elvin's car. A new deal was formally in place.

16

THE HAVERFORD FAIR

I love to jump. I do my job well.

BIRD HAD TROUBLE SLEEPING. It was four thirty on Saturday morning, and there was a lot on her mind. Today was the Haverford Fair! She'd never get back to sleep if she thought about it, so she forced herself to think of other things.

School started on Tuesday. She had new school clothes and a new friend in Kimberly, who had decided to stay at Forks of the Credit School. Julia was also enrolled, and Bird was extremely happy that she and her sister would go to school together every day.

The very prospect of school, however, was daunting. Kids mimicked the way she communicated. They laughed at her behind her back—and right in front of her face. It was surprising how people assumed you couldn't see or hear if you couldn't talk.

She rolled over and tried to find a more comfortable position, pushing away thoughts of Sunny cantering into a difficult combination of jumps.

Alec Daniels would be at school, too. Maybe even in her class. An odd flutter tickled Bird's chest. How could she look him in the eye after what happened the last time she saw him? She'd painted herself pink, for heaven's sake, and virtually killed her own dog! Bird blushed and hid her head under the sheet.

Maybe she wouldn't go the first day. She could get sick. Maybe even die. Maybe then Alec would realize how special she was. He would cry for her at the funeral, and Bird would look down from heaven and watch as he mourned her death and regretted that he never got to know her.

She then envisioned riding into the ring with the stands full of applauding fans, including Alec, standing up and cheering madly. Bird scolded herself. Don't think about the horse show! You'll never get to sleep if you do.

Bird mused about her mother as she turned over onto her back. The last few days had seen a tremendous improvement. They were getting along much better, and Eva seemed genuinely interested in both her and Julia. Bird wondered how much Stuart Gilmore had to do with the change. Eva was in love with Stuart—that much was clear—and Stuart never stopped encouraging her to be an attentive mother. In the back of Bird's mind, however, doubts lingered. Was this an act? Another one of Eva's attempts to land the perfect man? Bird hoped not. She'd rather believe that Eva had trouble knowing how to love her kids, and that Stuart was teaching her.

Bird clutched her pillow. She needed her sleep. The fair was mere hours away! Her stomach lurched. She could avoid thinking about it no longer. They'd been practising all week. Sunny was fit and eager and ready for anything. Regardless, Bird knew that the results of the show would entirely depend on Sunny's mood at the moment.

Bird rolled over and bunched the pillow up under her head. No use. She might as well get up. The alarm was set at six, anyway—just an hour and a half from now—and there were always last-minute things to do. She'd go out and check the tack box, make sure the water tank was full, throw in some extra feed. Then she'd groom Sunny with special care. She wanted him to knock people's socks off when he backed off the trailer.

So as not to disturb Julia, Bird dressed in her barn clothes in the dark. She noted her show habit hanging neatly on the hook. It gave her goosebumps. Stealthily. Bird crept down the stairs and outside.

In his stall, Sunny raised his head from his hay. *Is it time already, Bird girl? It's still dark.*

No, it's not time yet. I just couldn't sleep.

That makes two of us. I'm nervous.

There's nothing there that'll test you, Sunny.

I know.

Then what?

It's just a feeling I have.

About the show?

No. Those men. I don't trust them.

You got your way last time, Sunny. Nobody rides you but me, and nobody keeps you but Hannah.

That's the problem. I got my way last time, and they like to win.

So do you, Sunny. And so do I.

Sunny nuzzled Bird as she stroked his neck and rubbed his ears.

So what's my problem, Bird girl? We'll go out there and win.

When Hannah and Bird arrived at the grounds with Sunny in the horse trailer, the parking lot was almost full. There was always a huge crowd at the Haverford Fair, and this year was no exception. The competition would be stiff, Bird knew. She clutched her stomach to squelch her nerves.

"Nothing to fear but fear itself, Bird. Franklin Roosevelt," Hannah said.

Bird grimaced. Eat my shorts, Hannah. Bart Simpson.

She tried to take comfort in the cloudless blue sky and the light breeze. The day could not have been more perfectly suited to a horse show; warm enough that the horses were mellow, cool

SUNDANCER

enough that they had energy. The grass was still green but had started to brown in patches. A sure sign that fall was coming.

Together, Bird and Hannah unloaded Sunny and tacked him up. The plan was for Bird to warm him up in the exercise ring, then walk around the fair for a while to acclimatize him. Hannah would sign them up and get Sunny's show number.

"Take it easy, Bird," instructed Hannah, as she gave her niece a leg up. "It's important that you stay relaxed. Sunny feels every emotion you have."

No kidding.

As they walked to the big warm-up ring, they passed rows of temporary stalls made of sturdy steel rods covered in white canvas. The ring was full of horses and riders in various stages of exercise. Some were trotting; some were cantering; and some were jumping, with help from their coaches, over obstacles set up in the centre of the ring. It was busy and somewhat overwhelming, especially when small ponies darted past, seemingly out of thin air. Bird felt Sunny tense up.

Problem, Sunny?

Fancy Pants. Over by the biggest tree.

Bird looked. There was Leon, astride a handsome silver stallion. The horse was jumping around nervously. Leon held him tight and cursed at him. The horse was frantic and refused to comply. He was lathering up.

Let's pay them a visit, Bird girl.

Are you crazy?

Probably.

They trotted over to the big tree. Sunny got as close to the stallion as he could. *I call your person Fancy Pants. What do you call him?*

The silver stallion snorted. *I like that. Fancy Pants. It suits. What do you call your person?*

Bird girl.

Why?

Because that's my name. Bird looked at the stallion.

She can talk!

I know.

I didn't know humans could do that!

They mostly can't.

You're lucky.

I know.

Leon felt his horse calm down. The silver horse stopped dancing around and throwing his head.

"Finally!" breathed Leon. He looked up and noticed Bird on Sundancer. "So, you're here, are you? If you think you're going to win on that lunatic, you got another thing coming. Hurricane and I have it wrapped up."

Bird shrugged.

Leon glared at her with a look of pure anger in his eyes. Then he mimicked her shrug. "What's that supposed to mean? Why don't you talk?"

Bird shrugged again, this time with an added smile. It would annoy him, she was sure.

Leon narrowed his eyes. "You creep me out. And your horse is dead meat." He laughed suddenly, as if he'd just told a joke. "Literally! He's already buried! Dead meat!"

Bird peered hard at Leon. What did he mean by that?

"You don't understand? Read my lips, dummy." He cackled now, an ugly sound that carried over the usual horse show noises. "Prince Redwood. Is. Dead."

Bird's eyes widened.

"I shouldn't have told you. But who cares? It's not like you'll tell anybody, anyway." Leon laughed hard. "You can't talk!"

He's on the white powder again. The silver horse shook his mane sadly. *It makes him unpleasant.*

Too bad. Sunny sympathized. *I had a rider once like that. Drugs.*

Nothing worse. You never know what they'll do. They get mad fast.

I'm sorry, Hurricane. See you later.

Call me Silver. Everybody does.

Sure. Call me Sunny.

Bye, Sunny. Bye, Bird girl.

Bird responded: *Bye, Silver.*

Sunny and Bird warmed up for half an hour. They did some trotting, some cantering, some circles and lead changes, then hopped over the jumps a few times after Hannah came in to supervise. Bird knew that Sunny felt good. He took everything as it came, and remained settled and calm.

More and more big-time riders came in to warm up. A kid about her age trotted by on a large brown and white spotted pony. What's wrong with this picture? thought Bird. I'm competing against these pros? I should be back in the pony ring. Her stomach began to ache.

She heard applause. Leon and Hurricane were impressing the crowd by taking bigger and bigger jumps. Bird admired the way the stallion moved. Perhaps he would be their main competition.

Don't worry Bird girl. He's got Leon and I've got you.

Leon's one of Canada's top riders!

So? I'm Canada's top horse.

Bird smiled and patted his neck. He'd need that confidence today.

They walked around the fair and enjoyed the hubbub. Little ponies and their kid riders, families out for the day, stressed riders and their nagging mothers. People were bathing horses, mucking tent stalls, carrying water, feeding carrots, throwing hay. Golf carts and motor scooters buzzed around as riders signed up for classes or hurried to the far ring. Everyone was energized, intent on their next class, hopeful that this time, the first-place ribbon would be theirs.

The Grand Classic Event was due to start in twenty minutes. Bird and Sunny came back to the trailer for last-minute preparations.

This class was open to all comers. There would be twelve jumps—maximum four feet three inches high and six feet wide, with a twelve-foot water jump. There would be a time limit. The purse was thirty thousand dollars, with the winning rider taking all. It was no wonder that so many of the professionals came out.

Today, however, there was an unusual twist to the rules. In the final stage of the judging, the top four contestants would switch and ride a different horse over the course. It was called the Switcheroo. They would draw numbers to decide which of the other three winning horses they'd ride, and their ability to take a horse over a difficult course without having ridden it before would be the deciding factor. The Grand Classic Event was billed as the highlight of the fair for very good reason. Anything could happen.

Hannah tied Bird's number around the girl's waist and adjusted the collar of her jacket. "You'll be just fine. Just go out there and pretend you're practising at home. Remember to breathe. And count your strides out loud. It will help Sunny relax when he hears your voice."

Bird poked her aunt in the arm and grinned.

"Right. Sorry. I'm babbling out the stuff I tell all the kids. I guess I'm a little nervous."

That makes two of us, thought Bird.

Three. Sundancer piped in. *I want to win for you.*

Bird patted Sunny's neck and kissed Hannah on the cheek.

"I'll be up in the stands with your fan club, Bird," said Hannah smiling. "Everyone's here—your mom, Julia, Stuart, Abby, and the Piersons. Paul's the vet on duty, but if there are no emergencies, he'll sit with us. Your grandfather'll be watching, too, but he's with Lavinia and she still won't talk to me. You'll be fabulous." She paused for a moment, laughing at herself. "I'm babbling again. I won't say another word."

Bird walked Sunny over to the big ring, then she sat down, quietly waiting her turn. She'd drawn the tenth ride out of thirty contestants. Other riders were in the warm-up ring, popping their horses over four-foot jumps or practising leg yields to get their full attention.

She looked up into the stands, and tried to see where her family and friends were sitting. Amid the packed crowd, a pure-white object caught her eye. It was Kimberly, with her arm and shoulder in a shiny new white cast. Bird smiled to herself. Kimberly was sitting beside Julia and the whole group, halfway up the bleachers. It was a comforting sight.

Hold on. Who was that sitting on the other side of Kimberly? Bird suddenly felt a shiver of nerves. Alec Daniels. She took a deep breath. She must not let anything distract her, especially not a boy who probably thought she was an idiot.

The first horse was called. "Number 238, Razor's Edge, owned by Tamblyn Farms, ridden by Hal Childs."

Bird watched the jet-black gelding trot confidently through the entrance and canter past the starting gate. He was lovely to watch. He loped along, covering ground easily and soaring over the jumps without a care in the world.

He's too slow. They'll start making up time now.

Think so? His stride is long. It might be deceiving.

It doesn't deceive me. He's slow.

Just then, as Sunny predicted, the rider sped the black horse up. Razor's Edge didn't like the faster speed—it was harder for him to get his strides right. He plowed right into the water, cleared the first jump of the triple combination, then crashed through the second and third. Bird felt sorry for him; he'd been doing so well.

Don't cry too hard, Bird girl. Better for us.

The second and third riders had eight faults each. The fourth had twelve. The fifth had eight with two time faults, making ten.

Everyone has trouble with the water, Sunny. Why?

It's not paced out right. Don't worry. I've figured out what to do.

The sixth rider was Leon. "Number 276, Hurricane, owned by Owens Enterprises, ridden by Leon Parish."

Leon and Hurricane passed them on the way into the ring.

Don't let him scare you, Silver, cautioned Sunny.

Thanks, Sunny. I've been here before. You have a good round, yourself.

Sunny and Bird watched with full attention as Leon expertly guided Hurricane over every hurdle. They sailed over the dreaded water hazard and easily cleared the triple. He was a talented animal. Their time was under the limit, and the crowd was on its feet.

The announcer boomed, "We have a new leader folks. Leon Parish and Hurricane will be hard to beat."

I told you, Bird girl. Fancy Pants is a good rider.

Hurricane is no slouch, either.

Is that a challenge? Bird felt her mount tense.

Never. We all know you're the top horse.

Right answer.

The next three riders crashed into poles and generally made a mess of the course. Bird speculated that Leon's ride had demoralized them. Now it was their turn.

"Number 297, Sundancer, owned by Owens Enterprises, ridden by Alberta Simms."

Bird knew that her little fan club would be stamping and applauding. She thought of Alec Daniels and felt a tightening in her chest. What if she screwed up? What if she looked like an idiot again, like every other time he'd seen her? She pushed the thought away.

No one else in the stands would have heard her name

before. They were all probably wondering how she had the nerve to compete with this quality of rider. Bird swallowed hard. She wondered the same thing.

They'll know your name after today, Bird girl.

In a good way, I hope.

Sunny shook his whole body so violently that Bird had trouble staying on. Then he stretched his back, almost collapsing in front then sinking in rear.

What's going on, Sunny? It's our turn!

Cool it, Bird girl. I'm doing my stretches.

Now?

I'm limbering up. Okay, I'm ready.

You're making me crazy!

Relax, Bird girl. Let me do this, and just go along for the ride.

As they entered the enormous grass ring, Bird knew that all eyes were on her magnificent mount. Sunny's muscled body with its glistening chestnut coat shone in the sunlight as he saucily threw his legs forward in a bouncy, rounded canter and played. He arched his neck down to his knees and lifted his hind end high with each stride.

Sundancer reared up, then sped through the starting gate.

Sunny, slow down.

It's just a crowd-pleaser. Don't worry so much.

With that, he gave a buck. There was a collective cheer from the crowd. *See, Bird girl? They love me.*

With his theatrics out of the way, Sunny got down to business. The first jump was a four-foot white vertical with an ominous plastic owl sitting on the left standard.

Oooo, scary. Sunny lifted over it and landed softly. After two strides they made a sharp right turn and headed toward a multi-coloured in-and-out with two strides between jumps. Bird made sure she kept light in the saddle with little contact on his mouth.

Very good, Bird girl. That's the way I like you to ride.

I'm trying, Sunny.

As they landed each jump, she pushed her hands up his mane to allow him to stretch out his neck. Everything was going smoothly.

The fourth hurdle was coming up, and Bird could feel Sundancer's confidence growing with every stride. It was a huge brown oxer with no ground lines to help judge distance. The wings of the standards were festooned with pots of pink geraniums.

Then, just as Sunny was preparing to jump, the unthinkable happened: a small brown and white dog scooted onto the course, and directly into their path. To avoid the animal, Sundancer stepped sideways, forcing an awkward takeoff. He sprang with all his might to clear the top rail. He didn't touch a single geranium leaf, but his landing was bad. He tripped and stumbled.

Bird was thrown forward as Sunny fell to his knees. With great effort, the powerful animal pushed up and tossed Bird back into the saddle. He cantered on with minimal time lost.

Well done, Sunny, but I can't see and I've lost a stirrup.

Stupid dog.

With the back of her hand Bird pushed her riding cap off her nose as her left foot found the stirrup. The optical illusion jump was three strides away. Again the dog came running. It nipped at Sunny's heels then attached himself to Sunny's tail with his teeth.

You're asking for it, stupid.

The announcer called, "Would the owner of this Jack Russell terrier get him out of the ring? Pronto."

Sunny couldn't wait. He flicked at the dog with a rear hoof and never missed a beat. The Jack Russell rolled away like a rugby ball, then scrambled to his feet. He yapped and snarled and charged at Sunny again as they turned into the line of difficult jumps.

Bird glanced down at the angry terrier. *Go away! Go! It's my job!*

I'll give you a bone if you stop.

Promise?

Yes. Find me after.

The little dog turned and ran out of the ring. Bird would have to get her hands on a bone somehow, but she couldn't worry about that now.

The line of four jumps curved diagonally across the ring, from one corner to the other. They were all different and spaced differently as well. The first was made of wooden blocks painted like a red brick wall. There were three strides to a curved white plank fence, then five strides to large bicycle tires lined up between two steel standards. The last jump was four strides after that, and the oddest of the line. It appeared as if three black and white cows were looking at them, face forward.

One at a time, Sunny.

How else do you expect me to do this? Look over them, Bird girl, not at them.

Sunny didn't glance at any of them. He took one after the other without a care in the world. Now, there was the water jump followed by the triple combination, and the course would be complete.

Leave this to me, Bird girl. I've figured it out. Just sit tight, heels down. Give me lots of rein, and, again, look over the jumps.

Sunny gathered himself on his haunches and sprang over the water. The triple combination loomed up in front of them. Sunny's ears went up and he lifted off. They landed the first. Two strides to the second. Take off. And over.

The dog was back. Right on the landing spot.

Sunny was surprised. He avoided the dog but crashed through the last jump of the triple combination.

No bone for you!

I don't care. The brown and white spotted dog disappeared into the crowd.

Bird and Sunny walked out of the ring. His head drooped.

It wasn't your fault, Sunny. You know that.

I should have landed on him and killed him.

You did the right thing. We're still in second place.

Yes. For now. There are twenty more horses in this class, and they smell blood.

The announcer's voice rang over the sound system. "The judge has been asked to review the last round. Interference has been called, due to an unrestrained animal on the course." There was a murmur in the stands as everyone discussed this unexpected turn of events. "We will continue with the show and announce the judge's decision in due time."

Bird was pleased. Someone had objected.

"Number 316, Genesee Valley, owned by Prescott Stud, ridden by Holly Fergus."

The young bay gelding spooked at the plastic owl on the first fence and had a difficult time regaining his confidence. By the time he faced the row of cows, he was finished. He spun on his haunches and raced for the exit. The harassed rider excused herself as her mount pushed past the waiting horses. "Sorry!" she called. "Excuse us! Sorry."

Bird felt bad for horse and rider, but her mind was elsewhere. Now that she thought about it, that little brown and white dog looked familiar.

Sunny, that dog. Did you recognize him?

Sure. That's Buzz.

Buzz?

The Tall Man's dog.

Now I remember. At the Rockhill Show. You don't think...

Yes, I do.

Why didn't you say something?

You didn't ask.

Hmmm. Let's go for a walk.

Bird and Sunny walked around the tent stalls until they found
the ones belonging to Owens Enterprises. Navy-blue curtains
with gold lettering. Nobody was there. Presumably, they were all
out watching the show. A whining noise came from a curtained
stall decorated with red and blue ribbons.

Bird asked, *Is that you, Buzz?*

Yes. He locked me up.

Tsk, tsk. And after you did such a good job of upsetting us.

He told me to go get 'em! I do what I'm told or else.

You could've been hurt.

I'm quick! I never get hurt.

I hope not. Bird meant it. She was about to tell him not to do
it again, but she knew he wouldn't listen. Terriers never do. Jack
Russells especially.

They walked back to the ring, coming around a different
way. The tiny judge's booth was crowded with people. Bird saw
Kenneth Bradley, Elvin Wainright, Pete Pierson, and two other
men. One was the judge, Bird guessed. She didn't know the other.

She watched as Mr. Pierson painfully descended the steps,
looking quite angry. So he was the one who had cried foul. Good
old Mr. Pierson. Bird felt a stab of gratitude in her chest.

Elvin followed. His wide-brimmed hat obscured his expression, but Bird sensed a smug energy. Her grandfather and the
stranger came last, leaving the judge alone in the booth. He
spoke quietly into a phone.

Thirty seconds later, the loudspeaker crackled. "May I have
your attention, please. The judge has made his decision regarding
the interference call. No concessions will be made due to natural
causes. The round will stand as it is. Number 297, Sundancer,
ridden by Alberta Simms, has four faults. They are currently in
second place, before the jump-off round, with sixteen rides
completed and fourteen more to come."

Bird was resigned. They'd done their best.

Sunny was upset. *It's not fair! I would have gone clear!*
We'll have another chance at it. If not today, another time.
That's not the point! They cheated.

Bird observed her grandfather with his arm around the stranger's shoulder, walking toward the tent stalls.

The show went on. "Number 238, Whiskey Road, owned by Seabright Stables, ridden by Alicia Cawthron."

Bird and Sunny casually followed the men, staying out of their line of vision. The two men disappeared into the curtained room at the Owens Enterprises stalls.

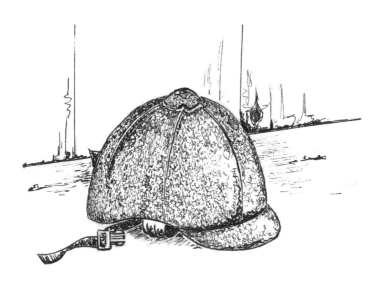

17

THE SWITCHEROO

I'm big. I'm a bit of a stallion.

THE ANNOUNCER'S VOICE ECHOED AGAIN throughout the fairgrounds. "May I have your attention please. The four finalists in our Grand Classic Event today are as follows, from first place to fourth."

Bird was frozen with anticipation. Sunny's ears flicked around.

We've got fourth, Bird girl, if I'm right about the paint's timing and the skinny mare's foot in the water.

"First is number 276, Leon Parish on Hurricane. Second is number 372, Jen Jefferies on Paramour. Third is number 310, Harold Smart riding Southern Comfort. Fourth is number 297, Alberta Simms on Sundancer."

Bird could hardly believe it. She sat on Sundancer in stunned silence.

"Again, numbers 276, 372, 310, and 297. Please come to the judge's booth to make your draw for the Switcheroo."

Hannah and Abby came down from the stands to help Bird. Both women were grinning ear to ear.

"I can't believe they didn't give you a break on the dog incident, Bird," said Hannah as she finished brushing the dried sweat from Sunny's coat.

"They rarely do," Abby said. "Stuff happens. Sometimes the

wind comes up and knocks over a flowerpot. Sometimes it suddenly starts to pour. I had a toddler run out on the course once. His mother ran after him and scooped him up, yelling like crazy. Dancer kept on going, like Sunny did today, but another horse might have reacted badly. You take your chances and go with it." She smiled at Bird and continued wiping down the tack. "You handled it beautifully, Bird, even with all that interference. You only had one rail down."

Hannah brushed some dust off Bird's jacket and bent down to wipe her boots. She straightened the cardboard number on Bird's back. "Now, away we go. You can ride the pants off any of those riders."

"Absolutely," said Abby as she held Sundancer's lead shank. "You have the advantage. Show me a horse that you can't connect with."

Should I win or should you win, Bird girl?

I wouldn't put it like that.

No? Well, if I have a clear round with my new rider and you don't, then I win. I can make that happen or not.

Bird rubbed his ears. *You're a better horse than I am a rider. Go out there and look good. Do your best, Sunny, and so will I.*

So you don't care who wins?

If you win, I'll feel as good as if I win. We're partners. I just hope that one of us wins.

Abby held Sundancer while Bird went to the judge's booth. Hannah went along to make sure that Leon didn't try to pull a fast one.

Just one thing, Bird girl.

What, Sunny?

Whatever you do, don't let Fancy Pants draw me.

I'll do my best, but the odds are a problem.

Leon sauntered across the ring at the same time, ignoring them completely.

Harold Smart and Jen Jefferies were already in the booth when Hannah, Bird, and Leon stepped in. It was quite crowded.

"Leon Parish, you go first. Reach in and pull out a name. If you draw your own horse, draw again."

Leon put his hand in the blue jar and brought out a folded piece of white paper.

"Give it to me," requested the judge.

Leon did as he was told.

"Sundancer. You will ride Sundancer fourth."

Oops, thought Bird.

"Can I draw again?" Leon looked aghast. "I grabbed two and dropped one, but I meant to drop this one."

The judge gave Leon a stern look. He simply replied, "No."

"I ride last?" asked Leon. "I don't like to ride last."

"As outlined in the rules, contestants ride in the spot designated by the placing of each horse. Now, Jen Jefferies, please."

Jen was an affable woman in her mid-thirties. Everyone liked her, mostly because she was genuinely nice to people and didn't involve herself in horse show politics. She reached into the blue jar.

"Southern Comfort. You will ride third."

Jen nodded. "Thank you. Do we get a practice jump?"

"Yes. You get two practice jumps in the warm-up ring. I will supervise that after the draw. Okay, then. Next name. Harold Smart."

Harold, dapper and lean, could be seen modelling riding apparel in several horse magazines. One benefit for him was that he got his clothes free of charge. All the young male riders tried to keep up with his changing styles, but he was always one step ahead of the fashion trends. He pulled a slip of paper from the jar and gave it to the judge.

"Paramour. You'll ride second."

The judge turned to Bird. "By the process of elimination, you will ride Hurricane, and you will go first. This worked out very nicely. No one drew their own horse. We'll proceed to the warm-up ring now, and get this show on before the crowd gets bored and goes home."

Hannah and Bird found Abby and Sundancer where they'd left them. Hannah filled in Abby about the draw.

"You're serious?" she asked Hannah. "Leon on Sunny?"

Hannah and Bird nodded together. They all started to laugh.

I don't see what's so funny.

You don't, Sunny?

No. Fancy Pants has some nerve to get on my back again.

That's exactly what's so funny.

Funny for you, maybe. I can't stand him.

The riders put their own saddles over the saddle pads of the horse they had drawn. Each mounted carefully, unsure of the temperament of the unknown horse. Bird felt Hurricane's power and sanity immediately.

I'm glad you're riding me.

I'm glad I drew you, Silver. You're a wonderful horse.

They walked into the warm-up ring. The judge instructed two teenaged grooms on how to place the practice jump, and one at a time the riders took their new mounts over. Hurricane had a gorgeous round form over jumps. Bird smiled with pleasure.

The pole was raised. Again, the riders rode over the jump. There were no problems with any of the horses, and Sunny behaved himself like an old school horse.

Good boy, Sunny.

Don't worry. I'll be good if he will.

Suddenly, without warning, Hurricane bucked. It was a huge nose-diving, kick-the-moon type of buck, and Bird was not prepared. She was thrown off his back and hit the ground hard.

What did you do that for, Silver?

You stabbed me!

I did not.

Yes! On my back.

Let me look.

Get away from me! Silver backed away with his eyes bulging wide. The grooms came running. One caught him before he could bolt.

I wouldn't hurt you, Silver. I just want to see what's going on.

You stabbed me in the back! It hurts.

Where?

Under the saddle.

How could I have done that? I was sitting on the saddle. Let me look.

Silver considered this, then calmed down.

Bird quietly walked over to Hurricane. She stroked his long neck, then unfastened the girth.

"What do you think you're doing?" yelled Leon from Sunny's back.

Bird ignored him. She slipped her saddle off Hurricane's back and placed it on the ground.

Leon jumped off Sunny to stop her.

Before he could reach her, she'd removed the saddle pad. Everyone gasped. An open stock pin was wedged into the muscle beside the spine on Hurricane's back. Blood had soaked through the Owens Enterprises saddle pad that was now laying on the ground. Bird turned to stare at Leon.

"What are you looking at? You stuck a pin in my horse!"

The judge irritably stalked over and took a good look. He reached into his pocket and pulled out his cellphone. "Herb Rawlie here. Get the vet. Now. To the warm-up ring beside the Grand Prix."

I see what hurt you, Silver.

What is it, Bird girl?

A big pin. The kind that riders wear at their necks. It's stuck in your back.

Abby and Hannah quickly arrived on the scene. Hannah hugged Bird and checked her from top to bottom to see that she was all right.

"Can you see clearly?" she asked.

Bird nodded.

"What day is it?"

Bird rolled her eyes and pointed to her mouth. Then she made the gabbing motion with her right hand and shook her head.

Hannah and Abby smiled. "She'll be just fine," Abby said as she put her hand on Bird's shoulder.

Paul Daniels' truck stopped beside the ring. He came running with his medical bag. His eyes took in the entire situation and he went directly for Hurricane. He pulled on latex gloves and examined the horse's back. With cotton pads soaked in antiseptic solution, Paul quickly removed the pin, then applied pressure with the pads. He stood beside the distressed animal and waited for the blood to coagulate.

Hannah asked Paul, "How did this happen?"

Paul pursed his lips. "If this is an accident, I'm a monkey's uncle."

"You think someone did this on purpose?"

Herb Rawlie interrupted them. "I'd ask that no one speculates about how this happened. I don't want to accuse Alberta of wrongdoing."

"Alberta?" gasped Hannah. "Why would she sabotage her chances of winning?"

"I don't want to accuse anyone of anything until we can sit down and piece it all together. The question now is whether the horse is capable of continuing."

Paul was astonished. "This animal has been punctured by an

unsterile object, deep into his latissimus dorsi. Edema is occurring rapidly, and the position of the wound is unfortunately situated directly under the saddle."

The judge looked blank.

Hannah translated. "It's infected, it's swelling up, it hurts, and to put a saddle on it would be cruel and unusual punishment." Paul nodded.

"So the answer is no?"

"The answer is no." There was no hesitation in Paul's tone.

Bird felt deflated. A tear fell from her eye as she patted Hurricane's neck.

Another time, Silver.

I hope so. We could've won, you know.

Paul gave Hurricane a shot of Banamine to ease the pain and a shot of penicillin for infection. A groom from Owens Enterprises arrived and led the injured animal back to his stall.

Bird stood forlorn, saddle on her hip, without a horse to ride.

The judge said briskly, "Now it's down to three. Let's get the show on the road."

Leon couldn't disguise his glee. He rode up on Sunny and said to Bird, "The luck of the draw. Too bad for you."

Bird stared at him, amazed.

No, Fancy Pants. Too bad for you.

Easy now, Sunny. You've got to win.

I can't. He makes me furious. I feel dangerous when he rides me.

Then scare him a little. But go fast and clean.

Give me one reason to make him look good.

Because that was our deal. One of us should win, and now it can't be me. Go out there, Sunny. Make us all proud.

Sunny stretched his neck to the ground and bowed at Bird's feet.

"What's he doing? He's gonna roll!" shouted Leon. "Get up, you stupid horse!"

If you say so. Sunny threw up his head and jumped up with his front legs. Leon was thrown back. He almost tumbled but caught himself in time.

Bird covered her mouth to hide her smile.

Have some fun, Sunny. I'll be watching.

I'll do it for you. Not for Fancy Pants.

Bird couldn't go up to the stands; she was too agitated. She stood at the rails where she could see and hear everything. Abby stayed with her for moral support, while Hannah went back up to sit with the others.

The announcer's voice rang out. "Attention. Attention. Thank you for your patience, ladies and gentlemen. We now have three finalists, not four. Number 297, Alberta Simms, riding Hurricane, has withdrawn from the competition due to injury. Hurricane is expected to make a full and speedy recovery. The show will now commence. The Switcheroo will take place immediately, starting with Harold Smart, number 310, riding Paramour, Jen Jefferies' mount. Once again, thank you for your patience."

Harold Smart looked immaculate but nervous. He breathed in and out twice, then gathered Paramour's reins.

"He takes hold turning right and runs away," whispered Leon. "Watch out for that."

Harold looked even more nervous. "Really? Thanks for the tip." He trotted Paramour into the ring flexing his head to the right. Leon chuckled.

Bird stared at him in disbelief. She could not believe that a person would mislead his competition so blatantly at such a vulnerable moment.

Paramour, a tall leggy gelding with a bright bay coat, cantered through the starting gate and headed toward the white fence. He cleared it beautifully and landed lightly. They had to make a hard right to the multicoloured in-and-out. Harold heeded Leon's words and held back his horse, so they came into the first of the two jumps too slowly. Paramour cleared the first jump but couldn't get enough propulsion and stopped at the second. Harold circled and took the in-and-out again, this time with vigour. By the set of his jaw, Bird knew that Harold had figured out Leon's game. Too late.

They soared over the brown oxer with the pots of geraniums. The optical illusion caused no problem for this seasoned jumper, but Harold didn't get him in straight to the red brick wall. The top layer of wooden boxes slid off and crashed to the ground. Paramour's ears flattened and he kicked out. He didn't like knocking down jumps. His hind feet rapped the white planks, and then, because he'd picked up too much speed, he had no room to jump from the base of the bicycle tires. He stopped again.

Harold Smart and Paramour were whistled out.

Bird thought they'd done remarkably well, considering that this was the first time they'd partnered each other. Not to mention the bad advice that Leon had given him going in.

"Number 372, Jen Jefferies, riding Southern Comfort. Southern Comfort was ridden earlier this class by Harold Smart."

Jen had been smart. She'd stayed far away from Leon who had been flirting outrageously with her, so she rode in with no preconceptions. Southern Comfort, a big rangy chestnut with a blaze and snip, trotted in loosely and proudly. His flaxen mane and tail gave him a friendly look, like an overgrown Welsh pony.

By the time this duo was sailing through the line of four jumps down the diagonal, it was clear that this was the winning round. They got along comfortably, as if they'd been partnered before.

They headed toward the water jump. One foot splashed slightly on takeoff. The crowd groaned. Southern Comfort completed the triple combination with ease, and they trotted out of the ring. Four faults. All because of a little water. Bird felt badly for them.

You said to scare him a little?

Bird turned to Sunny. *If you must.*

I must. Watch me.

"The last of our finalists is coming in now. Number 276, Leon Parish, riding Sundancer. Alberta Simms rode him in the qualifying round."

Sunny burst through the entrance and galloped through the starting gate. Leon held on for dear life and, try as he might, couldn't control the angry animal. Sunny hurled himself over the white vertical, and to add some zest, kicked the plastic owl right off the standard. Laughter filled the stands, encouraging Sundancer in his antics.

The multicoloured in-and-out was designed for two strides between jumps, but Sunny raced so fast that he did it in one. He screamed toward the brown oxer and tore over it, bucking as he landed. Leon Parish was now saying his prayers aloud.

The optical illusion was an obstacle that appeared straight from several angles, hence its name. Sunny took it from the extreme right so that he could shave off two strides into the line of four. Leon wasn't expecting that, so his balance was off. Sunny made a valiant effort to readjust his weight, and the two landed together.

The "brick" wall, land, two strides instead of three to the white planks. Land, four strides instead of five to the bicycle tires jump. Land, then three strides instead of four to the cows. Sunny was galloping full out. Leon's face was bright red. He was so rigid with fear that Bird thought he looked like a scarecrow tied to the saddle.

Sunny began to slow as he neared the water jump. Bird sighed with relief. She was glad that he remembered the tricky pacing. Now Sunny slowed to a crawl. He appeared to be cantering in slow motion with tiny strides. Then he suddenly hurled himself over the water. From where Bird was watching, it appeared as if he'd gone eight feet in the air and landed an entire stride away from the lip of water. Leon most certainly had not expected this and he barely stayed on. He lost the reins and his stirrups. He groped fruitlessly for the reins as his feet searched in vain for the stirrups. They took off at the first of the triple. Sunny ignored the wailing Leon, the flapping reins, and the pounding stirrup irons, as he jumped lightly and surely over the three last jumps and galloped through the timers.

The crowd was on its feet. Sunny danced along joyfully. He hop skip jumped to the centre of the ring. He did a short dressage demonstration, with grand jettes and airs above the ground. Majestically he pulled himself up on his hind legs, then took a deep bow. First to the east, then to the west.

Now that he'd found his stirrups and gathered the reins, Leon began to relax. Bird knew by the smile beginning to creep across his face that he realized that he'd won. Thirty thousand dollars plus the prestige. Leon took off his riding cap and waved it in the air. He stood up in his stirrups and bowed to the crowd.

Bird whistled under her breath. Big mistake. Sunny's ears went flat. With Leon in a vulnerable position, Sunny reared and shot out of the ring. Leon grabbed at Sunny's neck and managed to keep it together until they were past the exit. Safely out of the ring, therefore not eliminated by the rider touching the ground, Sunny dumped Leon face first on the hard ground.

Sunny trotted right over to Bird. He was so overcharged with adrenaline that Bird could hardly make out his thoughts.

Victorious! Completely victorious! Job done! Fancy Pants gone!
Calm down, Sunny.
Time perfect, no rails down! Tell me! How fabulous am I!

Bird laughed and patted his neck. The gelding pushed her chest with his nose and rubbed his face on her jacket. Bird scratched his ears happily.

You are totally fabulous.

I won! I won! Come for a victory lap!

No, Leon won, not me.

I won! Are you kidding? He's never getting on this horse again!

Sunny wouldn't take no for an answer. He twisted her in his snaking neck and pushed her toward his side.

Okay, Sunny. It's in bad taste, but who cares? It's your day!

Bird stuck her riding cap on her head and climbed up into the saddle. The two of them trotted into the ring. The audience was standing up to leave but sat when they realized that the show was not yet over. Sunny collected himself and arched his powerful neck. He cantered gracefully around the ring twice to a standing ovation and exited at a humble walk. Gone was the wild, crazy horse that had careered around the course at breakneck speed just a moment before.

"Please stay in your seats as we make the presentation to the winner of the Grand Classic Event. Let's call in Leon Parish on Sundancer to receive his first-place ribbon, the Classic trophy, *and* a cheque for thirty thousand dollars! Mr. Leon Parish, please enter the ring on Sundancer!"

Bird hopped down from the saddle and handed the reins to Leon as he stumbled past.

Leon shook his head. He spoke with difficulty through his split lip. "Are you inthane? Do you think I'm inthane?" His face was covered in blood and dirt. His left eye was swelling up.

He certainly looks insane, thought Bird.

"I'm never, never—read my lipth—never getting up on that horse again."

What did I tell you, Bird girl? Right again!

With that, Leon turned and hobbled into the ring to receive his award.

All at once, Bird was aware of being watched. She looked around, trying to locate the eyes she felt on her. Cody's furtive face peeked around a nearby fencepost.

Go fast, Bird girl.

Trouble, Cody?

The horse who calls himself Silver. He wants to talk to you.

Bird quickly handed Sunny's reins to a surprised Abby.

Stay here, Sunny. This must be important.

She raced off to find Silver. When she got to the Owens stalls, the one marked "Hurricane" was empty. Bird thought fast. The wash stalls. She checked. No, not there.

Bird had no idea what Silver could want, but it must be serious for him to send Cody. She dashed up and down the busy stall area, then caught sight of the rows of horse trailers. Maybe they were taking him home.

Bird saw Cody peeking from under a trailer.

Over there, Bird girl. In the second row. He popped back out of sight.

She ran. Around the second row, she saw the ramp of the Owens Enterprises trailer. Three grooms plus Elvin Wainright were trying unsuccessfully to load the big silver stallion. He was putting up a fuss—rearing, kicking, resisting everyone—and sidling this way and that to avoid the ramp.

I'm here, Silver. Cody found me.

What took you so long? I can't keep this up.

I ran as fast as I could.

The horse stopped fighting. The groom who was leading him panted with exertion. "Good boy, Hurricane. Now, just walk on quietly and we'll take you home."

I'll tell you fast. The big pin. Does it sparkle?

I'm not sure. Maybe. I didn't get a good look at it.

Leon wears one with a sparkle in the middle.

He does?

And he's not wearing it now. That's all I wanted to say.

With that, the big horse walked straight on the trailer and

stood quietly as the exhausted grooms secured his lead shank and lifted the ramp.

Elvin turned to Bird, a suspicious look on his face. "I don't know what just happened here. As soon as you turned up, Hurricane settled down and walked on the trailer. What did you do?"

Bird looked at him. She smiled and raised her eyebrows.

"Keep your secrets. There's something witchy about you."

With a small chuckle, Bird turned to go. She wanted to get Sundancer home, and she needed to find a way to tell someone what Silver had told her. She was not going to let Leon get away with hurting him.

"Not so fast," Elvin said sternly. "We're not finished talking."

Bird stopped and faced him.

"You don't fool me. I'd like to know why you stabbed Hurricane with the pin, and I'd like to know what you did to Sundancer to make him crazy when Leon rode him in the Switcheroo."

At that exact moment, Buzz, the little brown and white terrier, hopped out of the truck window and lifted his leg on the trailer tire.

Bird looked at Buzz, then she looked at Elvin. She smiled. So you think I'm a witch, do you? She pointed to her chest, indicating herself, then to her head, meaning knowledge. Then she pointed to Elvin, then his dog. She mimed little legs running and horses spooking. Then she winked.

"You *are* a little witch!" exclaimed Elvin, "but you can't prove anything." He yelled out orders to his grooms. "Bert. Get these horses home, then come back for the rest. Bill and Gord, pack everything up and wrap their legs for shipping."

Now he glared at Bird. "I warn you. We will get what we want. If not today, then tomorrow."

Bird had had enough of this nasty man. Shivers coursed through her body as she took off running back to the ring to find Abby and Sunny. There, she was surprised by her entire cheering section. Hannah, Julia, Eva, Stuart, the Piersons, and Kimberly. Alec stood to one side, looking nervous. Everyone spoke at once.

Kimberly gushed, "You were great, Bird! Too bad about Hurricane."

"You would've won the whole thing," agreed Stuart. "No question."

Laura gave her a hug. "What a treat to see you ride. Such a big horse for such a dear, dear, little girl!"

Julia grabbed Bird's waist and wouldn't let go. "I'm so so so proud of you, Bird!"

"Me, too." Pete laughed and mussed her hair. "You showed real character."

Bird looked at Pete. She put her hand on her heart and bowed her head. She wanted to thank him for calling a foul on her behalf.

"You're welcome, Bird," said Pete. "They didn't listen to me, but not for lack of trying. That dog was a menace."

Eva had been standing with Stuart, watching. She walked up to Bird and crouched in front of her, looking directly into her eyes. "All my life I wanted to ride horses because I knew it would make my father proud of me. But I was too afraid of getting hurt. You are so brave, Bird. You are the girl I wanted to be. I love you, honey."

Eva and Bird embraced. Bird felt Eva's love—pure and strong and unquestioning. Her mother said she loved her, and for the first time in her life, Bird believed it.

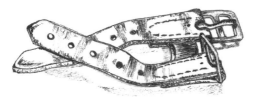

18

DOUBLE-CROSS

No one's going to hurt me real bad.

IT WAS TIME TO GO HOME. The Grand Classic Event was over, and the cars and vans were lined up at the exit. It had been a long, hot day and a peaceful fatigue had settled on everyone.

The Piersons waved their goodbyes. Eva and Stuart headed off with Julia and Kimberly. Paul had yet another emergency and raced off with Alec to deal with it. Abby and Hannah packed up the tack and prepared the trailer, while Bird spent some time alone with Sunny. She lovingly brushed the sweat from his coat while they waited for the lineup at the gate to ease.

Sunny, you won the day. Congratulations.

I didn't hurt Fancy Pants. At least not badly.

I'm glad about that.

I really wanted to.

Sunny, I have so many questions on my mind.

About what?

About what Leon said—that you were dead meat. What did he mean? And Silver told me that the pin that stabbed him probably belongs to Leon.

You have to tell someone. Tell Hannah.

I'll try.

Bird girl, you must learn to talk to humans.

I said I'd try! Bird put her brush back in the grooming kit and found the hoof pick. She thoughtfully picked the dirt and gravel out of his hooves.

Tell someone.

Bird decided not to tell Sunny what else was bothering her. He'd probably think it was silly. Alec had just walked away, without saying anything. She'd had such high hopes, too. Alec and she seemed to have been developing something. Some connection. And her performance today should've impressed him. She'd really hoped it would. But he wasn't interested. She'd have to accept it. Bird felt like an idiot. Again.

Bird led Sunny onto the trailer and clipped him in. The three exhausted females and their sleepy horse pulled out of the park just as the sun was beginning to sink in the late summer sky.

Not one of them was prepared for what they found when they got back to Saddle Creek.

Balloons and colourful crepe streamers hung from tree branches and fence posts up the lane. A long yellow banner was strung across the driveway with "Welcome home, Sundancer, champion of the Grand Classic Event!" painted in huge, still dripping, letters.

Bird smiled as she saw her sister duck into the bushes.

After unloading him, Bird quickly tucked Sundancer in his stall with feed and water, eager to join her family inside. He took a long drink, then sighed with contentment.

Have fun at my party, Bird girl.

Do you want to come?

No. I'm beat. But it's nice that they're celebrating.

Everyone is very, very proud of you, Sunny.

I'm glad. I'm really glad.

Bird rubbed his forehead and smiled. *I'm especially proud that you left Leon alive.*

That was probably a mistake.

Bird chuckled.

After cleaning and putting away the tack and trailer, Abby, Hannah, and Bird wearily entered the house. The festively decorated lane gave them the expectation of a surprise party, with everyone jumping out from behind chairs.

Nothing. Not a sound. The lights were off.

"Now I'm disappointed," said Hannah.

"Me, too," agreed Abby.

Bird heard something. She grinned. She walked over to the kitchen door and flung it open. Everybody was there: Pete and Laura Pierson, Eva and Stuart, Julia and Kimberly. And Paul and Alec.

"Surprise!" they all shouted, then began to cheer.

"I thought you had an emergency to attend," Hannah said quietly to Paul, amid the chaos.

"I made that up. We came here as fast as we could to get ready for the surprise." Paul looked at Hannah. "Are you mad that I lied?"

Hannah smiled. "Are you kidding? It was for a good cause."

There was potato salad, leafy green salad, hot French bread, and steaming chicken legs on the kitchen table. On the side table rested a huge decorated cake for dessert, with "Hooray for Bird and Sunny" written carefully in green icing.

"Who made the cake?" asked Abby. "It's beautiful!"

Pete answered proudly, "My extremely talented wife."

"How did you make it so fast?" asked Hannah, incredulously. "The show's barely over!"

Laura smiled mysteriously. "You'll never get my secrets out of me." Then she leaned over to Bird and whispered, "I made it yesterday. Even if you hadn't done well, it still would've been an achievement to compete."

Bird smiled broadly at Laura, and then, without even thinking, reached out and hugged her. A few days ago, this woman had been a mere acquaintance—someone to smile at or wave to in a store or on the road. Now she felt like family. Bird was grateful for her love and support, and hoped the hug would say that to Laura. Laura hugged her back—a wonderful tight squeeze. Then, she held Bird at arm's length and looked her straight in the eye. "You're a very special girl, Alberta Simms—and you must be starving." Bird swallowed the lump in her throat and nodded.

Everyone took a plate and loaded it up with delicious food. There was much chatter about the show and Leon and Hurricane and Sunny. The house was full of love. Bird felt included and warm inside. She caught sight of Alec across the room. He saw her and grinned. He put down his lemonade and applauded her. Bird blushed crimson. This day could not possibly get better.

There was an impatient knock on the front door. Bird froze. It could only be one person. Bird quietly followed Hannah as she went to open it.

Kenneth Bradley stood on the doorstep.

"Dad!" said Hannah, surprised. "Come on in! We're all in the kitchen."

"Who's here?" asked Kenneth.

Hannah answered uncertainly, "Paul, Alec, Eva, Stuart, Julia, Kimberly, Abby, and the Piersons. And Bird, of course, and me."

"Kimberly's here?"

"Yes."

"Did you ask her mother?"

Hannah furrowed her brow. "She's been with us all day, Dad. Lavinia knows that."

"Nobody asked if Kimberly could come home with you. Lavinia's in the car. She's very angry."

"Oh, no." Hannah looked out and saw Lavinia sitting stiffly in the passenger seat. Hannah waved. Lavinia didn't wave back. "Look, let me go out to the car and invite her in. You go into the kitchen and fill up a plate."

"Actually, we're going out to dinner. I'll tell her that Kimberly is safe. She'll stay here tonight."

From her position in the kitchen doorway, Bird felt herself growing angry on Hannah's behalf. When would people stop taking advantage of her? Of course Hannah wasn't going to say no to her father's request, but he hadn't given her much of a chance.

"Sure, Dad, Kimberly's always welcome here." Bird heard an emptiness—an unhappiness—in her aunt's voice.

"Good." Kenneth rocked back on his heels and smiled mirthlessly. He watched Hannah closely as he said, "Oh, one more thing. Sundancer is sold to a good stable in California. He's being picked up tomorrow morning at nine o'clock."

Hannah's jaw literally dropped open. "Sunny? Sold?"

"Yes. Do you have a problem with that?"

"Of course I have a problem with that."

Kenneth stood ramrod straight. "You have no right." He spoke with a controlled anger. "The horse belongs to Owens Enterprises. You merely train him and board him. I thought that was clear."

"We had a deal. Bird was to ride him in shows, and he was to live here."

"That's what I said. You train and board him. We own him, so we can sell him."

Hannah watched, dumbstruck, as her father calmly walked to his car, blithely taking all his granddaughter's hopes and dreams with him.

A million thoughts raced through Bird's mind. She needed to do something, and she needed to do it now. Hannah had to know about Silver and Leon. It might make a difference.

"Ha...nn...ah?"

Hannah turned quickly, surprised at both Bird's presence and the sound of her voice. "I'm so sorry, Bird. I'm so sorry you had to hear it like that. He's right. They own him, so they have the right to sell him. I don't think there's anything we can do."

Bird had no intention of giving up so easily. She put her hands on Hannah's arms to keep her from walking away. "Leon...dea...d m...eat. Pin. Leon." It was a big effort, and Bird felt exhausted.

Hannah tried to understand. "What about Leon? And dead meat? And what pin?"

Bird sighed. She'd have to think of another way to tell Hannah. But how? Speaking was simply too hard, and it wasn't fair to make Hannah guess. She'd write it down on paper. That's what she'd do. But all at once, she had another thought. Paul! He'd know what she was trying to say! Bird ran into the kitchen and found him, helping himself to another piece of chicken. She grabbed him and pulled him out into the hall.

"What's up, Bird?" he said good-naturedly as he wiped his mouth with a napkin.

Hannah answered hollowly. "My father was just here. I guess Lavinia didn't know where Kimberly was. And then he mentioned, rather casually, that Sunny was sold. Bird was trying to tell me something about Leon and dead meat and a pin, then she ran and got you, I don't know why..."

"Hold on." Paul raised his arms to stop Hannah from continuing. "That's a lot to absorb. As for Kimberly, I know that Lavinia saw her leave with Eva and Stuart and Julia. They waved goodbye to each other."

Bird tapped him impatiently on his arm. Frustration was welling up inside her. Why were they wasting time talking about Kimberly? She put out her hand, palm up. "P...in?"

"Pin?" Paul looked puzzled. "What pin?"

Bird trotted like a horse, then jumped up in the air howling with pain. She put her hand on her back.

"Oh, the pin that was stuck in Hurricane's back."

Bird nodded eagerly, then stuck her hand out again.

"Are you asking if I have it?"

Bird nodded.

"It just so happens that I do." Paul reached into his back pocket and brought out a small tin box. He opened it. Inside was a silver pin, about an inch and a half long, with a tiny diamond embedded in the middle. "I didn't have time to change. Good thing you asked. I'd forgotten all about it."

Bird looked at it closely. Sure enough there was a "sparkle" in the middle, as Hurricane called it. A small diamond. "Le...on's."

Hannah and Paul glanced at each other. "It's Leon's stock pin?" asked Hannah.

Bird nodded. She had no doubt about it.

"Why would he do that to Owens' best horse?" asked Hannah.

"For thirty thousand dollars," asserted Paul. "Bird would have done quite well on Hurricane. He eliminated the competition."

"How could he have done it, though? Logistically, I mean. Bird put her own saddle on Hurricane."

"But the Owens Enterprises saddle pad remained on the horse. Leon could've stuck the pin in the saddle pad when he removed his saddle, then waited for it to stab Hurricane."

Hannah grimaced at the thought.

"It would have moved around under the saddle when Bird was warming up, until it eventually stabbed right into his flesh."

Hannah shook her head. "Do you think Elvin had anything to do with this?"

"It's not his style," answered Paul. "He's a lot of things, but he wouldn't hurt a valuable horse like Hurricane. Elvin would've wanted him to win, anyway. Upped his value."

Bird agreed with Paul's assessment. But there were a few things about Elvin that these two didn't know. She made dog-yapping noises and mimed Sunny spooking at a jump.

"Are you saying that Elvin sent that dog out to ruin your ride?" asked Hannah in disbelief.

Bird put her hand on her heart and nodded forcefully.

Paul pursed his lips. "I wondered if that was his dog."

Bird said, "Bu...zz."

"If Elvin finds out who planted the stock pin, he'll be furious." Paul closed his fingers around the pin. "It'll be easy enough to prove if this is Leon's pin."

Bird had more to say. "S...unn...y d...ead m...eat. Leon."

Paul and Hannah exchanged confused glances. A second later, though, Paul dropped to his knee in front of Bird. "Bird." He spoke with a seriousness in his tone that she was not used to hearing. "Did Leon say that Sunny was dead meat?"

Bird smiled in relief and nodded.

Paul stood again and ran his fingers through his hair. "I'm just guessing here, but I think he meant that Sundancer is dead on paper. In other words, he's been pronounced dead—as I suspected from the first—and they've collected the insurance money for him." Paul began to pace. "Very interesting. And now Kenneth has sold him far, far away to California. For more money. Very interesting. I'm not sure we can prove anything, though. I have no access to the insurance company."

"What a bunch!" exclaimed Hannah. "Elvin doesn't know what Leon's up to and Leon doesn't know what Elvin's up to, and my father doesn't know what either of them are doing, but he trumps them all in the underhanded department! Should we involve the police?" she asked.

Paul considered it. Eventually, he shook his head. "We don't have enough to tell them yet. At this point, we're just speculating."

Bird's stomach flipped and flopped. A moment ago she'd been ready to eat a big meal and finish it off with cake. Now she felt as though she might be sick. It wasn't fair! They were up against dishonest people, and the bad guys were winning. She couldn't let Sunny go to California. She had to do something—and she only had until nine the next morning.

The kitchen door opened and Eva came out. "There you are! Everybody's asking about you."

Hannah said, "We'll be just a minute, Eva. Keep the party going."

Eva put her hands on her hips and looked at Bird. "The guest of honour has to cut the cake. For good luck."

Bird managed a smile for her mother's sake. Eva had no idea how much luck Bird would need.

Paul was still pacing. "I wonder what papers they're using to sell him. If they're using Prince Redwood papers, then we need to prove that they've collected insurance money on his death, and the deal is off. If they're using the passport with Sundancer as his name, then we must prove that Sundancer is really Prince Redwood. I can do that with DNA. Prince Redwood's DNA is on file because he's a registered Canadian Sport Horse. They owe me a favour at Equine Research in Guelph. I'll get a few hairs from Sunny and trot on down to the lab."

"Right now?" Hannah asked.

"There's no time to waste." Paul stopped at the door. "Unless you want him sold, Hannah. Tell me now. It might not be a bad idea."

Hannah looked at Bird, who'd gone rigid. "No, Paul, I don't want him sold. I want him to stay here with Bird. He's her horse."

Bird's face relaxed. She ran out the door with Paul. She was going to help in every way she could.

They turned on the lights in the barn. All the horses leaned out of their stall doors, blinking as their eyes adjusted to the light. Pastor yawned loudly, and Zachary began to relieve his bladder, which sounded like a water bucket overflowing.

Sunny was lying down. He was unhappy about being disturbed. *I've had a long day, Bird girl.*

Don't get up. We need to take a few hairs from your mane.

Why?

For a test. That's all.

What kind of test includes mane hairs?

A DNA test. It'll tell us who your mother and father are.

You want to know who my father is? Now?

Stop asking questions, Sunny. It's no big deal.

Do it fast. I want to get back to sleep.

Bird walked into Sundancer's stall and bent over the resting horse. She quickly pulled four hairs—with roots attached—from the big chestnut's mane and patted his neck. *Thanks, Sunny.*

Go away. I'll see you tomorrow.

Right. See you tomorrow.

Wait. Something's wrong. Tell me, Bird girl.

Nothing's wrong. I'll see you tomorrow.

You're a bad liar, but I'm too tired to argue.

Bird and Paul walked out of the barn after turning off the lights. The hairs were safely folded into a small plastic bag in Paul's pocket.

"Thanks, Bird. You got those hairs much more easily than I could have. He trusts you."

Because I can talk to him, Bird thought. In his own language. Nobody else does that.

"It's almost like you talk to him," said Paul.

Bird was startled. He was a perceptive man.

"I'm going directly to the lab to get this organized as quickly as possible." Paul opened the cab of his truck and jumped in. "I'll be back for Alec in a bit."

Bird pointed to herself then opened her hands and lifted them. She wanted to help.

"Thanks, Bird, but there's nothing for you to do. Don't worry. The DNA test will be done well before the truck arrives."

SHELLEY PETERSON

Paul started up the engine. "You did great today, Bird. You rode brilliantly, plus you proved to us all that Sunny needs to stay here. Get a good night's sleep, and we'll figure it out tomorrow."

Paul Daniels drove away, leaving Bird on the driveway. She felt a presence beside her. It was Alec.

"Bird, I have to say, I was, like, really impressed today. I didn't know you could ride like that. I sure couldn't."

Bird smiled at the handsome boy. She put her hand on her heart.

"I wish you could talk, Bird. I don't know what you think, or anything." He stood on one foot, then the other. "I just wanted to tell you that. That you were great. No matter if you won or not."

Bird woke up after a few hours of sleep. The surprise party was long over and the guests were gone. The dishes had been washed and put away. She tried to drift off again, but she could not get comfortable, no matter which way she tried to position her body or the pillows.

It had been a really nice party, Bird thought. They'd waited for Bird to come back from the barn, and then everyone had sung "For She's a Jolly Good Fellow" while Bird cut the cake. Alec couldn't sing on key, but somehow that made Bird like him even better. And the cake had been delicious. But still, Bird's heart had not been in it. She kept thinking about Sunny. She still was.

Bird looked at her bedside clock. Three minutes past three. Should she run away with Sunny, like the last time? But where? Not to the Piersons. That would be the first place they'd look.

It wasn't fair! Sunny jumped beautifully at the horse show, so he gets punished by being sold? To whom? Hmm. Bird thought back to the man with her grandfather at the show. The one who was in the judge's booth then went to the Owens stalls with him. That must be him. He had a California tan. He seemed like a nice enough man. He probably had no idea that he'd just bought a horse that might kill him. Not on purpose. But still.

Bird could not stay in bed for another minute. She got up and pulled her jeans and T-shirt on over her nightie. Downstairs she crept, step by step, careful not to wake anyone. She took a drink of orange juice, right out of the carton, and put it back.

As she closed the refrigerator door, she noticed a light moving on the driveway. She went to the kitchen window to get a better view. The light was coming from the dashboard of a truck. The truck had no headlights on, and it was pulling a two-horse trailer slowly up the driveway.

Her grandfather had said they were coming at nine in the morning. It was three. Something wasn't right. She slipped out the door and followed the truck to the barn.

The night air was much cooler than the daytime heat. Fall was coming. Soon she wouldn't be able to walk outside barefoot, Bird mused, as her feet felt the moisture of the grass along the driveway. Then again, by fall she hoped her nighttime visits to barns would be a thing of the past. She neared the barn door.

Elvin Wainright got out of the truck. He felt his pockets for something, then pulled a small syringe from his breast pocket. Bird watched, then followed as he entered the barn, feeling his way cautiously in the dark. As he neared Sunny's stall, she flicked on the lights and stepped out of the shadows.

"Bird!" Elvin stammered. "You scared me out of my wits."

Good. Bird darted in front of Elvin and planted herself firmly in front of Sunny's stall. She put her hands on her hips and stared at him.

What's going on, Bird girl?

Nothing. If I can help it.

"The plan has changed. Our client wants Sundancer shipped down sooner. We're getting a head start. Please step aside. Let me do my job."

Bird didn't budge.

The Tall Man. He's here to take me away.

Not if I can stop him.

"Look, Bird, please. Move out of the way. I'm asking you nicely." Despite his words, Elvin's tone was getting less nice.

Bird pointed to Elvin's hand, which still held the syringe. He'd slyly hidden it behind his back.

"He'll need a little Ace for the long ride. To keep him calm." Elvin's patience had just run out. "Bird, I'm telling you to move out of my way. Sundancer's sold. It's a done deal."

He said sold.

Yes.

You didn't tell me.

I found out last night.

And now you plan to stop him?

Yes.

How, Bird girl? He's much bigger than you.

I don't know, Sunny.

Bird tilted her head and continued to stare at Elvin.

"You are a freak show." Elvin grabbed Bird by the shoulders, spun her around, and picked her up. "Don't say you didn't ask for it."

Elvin carried Bird to the dark tack room and tossed her inside. He closed the door firmly as she rolled into the saddle racks and crashed to the floor. Bird struggled to get up. She heard something heavy being dragged across to the tack room door.

She also heard Sunny kicking and whinnying. He was putting up a fight. So could she. Bird staggered to the door and tried to push it open. It wouldn't budge.

Get help, Bird girl! Get help!

I'm locked in here, Sunny!

Just then she remembered the phone. It was hidden in a cupboard behind the horse coolers, to keep the cats from knocking it off the hook. Bird opened the cupboard and picked up the phone. Above it was a list of important numbers. Bob Kleinpaste the farrier, Jim Lyons the hay supplier, Bill the carrot man, Robert McCarron at the Victoria feed store. And at the very top was Paul Daniels, the veterinarian.

Bird couldn't remember the last time she'd used a telephone, but she picked it up and dialed Paul's emergency number, praying that he was on call. It rang once. Bird waited. It rang again. Each second felt like an hour.

"Paul Daniels here." Paul's voice sounded hoarse and groggy.

"Co...me!" Bird whispered.

"Who is this? Speak up, please."

"B...ird. Come! Ba...rn."

"Bird? What happened?" He didn't wait for an answer. "I'll be right there."

Bird hung up, then dialed the house. Hannah picked it up on the first ring. "Hello?"

"Co...me b...arn. N...ow!"

"Bird is that you? Are you all right? You said the barn?" Hannah was clearly disoriented from sleep.

"El...vin."

"Elvin's here? Now? It's three in the morning!"

Bird hung up. She listened. Sunny was making a terrible noise. It sounded like he was choking to death. Bird started pounding on the door.

"Shut up, kid!" yelled Elvin. "I've got enough trouble here with the horse!"

Sunny? Are you all right? Bird tried to reach him.

I'm fine.

What's all that noise?

Does it sound good?

No! It sounds like you're dying.

That's what I'm going for.

Good boy. Paul and Hannah are coming.

Sunny's throaty coughs and chokes and gags got louder. Another horse started to cough. Soon, the entire barnful of horses was snorting and hacking. Even in her desperation, Bird stifled a laugh. She'd done all she could. Now, she simply had to wait.

It didn't take Hannah long to get to the barn. She'd thrown a coat over her nightgown and slid her feet into sneakers. "I saw the lights! What's going on?"

Elvin spun around, fear etched on his face. "Hannah!"

Sunny continued to hack and rattle. The others fell silent.

"What have you done to my horse? He's choking to death!" Hannah rushed to his stall.

"I didn't touch him, I swear! He just started making all these...er...sounds."

"Did you give him anything? What's in that syringe?"

"Ace. I haven't been able to get near him. I promise."

She opened Sunny's stall door and stepped in. "Easy boy." She stroked his throat. "Easy, Sunny." The big horse suddenly stopped choking.

"Look, Hannah," started Elvin uncomfortably. "Look. The client wants him sooner than we thought, so I came..."

"You came to make sure we didn't pull a disappearing act. I wondered if this might happen."

Elvin pulled himself up to full height. "Yes. That's right. No point pretending. The last time we came to get him, Bird ran away with him."

Hannah cleared her throat. "I meant, I wondered if this might happen because this is exactly what you pulled last week. Remember? Leon stole Sunny from the Piersons' barn in the dark of night."

"Let's just say that there's not a lot of trust on either side."

Paul's truck screeched to a halt at the front door of the barn. He jumped out, slammed the door, and ran in. "Hannah! Where's Bird?"

Hannah's eyes opened wide. "Oh, my gosh. I completely forgot!"

Bird started pounding on the tack room door.

"The tack room." Hannah and Paul spoke at the same time. Together they pushed the ancient oak tack trunk away from the door.

"This weighs a ton," said Paul.

Bird opened the door and stepped out. Hannah gasped when she saw the bloody gash on her head.

"What did you do to my niece?" demanded Hannah.

Bird mimed being man-handled and thrown into the tack room.

Hannah spoke sharply to Elvin. "We're pressing charges."

"Let's all calm down. I'm sure we...," Elvin began.

"No!" snapped Hannah. "Let's *not* calm down. You came here in the dark of night to remove a horse from my premises without permission. And you roughed up and injured my niece. I'm calling the police."

Elvin clamped his wrists together, miming handcuffs. "Take me away in chains. Guilty as charged. But look at it my way. We've just sold this horse for three hundred thousand dollars, U.S. I want to have him at my barn, under my care, until he gets on the trailer tomorrow."

"Why didn't you simply ask me?" Hannah was not placated. "Why come like a thief in the night?"

"And there's no excuse, ever, to hurt a child," added Paul. Bird was sitting bravely on the oak tack trunk. Paul had already swabbed the cut with antibacterial soap, and was applying antibiotic ointment and a bandage.

"I'm sorry. Look, I'll leave now. I'll be back for Sundancer at nine. I would appreciate it if we can forget all about what happened tonight."

Hannah glared icily at Elvin. "I make no promises. And

Elvin, Sundancer will be under guard for the remainder of the night. Don't try anything stupid."

Elvin tried to manage a smile, but it looked strange. "Don't worry, I won't. By the way, I need Sundancer's passport. It goes with him."

Paul looked up from his patient. "The passport? You're using Sundancer as his name?"

"Yes. It only makes sense. That's the name he's been showing under."

"But surely his papers say Prince Redwood?"

Elvin turned to go. "Leave the details to us. And Hannah, send the bill for board and training directly to me. I'll pay it promptly and add a little extra to compensate for tonight."

Stunned, Paul, Bird, and Hannah watched as Elvin turned the truck and trailer around and drove out the lane. This time the lights of the truck were on.

19

DANCER

I like to be scratched under the chin.

BIRD HAD MADE HER DECISION. She would remain with Sundancer for the rest of the night, and nobody was going to talk her out of it. She had no idea what would happen in the morning, but each time she thought of Sunny leaving she felt a sharp pang in her chest.

Hannah and Paul went into the house to make coffee. They decided to take turns guarding the barn with Bird while the other napped.

Bird got herself comfortable in a nest of hay and rested against the wall of Sunny's stall, tucked into a soft horse blanket. Sunny was content. After the Elvin incident, he was happy for Bird's comforting presence.

Thank you, Bird girl.

For what?

For using your voice. You got help for me.

I did, didn't I?

That was good.

I surprised myself. I haven't used the telephone since I was six.

Maybe you can talk now. To humans, I mean.

Maybe. It hurts, though.

Why?

To answer that question, I'd need all night.

As it happens, that's exactly the amount of time I've got.

Bird paused for a very long time while she gathered her thoughts. Sunny took a sip of water from his bucket and munched some hay. He circled a couple of times, then lay down in the wood shavings beside her.

Go ahead, Bird girl. Tell me your story.

Bird patted his long neck and took a deep breath. She wasn't sure what she was feeling, and she didn't know how to explain. She'd have to feel her way through.

I was six and a half, and I just stopped talking. Period. Overnight. Sometimes not speaking is inconvenient, but it's amazing how well a person can get along. People react in different ways. Some think I'm crazy, or stupid, or willful. It doesn't bother me much, mostly. People don't talk to me, either, but I know what they're thinking. And they don't often say what they mean anyway, so what's the point? The funny thing is, when I do talk, nobody listens.

Sunny continued to crunch on hay. *Okay, but other humans speak. Why not you?*

I've been trying to figure that out. I think it started with my mother. Sometimes I wonder if it started with my father. He didn't even want to know I existed! But that can't be it. He didn't know me so I can't take it personally, right? He didn't want to know about any baby, period. If he knew me and rejected me it would be different. That takes me back to my mother. She heard only what she wanted to hear. She saw only what suited her. She liked to paint pretty pictures in her head and make them real. She forced them to happen.

If it wasn't perfect, it scared her?

Exactly. And I wasn't perfect. I wasn't what she wanted from the very beginning. I look like my father, who she doesn't want to remember, and she could never understand my relationship with animals. It made me different from other kids—my friends teased me when I told them I could talk to the dog. I didn't care—it was their loss—but it totally embarrassed her. She wasn't able to force me into her picture. I tried, Sunny. I tried hard to fit into her world, but I couldn't.

Bird wiped her eyes. She tried to take a deep breath, but it caught in quick gasps. *I smiled and laughed like she wanted me to, but I was faking and she knew it. The clothes she got me to wear made me feel stupid. I hated how she wanted me to be, and how she made me feel.*

Bird paused for a moment, remembering. *Mom always had boyfriends. And it was very important to keep the boyfriends happy. Even if they were creepy. Like Bill. I could read his mind and I knew what he was thinking about me. It was disgusting. So I told Mom and she didn't believe me. She said I was making it up. That I was a liar. She was really, really angry. And whenever I tried to explain what our animals were saying, she freaked out. You see, every time I said something important, Sunny, she told me I was lying. We grew further and further apart until we hated being near each other.*

Sunny yawned and stretched his neck. *So you hated her.*

It's not just that I hated her. I hated me for hating her, and I hated that I cared so much that she hated me! Then one day, it was like I didn't have the energy to speak. It wasn't really a decision or anything. It was just...easier. And it worked in a way, because Bill got mad and then he left. But then Mom hated me even more. Bird slumped against the stall wall, tears rolling down her cheeks.

Sunny chewed on hay. *That was a long time ago, Bird girl. She doesn't hate you now.*

Bird looked at Sundancer. His remark caught her by surprise. *You're right. She doesn't hate me now. She's trying hard to learn to love me. But really, what's more important is that I don't hate her any more. It still hurts, but I understand more now, and I can forgive her.*

Sundancer put his nose on her arm. *Understand what, Bird girl?*

Understand about my mother. She has a hollowness inside, Sunny, from how she grew up. Same as Hannah, but it shows in different ways. My grandfather is not a nice man, and he wasn't a good father. I never thought about that until lately. I mean, I never thought about why Mom is how she is. What her life was like when she was a kid. I only cared about what she was, how she acted, how she treated me, what she thought of me, and why I mattered so little to her. But mostly I thought about how I hated her.

Hate is fun for a short time, Bird girl, then it gets very wearying.

I know what you mean, Sunny. It's an exhausting emotion. It takes away energy. It took away my ability to speak.

Yet you speak to animals, Bird girl. No other human that I've ever met can do that.

Some must, Sunny, but don't you see? That's my biggest problem! That's what makes me weird.

Do you wish you couldn't?

No! It's my biggest problem, but it's also my greatest skill. I don't know how other people get along without it. If people just tried to communicate with animals, they'd understand more about humans. About how confusing we are...to animals, but to other humans as well. Animals are direct. They're not deceptive or manipulative, and they don't have secrets. I prefer them to people, for the most part. Bird found that Sunny's question had distracted her. She felt calmer now.

I was messed up by humans, too, just like you.

I know. But we survived, didn't we? We're both survivors. We did what we had to do. I guess for me that meant being quiet for a while.

Sunny took a bite of hay. *I started hurting people before they hurt me.*

I know that, Sunny. But most people still don't understand why you do the things you do.

Some days are bad days and some days are good days.

You have fewer bad days now.

True. It's because you explain things to me, and my troubles go away.

Partly. But you had to be willing to let go of your hatreds and fears.

You helped me do that, Bird girl.

And you helped me, too, Sunny. More than you know.

Bird thought about the last few weeks—her school troubles, her mother's visit, her grandfather's tricks and schemes. Would she have been able to make it through without Sunny? She doubted it. If she made his troubles go away, then he did the same for her. When she was on his back—or even just near him—she felt strong and capable and loved. She felt like she could do anything—forgive her mother, forgive herself, even talk. She leaned forward and rubbed his ears.

And now, I need to take my own advice.

What are you talking about?

You were willing to let go of your fears, Sunny. Now, I have to let go of mine.

Hannah had not slept well. Taking shifts on watch with Paul, the time evaporated into stress-filled thin air.

Stuart showed up at the house for breakfast at eight thirty. Without knocking, he walked right into the kitchen with a cheerful smile. "Good morning, Hannah! Lovely Sunday."

Hannah sat alone, hunched over the table. She peered at him over her coffee mug through puffy eyes. "Morning, Stuart. You almost live here, lately."

Stuart nodded happily. "Seems I do. Is the beautiful Eva up yet?"

"Yes. She's shaving her legs."

"Wonderful. Wonderful." Stuart whistled as he poured himself a coffee. He peeled a banana and crammed a day-old blueberry muffin into his mouth.

"Help yourself to coffee, Stuart. And please, get yourself something to eat." Hannah didn't bother to conceal the sarcasm in her voice. "Tell me, Stuart. Why exactly are you so happy today?"

Stuart winked at her. "Hannah, all will be revealed. I have a surprise guest. He should be here any minute. Trust me, today will be a very happy day for us all."

"You're proposing to Eva?"

"Great idea! I think I may. It might be rushing things a bit, but she is the most perfect woman I've ever met. But first, I have a little surprise."

Hannah steeled herself. "Stuart, I can't imagine that you didn't notice, but I'm in a terrible mood. Sundancer is leaving in half an hour and Bird will be wretched. Surprises are not welcome today."

"This one will be."

There was a rap on the door.

"My guest!" Stuart opened the kitchen door with a flourish. Standing there was a sturdy man of about fifty years of age. He had short-cropped greying hair and a friendly smile. He wore jeans, a plaid shirt, and workboots, which he leaned over to remove.

"Don't worry about your boots, the place is a mess," said Hannah, too tired to rise.

"Hannah, this is my brother-in-law, Mack Jones. Mack, meet Hannah Bradley."

Hannah took another look at the man. "Mack Jones? Not the police chief?" She found herself standing.

Mack nodded. "I'm in my weekend clothes. Stuart explained your little problem and I think I can help."

"Help? Really? How?"

Stuart put a finger to his lips. "All will be revealed."

"Stuart, you're driving me crazy!" Hannah snapped.

Eva appeared at the hall door. "Hannah! Don't talk to Stuart that way."

"Eva, my darling!" said Stuart. "It doesn't bother me one bit. Have you gotten rid of all unwanted hair?"

"Stuart! What's gotten into you? And who is this?"

"Eva, it's time you got to know my family. I'd like you to meet my brother-in-law, Mack Jones. Mack, this is Eva Simms. You might remember her. She's Hannah's sister."

Mack smiled warmly and put out his hand for Eva to shake. "I certainly do. It's been a while, but you look exactly the same."

"Thank you, and I'm pleased to meet you," said Eva, returning his smile. "Again."

"I asked Mack to come this morning. To meet you, of course, but he may be able to help."

"Help? How?" asked Eva.

Hannah and Stuart said in unison, "All will be revealed."

Eva gave them a perplexed look, lifted her eyebrows, then turned to get some coffee.

Paul Daniels entered the kitchen and went right to the coffee pot. He'd driven to Guelph for the DNA results, and then checked on the situation at the barn. "Hi, Stuart, hello Mack," he said as he passed by.

"Hi, Paul. How's it going?"

"Fine, with the help of a cup of fresh coffee. What brings you to Saddle Creek this fine Sunday morning, Mack?"

"My brother-in-law," Mack answered.

Paul poured his coffee, then slowly turned to face Mack and Stuart. "Good idea, Stuart. Why didn't I think of it?"

"Think of what?" asked Eva.

"What are you going to do?" Paul asked Mack.

"All will be revealed," chimed Eva, Hannah, and Stuart. They burst out laughing. Now it was Paul who looked confused.

"Don't worry, Paul. We're all in the dark except Stuart and

Mack." Hannah gave him a reassuring smile.

"Where's Bird?" asked Eva.

Paul answered, "In the barn. She's asleep beside Sunny. Don't wake her, she's been up most of the night."

"Poor girl," said Mack. "This must be very tough on her."

The rumbling sound of a big diesel engine interrupted their conversation. They all knew what it meant.

"It's here." Stuart was the one who said it aloud.

Up the driveway rolled the biggest equine transport truck that any of them had seen. It was pure white, with enormous red and white Canadian flags emblazoned on the sides. The jolly driver waved as he hauled it past the house toward the barn.

"Where is he going to turn it around?" Hannah murmured aloud.

Eva gasped, "It's bigger than a moving truck!"

"It's a recreational vehicle for horses," said Stuart. "A barn on wheels!"

"How many horses does it carry?" wondered Paul.

Hannah answered, "Enough to clean out my barn."

"Let's go," said Mack, opening the kitchen door. He held it for Hannah and Eva.

Out they went to face whatever must be faced. Only Stuart seemed confident. "Good morning!" he called to the driver.

"Good morning!" the driver answered with enthusiasm. "Great day for a drive. The weather's perfect from here to Utah. Little weather there, but the system might have moved by the time we pass through. Nothing we can't handle with a truck this size. I'm Andy, by the way."

Paul introduced himself and everyone else, then said, "We have to wait for the owners, Andy. They've got the travelling papers."

"Good, good."

"Can I get you a coffee?" asked Hannah.

"No, no. I'm in good shape, thanks."

A black Cadillac stopped beside the transport. Out stepped Elvin and Kenneth. Both men looked stern and businesslike. Kenneth, dressed formally in a suit and tie, handed a brown manilla envelope to Andy.

"Papers are in order. Stamped this morning by my vet. Let's get Sundancer aboard." Kenneth sniffed impatiently.

Andy smiled broadly. "Sure, sure. I'm ready when you are."

Elvin turned to Hannah. "Did you sign over Sundancer's passport?"

"I've got it in the tack room. I'll get it now."

Stuart Gilmore smiled at Kenneth as Hannah made her way to the barn. "Mr. Bradley, I'd like you to meet my brother-in-law, Mack Jones. Mack, this is Mr. Kenneth Bradley."

Kenneth's face dropped. "Mack! I didn't see you." He immediately became very charming. "It's been a long time, and I've never seen you in civilian clothes."

"No problem, Kenneth." Mack turned to Elvin. "Elvin Wainright, is it? Remember me? It's been a while since I've seen you, as well. Things good?"

Elvin's eyes darted from face to face. "Nobody said anything about bringing in the police."

"Oh, don't worry. This has nothing to do with your assaulting Bird last night." Stuart consoled him. "He's my brother-in-law. I invited him over to meet Eva and have a cup of coffee."

Elvin was about to say something but thought better of it and clamped his mouth shut. Wet patches appeared on his blue cotton shirt.

In the barn, Hannah got Sunny's passport from her tack room and went over to his stall. She looked over the door. Bird was curled up in a ball in the far corner of the stall, asleep in a nest of hay. Sunny stood right beside her, between Bird and the door. Exactly like mares do with their newborn foals, to protect them from the world. He lifted his head and looked at Hannah squarely.

Bird's eyes opened. "Hannah," she said clearly.

"Bird, you're awake. They've come."

"I kn...ow." Bird stretched and yawned. "I heard the truck. It sou...nds huge." She rose to her feet and brushed herself off. She put her arms around Sunny's neck and stood quietly with him.

I don't want you to go.

I'll escape, Bird girl. I'll run back.

California is a long, long way away.

Your mother came here from there. I can, too.

She flew in an airplane.

Like a bird?

Yes, Sunny. Like a big bird.

Like you, Bird girl. You can fly.

No, Sunny.

Yes, you can. I heard you talk right now to Hannah. If you can talk to humans, you can fly. Nobody can stop you now.

Bird's heart swelled with love for this animal. His confidence in her was overwhelming.

I feel empty inside that I must leave. Hollow.

You must behave there, Sunny, or they will hurt you to try and fix you.

I know. Come down and take me back home. Soon—I can't behave for long.

I'll save all my money. I'll buy you back and bring you home.

I know you will, Bird girl.

Hannah stood beside the stall. Her niece's cheeks were wet with tears. The gelding's head was cradled in her arms and his ears flopped forward.

If her father could see this—really see it and understand it—Hannah thought, then he would never send Sundancer away. Not for any amount of money. Hannah knew, however, from a lifetime of experience, that Kenneth's heart was two sizes too small. Like the Grinch who stole Christmas.

She shook her head sadly and left Sunny and Bird alone.

Outside again, Hannah heard Mack Jones ask, "Kenneth, which horse are you selling?"

"Oh, a real troublemaker. We've had problems with him since the day he was born."

"Really? Well then, it's good to get rid of him. What's his name?"

"Ah, well." Kenneth shot a glance at Elvin. "Sundancer. Bird's done well with him. Won the Grand Classic Event yesterday."

"Wow. Big time." Mack nodded. "At the Haverford Fair."

Kenneth nodded, too.

"What's Sundancer's parentage? Is he one of yours?"

"Yes. California Dreamin' out of Princess Narnia."

"Well bred. Interesting that he's going to California. He's not just California Dreamin'."

Everybody laughed at Mack's joke, nobody louder than Kenneth.

"You had another horse of that breeding, didn't you." Mack stated this rather than asked. "By the name of Prince Redwood."

Kenneth nodded. He gave Elvin a warning look as he clenched and unclenched his fists.

Mack continued. "I checked into it. I spoke directly to Henry Irving. Irving Insurance paid out a quarter of a million when he was destroyed last month. Lot of dough."

Paul and Hannah exchanged astonished glances. This was news to them. Hannah's stomach knotted up. Stuart smiled happily.

Again Kenneth nodded. "Where is this going, Mack?" he asked as jovially as he could. "Irving insures a lot of horses. Some worth far more than that."

"He was telling me," Mack scratched his head and took his time, "he was telling me that they never requested an independent veterinarian's evaluation. Never even examined the body. Odd."

"That's Irving's problem," snapped Kenneth, then quickly regained his composure. "The body was taken by the dead stock removers and incinerated. All authorized by Irving. If you want an inquest, it's too late."

Mack's eyebrows lifted. "Not really. I've come to check Sundancer's papers. Before he's out of our jurisdiction."

"This is highly irregular." Kenneth brushed the sweat from his forehead. "I don't need to comply."

"If everything is proper you should have no problem."

Kenneth considered his options. "Go ahead, look at the papers. They're in order. I don't know what you expect to find."

The driver handed the manilla envelope to Mack. Mack opened it and removed the travelling papers signed and stamped by a veterinarian, which described the horse and his markings, and included proof of a Coggins test and inoculations. This was all in order. In a different envelope were the registration papers.

Mack read aloud. "Sundancer, male, date of birth May 29th, 1998. Sire, California Dreamin'; Dam, Princess Narnia."

"There. You see?" said Kenneth brusquely.

Mack pulled another document from his pocket. "I just happen to have the death certificate for Prince Redwood in my pocket. Let me see. Date of birth May 29th, 1998. Two horses born on the same day, with the same dam?"

"Simple. She had twins. Now let's get the horse out of the barn and get him on the road. It's a long drive."

Mack smiled humourlessly. "There's no need to rush anything. I have a few questions. The registration document for Sundancer is dated last week." He held up the breeding papers. "Now, why would that be? Unless you had the name changed from Prince Redwood to Sundancer?"

"We lost the original and had it reissued."

"Of course. Happens all the time."

"Yes, it does!" Kenneth had no patience left. "I've had enough of this. If you have a reason to detain Sundancer, get a warrant. I'll call my lawyer." He reached into his jacket pocket and pulled out his cellphone.

It was time. "Perhaps that would be a good idea," said Paul Daniels. "Because Sundancer's DNA matches Prince Redwood's. He's not a twin, he's the same horse. Dr. Samuels was the attending vet, and he confirmed last night that it was a normal, single birth."

"You might find this interesting, too." Paul continued to speak, casually brushing some dust off his sleeve. "This horse's DNA is not a match with the declared sire's. Prince Redwood— or Sundancer, if you wish—was not sired by California Dreamin.'"

Kenneth Bradley was dumbfounded. "That's not possible. Not possible." He turned to Elvin. "How is this possible?"

Elvin blushed a crimson red.

"There is no way that California Dreamin' could be Sundancer's sire." Paul produced his DNA report and handed it to Mack Jones.

Mack looked at it and sighed. "This gets more and more complicated. Where does this leave us now?"

Just then they heard a loud whinny. Everyone turned to look.

A big chestnut horse was trotting up the driveway. His coat was glossy and fine. His legs were long and strong. His head was held proud and his manner was regal. There was no question who this was. This was Dancer.

Abby Malone rode the old jumping champion with pride. He strutted past the house like he owned the place.

Julia ran out the kitchen door, shouting, "Abby! Hey, Abby! Is that Dancer? I've only ever seen pictures of him before!" Dancer snorted and shook his silky mane. Abby nodded and

waved happily as they continued trotting on toward the barn.
Julia followed at a run.

"Well, I'll be a monkey's uncle," Elvin whistled under his
breath. "It's the king of them all."

And a king he looked. Every inch of him from nose to tail.

Abby halted Dancer at the stable door. She took her feet
from the stirrups and slid down to the ground. "Good boy." She
patted his neck. Dancer nickered softly.

Abby looked from one person to another, then stated, "I
wanted Sundancer to meet his father before he left." She smiled,
enjoying the stunned reaction all around.

"This is preposterous!" exclaimed Kenneth Bradley. "You
should know better than to say a thing like that without proof."

"I took the liberty of contacting the Canadian Sport Horse
Association. They have DNA records of all registered horses on
file."

"Do you have Dancer's record with you?" asked Paul.

Abby grinned. "I just happen to have it right here." Abby
pulled a paper out of her back pocket and passed it to Paul. "Our
friend Jewel from the horse show was extremely helpful." She
looked at Hannah with a smile.

Paul read it carefully, and checked back and forth between
Dancer's and Sundancer's tests. Two minutes passed.

"It could very possibly be a match. I'll have to send it to
Guelph to be sure." Paul handed the two reports to Mack Jones.

Dancer whinnied loudly. His deep neigh echoed throughout
the neighbouring fields and farmland. All the horses on the
farm returned his call. For a moment the air was full to overflowing with equine communication.

Then, there was an answering whinny from the barn, equally
powerful, but slightly different in tone. Sundancer, led by Bird,
stepped out into the sunshine.

The similarities were undeniable. The shape of the heads;

broad at the forehead and full at the jaw, with good-sized ears and intelligent eyes. Their heights were comparable. Their coats were of an identical fiery copper hue. Their legs were shapely and correct, with strong, black feet. Their tails were set at the same angle.

It was the attitude, however, that was most remarkable. Both horses had the same haughty confidence and looked down at the people with the same arrogant cock of the head.

Dancer, you are a legend. My name is Bird.

You're the girl who talks to horses.

Yes.

I'm pleased to meet you. We've all heard tell of you. Dancer bowed to Bird with respect.

Thank you. Bird was touched. She lowered her head modestly.

Sundancer stepped forward. With arched necks, the two chestnuts introduced themselves. Sundancer bowed deeply to his regal sire and stayed down. Dancer then returned the compliment to his talented son.

There was no doubt left in anyone's mind. The sight of these two magnificent horses bowing in unison was conclusive. They were surely of the same blood.

Mack Jones spoke. "Do we need more proof?" He gathered up all the papers and documents. "Andy, we'll not need your services today, but send Owens Enterprises an invoice for your time."

Mack took a notepad and pen out of his pocket and continued: "Who rightfully owns this horse is unclear at the moment since he has no valid papers. There are penalties for that—and even graver consequences for people who commit insurance fraud. Kenneth Bradley, Elvin Wainright, you should contact your lawyers. Once we sort out this mess, you'll need them."

Elvin and Kenneth stood together. Silent.

Mack Jones continued, "I'm appalled that after collecting two hundred and fifty thousand dollars in insurance for the death of this animal, you would have the gall to sell him for three hundred thousand more." Mack shook his head sadly. "It's greed that tempts people, and greed that catches them. Kenneth Bradley, you, of all people, should have learned that lesson by now."

"Sundancer. Son of Dancer." Abby smiled at Bird. "You sure gave him the right name, Bird."

Bird nodded shyly. She softly said, "Thank you, Ab...by."

"Bird!" Abby saw how Bird blushed at her reaction. She decided to let it go. Bird had chosen to speak to her. She was glad. That was enough.

Hannah spoke as she gave Bird's shoulder a supportive squeeze. "The name fits perfectly, doesn't it? Tell us, Abby, how you figured this all out."

Paul nodded. He was about to ask the same thing.

"One of Owens' ex-grooms is a friend of mine. Yesterday he let it slip that Dancer actually sired this foal." Abby looked at Elvin and Kenneth. "I'm not telling who it is, so don't look at me like that."

Mack said, "Keep talking, Abby. This is important."

"I'll start at the beginning. You know that the Jameses could never keep Dancer fenced at Hogscroft. He'd jump out in the night, and he'd be back in the morning. Nobody the wiser. He never caused any trouble, aside from the obvious. Mares got in foal." She stroked Dancer's sleek neck.

"You had a Dancer foal, didn't you?" Mack prodded.

"Two. Both times were unscheduled breedings, if you know what I mean." She smiled. "And Moonie's two fillies are fabulous. I could never have afforded the stallion fees. That's why there have never been any complaints. Dancer's the best stallion around."

"So what you're telling us is that Dancer impregnated Princess Narnia on the Owens property?" Mack asked. "Dancer came to the Owens stables?"

Abby grinned. "Yes, exactly that. There sure is irony."

Everyone nodded. They knew the story. Hilary James, whom everyone knew as Mousie, had won every competition she'd entered on Dancer. Samuel Owens noticed and wanted to own him. When Hilary James refused to sell, he'd become obsessed. When he couldn't own Dancer, he tried to kill him. Owens underwent treatment for mental instability, but when he was released, his need for revenge caused chaos in the area until he literally self-destructed at the opening night of the local theatre.

"Owens must have been elated to have a Dancer baby," Mack stated.

"He never knew," Abby asserted. "According to my source, his staff knew, but they were too afraid to admit that it could have happened under their watch. So they trumped up the story about Princess Narnia and California Dreamin'. Forged the papers. Paid people off."

Kenneth stared at Elvin. "Is this true?"

Elvin looked like he might have a heart attack. His face was red and his eyes bulged. He blurted, "Mr. Owens would have gone crazy if he thought that a stallion had access to his stable. He would've fired everyone with no warning, no severance, no references."

"Even for a Dancer foal?" asked Hannah.

"Nobody wanted to take the chance," whined Elvin. "Would you? Surely you must remember? That man was a maniac. Certifiable lunatic."

"When did it happen, Abby, this immaculate conception?" Paul wanted to know.

"Another irony. It happened the night Dancer was held prisoner on the Owens property. Owens ordered his man, Chad Smith, to steal Dancer from Hogscroft, remember? They dyed him black and called him Spirit?"

"I'd forgotten." Paul shook his head. "Oh, the hoops he went through."

"Well, Dancer knew there was a mare in season, and he found her. Jumped right into her stall and out again. You know they can smell them two miles away."

"And will jump any fence along the way," added Paul. "So how long ago was that?"

"Eight years ago, when you count the eleven-month gestation period."

Mack nodded and put away his notebook. "Thank you very much, Abby. You've solved an intriguing riddle." He glared at Kenneth. "Sundancer stays here. The courts will decide on his custody. And Irving Insurance will be notified immediately. Kenneth Bradley and Elvin Wainright, contact your lawyers. You will not be leaving the country any time soon."

Stuart grinned like a boy. "What did I tell you, Hannah? Today turned out to be a very happy day." Then he dropped down on one knee at Eva's feet and took her hand. "Eva, will you marry me?"

20

NINE A.M.

All my troubles are behind me.

THE FIRST DAY OF SCHOOL was beautifully bright and clear. The sky was blue, the lawns were green, and flowers of red and white and pink grew lushly in the gardens around the old red brick building.

It was almost nine o'clock, just before the bell, and Julia, Kimberly, and Bird met as planned on the wide stone steps. They all gave each other a big hug.

"Look at you, Bird," exclaimed Kimberly as she hugged her friends. "Your haircut is too wicked for words. I love your jeans and jacket! And that colour blue is perfect on you."

"Tha...nks, Kimby. You lo...ok great, too." Bird felt happy from the top of her head to the tips of her toes. When Eva dropped her and Julia off, she had told them how much she loved them and how proud she was of them. And she meant it— Bird knew that. More importantly, Bird was ready, finally, to let Eva be her mother. After all this time, she thought she could trust Eva enough to allow her to try. And if Eva was willing to try, then she should try, too. It looked possible, even probable, that they could truly become a family.

Eva would never understand Bird's ability to communicate with animals, but that was okay. Most people didn't. Bird would keep her secret. It was better off left between her and the animals.

But the fact that words were beginning to come freely from her lips whenever she wanted was absolutely thrilling. She fit in, for the first time that she could remember. Sunny was right, Bird thought. Now I can fly.

Kimberly was still gushing happily. "Julia, your hair is sooo pretty! I totally love that clip. You'll be the 'it' girl of your grade!"

"Stop, Kimberly. No, no, keep going!" Julia laughed cheerfully. "You look great, too. And your sweater even matches your new cast." Kimberly wore a bright-green cast on her healing arm. A few more weeks and it would come off.

"Pas...tor will be glad when you can ri...de again," said Bird.

"You think? Well, when I do, I'm going to be nicer to him. He's a good horse for me."

Bird nodded. "I th...ink so, too."

Two boys Bird and Kimberly's age walked past them, up the stone steps toward the old double doors. One had dark hair and the other sandy blond. One did a double take when he noticed Bird and nudged the other.

"Bird, don't look. Alec Daniels and Josh Prokosh are looking at you!"

Bird blushed.

Julia took at good look at them. "They're both hot, Bird. I never noticed how cute Alec is. And Josh...if I was just a little older..."

"They're still looking at you, Bird." Kimberly took a quick peek at Josh then turned away before he caught her looking.

"I kn...ow," said Bird shyly. "I've had a cr...ush on Alec for...ever." As soon as the words were out of her mouth, Bird gasped. She couldn't believe she'd just admitted it! It was a hazard of being able to talk. She'd have to remember that and be more careful.

"Ooooh!" Kimberly and Julia teased her.

"Maybe he'll be in your class, Bird," Julia wished for her sister.

"I'll find out soo...n." Bird felt shivers of expectation and fear mingling up and down her spine. Her stomach clenched, then settled.

"I'm so glad that I'm back here again this year," sighed Kimberly, looking at the old familiar doors the boys had just entered. "It feels so good. I didn't like CCS."

"Because there are no boys?" Julia asked impishly.

"For sure," answered Kimberly, laughing. "But mostly because the girls all looked at me like I was so beneath them. My mother couldn't afford it anyway—especially since she and your grandfather broke up."

"Was Gramps going to pay?" asked Julia.

"I guess," answered Kimberly. "He wanted me to board there. I don't think he wanted me around. Not a problem now!"

"I'm gl...ad you're here," said Bird slowly. It still took some effort to talk, but less and less. "I need help making fr...iends. You g...uys are it."

"Stick with us and you'll go places," joked Julia. "What am I saying? I just got here! I don't have any friends either!"

"Three is the perfect size for a beginners clique." Kimberly struck a haughty pose and flipped back her hair. "We won't let anybody in, then everybody will want to be our friend."

"That's just about it."

The three girls turned to see who'd spoken. Stuart Gilmore, the school principal, had joined them. He radiated hearty optimism.

"Welcome, ladies, to your first day of school. It's going to be a fabulous year at Forks of the Credit, I can just feel it."

"Tha...nk you," Bird spoke seriously. "For let...ting me come back."

"It's a whole new ball game, Bird. This was a special summer for you. You're still the unique, remarkable young lady that you've always been, but now there are no restrictions to your growth."

Bird glowed with warmth. "I never thought it would h...appen."

"Just don't expect special treatment because I'll be your step-father," Stuart said proudly. He smiled and gave them a wink.

The school bell rang—long, loud, and harsh. Bird looked over to the bushes, where a small coyote hid from the crowd.

I'll be okay, Cody. You don't have to stay.

I want to, Bird girl. I have nothing else to do today.

Thanks. See you later.

The three girls excitedly picked up their bags, gave each other another quick hug for good luck, and ran inside. Soon they would discover what this new school year had in store.

At the kitchen table at Saddle Creek Farm, Eva and Hannah sat chatting over coffee.

"Eva, I didn't think I could last three days when you first came to visit. Now, I wish you and Julia and Bird could stay here forever."

Eva smiled gratefully. "You know we can't."

"I know." Hannah fought back an unwelcome rush of emotion. "I can't believe Bird won't be living here any more."

"Hannah, I'll never in a million years be able to thank you." Eva plucked a tissue from its box and gently wiped a tear from Hannah's cheek. "You took her in when I couldn't cope. I was selfish and self-absorbed, I see that now. I hope you can forgive me."

"Of course I can." Hannah was sincere. "Let's make a toast. To us. May we always accept and understand each other."

Eva held up her cup, and Hannah clinked her cup with Eva's. "Let's drink to love, without judgement."

Thoughtfully, Eva took a drink of coffee. She said, "Stuart and I are looking at houses. Three bedrooms, with a good-sized yard. Something cozy and manageable, but not too crowded for the girls. We were thinking that the girls and I would live there until Stuart and I got married, then he'd sell his house and move in with us."

"Have you seen the right thing yet?"

"That depends on whether or not you want us close by."

"I do!" Hannah spoke earnestly. "Sunny's here, so Bird needs to be close or you'll be driving her all the time. And Julia's doing so well with her lessons that soon she'll want a horse of her own. I want them—and you, Eva—to stay a big part of my life."

Eva looked relieved and happy. She took her sister's hand. "Then we've found the right house. It's just down the road."

"This road? Not the Stevenson house?"

Eva nodded.

"It's perfect!"

The sisters embraced.

At nine o'clock that same morning, Laura and Pete had just finished their breakfast at the sunny kitchen table. Laura rose to clear the dishes.

Pete put down his newspaper and looked at his wife. "Says here that Leon Parish won the International class at Spruce Meadows."

"He's a good rider, Pete."

"Yes, he is. Shame that Sundancer banged him up like that." His eyes twinkled.

Laura chuckled as she rinsed the dishes.

"I'm glad things worked out for Bird." Pete was thoughtful. "She's got some mystery to her. Some magic. The way she relates to horses. All animals, really. I'm glad she'll get to keep Sundancer after all."

"It's the right thing," said Laura firmly. "That horse was miserable before he came to her, and he would be miserable if he had to go."

"I had a horse like Sundancer once."

"I remember that horse. Piperson. He scared everyone."

"I just couldn't figure him out. I thought he was mean. Mentally ill. Finally, I put him down for safety's sake. If Bird had been around then, she could've straightened him out."

"You had no choice, Pete. You couldn't have sold him; someone might've gotten killed."

Pete nodded his agreement. "A horse can suffer a fate much worse than being humanely euthanized. That old adage goes, 'When they're in the ground, you know where they are.' They're not starving or dying of thirst. They're not freezing or being eaten alive by bugs. Or exposed to the hot sun without shelter. And they're not being abused by some so-and-so who doesn't know what else to do with a 'bad' horse."

"You still feel bad about it, don't you Pete? Well, you shouldn't."

"I know. I did the right thing with Piperson. I'm just saying that without Bird, that would have been Sundancer's fate as well."

"You're right."

Pete nodded sadly. "But so many times—so very many times—I wished he could talk to me."

Dr. Paul Daniels drove his truck down the gravel road. It was only nine in the morning and he'd already been at three barns, dealing with everything from thrush to a milk rash on a month-old foal's bottom.

He was leaning forward to call his office on his portable phone when he noticed something small and brown and furry on the road ahead. As he got closer, it moved. He pulled over to the side of the road and got out.

"Well, I'll be." It was a brown puppy of mixed heritage, only three or four months old. His chest and feet were white, and his tail had a little white tip. His short, floppy ears shook nervously as he looked up at Paul with huge, fear-filled eyes.

"Somebody threw you out of a car, didn't they, boy?" This

was not the first time he'd found an unwanted animal on a country road. Paul scooped him up carefully, and the little dog yelped with pain. He carried him to his truck and gently examined him. Broken leg. Sore ribs, maybe cracked.

Paul gave him an injection of antibiotic, and one of pain medication. He put the broken bone in place and fashioned a splint.

"There you go. Feel a bit better?" The puppy licked his face. "A dear friend of mine lost her dog not so long ago. Her name is Hannah. You won't be expected to replace Hector, but you'll make her feel better. And I'll tell you a secret. She's the woman I'm going to marry."

He whistled cheerfully as he drove up the lane to Saddle Creek Farm.

Kenneth Bradley was angry. "What kind of a lawyer are you?"

"The honest kind. You'll have to find someone else to appeal your case."

"Are you crazy? I can make you rich, Earl. What's your problem?"

"You asked me to falsify documents. My assistant will show you out."

Kenneth Bradley rose to his full height. "Do you have any idea of what I can do to you?"

Earl Maddox rose, too, and looked him in the eye. "Threats will not make me change my mind. You are a man who believes that laws were made for other people, Mr. Bradley, but the evidence sinks you, and no amount of money can fix that."

Kenneth Bradley smiled the smile that always made Bird think of a shark about to bite. "I'll make sure you regret this day, Earl Maddox. You have nothing."

"No, you're wrong, Mr. Bradley. I have ethics."

Kenneth Bradley stormed out of the young lawyer's office.

Earl took in a deep, cleansing breath. He looked at his watch. Nine A.M.

Elvin Wainright waited for the nine-fifteen bus. In a carry case on the bench beside him sat the miserable Buzz, who hated being cramped up. On the linoleum at his feet, in two huge suitcases, were the things that Elvin had chosen to bring with him. Today was Monday. His day off. Horseman's holiday. He wouldn't be missed until tomorrow.

He was heading north, where there was work at a breeding farm eighty miles from Sudbury. Obscure little farm outside an obscure little town named Fleet. No one would find him for a while. Enough time to figure out where next to go. Perhaps the Cayman Islands. Or Dubai.

Outside, a policeman strolled past the window of the terminal. Elvin pulled his fedora over his eyes.

Abby Malone looked out of the airplane window. It was nine o'clock, and she was high above the clouds. She wondered about the theatre school she was about to enter. It was expensive. And living in New York would be, too. She'd worked hard and had saved every penny for two years.

But this was her dream. Ever since her debut in The Stonewick Playhouse's production of *Pinocchio*, Abby had wanted to give the magical, mysterious world of theatre a try. Her skin tingled as she remembered the dressing room below the stage with its lingering smells of greasepaint and old costumes and sweat. And her ghostly friend, Ambrose Brown.

Only one thing had worried her as she'd planned for this adventure. Cody. The little coyote doted on Abby. What would happen to him if she left? Luckily, the problem had solved itself. As Abby readied herself for her move, Cody began to spend more and more time with Bird. That girl was the only other human that Cody was comfortable with.

Abby smiled as she watched the cloud formations move and swirl before her eyes.

Alone in the paddock, the sleek chestnut gelding grazed. Sundancer methodically trimmed the blades of grass close to the ground, left to right, right to left, as far as his neck could reach in each direction. He then took a step and began again. Row after row. Step after step.

Suddenly, he lifted his head. *Bird girl.* The one he trusted. The one who, very soon, would ride him to greater glory than he could imagine. His eyes clouded with concentration, and his delicately pointed ears twitched.

Bird girl. Are you all right?

Bird looked at the back of Kimby's head, and glanced at the dark, curly-headed boy sitting two rows over. She smiled.

She pictured Sundancer in his lush pasture: stately, handsome, and content. The horse of her dreams.

Yes, Sunny. I'm all right.

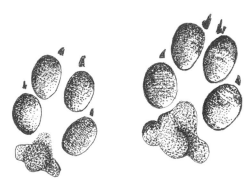

Author's Note

THE HORSE IN THIS STORY is based on a real horse.

My Sundancer was a mystery that I could not solve. In these pages, I use Pete Pierson's voice to explain the agonizing conclusion that caring horse people might come to when a horse is dangerous to humans and all avenues to reform him have been intelligently exhausted.

Over the course of his troubled life, Sundancer was sent to many hard-working, conscientious professional trainers. Nine, to be exact. Putting their egos aside, each one came to the same conclusion: He could not be trained.

In desperation, one of these trainers asked me to telephone Indian Fred for advice. He was a very old man (who's since died) who lived in the mountains of California and was reputed to have an uncanny knack for speaking directly to horses. I confess that I thought it odd, but I called. I had nothing to lose. The results of what I learned about Sundancer during that call appear throughout the book. They are the words—Sundancer's words—that start each chapter.

Often, during those long, frustrating years when I tried and tried again to figure Sundancer out, I fantasized about being able to talk to him. To listen to his fears. To understand why he did the things he did. Of course I couldn't, and thus this story.